DARKNET

Darknet

First edition
March 11, 2015

Copyright © 2015 by Matthew Mather
Published by Matthew Mather ULC

ISBN: 978-1-987942-00-2
Cover image by Michael Corley

AUGUST 10th

Wednesday

1

Central London
England

One hour until the next assassin deadline. *Dead*-line. An appropriate word. Sean Womack checked his wristwatch. Tried to steady his shaking hand.

It was noon.

Clang. Clang...

The clocks of London chimed their consensus. *Sixty minutes until the next assassin's bet*, but he only needed half that. The Assassin Market—a crowd-funded murder collective—was on the hunt for him.

Sean sat on a granite bench beside a statue of Queen Anne, balancing a thick manila envelope on his knees while he stopped and rolled up his sleeves to relieve the sweltering heat. *My God*, he didn't know England could be this hot.

Buses and cars rumbling past, tourists staring at maps, children on summer outings squealing with excitement—the hustle and bustle of the city surrounded him. Next to Sean, a man in a tailored suit had his brown-bagged lunch spread out on his lap. The man chewed thoughtfully on a whole grain sandwich while staring at a flock of pigeons that scratched and cooed in front of them.

Glancing at the man beside him—perfect silk tie, coiffed hair, polished brown shoes—Sean wondered, is *he* the one? The man didn't look the part, but then it was impossible to tell anymore.

Sean's stomach growled. He hadn't eaten in a day—maybe two—but had no appetite. He wiped the sweat off his forehead and adjusted his sunglasses.

Staring at the immense face of St. Paul's cathedral in front of him, Sean wondered why there was only one clock, or at least, only one clock face, located on the right side. On the left, there was an empty space where a clock face should have been. Had it been designed like that? He didn't think so. As scared as he was,

the inconsistency of it annoyed him. He reached for his phone—
to do a web search and find out why—before stopping himself.

He didn't have one.

No cell phone, no computer. No electronics of any kind.

Sean glanced back up at St. Paul's. His mind deconstructed it,
visualizing where the flying buttresses, hidden behind the
towering walls, lined up to support the dome in the middle. In his
mind's eye, the stones of the cathedral hovered in space, great
wooden arches coming up around them, his brain recreating the
systems and sequences of events needed to build it hundreds of
years ago.

He couldn't help himself. His mind never stopped planning,
creating systems, imagining possibilities.

Sean checked his watch again.

Fifty-six minutes.

Looking at the envelope on his knees, he pulled a pen from his
pocket and scrawled an address on it. Taking a deep breath, he
closed his eyes. When he opened them again, he scratched out the
address and wrote a different one, then pulled a scrap of paper
from his pocket and scribbled something else on this and inserted
it into the envelope. Satisfied, he rocked to his feet and pocketed
the envelope, then walked forward to join the line of tourists
going into St. Paul's.

A sign on a stone box at the entrance suggested a donation of
five pounds. Sean fished in his back pocket and stuffed the last of
his cash into the box. Walking inside, he followed the tourist flow
and gawked up at the marble arches, the gilt frescoes of gold and
blue lining the cavernous main dome, the wrought-iron
chandeliers dangling from vaulted ceilings. *Jake would love this.* They
would never have even dreamed of visiting a place like this when
they were kids.

Every few feet, Sean stopped to glance at the entrance.

Reaching the back, he stepped over the cordon rope into a
corridor, then turned and ran down the passageway. The sound of
his footfalls echoed off the stone walls. Reaching the end, he
banged on the lever of an emergency exit.

No alarm sounded.

Back outside, he squinted in the sunshine. A helicopter
hovered overhead, chop-chopping in the clear blue sky. A red
double-decker bus growled past, belching fumes as the driver

4

changed gears. Green trees swayed in the breeze. *Has the story already broken?* He looked at the helicopter. Another had joined it. Keeping his head low, he continued down the street, glancing back at the emergency exit.

Nobody followed.

Blue glass-and-steel skyscrapers rose past the dome of St. Paul's on his left, construction cranes balanced between them like insects atop termite mounds; building, building. He glanced at the helicopters again, then took a sharp right turn to duck down an alleyway, colliding with someone coming from the opposite direction.

"Can you help me?" the man asked.

Sean grabbed him. "Who are you?"

"Dave," the man squeaked, trying to step back. "I wanted to know if you'd take a picture of me and my family." He pulled free.

Sean looked up. The man's wife and kids huddled behind him. Sean glanced up higher, at a CCTV camera on the corner of a building. London had the highest concentration of surveillance cameras in the world. It was a risk Sean was well aware of, but one he needed to take.

"Sorry," Sean said to the man. "Sorry, I was just…" but he didn't finish his sentence as he jogged away from them, down the last steps of the alleyway.

He stopped at the corner.

Looked in all directions.

Glanced at his watch again.

Forty-four minutes.

Turning left onto Queen Victoria Street, Sean started back toward the center of the City of London. People thought that London was this huge city, but the City of London, proper, was contained in one single square mile. One of the smallest cities in Europe, in fact, but it was also the highest concentration of financial firepower on the planet—and the money laundering capital of the world.

More helicopters had assembled overhead.

After three more blocks, Sean found what he was looking for. A Royal Mail box, bright red, with the Queen's ER insignia emblazoned in gold on the front, standing at attention next to the entrance to the Bank tube station. It was in the middle of a roundabout in a five-way intersection of streets—Victoria,

5

Cheapside, William, Threadneedle, Prince—and in the shadow of the imposing Bank of England building. Next to the post box stood an equally red and iconic English telephone booth.

Sean slipped the envelope into the post box, double-checking to ensure it slid all the way in, then opened the door to the telephone booth while searching his pockets for change. No credit or debit cards, not since Amsterdam. Even if he didn't use them, he wasn't sure if someone could track their RFID tags. It was best not to take chances. Sean leaned against the inside wall of the booth and dialed a number he'd committed to memory.

Glanced at his wrist.

Thirty-eight minutes.

More than enough time.

The entrance to the Bank of England building was directly across from him, the Governor's limousine parked in front, waiting. The quarterly Bankers' Assembly meeting had started inside. Across the street was as far as he needed to get to finish what he'd started.

As he cupped the receiver to his ear, the line started ringing, and not the long muted tones of a UK or European number, but the short, familiar jingling of a North American one. He stared at the Bank of England across the street.

Three rings. Then four.

An answering machine picked up.

"You have forty seconds," announced an automated voice before connecting him, telling him how much time he'd paid for. He only heard the tail end of an answering machine message on the other end, "…the O'Connell residence, please leave a message."

Sean took a deep breath. "Jake, hi, it's me."

How to put this?

"Listen, I'm sorry I haven't been in touch for so long, but there's something I need to tell you…"

Behind him, a growling roar erupted, and Sean turned in time to see the front of a double-decker bus bearing down on him. It crashed into the telephone booth, crushing and dragging him across the center of the square.

AUGUST 11th

Thursday

2

Atlas Capital Offices
Long Island, NY

"I like the ring of it—*blood diamonds*." Danny Donovan, the CEO of Atlas Capital, held up his arms to show off his new cufflinks. Diamonds the size of gumdrops glistened on them.

Jake O'Connell held his gaze steady on his boss. "Nice," he replied.

They sat across from each other in the main conference room of Atlas Capital, at a mahogany table that stretched the length of the thirty-foot space, the room separated from the rest of the office by a glass wall. Nice, but not too nice. The table, scuffed in places; the chairs bought at a bankruptcy auction. Donovan liked to keep up appearances, but only to the outside. Few people, except those who worked here, ever came to Atlas's offices.

Atlas liked to say it was a Wall Street firm, but in reality, it was far from it—at least physically. Like the legendary garage start-ups of Silicon Valley, Long Island now housed more financial upstarts in abandoned shopping malls and reconverted warehouses than all of Manhattan combined.

"I didn't defraud them," Donovan added, getting back to their discussion. He maintained persistent two-day-old stubble below thick eyebrows that looked plucked and arranged, his black hair parted and slicked back to one side, his three-thousand dollar bespoke suit immaculate. "I'll admit to bending a few rules, but I didn't steal from those pensioners' accounts. I would never do something like that."

Jake watched a veil pull over Donovan's eyes like a translucent third eyelid to obscure the reptilian depths below. Probing. Searching for weakness. The edges of Donovan's words were all too familiar to Jake.

"I know," Jake replied, the same way he'd always acknowledged his own father's lies. "I believe you," he added.

But he didn't.

9

If there was anything Jake knew about, it was psychopaths. His experience was as personal as it could get: his own father was one.

It was something that took Jake a long time to see for what it was. Growing up, Jake assumed every father treated his children as possessions. But one day in middle school, a kid taunted Jake, saying his dad thought Jake's was a psycho. Jake beat the crap out of the kid, but afterward he looked up the word in an encyclopedia. A great truth was revealed. Many things came into focus.

And a life-long obsession with psychopaths was born.

The popular media vilified 'psychos,' made them out to be ogres, but they possessed the exact qualities celebrated by the modern world: charm, ruthlessness, and a win-at-all-costs mentality. Psychopathy wasn't black or white, but more a multi-colored rainbow from Ted Bundy to the Dalai Lama, with everyone else fitting somewhere in between.

Jake often wondered why psychos seemed to surround him.

Did he search them out?

Or did he notice them more than most?

It was hard to tell.

Jake rated everyone he met on his psychopath scale, from full-Ted to deep-Dalai, even himself. He stared into the mirror sometimes, deep into the depths of his own eyes. Did a full-Ted psychopath know what he was? How? Everyone thought they were good people—even Hitler imagined himself a savior, bearing his cross for the greater good.

It was all a matter of perspective.

Jake spent his life trying to hide the void inside. He used to rely on anger and violence to do the job, but now his family and work fulfilled that role. Still, his life often felt like a show, a collection of learned behaviors.

Donovan pulled back from Jake and smiled. "I don't know which one of us is the better liar."

Jake forced a smile in return. "Do I have to answer that?"

"Not yet." Donovan grabbed his coffee cup from the table. "But soon you'll be answering questions. The Securities and Exchange Commission's lawyers are getting ready. It's not just my neck on the line, you understand?" Donovan pointed his cup at Jake. "Who would have imagined that an ex-con like you would end up a Wall Street trader? You want to keep it that way, you

10

play ball."

Jake nodded. "Understood." It was a point Donovan never let him forget. Ever.

Five years ago, Sean Womack, his childhood friend, started bringing Donovan into the bar Jake managed in the Meatpacking district, one of the hottest late-night party corners of Manhattan. Soaked in tequila and high on cocaine, night after night Donovan had promised to bring Jake into his new financial start-up.

Jake never believed it would happen, but he took to treating the guy with a few shots whenever he showed up. Then one day Donovan made good on his word.

Almost inexplicably.

Donovan flashed his cufflinks again. "Three carats. Not bad, huh?"

"They are nice." Jake couldn't care less about the cufflinks. He leaned forward, elbows on the table, and steepled his fingers together. "Listen, I need to know what to do with this Joseph Barbara guy. Who is he?"

Donovan smiled. "*Who is he?* You don't know?"

"I put a meeting on our schedule with him tonight, down at Johnny Utah's."

"Cancel it. Doesn't matter anymore."

"This guy sounded pretty upset." Jake needed some resolution. "His name's not on our official list of customers, so I don't know how—"

"I gave him your name." Donovan held his cufflinks up at a new angle.

"You gave him *my* name?" What was Donovan up to?

"Don't worry about it."

This set alarms jangling. Donovan might have taken Jake in under his wing, but he had the uncomfortable feeling of a big brother, like the one that used to hold Jake's head underwater in the bathtub when he was little. For the hundredth time he felt the impulse to quit, but there was no way he could get this kind of money elsewhere.

"Okay," Jake replied, unconvinced, "if you say so." He could do his own research. Just then he saw someone he wanted to talk to walking by outside. Jake excused himself to Donovan, "Just a second," as he jumped up and opened the conference room door. He stretched his hand out. "Mr. Viegas," Jake said, projecting his voice.

Vidal Viegas, the chief operating officer of Bluebridge Capital, turned to Jake and blinked, his watery left eye drooping from some long-ago illness. Bluebridge was doing an audit on Atlas's accounts today. Viegas looked more clean-cut than Jake remembered, his hair thicker. They'd met a few times over the years, but Viegas was a financial superstar now—no longer the obscure university professor he used to be. Maybe he didn't remember Jake.

They stared at each other. Jake's hand hovered in space between them. He was about to pull it back when Viegas finally took his hand.

"Ah, yes, Mr. O'Connell. How are you?"

"Good." Jake gave two firm shakes, then Viegas's hand slithered out of his. "Have you heard from Sean lately?" Jake asked.

Another pause. "No, I haven't." Viegas flashed a weak smile. "Please, excuse me." He turned and started for the front. Another man, limping, walked beside and behind Viegas, following him.

Jake watched him go. On the wall of plasma TVs lining the front of the office, Senator Russ talked on CNN. It was coverage of the presidential debate on the conflict in the Middle East. Eleven weeks to go until the election, and Russ was twenty points ahead. Jake closed the door and sat back down with Donovan.

"It's those bastards at Bluebridge who are setting me up." Donovan thrust his chin at the disappearing silhouette of Viegas. "They're paying big money to back Russ in the elections. Something weird is going on there. How do you know him?"

"Through Sean. You remember Sean Womack?"

Donovan scowled. "Of course."

"Viegas was his thesis advisor at MIT." Jake turned his Silver Eagle dollar coin over and over in his pocket. An old habit.

"Viegas was Sean's thesis advisor?" Donovan hissed. "He never told me that—"

"You still talk to Sean?" Jake asked. He hadn't talked to his old friend himself in months, but there were more pressing issues. Jake took a deep breath. "Look, we need to talk about this SEC investigation. I want to know what I should do if they come for you. I'm worried."

"Me too," Donovan sympathized.

But Jake knew he wasn't. Not really.

Jake had ranked Donovan a half-Ted psycho the moment he walked into Jake's bar for the first time; his well-oiled smile and piercing eyes were dead giveaways. Right now, Donovan's eyes did their best to project concern and sympathy, but Jake imagined what was going on behind them.

To a psychopath, there were no dark clouds, only silver linings. There were no moral hazards, only opportunities. Even with an impending arrest and possible jail time, Donovan was probably thinking he'd get a movie deal when he got out in a few years, cement his fame as the Lion of Long Island. People saw Wall Street executives being dragged away in handcuffs after stealing the life savings of millions of retirees and asked, "How could someone do something like that?" when the real question was, "How couldn't they?"

Donovan's phone buzzed. He looked at the message on it. Jake watched him clench his jaw, a vein popping out in his neck. He was only a half-Ted. He felt some stress. Donovan looked at Jake, down at the message again, then back at Jake. "I need to talk to you, too."

Jake stared at Donovan for a long second. "Anything I should be worried about?"

Donovan paused. "This is going to sound nuts, but they have audio recordings, even video, of me saying and doing things that I…didn't…do."

It was odd that Donovan kept insisting he was innocent. The lies were usually casual—obvious, even. So why keep up the pretense? Most of the time Jake could parse what Donovan was up to, but not now.

Donovan's father had been a school teacher in the Bronx, his mother a secretary. He fought his way up, graduating from Harvard on scholarship before making a rapid ascent through the ranks of JP Morgan, the largest investment bank on Wall Street. These were the things Jake genuinely respected him for—hard work, coming up from the bottom, working class roots. After only three years at JP Morgan, Donovan led a rebellion in the high frequency trading group and dragged some of their best minds out here to Long Island for his own start-up. It was a risky move that paid off. Rumor had it that Donovan cleared two hundred million the year before.

"Between you and me, I'm no angel," Donovan continued. "I've done some stuff that's a little off the books to get this place where it is." His pasted-on prep school accent was sliding into his old Bronx slang, a sure sign of agitation. "I'll admit to that, but not this stuff they're trying to stick on me." He slid a memory key across the table to Jake. "Put this in your pocket."

Jake picked it up, held it between his fingers like it was radioactive. "What the hell is it?"

"We ain't got much time. That text I just got? They're on their way."

"I can't have anything to do with this." Jake put the memory key down, pushed it back across the table. "I've got a family to protect."

Donovan laughed. "How do you think you got this job?"

An ominous current slid down Jake's back.

"Your friend, Sean, he helped me out. So I helped him out. Hired you." Donovan pushed the memory key back to Jake. "There are encryption keys on there for some locked accounts. You keep that safe. We're in this together."

A commotion erupted in the front of the office. Through the smoky glass walls of the conference room, Jake saw a group of men massing at the front, one of them holding a piece of paper above his head. They wore bulletproof vests and spoke in loud voices. After more angry shouting, the secretary at the front pointed toward the conference room. The men in vests advanced toward Jake and Donovan, handcuffs out. Jake looked Donovan in the eye and grabbed the memory key, stuffing it into his suit vest pocket.

Donovan straightened his sleeves and admired his diamond cufflinks again, nonplussed. "You take care of that, Jakey."

AUGUST 13th

Saturday

3

Upper West Side
New York City

"Tur…"

Jake propped himself up on the couch and leaned over his five-year-old daughter Anna's shoulder. "Just sound it out," he encouraged. "Tur…bu…"

"Turbulence!" Anna squealed.

Jake nodded. His daughter was a prodigy when it came to reading, something she must have gotten from his wife. Anna had decided she wanted to read to him from his *Pilot and Plane* magazine. He'd started taking flying lessons, and his daughter was fascinated with the idea that he'd be able to soar into the sky.

"Turbulence can a…" continued Anna, "…rise from a number of sources. Muh…"

Jake intervened again. "…can…eh…"

Anna waved him away. "Mechanical, mown…tane wave, frontal activity…"

"Good," Jake encouraged.

"But in summer," continued Anna, "the primary offender is convek…shun." She nodded, trying to convey the seriousness of what she was reading. "As the sun heats the ground, convection turbulence chops up the sky…"

She stopped and turned to Jake, frowning. "Can something really chop up the sky, Daddy?"

"It's just a figure of speech." Jake smiled. "The sky doesn't get chopped up."

"Oh, okay."

"Anna, time to get ready," Elle called out from the kitchen.

Jake turned to see his wife's head poking around the corner, smiling, her brown eyes twinkling. She was getting the lunch bags ready. Anna had piano lessons on Saturday mornings, then ballet in the afternoons. Elle wanted to take her for a walk in Central Park in between and have a picnic.

17

Anna squealed, "Okay, Mom!" and dumped the magazine into Jake's lap before running around the dining table and heading for her bedroom.

Jake smiled as he watched her go. He was filling another role now—that of the doting father, teaching his daughter to read. Swinging his legs off the couch, Jake stood and stretched, admiring their apartment. "You've done an amazing job fixing the place up," he said to his wife.

They bought the place two months ago, moving to the Upper West Side next to Columbia University, from their old—and much loved—loft in Chelsea. The new apartment had three bedrooms, and the area had access to better schools. All for Anna, of course, but Jake had emptied his bank account to make it happen, and the mortgage was crippling. With Atlas under investigation, the noose seemed to tighten around Jake's neck.

"It's been a team effort," Elle replied, disappearing back into the kitchen.

Jake walked into the kitchen and leaned against the wall. "What y'all doing tonight?" He wasn't Southern, but Elle was, and he liked to poke fun at her by using 'y'all' sometimes. "Still going to the Necrosis show?"

"Of course." She brushed past him to the entrance, leaning down to grab a backpack from the doorway closet.

Jake lowered his voice. "Are you sure that's a good environment for Anna?"

Back in college, his wife had started managing punk rock bands as a way of drawing her favorite groups to the small town of Charlottesville. Now she worked full time at Columbia as a researcher of infectious diseases, but she continued with the band management as a labor of love.

Jake first met her when he was twenty-three at one of her gigs down in the East Village. It was a few years after he and Sean moved to the city from upstate New York. Jake was tending bar when he heard screaming out back. Going out to investigate, he'd found Elle holding the lead singer of the band the bar had booked for the night. The singer was crying, cursing, and Elle was singing him a lullaby, cradling the two-hundred-pound-tattooed-and-Mohawked baby in her arms.

Jake was smitten on the spot.

Elle dropped the backpack onto the entrance table and stuffed the lunch bags inside. "Are you serious? You think *my* environment is bad for her?"

This wasn't an argument he could win, not after the police had carted his boss off in handcuffs. To Elle, Donovan's fate was a confirmation of her intuition. She never liked the man.

Jake wisely remained silent.

"Are you going to join us after your flying lesson?" asked Elle.

His fourth one was this afternoon. Jake's early birthday present to himself for his upcoming thirty-fifth birthday, now two months away. "No, I have to go into the office and sort things out a bit. But I'll walk to the piano lesson with you."

"So you're going to be away from home all day and night," Elle stated more than asked. "It's the weekend."

Jake slumped into the couch. He felt the edge in her voice. "This isn't easy, Elle."

Her face softened. "How bad is it?" She meant what was happening with the fraud investigation at Atlas.

"Pretty bad." Jake rubbed his face.

She paused.

"Is there anything you need to tell me?"

He paused.

"No," he lied, feeling the memory key in his pants pocket.

Friday had been a disaster at work, with the police digging through Donovan's office on the one hand, and calls from frantic clients wanting to pull their money from the company on the other. All the chaos had barely given Jake a free moment to think about the memory key. This morning, though, he could think of little else.

Sean was involved.

Something was going on.

Elle watched him. "Have you thought more about my idea?"

A hotel-restaurant in Virginia Beach, near her family, had gone on the market. Elle thought it would be the perfect situation for them. With his experience he could manage the place; she could book live gigs. It would whisk them away from the craziness of the city, and Anna could grow up nearer Elle's family. Elle also had an opportunity for a research position at Old Dominion University.

"Yeah, I did." Jake rubbed his face. "But the timing, it's…"

"Uh huh." Elle turned, shaking her head.

19

Jake exhaled.

They needed more money before they could do something like that, even if he liked the idea. Everyone he worked with had their 'number,' the hypothetical amount of money needed in their bank account before they could stop the madness, call it quits and head for the beach. In all the time Jake had been in the financial world, though, no matter how much money he saw people rake in, nobody left.

But he'd be different.

He just needed a few more years.

Jake pulled his sneakers over to put them on.

Anna appeared, ready to leave, done up in a black leather coat and sunglasses with a pink beret. Kids didn't come cheap these days. She was on her phone—an old one of Jake's he'd given her as a toy—talking to one of her imaginary friends. It was a real cellphone, but not connected to the network. The phone linked into the Wi-Fi in the apartment, though, so she could play web games on it. Carrying it around made her feel like an adult.

"Did you get that message from Sean?" Elle asked.

Jake looked up, one sneaker half on, his heart skipping a beat. "Sean left a message?"

There weren't any new messages on his phone or email—he knew, he'd been checking. Jake almost called Sean at six that morning, but Anna had already been up.

"On the machine. Must have been from yesterday or the day before."

Sean never left a message on their landline. Jake was surprised Sean even knew the number. He hadn't heard from his friend in two months—which was unusual as they normally talked every week or two—but then Sean was jetting around the world dating models and setting up banks.

Jake squirmed around on the couch and grabbed the old-school answering machine they still had. He punched the 'message' button.

"You coming?" Elle asked.

"Jake, hi, it's me," Sean's voice echoed from the playback. Traffic growled in the background. *"Listen, I'm sorry I haven't been in touch in so long."* A car honked in the pause. *"But there's something I need to tell you…"*

The recording ended with a loud crashing sound.

That was odd. Jake pulled his phone out and dialed Sean's private number. It rang four times before going to voicemail. Jake searched his contacts and found another number for Sean, the public one for his business, and dialed that next.

Elle and Anna stared at Jake from the entrance. "Are you coming?" Elle asked again, the frown on her face mirroring her impatience.

Jake held up one finger. "Sorry, just a second." The number rang three times, and he was about to disconnect when it picked up.

"Sean, you there?" Jake said into his phone. Dead silence. "Sean?"

"I'm here," came a reply, slightly garbled. "How are you, Jake?"

"I'm good." Jake frowned. Sean sounded…weird. Not like himself. "Are you okay?"

"I'm fine." Another pause. "I heard Donovan was arrested."

Jake turned away from his family. "Yeah," he whispered, "and he gave me something."

"Oh yeah? What?"

"I don't know. But he said you made it for him."

More dead space.

"Jake!" Elle stamped her foot. "Are you coming?"

He turned to face her, nodding. "Just *one* second." He turned back away. "Listen, Sean, can I call you back? I really need to go."

Two or three seconds passed before there was a reply: "Sure. And Jake, don't worry about it."

The line disconnected.

4

University Medical Center
Hong Kong

Mr. Yamamoto eased himself off the examining table and buttoned up his shirt. The doctor's office looked nothing like the traditional ones at home in Japan, but he preferred the clean, antiseptic feel of a western-style executive clinic.

"How are the results?" Yamamoto asked.

"Perfect," the doctor replied. "You are making an excellent recovery. Just make sure to get some regular exercise." The doctor bowed and excused himself, leaving Yamamoto alone in the examining room.

They spoke in English. Despite the reversion to Chinese control, Hong Kong retained a strong undercurrent of its colonial roots. Yamamoto preferred to keep referring to it as Victoria City, something he knew irritated his Chinese counterparts, and the surprise he had in store for them today would perform even better in that capacity.

But perhaps he was giving them a great gift, as well.

Looking at himself in the mirror, Yamamoto executed a perfect Windsor knot in his tie with practiced ease. Dusting off the shoulders of his suit jacket, he put it on before inspecting himself one last time. He felt better than he had in years. Opening the door, he strode down the corridor, flanked by his two bodyguards who were waiting outside. His assistant was in the reception area with a cup of jasmine tea.

"Have you arranged everything?" Yamamoto asked in crisp English. It was the weekend, so arranging a meeting with the heads of several of China's largest banks was no small feat.

"Yes, Chairman, we will be meeting at the head offices of Goldman Sachs."

"Good." Yamamoto nodded.

Neutral ground, and right next to the Bank of China complex. It was a straight shot down Victoria Road from here, past the glass canyons of the city. It was also next to Hong Kong Park. Perhaps he would take a short walk afterward.

Outside, his driver stood at attention with the limo door open. Yamamoto slid into the cool interior, one bodyguard ahead of him and one behind, while his assistant opened the front door to sit beside the driver. Hong Kong had some of the worst traffic in the world, but he used this car as his traveling office. Someone was waiting inside for him, an outside consultant.

Yamamoto didn't trust his own staff enough to share the details of his special project with them. No one besides Yamamoto and the consultant knew about it.

The car pulled away into traffic.

"Is Atlas Capital involved?" Yamamoto asked the consultant, Shen Shi Heng.

Shen Shi shook his head. "Not directly, but Danny Donovan was formally indicted on federal money laundering charges yesterday."

The meme of the Western cowboy ran deep; Mr. Donovan had allowed it to consume him, leading to his downfall. Still, Yamamoto suspected Donovan would pop to the surface again, like a turd in a communal swimming hole.

"Do we have any exposure?" Yamamoto asked. He meant any risk of financial loss associated with the downfall of Atlas.

"Not according to the connections I can see," Shen Shi replied. "But I haven't had a lot of time to investigate that aspect of it. Why don't you let me connect with your staff?"

Yamamoto let the insolence slide. For now. He'd made it clear that there was to be no contact with his staff. His bodyguards remained impassive by his sides.

"Did you prepare a map of the nodal points?" For months, Yamamoto had suspected a massive conspiracy in the banking world, and the data Shen Shi was collecting could prove it.

Shen Shi nodded and handed over a tablet. Yamamoto inspected the connection points, a smile spreading on his face. Many of the connections led into the Chinese Politburo, several others into the Peoples' Liberation Army, and from there to a network of holding companies. His assistant pinged him with a message—they'd arrived.

"You are to come up to the meeting with me," Yamamoto told Shen Shi, "but only speak when spoken to, and only answer my queries. Is that understood?"

Shen Shi nodded.

They exited the limo. Yamamoto stopped, again flanked by his bodyguards, to inspect the crisscross pattern of the Bank of China building beside them, and then entered the seventy-story glass tower of Goldman Sachs, where he and the consultant and bodyguards were whisked to the top floor. An administrative staffer greeted and ushered them into an expansive conference room with twelve-foot ceiling-to-floor glass walls. A glistening black oval table sat at the center, and seated around it were representatives of ten of the world's largest banks.

Yamamoto dispensed with pleasantries. "Gentlemen, today I…" He stopped halfway from the doorway to the table.

Why was it so hot in here?

Yamamoto closed his eyes and tried to take a breath, sweat blossoming on his forehead. It felt like a python had wrapped around him, squeezing the air from his lungs.

"Yes?" the envoy from the Bank of China demanded. "Why did you drag us up here?"

▲ ▼ ▲

Shen Shi hung back at the doorway, two steps behind, unsure whether to step forward. From behind him, the two bodyguards sprang forward to grab Yamamoto as he faltered and fell forward, gagging and convulsing.

"Get a doctor!" one of them yelled into his walkie-talkie.

AUGUST 15th

Monday

Atlas Capital Offices
Long Island, NY

"Mr. Sinclair, I assure you that your money is safe," Jake said into the telephone. "Whatever Mr. Donovan was—"

Angry shouting on the other end. Jake pulled the receiver from his ear.

"Yes, I know he's the founder of Atlas," Jake continued when the yelling subsided, "but you and I have a relationship—"

Now came a rush of expletives. Jake cringed. "I understand. I'll start the paperwork, but in a few weeks…" His voice trailed away. Mr. Sinclair had already hung up.

Jake rolled his shoulders and stared at the lights flashing on his phone—two calls waiting. Two other clients scrambling to get their money out. Five years of work, all going down the drain since Donovan's arrest.

As much as Jake liked to think of himself as a trader, he spent most of his time at Atlas Capital as a glorified go'fer for Donovan. Jake spent three years learning the ropes, verifying trades, running tickets, and last year he finally started making his own trades. Atlas did most of its trading electronically, automatically—half of the money it made was through algorithms designed by the geek group in the basement.

If half of what Atlas made was through automated systems, the other half was still earned the 'hard' way—through relationships and working the human side of the system as a 'buy side' trader. That was where Jake fit in, working the angles from the inside, talking to people and making deals. It made for a lot of late nights, and when Donovan said jump, Jake still asked, "How high?"

The question now: could he jump high enough to escape this mess? What nasty surprises might be lurking in the memory key Donovan gave him? Jake didn't want to carry it on him or leave it at home, so he'd stuffed it into a potted plant in the entranceway.

An FBI agent walked by the open door to Jake's office, staring hard at Jake as he passed. There were a few new rules in the office this week. No closed doors. No paper shredding. No deleting of any files, not while FBI agents tore through Donovan's office like an angry pack of dogs.

"Susie," Jake called out, "could you pull up all of Mr. Sinclair's files?"

The cubicle pit was a mess—people yelling, telephones ringing. The phone lines were jammed, so shouting was the easier channel of communication. Trying to act normal, with the FBI running from office to office, was like trying to carry on a conversation when having a colonoscopy.

"Susie! SINCLAIR, please!" Jake exhaled and waited, but got no response. "Susie!" he yelled again.

"Get it yourself!" came her angry reply. She scowled and ducked behind her cubicle wall. She didn't like Jake ordering her around, even though that's exactly what assistants were for.

"I'm sorry, are you in the middle of another online shoe shopping bid?" Jake said loudly.

Sometimes a little public shaming was the only way to get things done with her. He was going to have to fire her. Sure, the past week was crazy, but he'd been having problems with her for months. Closing his eyes, Jake leaned his head back. One other new policy from the feds. No hiring or firing.

Atlas wasn't closed, not yet, but at the rate clients were leaving, it wouldn't take long for the inevitable. This morning, everyone stared at each other around the coffee machine, trying to remember what deals Donovan did with them, how they might be exposed.

Another light lit up on his phone. Groaning, Jake punched the button. "Jake O'Connell here."

"Jake?" replied a trembling voice. "Is that you?"

"Yes, it's Jake, who is…" He frowned. "Mom?"

"Hello, Jakey," his mother said over the line.

She never called him at work. She never usually called at all. He didn't know she even knew his number. It had to be something to do with his father. "Are you okay?" Jake asked breathlessly. "What did he do, did he hurt you?"

"No, no," his mother answered, her voice barely more than a whisper.

Jake plugged his other ear. "Mom! Speak up, please, I can't

hear you. What's wrong?"

Silence.

"Mom, are you okay? What's going on?"

"Sean's dead."

The paper shuffling and shouting faded out of Jake's senses. "Wh...what did you say?" he stammered. "Did you say something about Sean?"

"Sean's dead," his mother repeated.

Blood rushed into Jake's face, his fingertips tingled. "Sean's dead? Sean Womack?"

"Yes, little Sean. His aunt called me early this morning. Said there was a traffic accident in London, or something like that. You should call her."

"Sean Womack, you're saying something's wrong with him? I just talked to him on the weekend."

"He's dead, Jakey. I'm sorry. Call his Aunt Rita. She knows more. I'm sorry."

Jake's hands went numb. He stared at the phone in his hand. "Okay. Thanks." He hung up.

An image formed in Jake's mind, of the first time he met Sean. In a darkened room, bunk beds lining the walls, a foster home when he was six years old. Sean's face appearing in the darkness, talking about a fort he built out back. About playing with goats.

Goats.

That's what came to Jake's mind.

What did he feel?

Nothing. He felt numb. What should he feel?

The last time Jake spoke to Sean was Saturday, two days ago, and he hadn't called him back since then. Why hadn't he called Sean back again? When they spoke, Sean told him not to worry about it. That's the reason Jake was trying to tell himself, but that wasn't true.

He'd been avoiding it, to be honest. Didn't want to believe that Sean was involved in something illegal, not after getting that memory key from Donovan. Didn't want to hear it. Sean had been the one to rise above it all. Though a part of him had been desperate to talk to Sean, he hadn't made the call.

And now he couldn't.

Not ever.

6

Shenzhen
China

"So Yamamoto just dropped dead?" Jin asked.

Shen Shi looked up with a mouthful of noodles and nodded. He raised one arm and then let it fall to the table, slapping it down hard. "Boom, like that. Fell over dead, right in the Goldman Sachs main conference room with everyone watching. It was awful."

They were having lunch on the top floor of Building Two of the Shenzhen Nanshan Hi-Tech Incubator. Shenzhen was the city next to Hong Kong, more working class—with much lower rent—than the financial metropolis across the bay. Hong Kong, Shenzhen and the city of Guangzhou spanned a single urban area.

The noise Shen Shi made hitting the table earned disapproving glances from people at other tables in the cafeteria. The Hi-Tech Incubator building they had their office in was a serious place.

Or it was supposed to be. Jin and Shen Shi were rarely serious.

Jin would have giggled at the stares from the stern men in suits, but Shen Shi wasn't smiling. Yamamoto's death must have really affected him, and she could see it in Shen Shi's eyes.

Jin and Shen Shi had known each other their whole lives. Jin was born in Boston, and Shen Shi here in Guangdong province, but they were the same age and had spent most of their summers together growing up. Jin's parents went to America in the mid-1980s, before Jin was born, part of an early scientific exchange program of researchers between Northeastern University and Guangdong. It was only supposed to last for a few years, but her family had stayed, becoming American citizens.

When Jin was snared in a hacking investigation four years ago in Boston, part of a botched intrusion testing program, Shen Shi had offered to help her start a business in China. She'd jumped at the chance. From an office on this floor, they now ran a data mining business that searched through huge repositories of digital information for their clients, which included banks and government ministries. Jin was more of the geek side of their team—reserved, shy—while Shen Shi was outgoing, a real go-getter businessman type. A perfect partnership.

"So you were in the limo that picked him up?" Jin was curious to get a first-hand report. "Right from his doctor's office?"

Yamamoto's death was front page news in the *Shenzhen Economic Daily*. Though he'd died on Saturday, the press hadn't found out until late on Sunday. It wasn't surprising. The local government kept tight control over the media.

"That's the weird thing." Shen Shi shoveled in another mouthful of noodles. "Why would he drop dead right after getting his heart checked out?"

It was common knowledge that Yamamoto, the chairman of Japan's largest financial fund, had had a heart attack the previous year. The news stories had been rife with speculation, but none had mentioned that he'd been at his doctor's office minutes before his death.

"Just a coincidence," Jin offered. "I mean, it's called a heart *attack* for a reason."

"That's what I thought, too."

The way Shen Shi said it invited speculation. "Until what?" Jin asked.

Shen Shi grimaced and looked out the window.

"Are you okay?" Jin asked. She'd never seen her cousin like this. Distracted. Distant.

"It's not just Yamamoto…" Shen Shi's words drifted off.

"Then what is it?" Jin asked.

Shen Shi looked her in the eye and worked his mouth around as if he tasted something terrible. "Sean Womack, you remember him?"

"Sure." Jin nodded. They'd worked on contracts at the Bank of China with Sean, many years before. Sean even helped her with lawyers when she was snared in the hacking investigation in Boston.

"He died yesterday, in London. Just saw a news article today, some random traffic accident."

"My God, really?"

"I didn't tell you before, but he was the one that recommended us to Yamamoto."

Jin had one hand to her mouth, still trying to process the news.

She wasn't close to Sean, not in years, but still, he was a friend. It didn't surprise her that Sean had recommended them to Yamamoto—Sean knew everyone in the financial world.

Jin spoke through her hand. "Sean sent me an odd email three weeks ago."

"What did he want?"

"I don't know, and he didn't respond when I asked him." And now I can't, Jin realized with a sinking sensation that settled in her stomach.

Shen Shi frowned until his forehead creased into red ridges. "All I know is that some of the chairmen of the big banks were present at that Yamamoto meeting. Something big was going down…"

Jin connected the dots. "Wait, so you think Yamamoto was *killed?*" She couldn't help the excitement in her voice.

None of the newspaper articles said anything except that it was a heart attack. She tried to keep quiet. They spoke in English— Jin's Cantonese was rusty—so it was doubtful they'd be overheard. Not here, anyway.

Shen Shi pushed away his plate of noodles and opened his laptop. He moved around the other side of the cafeteria table to sit next to Jin as it started up.

"I don't know." He started up a data visualization tool. "Yamamoto had me investigating the connection between shell companies spawned by decentralized autonomous corporations."

Jin frowned. "Like bitcoin companies?" It wasn't her area of expertise. She pulled up a web definition on her laptop:

A Decentralized Autonomous Corporation (DAC) is a network of artificial intelligence agents which divides its labor into two parts: (1) tasks it pays or incentivizes humans to do, and (2) tasks which it performs itself. It can be thought of as a corporation run without any human involvement, under the control of an incorruptible set of business rules.

Shen Shi nodded. "Bitcoin was the first autonomous corporation, if you want to look at it that way. You can look at them as currencies, but you can also look at them as equities, like companies on regular stock markets. Their value is already in the tens of billions. At this rate they'll become some of the most valuable corporations on the planet in a decade." He pulled up a graphic on screen. "And nobody's in charge of them."

"Nobody?"

"Well, they're in charge of themselves."

"And these autonomous corporations Yamamoto was looking at, they're not cryptocurrencies? What are they for?"

Shen Shi slid closer and lowered his voice. "From an outside view, it looks like they're sending money into the accounts of Politburo members and organizations affiliated with the cyber wings of the PLA."

The Peoples' Liberation Army. Jin and Shen Shi did contract work for them from time to time. Everyone did. It was a massive organization in China.

Shen Shi opened another window on his screen. "After Yamamoto died, I went and pulled data sets across all the banks we work with to see if there were more connections."

It was a common practice. By reviewing data across numerous platforms, it was possible to detect cross-channel schemes— systems that criminals used that hopped from one network to another, making them more difficult to track. He moved his laptop in front of her.

"So what am I looking at?" Jin tried to make sense of the information on the screen. It was a list of individuals, with a dozen parameters correlating them together. "Are these people Yamamoto suspected of fraud? Was he going to the heads of the banks with this?"

Shen Shi shook his head. "I'm not sure. These people, they're acting in strange ways."

Fraud detection used to mean keeping track of obvious things like if someone started buying expensive jewelry at three in the morning, or bought something in Amsterdam and then in Atlanta ten minutes later. Now, though, they looked at the amount of time it took a user to type in their password, how long they stayed online, who they interacted with, and more by drawing on a huge amount of data to find anything that looked unusual.

"Do you think it's identity theft?" asked Jin.

It was a growing problem. Working for multiple banks on fraud investigations, Jin and Shen Shi had access to a range of commercial and government data sources—medical, police, social media, credit card, and financial records. Not all of it was legal to access, although "legal" was a malleable word in China.

"No," replied Shen Shi, whispering even lower. "At least, not in the usual sense, because nothing is ever reported. These individuals don't call in about stolen money or fraudulent credit cards. Not ever."

Jin studied the data maps. A chill ran down her back. She closed the laptop. "Let's get out of here, go back to my place." There were too many people around them.

Shen Shi nodded.

They gathered their coats and bags and walked down the long corridor to the elevators. Shen Shi punched the down button. "You see what I mean? Isn't it strange?"

Jin nodded. "But you can make enough data look like anything."

The elevator pinged to their floor.

"Maybe, but *that* many people correlated together like that?" Shen Shi looked Jin in the eye. "That's an extreme outlier."

An outlier, something so far outside of the norm that the data point laid by itself. The signal of something unusual, that wasn't a part of the rest. Or something that wasn't right.

The elevator doors opened. Shen Shi turned, took a step forward, and disappeared.

Jin didn't even hear her cousin scream as he dropped down the elevator shaft, just the thud—thud—thud of his body hitting metal girders, over and over as he fell twenty floors.

AUGUST 16th

Tuesday

7

Upper West Side
New York City

"Is that him?" the new guy asked.

Cormac Ryker leaned forward and squinted, trying to see through the glint of the afternoon sun shining on the windshield of the old Caddy they were doing surveillance from.

"No, that's not Jake O'Connell." Cormac opened the file sitting in his lap and shuffled through a few pages. They were only here to gather information, at least for now. He held a picture up. "I think it's his brother."

"You sure?" His new partner opened his own file folder. "O'Connell's brother is in jail."

Cormac frowned. *How did I get stuck with this idiot?* "Weren't you supposed to verify that last week?"

"I did. He was still in Attica, doing a dime for armed robbery. Wasn't due out for another year."

"Well, he's out now."

His partner nodded. "I guess so."

And that was it. No apology for messing up, no ownership of the mistake.

Cormac let it go.

This time.

It was nice to be back up north, to have some fresh air to breathe. Cormac's new employer seemed to want him in and around New York, which was fine by him. Maybe he was getting too old to be out in the wild. If he didn't eat another taco for as long as he lived, that would be fine by him.

Officially, he didn't know who his new employer was, or at least, his employer had chosen to remain anonymous. But Cormac still had a good idea. Intelligence was a key skill of any operative, so he made it his job to find out who—and what—he was dealing with. And he knew this was one big fish. The paydays made it feel like Christmas.

He laughed to himself.

During his two years in Mexico, he'd found out that there was a new Santa that people got presents from, but this one wasn't a jolly old man. The cartels he'd worked for worshipped the Santa Muerta—the patron saint of death—whose shrines made the Saint look like a grim reaper in drag. It was a serious deal for them. *Narco cultura.* The pushers and dealers, mules and pimps, and even the human traffickers needed someone to pray to.

Cormac never understood the need for a higher power. He figured other people made it up to hide their fear and trembling—but his hands were steady. His eyes were as clear as his conscience.

Cormac's new partner turned to look at him. "You're Hard Core, aren't you? I've heard of you."

Cormac glanced at him and shook his head, then returned to staring at the entrance of Jake O'Connell's apartment building. His partner tried to introduce himself the first time they met, but Cormac had stopped him. Wearing Ray-Bans, camouflage shirtsleeves rolled up, the man looked like he was showing up for a film audition for the part of the generic bad guy. Cormac's greatest skill, like a chameleon, was to blend in, become a part of the landscape.

Make them think you're weak.

The little guy.

Then they never saw you coming.

The skill of surviving in hostile environments wasn't about muscle or even firepower, but more about intuition—about knowing the enemy's customs and rituals, knowing what the right thing to do was in any given situation.

Right now, the thing to do was to try to ignore his partner as much as possible.

How some of these idiots got through Q Course was a mystery to Cormac, but then, he came from a different generation. Even so, it was a small community, and they all knew each other. His new partner was staring at him, still waiting for a response, smiling at his own cleverness. He didn't realize it, but he had just done something dangerous.

"Some people call me that," Cormac replied.

'Hard Core' Cormac Ryker was a nickname he earned early in his career. Cormac was top of his class in Jump School and the

38

Special Operations Preparation Course and Assessment—SOPC
and SFAS—at Fort Bragg after two tours in Afghanistan. He had
a special skill with languages, and went deep on several missions.
Left alone out there, things sometimes got turned around. It
wasn't all black and white. But when it came down to it, the
problem wasn't what Cormac had done. It was that his superiors
caught him.

After an IED attack on a convoy of marines in the western
Iraqi province of Al Anbar killed one of his special ops buddies,
Cormac had taken it upon himself to find some justice. Armed
with a blowtorch and pair of pliers, he'd gotten the names and
locations of those responsible. Late one night, he'd slipped out
under the wire of the Al Asad Airbase where his 82nd Airborne
Division was stationed. Went out into the town and attacked the
Al-Qaida compound his sources had named.

Killed everyone inside.

To send a message.

That the message included the deaths of twenty-four unarmed
Iraqis, half of them children, didn't bother Cormac, but it did
bother the brass. A special investigation ensued. Surveillance
images were shown of Cormac behind the supply depot, slipping
under the chain link fence. As far as the world knew, the incident
was another senseless massacre by unknown forces. The media
pegged it as a Shia-Sunni internal conflict, but everyone inside his
unit knew who was responsible.

"That's him," Cormac said, pointing at Jake O'Connell walking
across West End Avenue and stopping at the corner of 104th
Street.

"Should we get out?" his partner asked.

"No. Wait." Cormac looked at him again. "I better get
changed."

The truth was, the Middle East never confused Cormac. Death
fascinated him, and that scared other people.

Which was good.

Fear was an effective weapon.

After a hushed discharge, Cormac did a rotation through the
private security services, Academi and the rest, but he didn't like
to take orders. So he branched out on his own. Getting kicked out
of Special Forces was an inconvenience, mostly because it
removed his easy access to his favorite toys, but it opened a vista

of new opportunities. In Special Forces, killing was just a part of the job, a reward for the low pay.

But on the outside, it was amazing how much you could get paid for murder.

▲▼▲

Jake fumbled with his keys, trying to open the apartment door. Elle opened it. "Your brother is here."

"What?" Jake replied, not understanding. It had been a long day at the office.

She swung the door in. Someone was on the couch. Eight years had passed since they last saw each other, but Eamon looked the same. He smiled at Jake.

Jake didn't smile back.

"Why don't you take Anna out to the park?" Jake whispered to Elle, striding in, throwing his suit jacket and briefcase on the entrance table. Under his breath he added, "Why didn't you call me?"

"I did, but you weren't—"

"Uncle Eamon is here!" Anna squealed from behind Elle, gripping the fabric of her mother's skirt and glancing furtively at her uncle on the couch.

"I know, baby." Jake stooped to catch his daughter and swung her off her feet. "And me and your uncle need to have a chat." He brushed her blond hair back. "Is that okay? Do you think you could go for a walk in the park?"

Anna scrunched up her face in solemn deliberation. "Yes."

"Good girl." He put her down gently.

Jake waited until Elle and Anna were gone before walking into the living room. Rather than sit on the couch, he stood and faced his brother. He studied Eamon, that sledge of a nose broken in a schoolyard brawl but never fixed, the four-leaf clover tattooed on the side of his neck still proudly Irish. Now that he was closer, he saw Eamon's eyes had aged and the confident mop of blond hair on his head was showing gray in the shaved sides.

"Didn't know you were out."

"Been a week already." Eamon laughed. "Looks like we're about to switch places."

He must have heard about what was happening at Atlas. "I had

40

nothing to do with it."

"I bet that's what that Donovan fella is saying, too." The smile slid from Eamon's face. "I spent a lot of time inside, and there's one thing everyone in there has in common."

"What's that?"

"They're all innocent."

Jake rubbed his temples and sighed. "What do you want, Eamon? Come all this way to gloat?"

"That's not nice, is it?" Eamon leaned forward on the couch, perched on the edge. "You don't need to be an asshole. Never even invited me to your wedding. Never met your kid before." He shrugged. "Beautiful girl, your Anna, and Elle is still the stunner."

"What do you want?" Jake repeated.

His brother only ever showed up when he needed something, usually money, and trouble was never far behind. He must have gotten Jake's address from their mother, but she hadn't asked Jake for permission.

"Just wanted to say hello to my little brother, see if enough water had passed under the proverbial bridge." Eamon held his hands wide. "Forgiveness and all that."

"Give me a break."

Jake stuck his hands in his pockets and rubbed his Silver Eagle coin with his right hand. With his left, he gripped the memory key Donovan had given him. Though he spent hours examining its contents on his computer, the only thing he understood offhand was a database with stacks of financial records connecting shell companies all over the world. That alone might be damaging, but there were directories of software as well. He didn't trust any of the IT people at Atlas to have a look.

Eamon hung his head. "I'm here because I heard about Sean." He looked up and stared Jake in the eye. "He was my friend, too." Eamon stood and placed a hand on Jake's shoulder. "Are you okay?"

Jake called Sean's Aunt Rita for details the day before. She said a bus killed him, a random traffic accident. It took two days for the police to identify him, from immigration cameras at Heathrow, because Sean hadn't been carrying a wallet or any ID at the time of the accident.

Jake stood in silence, staring into space. He rubbed his face. "Yeah, I'm okay." Having his brother there added to the surreal

41

texture of the day.

"Want to get a drink?"

At least that was one thing they had in common. "Yeah, I do," Jake replied.

In a few minutes they were next door in the Colcannon. You couldn't throw a stone in New York without hitting the window of an Irish pub. It was nearly empty, and Jake and Eamon seated themselves at the bar, ordering two pints of Guinness and two shots of Jameson whiskey.

Just like old times.

Only two other people were in the place, quietly talking in a dim corner, and another man, limping, came in behind them and seated himself further down the bar.

"You go home and see Mom and Dad yet?" Jake asked.

"Not yet. And neither of them came to see me inside the last two years. You?"

"I go and see Mom from time to time, but she doesn't come out of her bubble." Jake looked at the floor. "I give her money, but I'm pretty sure Dad gets it somehow."

"I'm sure he does," Eamon agreed. "Do you know when the funeral is?"

Jake shook his head. It would cost a lot of money to fly the body home. Sean's aunt had no money, and Sean had few friends at home to help her. He hadn't thought about that. Sean had money, lots of it, but Jake had no idea what would become of his fortune now that he was dead.

Jake now realized how little he knew about what his friend had been up to for the past few years. We only see two things in people, Jake's dad used to say. What we want to see, and what they show us. Neither was the truth, and neither seemed to sum up Sean.

Eamon raised his shot glass. "A good funeral's better than a bad wedding. We should give Sean a proper send off."

"Yeah."

Sean would have liked that. A good party. Jake raised his shot. "Cheers." Downed it with his brother.

Eamon winced from the bite of the whiskey. "Are you going to come upstate, see the old boys?" He motioned to the bartender for two more.

Jake took a deep breath. "I have a family now, Eamon, and I

42

don't want all the bad stuff to come near us." They grew up rough, and while Jake had escaped that life, Eamon stayed close to the old gang, who still dabbled in petty crime—and sometimes more serious stuff, like the felony conviction that had landed Eamon behind bars.

"Can't ignore where you come from, Jake." Eamon took a deep drink from his Guinness. "Anyway, seems you've moved up the food chain. Whatever I did was small potatoes compared to that boss of yours."

"I don't want to talk about it."

Eamon finished his pint in two more gulps and dangled the empty glass in the air, asking for another. The bartender nodded as he brought their second round of shots. "You remember that place in the woods where we used to hide?"

Jake remembered. A treehouse he and Sean had built deep in the woods. In a rare act of camaraderie, Eamon had helped, stealing timber from local construction sites. Rough boards nailed together, hidden in the branches. At the time it seemed like a palace, a sanctuary they could escape to from their foster homes. They spent weeks hiding in the woods sometimes, living off the land in the summer, starting when Jake was barely ten years old, Sean eleven, and Eamon fourteen. Runaways.

"Those were some good times." The second round of shots arrived, and Eamon picked up one and downed it.

They were. Jake remembered having fun, even with his brother. Days spent lounging in the sun, swimming in a nearby creek. Now that part of the forest was mostly new development, condos and strip malls, but the old farm was still there.

"He was my friend, too," Eamon said again as he placed his shot glass down. "There's something else I learned on the inside."

Jake looked away. "And what's that?" He didn't reach for the other shot next to Eamon.

"There's no such thing as coincidences."

"Which means?"

"Your best friend getting killed in a random accident when all this stuff is going on with your boss,—"

"So what do you think happened?" Jake cut him off. The accident report from London was definitive. The bus driver swerved to avoid a bicyclist and jumped the curb, hitting and killing Sean.

43

"What was Sean involved in?" Eamon asked. "Tell me Sean wasn't involved with Donovan in some way." He leaned close and stared Jake dead in the eyes. "Tell me that, and I'll go."

Jake gripped the memory key from Donovan in his pocket. He knew Sean had done something for Donovan in return for a favor—a well-paying job for Jake so he could provide for his wife and new daughter. Jake wanted to shout and scream about it, but he didn't trust his brother. The same way he didn't trust his father. Hard-won wisdom. But not saying anything said a lot.

Eamon lifted one finger and pointed it at Jake. "I knew it. I feckin' knew it. Who was Sean working for?"

Jake didn't know all the details, but he knew a little. "He was doing a lot of work for Bluebridge, here in New York, out in Hong Kong, all over."

"Bluebridge?" Eamon frowned, then his eyes widened. "Yeah, I heard of them. On TV all the time." His eyes narrowed. "Are they connected to Donovan?"

The connection dawned on Jake just as Eamon said it. "Donovan said Bluebridge was setting him up, framing him for stuff he didn't do," Jake blurted before thinking.

Eamon pounded the bar with one fist. Everyone turned and looked at them. "You see, I knew it. Tell me what you know, Jakey. These bastards might think they're above the law, but they'll not get past me."

It was all still a shock. Jake's mind spun, connecting the dots. But there was one thing he did know. "I shouldn't have said that."

He didn't want his brother involved, not in any way.

"What?"

Jake looked Eamon in the eye. "I don't trust you. Plain and simple."

"You've got to be kidding me."

"Go home, Eamon." Jake picked up his Guinness and took a sip, then put it back down. "Wherever home is for you now."

Eamon didn't move. "How many times do I have to say I'm sorry?"

"Go home," Jake repeated.

"Jesus Christ, Jake, we were kids. I'm sorry."

Jake stared at his beer, an image forming in his mind of the frozen interior of a car. "Just go."

44

8

Outskirts of Shenzhen
China

Jin rubbed her eyes. "Can I come in?" she asked.

Wutang blinked at her through the open door of his apartment, a mop of unruly black hair disheveled above his boyish face. "Jin?"

"Who do you think?" She rolled her eyes. She was right in front of him. "Can I come in?" she asked again.

"Uh, yeah." Wutang nodded, rubbing his face. "Just a second." He disappeared, but left the door ajar.

Jin heard him shuffling around. He had to be picking things up, trying to tidy. She'd dropped in without warning. "You don't need to clean up for me," she tried to tell him, but it was futile.

She knew he had a crush on her. They'd been working together on a Ministry of Public Security project for more than six months, on and off.

"I'm…" More noises from behind the door. "One second."

Something crashed. Wutang swore under his breath. Jin felt nervous and exposed in the hallway. She couldn't take it anymore, so she pushed the door open and stepped through.

Inside she found Wutang standing with an armful of clothes. A sock fell and he tried to grab it but missed. A flat plasma display covered one wall of the small apartment, a first person shooter game frozen mid-gunfire. Take-out containers covered the table in front of the couch.

"Sorry for appearing out of nowhere like this." Jin bowed her head. "Go ahead. Finish cleaning, I'll wait here, Wutang." This wasn't his real name. It was Liu Wei, but she knew that was what all his friends called him. "Can I call you that?"

Wutang nodded awkwardly and ran off with the pile of clothes. "It's horrible what happened to Shen Shi, I'm so sorry…" He disappeared into his bedroom with the pile of clothes.

Of course everyone knew.

45

It was all over the news.

Jin was still trying to erase the image of the yawning abyss of the elevator shaft. She had almost stepped into it herself, reaching out to join Shen Shi before she managed to stop herself, her mind realizing something wasn't right. The rest was a blur. The police seemed to arrive within seconds. There was confusion over what had happened. *Did he force the doors open?* No. *Did he jump?* No, it was an accident. *Did you push him?* What?

The terror in the back of her mind was that this wasn't an accident. Nobody knew that Shen Shi was working for Yamamoto, not even her friends—except perhaps Sean, but he was dead. It was a secret project. Nobody knew he was there when Yamamoto died.

Except her.

But that wasn't entirely true, she realized. The heads of the banks in that room had seen Shen Shi, as well as Yamamoto's body guards. So some people knew Shen Shi was involved, or at least, had seen his face, which was much the same thing. That room had been packed with powerful people, and one of them might have killed Yamamoto to keep him quiet.

And they might have killed Shen Shi as well.

Their data mining company was registered under Shen Shi's name—she didn't have a Chinese passport—so somebody investigating might not know she was involved, and nobody knew that he'd shown her the data. At least, she didn't think anyone knew.

Yet.

Miss, one of the policemen had said to her after Shen Shi's accident, *Miss Huang, we need you to come downstairs. We're going to look at the footage on the closed circuit cameras.* And that's when the terror really blossomed in her mind. *The cameras.* They lined the hallway leading up to the elevator. It was a new building, completely wired.

Completely monitored.

As soon as the officers allowed her to leave, she ran to her apartment and grabbed a bag. She started up an app for the augmented reality glasses she and Shen Shi had been working on as a research project. It did real-time facial recognition of the people you looked at, comparing them to scrapes of social networking sites. Ninety percent of people in Shenzhen had social media accounts. It was a powerful way to view the people around you.

After grabbing some personal things, she retreated to a café and sat with her back to the wall, watching the names and details of people flash in her augmented reality glasses. By cross-correlating with other databases, it pulled not just their names, but their addresses and even their occupations, compiling the information on her display. Anyone it couldn't identify was highlighted in red.

She'd spent a frightening day and night watching red haloed people come in and out of the café.

And she couldn't stop thinking of Shen Shi's laptop the whole time.

She had it.

The one with the data from Yamamoto.

Jin had picked it up from the table when they got up to leave, slipped it in her purse at the elevator. If somebody had been watching them, they might not have noticed, but now, after a day of investigating, it had to be obvious the laptop was missing.

There was only one other person who could have it.

Jin.

Was it a coincidence that Shen Shi fell into an empty elevator shaft two days after Yamamoto's sudden death? Yamamoto had survived a previous heart attack; perhaps a second attack had simply been a matter of time. When she looked up elevator accidents in the café, she found out thousands of people died that way every year. The poka-yoke—the fail safes—should have kicked in, but it was a new building. They were already calling it a faulty systems installation in the social media feeds. But what about Sean Womack? Adding a random traffic accident to this cluster of deaths seemed beyond chance.

Jin had two choices. Either it was a coincidence, in which case she made herself look suspicious by running and hiding. Or it wasn't, and some unknown forces were hunting down and killing people associated with the data Shen Shi dug up. It wasn't hard to decide on the cautious approach.

She needed to hide somewhere and look at Shen Shi's data in detail, figure out what it meant. The same filtering of social media sites she used could also be used against her, so she couldn't go to any of her good friends, not even old friends or associates.

She needed someone she could trust, but who was at a distance from her electronically.

Wutang had immediately come to mind.

▲ ▼ ▲

Wutang appeared from his bedroom and stood awkwardly in front of her, smiling. Jin hadn't accepted his friend requests yet. He was cute and nice, but she knew how he felt about her—he told her in a million silent ways—and she was wary of romantic relationships. To be honest, she was shy. The only place she didn't feel awkward was in front of a computer screen.

"I know this is crazy, but can I stay here for a few days?" she asked, fighting her own desire to turn and run, to go to Shen Shi's family—*her family*—and share her grief and terror with them, burrow into their warm embrace. But part of her knew that could be dangerous, for her and for them.

Wutang blushed. "Yes, sure, of course."

"I just don't want to be alone. Please, please…don't make a big deal of it," she stuttered.

"I won't, I mean, don't worry." Glancing sideways, he grabbed underwear off his kitchen counter. "Do you, ah, do you want a drink?"

"No." She noticed she was shaking, and held the counter to stop her hand from trembling. "Can I sit down?"

"Yes, yes, I'm being rude, please sit." Wutang motioned to the couch. "I'll get you some water."

Jin made her way to the couch and collapsed into it, dropping her bag on the coffee table. She hadn't slept the whole night before. Wutang appeared with the water.

"Thank you." Jin took the glass.

"I was about to go to my family." Wutang hovered over her, clearly unsure of what to do. "It's my grandfather's birthday. I can cancel—"

"No, don't." Jin stood, still holding the water glass in her right hand as she took Wutang's hand with her left. "Don't change anything you're doing. I'll be fine here for a few hours alone. I needed somewhere…" Her voice trailed off. "Wutang, I need you to promise me something."

She squeezed his hand.

Stared into his eyes.

"Anything," Wutang said.

"You cannot tell anyone that I am here."

Silence.

She held his gaze.

From the look in his eyes, she could tell he understood what she was asking. Something was going on, and if he accepted, he would be an accomplice by association.

A moment of truth passed, then Wutang squeezed her hand back. "No one, I promise."

Jin felt tears coming. "Thank you, Wutang. I'm sorry if I didn't return your friend requests, I've been—"

"Sit down and relax. I'll put some tea on." A warm smile spread across Wutang's face. "Really, don't worry."

For the first time since the accident yesterday morning, Jin felt some measure of safety. She kissed Wutang's hand. "Thank you."

Wutang blushed again, a deeper shade of red this time. Letting go of her hand, he turned and busied himself with cleaning up some more while the tea brewed. Then, apologizing profusely again, he excused himself and said he'd be back in a few hours; in the meantime, she should make herself at home.

Jin said she'd take a nap, and he provided a blanket and pillow. She asked for the router code, of course, so she could connect.

As soon as Wutang was gone, Jin started her laptop and logged into one of her darknet accounts through an anonymous browser. Then she took out Shen Shi's laptop. She stared at it for a few seconds, still unable to comprehend that he was gone. It was all so surreal. There had been no time to grieve yet, not with the blind terror that filled the space between every synapse in her brain.

She had to think. Shen said that Sean Womack had recommended them to Yamamoto. Three weeks ago Sean had sent her an odd email message: "Remember the nuggets." That was it. He hadn't responded to her email when she asked what he meant. It was the first direct message she had from him in months.

She turned on Shen Shi's laptop and entered his security code, then opened the Tor anonymous browser and typed 'Sean Womack' into the search box.

Sean's blog popped up as the first search entry, www.SeanWomack.com, followed by pages for several agent-based e-books he'd authored along with his social media pages. There was a new post on his blog, written the previous day, on the quarterly results for his cryptocurrency mining operations. It had to be automatically generated, but it was still creepy that it was signed Sean Womack.

She clicked his main social media page. It exploded onto the screen with hundreds of new messages from people expressing their condolences. He had an app running that automatically generated responses, thanking them for thinking about his death. If she hadn't known he was dead, she might be excused for thinking he was still a busy man. Digital death followed long after physical death.

She clicked on a link to a story about his accident: *BBC – Aug 12th —A London transit double-decker bus jumped the guardrails today, killing a tourist next to the Bank of England. The man, described as a Caucasian in his mid-thirties, had no identification, and police are asking…*

His body hadn't been identified for two days, and even then, there'd been no official time of death. Frowning, Jin dug through the connected news stories. Sean had always been wired—phone, tablet, smart watch, laptop—so it seemed strange that he'd been found without any of those things.

Most of the reports claimed that the driver had swerved to avoid a pedestrian. A social media post by the bus driver's son swore that his dad hadn't swerved, that the steering system had malfunctioned and the bus had caused the accident by itself. The story was buried amid others claiming that London Transit was testing new collision avoidance systems in its buses.

Had someone hacked the system?

It wouldn't be the first 'grand hack auto' story. She found a related story on Rolling Stone journalist Michael Hastings, who had been investigating military intelligence agencies a few years before. Hastings had died in a mysterious car accident the day after telling colleagues he was going 'off the radar.' There was evidence that he was the victim of a car cyberattack.

It was also strange that Sean had been carrying no ID. Jin remembered Sean as being careful, always aware of his surroundings.

Exhale. Let the stress out. She had to think. Maybe she should look at the data again. She opened a visualization app and loaded the information Shen Shi had shown her.

Yamamoto had given Shen Shi access to a wide range of databases, many of them technically illegal to access—Chinese ministry databases of medical files, police records—in addition to the usual social media feeds and commercial banking and credit card databases. The strange activity Shen Shi had flagged was from a group of people whose online behavior had changed, where they had started making donations to the Chinese Politburo and PLA.

Jin made a fresh pot of tea, then sat to begin a new analysis. She tagged unusual deaths from the police records and cross-correlated them with the groups of people flagged in Shen Shi's analysis. Outliers popped up right away: suspicious pacemaker failures, strange drug mix-ups.

By themselves, they were within the noise of probability distributions, but when linked with Shen Shi's data, it became obvious something else was going on. One way or the other, all these people liquidated most their assets just *before* their deaths.

On her screen glowed a connected trail of wealthy dead people that stretched all across China.

AUGUST 17th

Wednesday

9

Bluebridge Offices
Stamford, Connecticut

The receptionist smiled. "You can't go in, sir."

Jake glanced around the Bluebridge lobby. Big enough to be an aircraft hangar, its polished marble floors reflected the overhead chandeliers. Entering through the phase-shifting glass entrance doors, which lightened and darkened depending on exterior lighting, was an otherworldly experience, like passing through a time portal into the future.

The chandeliers hanging in the Bluebridge lobby were famous. Jake saw an article about them in one of his wife's architecture magazines—unique artworks by some Japanese post-modernist, forged in huge 3D printers from sintered quartz. In person, hanging from the thirty foot ceilings like shimmering angels, they seemed to say, *Herein lie the gates to power and wealth,* to anyone who dared enter.

Jake looked back at the receptionist, flashing his best high-wattage smile. "Like I said, I know Mr. Viegas. Could you please call him?"

He inspected her nameplate, then inspected her: flawless skin, hair done in a business-but-sexy bun, and a Burberry-pattern neckerchief tied in a neat bow. "Cindy, please, this is a personal matter," Jake added.

"Sir, you *cannot* meet with Mr. Viegas today. You will have to make an appointment." Cindy checked her screen. "I could put you in for a video meeting sometime over the next two weeks. Let me check the scheduling system."

No chance of getting anywhere with her. Cindy was a professional goaltender.

Nodding, Jake leaned onto the reception desk and looked at the display on his smartphone. He was researching some of Sean's businesses, trying to find out what he'd been involved in before the accident. Sean had been working in banking, designing automated trading systems. That much he knew.

His friend also mentioned something about cryptocurrency mining. Jake had heard of it, but wasn't familiar. He pulled up an online definition:

Cryptocurrencies are software-based online payment systems, the first of which, bitcoin, was introduced in 2009. Payments work peer-to-peer without a central administrator, which has led the US Treasury to call them decentralized virtual currencies—a cryptocurrency or digital currency. A key feature is that funds, and funds transfers, can be completely anonymous....

Jake continued reading while Cindy searched the scheduling system. *Cryptocurrency mining* was an activity used to generate new digital funds. So Sean had been involved in an online money generation scheme. This didn't surprise Jake. Cryptocurrencies could be pegged to US dollars, and even used to create "bit-shares" of virtual online corporations. Money shifted from one place to the other, all outside of governments and regulators. He read another webpage:

Digital currencies have been the subject of scrutiny amid concerns that they can be used for illegal activities, much like cash. In October 2013, the US FBI shut down the darknet Silk Road black market and seized 144,000 bitcoins worth $28.5 million at the time.

Jake sighed. What had Sean gotten himself tangled up in? And what was a *darknet?* He clicked another online definition:

A darknet is a private network where connections are made only between trusted peers, often associated with "underground" web communications and technologies, commonly associated with illegal activity or dissent. Darknets are anonymous, enabling users to communicate with little fear of government or corporate interference.

Jake could barely keep up with the jargon.

"Are you available on Thursday, two weeks from now, at 2:45 pm?" Cindy asked.

Jake looked up from his phone. "Sure, I'll take the meeting."

"Very good."

The interior courtyard was visible through the glass wall

behind Cindy's desk. Bluebridge headquarters was reminiscent of Egyptian or Mayan stepped pyramids, but with a hollow interior. Each floor had offices—he could see a smattering of people standing and walking on all levels—ringing its circumference, all of it chrome-and-glass, creating a semi-transparent structure with vines and plants hanging off the interior balconies like a modern Babylon.

The inside area was as large as a football field. Workers were busy setting up for the event tonight. A fundraiser in the inner sanctum of Bluebridge.

He'd tried to get a ticket. It wasn't possible, not even through his wide network of connections. Viegas was going to be here tonight, and Jake wanted—*needed*—to speak with him. In person.

"Could you place your finger on the scanner?"

Jake frowned. "Now? For an online meeting in two weeks?"

"We require everyone we schedule meetings with to bio-authenticate."

"Are you kidding me? What if I was remote?"

Cindy wasn't fazed. "Our procedure is to send out teams to authenticate remotely."

Jake stared at the scanner in front of him, his Atlas work email displayed on it.

He knew they were paranoid here. All the big financial funds—Vanguard, Cerberus, Blackrock—were secretive to varying degrees, but Bluebridge took the ribbon. Working here was like joining a cult. Management warned employees not to talk to outsiders about anything they did inside, and could only communicate via approved devices—whether work or personal. Bluebridge recorded every conversation and email. It was the only place he knew of that had four Chief Security Officers, all of them high ranking ex-CIA. It wasn't like the security apparatus of any other corporation.

Then again, Bluebridge wasn't like any other corporation. Henry Montrose III, the founder, had made a reported five *billion* dollars the previous year, with Viegas not far behind, making them the highest paid executives on the planet. That was as much money as run-of-the-mill billionaires made in a lifetime, but at Bluebridge they gave the impression they were only getting warmed up.

Jake glanced from the scanner to Cindy, then pressed his

thumb onto it. Something fluttered past him and Jake tensed up and turned around. He was about to tell Cindy that a bird had flown into the lobby when another of whatever it was buzzed past.

"Delivery drones," Cindy advised, smiling. "It does take a little getting used to."

Jake watched this one zip down the corridor. It was a four-prop helicopter, much like the ones carried in electronics stores, with a small package secured underneath. Two people walked up the hallway talking, oblivious to the device flying at them, and Jake was about to yell a warning when the drone executed a neat sidestep around them. The people didn't even look up or acknowledge its passing.

"Thank you, Mr. O'Connell. You will get a message the day before the meeting with instructions."

Jake lifted his eyebrows in response. "Sure." Who knew what he'd be doing in two weeks.

Yesterday, after his brother's visit, the SEC had served Jake formal investigation papers by a bailiff. They'd instructed Jake not to leave the New York metropolitan area. Not to contact Donovan. Not to erase any emails or documents.

Not a surprise.

He'd expected it to happen, so he hadn't paid it much attention.

What he had been doing was researching Bluebridge. Many of the shell companies listed on Donovan's memory key connected to it, through circuitous ownership networks spanning the global financial system. Was Bluebridge framing Donovan? Did it have anything to do with Sean's death?

Jake had met Viegas several times before shaking his hand at Atlas last week—a few times at MIT when visiting Sean, then once more at Bluebridge. Viegas scored low on Jake's psychopath scale, more Dalai Lama than the other way around. Sean might have been the brilliant one, but Jake's skill was reading people, noticing what they were thinking. He wanted to confront Viegas, see how he reacted.

Not a sophisticated plan, but he realized now that they wouldn't let him stand there and wait.

"I took the liberty of ordering you a car service," Cindy said. "I assumed you came in from the train station?"

Jake glanced over his shoulder to see a car waiting beyond the entrance doors. It wasn't a taxi. It was a limo. He nodded. "Thanks, Cindy." Elle and Jake didn't have a car. He had taken the Amtrak from Penn station to Stamford, then a taxi to Bluebridge. Cindy must have noticed him arriving in it.

▲▼▲

Cormac watched Jake get out of the limo and walk into the station. Rolling down the window of his Buick, he used binoculars to watch Jake through the glass walls of the enclosed second floor waiting area.

After ten minutes, the southbound Amtrak pulled into the station, obscuring Cormac's view of Jake. A minute later, it pulled out of the station, leaving an empty platform behind.

"We're good," Cormac keyed into the encrypted messaging app on his phone.

He was leaning forward to start his car when he spotted something from the corner of his eye.

A taxi headed out of the station, already up the road.

With Jake in the back seat.

Cormac swore under his breath and dialed a number. No answer. Swearing again, he keyed another number and fired off a hurried text message.

▲▼▲

The taxi driver dropped Jake off just before the entrance to Bluebridge. As he'd waited in the train station, the anger had built inside Jake and then sparked like a rushed ignition sequence when the train pulled in. If someone here was involved in Sean's death, he had to find out.

Now.

He was pretty sure Viegas wasn't involved. Viegas had been Sean's friend and mentor. If Viegas saw Jake, he would give him a minute. Maybe he didn't even know Sean was dead.

Going back and waiting outside the Bluebridge entrance seemed like a workable idea. He'd spotted a coffee shop across the street, and decided he could wait there until a limo or helicopter arrived. Then he could cut through the pines, past the exterior security, and try to confront Viegas. Not elegant, but better than nothing.

The moment Jake disembarked from his taxi, a black limo pulled in through the front security gate, the outline of Viegas's head visible through its tinted window.

Lucky, but it was perfect timing.

Ducking through the trees, Jake jogged to the entrance just as Viegas got out of the limo and passed through the front doors. Someone shouted behind Jake. He picked up his pace, ran harder, and in a few seconds he was at the doors. They slid open before him.

Cindy, the receptionist, saw him coming in and stood. "Mr. O'Connell? Did you forget something?"

"No, I need to use the bathroom."

Cindy was already picking up her phone, probably dialing security. "Mr. O'Connell, you cannot come in here."

Jake jogged past her desk and ignored her. He'd been here before with Sean, so he knew Viegas's office was to the left, past the pit of programmers on the first floor.

"Mr. Viegas!" Jake called out, rounding the corner. Viegas's head turned toward him. "I'm Jake O'Connell. We met at MIT a few times, and we shook hands at our office last week. I need to talk to you about Sean Womack."

Jake sprinted the last few feet, then skidded to a stop, holding his hands up. He knew the guards would be on him in seconds, but he figured Viegas would at least hear him out.

Viegas stared at him.

"Sean Womack," Jake repeated. "You were his thesis advisor, we got together in Cambridge. He...he's been working with your company for the last few years." Jake took a gulp of air. "Sean was killed in London, I wanted to—"

"I don't know what you're talking about." Viegas backed away.

"He's over there," someone said behind Jake.

"I know you were close to Sean. I want to talk to you for a minute. Just a minute, please."

Viegas's eyes remained blank. Frightened.

"Sean Womack," Jake repeated, pleading now.

Something seemed odd. Jake did a quick scan of the office space. It extended for at least a hundred feet on each side, the space filled with dozens of cubicles. He remembered it as a beehive of activity when he was here before.

Now it was empty.

Someone grabbed Jake's arms, pulling them behind his back as he stared at Viegas. He felt cold metal. Click-click-click. Handcuffs tightened around his wrists.

"What the hell?" Jake tried to twist around, but now two people held him, lifting him from the ground.

"Mr. Jake O'Connell, you have the right to remain silent…"

Jake craned his neck around enough to see police uniforms. Four of them were behind him, with more streaming into the lobby. Red and blue lights flashed and shimmered in the chandeliers overhead.

"…you have the right to an attorney…"

"Are you kidding? I just ran in here, you can't arrest me for that."

How did they get here so fast?

They continued to read him his Miranda rights.

"What is this?" Jake shuffled forward. Five police cruisers were parked outside the entrance. "Does this have to do with the SEC investigation?"

The front doors slid open in front of Jake, and the policeman standing on the other side answered his question. "No, Mr. O'Connell, you're being arrested for rape."

10

Shenzhen
China

Yawning, Jin pulled off the bed covers and called out to see if Wutang was home.

No response.

Getting out of bed, she opened the door and peered outside the bedroom. The apartment was empty.

Quiet.

And immaculate.

She hadn't even heard Wutang leave.

He'd been gracious to her when he returned from his family event. Rather than make some insinuation about the two of them sharing his bed, he'd insisted she take the bedroom. After changing the sheets and grabbing a pillow and covers for himself, he shepherded her into his room despite her protests, telling her they could talk in the morning.

After not sleeping the night before, she fell asleep as soon as her head hit the pillow.

Wutang's apartment was in a high-rise complex, one of a dozen cookie-cutter buildings that had sprung up almost overnight, towering residential mushrooms in the Yeuhai district. It was modern and comfortable, if small. The bedroom was the only closed room—apart from the tiny bathroom with its shower stall—leading onto an open-plan combined living room and kitchen. Not more than six hundred square feet, and painted stark white. Unimaginative framed prints of orchids decorated the walls. The main defining feature was the massive flat screen display that covered the living room wall, and above that, a mass of wires connected to several routers.

Most important, Jin felt safe here.

The days before seemed like a nightmare, but on the coffee table next to her laptop was a rude reminder that it wasn't a dream. The card from the policeman who had interviewed her after Shen Shi's "accident." She stared at it, willed it to go away, but it wouldn't.

The shock of her cousin's death was fresh. Jin felt flat, single-dimensional, her emotions a distant concept that belonged to someone else. On the counter was a note from Wutang saying he'd be back before noon. Had to go out to the office.

Instinctively, she checked for her cellphone before realizing she'd left it at her apartment. If someone *was* looking for her, a cellphone was a beacon that could pinpoint her. Better to be safe. But there would be a dozen messages on it from her mother and aunts.

Better check my email.

Reaching into her backpack by the door, she pulled out and opened her laptop, putting it on the coffee table. Jin had left emails for her family saying she was fine, staying with a friend, but they'd be frantic by now.

She should be frantic herself, but somehow, she wasn't. She felt numb.

Jin filled the kettle on the kitchen counter and turned it on, then walked over and opened the sliding patio doors that led to the small concrete balcony outside. Humid air and the noise of traffic ten stories below rushed in through the open doors. Rows of nearly identical skyscrapers stretched into the distance to the glistening waters of Qianhai Bay.

Her laptop pinged. Someone was messaging her. Sitting on the couch, she opened her encrypted messaging app.

>>*Wutang: You okay? Worried about you.*

She smiled. She liked that he was worried about her.

>>*Jin: I'm fine.*

The cursor blinked. Wutang typed on his end: *I've been looking up digital autonomous corporations, DACs, the stuff Shen Shi was researching for Yamamoto.*

Appended to his message was a list of web pages. Jin clicked on the first one, and an article popped up from *Forbes* magazine about the recent flourishing of autonomous corporations operating on darknets, linking them to organized crime: *IdentityDAC is a digital corporation that manages the valuation and disbursement of stolen identities and credit card numbers. The FBI and Interpol have been investigating the sudden explosive growth of IdentityDAC, but due to the distributed nature of its operations...*

>>*Wutang: Are you reading?*

Jin responded, *yes*, still scanning the end of the identity theft story. The article had links to another discussing BlackCorp, a criminal collective for hacking, and RansomCorp, which enabled attackers to use an encryption virus to ransom the contents of a target's hard drive.

>>*Wutang: I need Shen Shi's credentials, can you get them?*

Shen Shi's laptop was next to Jin. She knew his usual passwords. *Yes*, she typed back.

The list of autonomous corporations went on and on. Jin scanned them, a low-voltage tingling working its way down her back. Something related to this must have been what Yamamoto was planning to expose to the banks. What got him killed. What got Shen Shi killed.

>>*Jin: When are you coming back?*

>>*Wutang: A few hours. There's an emergency I need to fix.*

The cursor blinked.

She typed: *Are these corporations purely digital then, no humans involved?*

>>*Wutang: The autonomous corporation itself is, yes, but they pay people to do work in the real world—to hack, to steal—while they carry out their programmed missions in the digital world. And under US law they have rights as 'people'…*

People? Jin picked up her cup of tea and blew on it, taking a sip. *Corporations counted as people?*

>>*Wutang: I need to log off. Find those credentials. We'll do more when I get home.*

>>*Jin: Will do. See you soon.*

Wutang logged off the messaging app, and Jin sat back with her cup of tea. On her laptop screen, an alert flashed, advising twenty-two unread email messages. Deciding she didn't have the emotional energy to deal with that right now, she closed her laptop.

So autonomous corporations used humans to do their work in the physical world. She'd heard of them, glanced at articles on cryptocurrencies when going over the morning news, but she'd never considered the implications. Leaning forward, she grabbed her backpack and took out Shen Shi's laptop.

Shen Shi.

Her hand trembled. She put her cup of tea down, spilling some of it as the sobs came. The fear she'd felt since the "accident" all

64

turned to sadness. Shen Shi was gone. Her resolve hardened. Someone had done this to her cousin. They had to find out who.

She settled onto the couch with Shen Shi's laptop and found his encrypted password locker, opened it, and sent the contents to Wutang. Logging in as the administrator, she changed the password, then opened an anonymizing web browser.

It was strange that Sean had been carrying no ID. Jin remembered Sean as being careful, always aware of his surroundings. He had friends everywhere, and he wouldn't be without identification unless it was on purpose. Had someone stolen his wallet? Was it a robbery? It seemed unlikely.

She repeated the web searches she did the night before to see if she missed anything, then scanned the list of results. On the third page, a connection popped up that she hadn't seen before: *Vidal Viegas.*

Vidal Viegas had been Sean's thesis advisor at MIT. She remembered hearing about the mentorship from Sean, who used to joke about having someone at the top of the industry. Jin pulled up more searches clustered around Viegas: author of the machine-learning algorithms that she and all of her colleagues in the data business used. She found as many references to fundraising events with US-presidential-candidate Senator Russ as she did Viegas's technical work on automated agents and data mining.

A fluttering dread roiled Jin's stomach. Viegas was now the famous co-founder of Bluebridge, the world's largest hedge fund.

The strange email from Sean before he died. He'd written a single phrase in his message: *"Remember the nuggets."* Was it a warning, a coded message?

He had to be referring to the last time she'd spent time with him in person, years ago in a bar in Guangzhou. The memory stood out because he'd brought a dozen boxes of chicken nuggets to the bar with him, and within minutes, pretty young models had mobbed their table. The night had turned into an urban legend among their colleagues in the banking world. When they worked on data mining projects, they called influential outliers 'nuggets,' little golden pieces of information that seemed to have magical properties.

Remember the nuggets. She'd met Sean's friends that night in Guangzhou. What were their names? Max Lefevre was one of them, a French Canadian that Sean worked with, and another guy was there, Sean's *best* friend. Jin scrunched up her face, trying to force the name out.

Jake.

Jake O'Connell.

She remembered him as a nice guy. Good looking, clean cut, and nothing at all to do with the usual crowd of hangers-on that buzzed around Sean.

Jin opened her social media account and typed Jake's name into its search box. Yes. They'd friended each other. Details of Jake's life spilled out on her screen: well wishes for his daughter's birthday, location tags at restaurants around Manhattan. A life observed from a distance for the entire world to see.

She opened a new search box and queried Jake's name together with "Manhattan," then clicked the first story: *New York, Aug 17th—Jake O'Connell, an executive linked to the Atlas Capital fraud investigation, was arrested on rape charges...*

That didn't sound like the Jake she knew. She'd only met him that one time in person, but they'd friended each other on social media and she'd followed his postings. She liked to think she was a good judge of character. But maybe she was wrong. Taking a deep breath, Jin sent an encrypted email to Jake, asking him to contact her. No other details than that.

She decided to go back to the data sets she'd been looking at the night before—the trail of wealthy dead people. The big question: Was it real?

The problem with examining a lot of data at the same time, cross-connecting it and searching for outliers, was that eventually you'd find whatever pattern you were looking for. With enough data, you started seeing anything, like reading a medical textbook and deciding you had the symptoms of a dangerous disease when all that was happening was the regular mechanics of life.

She needed a second opinion.

>>Message>>Jin to Chen: Could you have a look at something for me?

Chen was a friend who she and Shen Shi had worked with on their last two Ministry projects. Even so, she made it a policy to contact everyone through an anonymous connection. You never knew who might be tapping the data stream. She leaned forward toward the tea set. Before she could finish pouring herself a cup, the messaging app pinged.

>>*Chen: Heard about Shen, so sorry.*

The cursor blinked as Chen continued to type on the other end.

>>*Chen: Very weird.*

Jin sighed, put down her cup of tea and replied.

>>*Jin: Yes.*

>>*Chen: Are you okay?*

>>*Jin: No.*

She waited. The cursor blinked.

>>*Chen: What can I look at for you?*

Uncrossing her legs from the couch, she put the laptop on the coffee table. Opening some online tools, she set up a data exchange, answering questions back and forth about what she wanted examined. She didn't want to tell him what to look for—that might skew what he found—so she only said that there were some unusual correlations.

>>*Chen: Do you want to get lunch?*

Jin blinked and stared at the cursor. She could use some company. Wutang wasn't going to be back for a few hours.

>>*Jin: Sure.*

She didn't want to say where she was staying, but she gave him the name of a noodle shop around the corner, a small one she knew to be quiet. They could discuss the results and see if Chen saw the same patterns.

One click of the 'send' button, and the data started uploading from Shen Shi's laptop into a secure cloud repository for Chen. Logging off the chat app, Jin checked the time. It was forty minutes past twelve. She needed to grab her shower.

Leaving her own laptop open, she picked up Shen Shi's and deposited it into her backpack. She smiled. Wutang had left towels out on top of the counter for her. Jin picked up the top towel and held it to her nose. It smelled fresh. What a sweetheart.

Her laptop issued an angry ping. An urgent message alert.

Still holding the towel, she leaned over the couch and squinted at the screen. It was a message from Wutang.

>>*Wutang: You need to look at this right now.*

Jin sat down, towel in her lap, and clicked the link attached to the message. A web article popped up:

The Assassin Market—a crowd-funding service that enables people to

anonymously contribute cryptocurrency funds toward a bounty on anyone. A
kind of Kickstarter for murder, this darknet site has resisted multiple
attempts by the CIA to bring it down as it spawns itself…

Her background low-voltage dread spiked into high-voltage
panic.

>>*Jin: Why are you sending me this??*

>>*Wutang: Sit down.*

>>*Jin: I'm sitting down.*

The cursor blinked. Then blinked some more.

>>*Jin: What?? What's going on??*

>>*Wutang: Don't go anywhere; I'm on my way home.*

>>*Jin: Why?*

>>*Wutang: I used the credentials you gave me from Shen Shi to log into*
the Assassin Market the article is talking about.

>>*Jin: And??*

Why hadn't Shen Shi told her? Why was Wutang making her
wait?

The next message pinged with an attachment. A spreadsheet.
She double-clicked it. A list of names appeared, each name with
fractional number of cryptocurrency funds, along with a dollar
equivalent next to it.

>>*Wutang: This is the Assassin Market hit list.*

$275,652 posted as bounty for the assassination of the
International Monetary Fund director.

$142,544 for the President of the United States.

Jin scanned down the list of names, which looked like the
typical crackpot—

A name popped out, floating disconnected from the rest of the
page: *Shen Shi Heng. Recent payout: $86,544.*

The apartment spun and her stomach churned. She held the
towel to her face, her hands shaking. There was one more name,
added just that morning: *Jin Huang—$103,233.*

>>*Wutang: I'm sure this is some sick joke. Stay there, I'm almost*
home—

Jin snapped the laptop closed and pulled her hand away as if it
was burning hot. She got up, knocking the table, spilling the tea.
She grabbed her backpack with Shen Shi's laptop. She had to get
out of there.

But where would she go?

She turned to the patio doors. Better close them. Pull the curtains.

Hide.

Behind her, the apartment door splintered and flew open. Men in head-to-foot black clothing forced their way in.

Jin shrieked and dropped the towel, spinning around and crashing into the coffee table. She was still holding her backpack with the laptop. One thought filtered to the top: they had to be after Shen Shi's data. Scrambling to stand, she swung the backpack out the balcony door just as one of the men grabbed her and pushed her to the ground. She watched the bag clear the balcony railing outside and fall from view.

Squirming, Jin tried to get up, but the man held her down, wrapping his arms around her. Two others stormed into the bedroom and kicked in the bathroom door.

A fourth man entered the apartment door slowly, pulling a syringe from one of his pants pockets. Jin's eyes went wide as she watched him hold it up and squirt liquid from its tip. She tried to scream, but the man restraining her had his hand clamped firmly over her mouth. The fourth man grabbed her arm and stuck the needle into it, plunging the contents of the syringe into her veins.

Her vision swam. The last thing she knew was white-hot terror as nausea overcame her and blackness descended.

AUGUST 18th

Thursday

11

District Courthouse
New York City

Jake almost cried when he found Elle sitting behind his lawyer in the courtroom. The judge set a two hundred and fifty thousand dollar bail, but Jake was released the moment he was shuffled back into the holding cell.

He hadn't thought she'd post bail for him.

Not that fast.

Not for something like this.

Released into her custody by the court, he followed her down the rickety wooden wheelchair ramp in front of the building.

"Can I get a hotdog?" Jake asked stupidly when they passed a street vendor. He was starving, having barely eaten in the past day, but Elle didn't turn, didn't respond in any way. She walked ahead of him until she found a taxi.

Once seated in the back of the cab, Jake slid closed the plastic divider between the passenger compartment and the front seat. He turned to his wife. "Thank you," he whispered.

After being arrested, he used his first call on his lawyer; the second, to leave a message for Elle. He'd tried her three more times with no luck, and she hadn't called him back.

Elle stared out of her window, keeping her distance. He tried to reach for her hand, but she shrugged him off, clenching her jaw. "What were you doing at Bluebridge?" she asked. "They said you tried to attack Vidal Viegas. You're lucky he didn't press more charges." She looked away.

The cab accelerated and passed Canal Street. Jake looked out the window at the street vendors selling fake Gucci bags and Rolex watches.

"The woman who accused me," Jake said, "Susie, my assistant, you met her at the cocktail party last Christmas—I was about to fire her." Susie's accusation was totally fabricated and inexplicable.

"Maybe this whole thing at Atlas has her scared and she needs money. I don't know."

"Like last time?" Elle stared hard out the opposite window.

"I'm sorry, Elle, I don't know what to say. I didn't touch her. I swear."

"The prosecutors for the Atlas case told you to stay in New York." Elle glared straight ahead, not looking at Jake, but not looking away either. "What possessed you to go to Stamford?"

Buildings and faces slid by outside the taxi window. "I think the executives at Bluebridge were involved in Sean's death."

"What happened to Sean was an accident," Elle said, still staring away from him when the taxi reached 52nd street to begin winding its way cross-town. "An accident, Jake. I read the police report. You read it, too."

Her face softened and she turned to him.

"I am truly sorry, Jake, I know how much he meant to you." A tear spilled down her cheek. "But I can't do this again. I don't know what's going on with you, but I can't do this again."

▲▼▲

"Get out of my way!" Jake yelled, pushing back the reporters and cameras.

Someone must have tipped them off about his release. A trader in the middle of the Atlas scandal, arrested for sexual assault and attacking Vidal Viegas—one of the richest hedge fund managers in the world—before a fundraiser for the leading presidential candidate. It was the hottest news item of the day.

"Sorry Mr. O'Connell." Their doorman, Karl, tried to shield Elle and get them inside.

A reporter shoved his way into Jake's face. "Mr. O'Connell, why were you at Bluebridge?"

"No comment." Jake shoved back and ducked through the front door to their building.

Karl closed it behind them, yelling, "I'll do my best to keep them out, Mr. O'Connell."

Inside wasn't much better. Since their apartment was on the first floor, it was right in front of the pack of paparazzi. Even with the blinds and curtains closed, Jake felt them buzzing outside like a high-voltage transmission line.

He threw his suit jacket onto the kitchen table. He'd slept in it.

"Elle, you've got to believe me. Somebody is setting me up. They must know about the dropped sexual harassment charge from a few years back and—" He stopped midsentence. "What the hell is *he* doing here?"

Jake's brother was sitting on their couch. Anna snuggled up beside him, watching cartoons on their giant flat screen TV. Eamon smiled at Jake. "Nice to see you, too."

Esmeralda, their housecleaner, appeared from the bedroom down the hallway. "Do you need me anymore, Mrs. O'Connell?"

"No, thank you, Esmeralda. I really appreciate you coming on such short notice."

"No problem, Mrs. O'Connell." Esmeralda smiled thinly at Jake. "Glad you are home, Mr. O'Connell." She picked up her purse and jacket from the table. "Goodbye, Anna." She blew her a kiss.

Elle waited until Esmeralda closed the door behind herself.

"What's your brother doing here?" She threw her arms in the air. "You got thrown in jail, so I figured it might help to have someone around who knew a thing or two about it. Do you think I have any idea how to raise bail?"

Jake blinked twice. "I, uh, I hadn't thought about it. I was so happy to see you."

"You can thank him for getting you out." Elle pointed at Eamon. "I would have let you rot in there for a few more days, but Eamon insisted on getting you out." Her lips trembled. "I had to put our home up as collateral." Turning, she stormed down the hallway toward their bedroom. "Anyway, you can use the company."

Jake said nothing. Exhaled. Time for damage control.

"Thanks for getting me out, Eamon," he said quietly. "I appreciate it."

"No problem. You okay?"

"More or less," Jake replied, but he felt like his life was spinning ever further out of control.

Could Susie, his assistant, have really cooked up this scam for money? True, she knew Atlas was a mess...and she undoubtedly knew he was on the verge of firing her. Still, it seemed out of character for her to concoct a scheme like this.

Jake took a few steps into the living room, dodging stuffed

toys and Lego sculptures to sit down next to his daughter, Anna, her eyes still glued to the TV.

"Daddy," she squeaked as he sat, finally peeling her attention away from the movie. She wrapped her arms around him. "I missed you," she said, looking up into his eyes.

"I missed you too."

She had her mother's almond eyes. Jake's mouth. There was an ache inside him, sitting here beside his soon-to-be-six-year-old daughter in the wake of a day he'd missed completely. Anna was the most perfect and beautiful thing he'd ever laid eyes on, and he felt, acutely, the loss of a thousand precious moments with this little person who would grow up sooner than he could imagine.

Did she know where her dad had been? Shame and fear snaked through Jake's gut, but Anna's eyes betrayed nothing. Leaning down, he kissed her forehead.

She scrunched up her face, said, "Yuck, Daddy," then squirmed free to return her attention to her cartoon.

Jake glanced around the apartment. Something was out of place. The luggage stacked by the door.

"Elle? What's with all the bags?" He stood.

"I told you I'm not doing this again." Elle appeared through their bedroom door, scarves and shoes in hand. "I'm bringing Anna with me to my sister's in Hoboken." She swept past him and stuffed the items into one of the bags by the door.

Jake felt his face flush. "I didn't do this, Elle. My assistant is setting me up, either she wants money or something else. Donovan said Bluebridge framed him. Maybe he was right."

Elle threw the last shoe she was holding toward an open bag, and it bounced off against the wall and skidded across the floor. "Why would they do that?"

"I don't know."

"So you expect me to take your word for it like I did last time?" She reached for a piece of paper on the entrance table, waved it in the air.

"I went ahead and checked your phone records. You called this girl, Susie, late at night, over and over." Wiping away tears, she gritted her teeth. "What do you have to say about that?"

"What? Let me see that." Jake never called Susie outside of work hours. "Honey, you have to believe me."

"Again?" She held the accusatory paper in front of her like a shield. "The meaning of life is happiness, right Jake? Isn't that what you told me when you asked me to marry you? You promised we would romp around the world like two kids in a playground, spreading our love. Well, you're spreading your love, all right."

Jake felt Anna gripping his wrist like a vice. He looked down into her frightened eyes, filled with tiny tears. Jake and Elle never fought in front of her. "Elle, can we talk in our room?" Jake asked, lowering his voice.

"Anna and I are leaving this…this *circus*, and that's final." She waved one hand toward the windows, toward the media buzzing outside.

"You can't split our family up, Elle, please."

Elle took two steps toward Jake and shoved a finger in his face. "You are the one splitting this family up. I don't need all this money you're chasing. I don't need"—she jabbed her finger toward the front windows—"*this*."

"I didn't do this," Jake pleaded, his voice barely more than a whisper.

"I thought I knew you, but you *are* like your dad." Elle's voice was steadier now, but harder. "You said you hated how your father gambled, yet here you are, doing the same thing with stocks. You hated how he conned people, yet look at you—you see rules and laws as guidelines, not mandates. Ethics only matter if you get caught, right? Isn't that what you said about your dad?" She sighed. "Go look in the mirror, Jake."

"Please, Elle," Jake begged.

"Insanity is doing the same thing, over and over, and expecting different results. That's another of your favorite expressions. I'm through with doing the same thing."

Elle took another step toward him, and he half-expected a slap in the face, but instead she knelt down and picked up Anna. "Come on, we're going to Auntie Julia's," she whispered to their daughter.

Jake wanted to get up and block the door, pull Anna away from her, but he watched as his wife got up and walked out the door. She left the offending telephone record on the dining table.

It would be better—*safer*—for her to be at her sister's, and for Anna to be away from the pack of reporters outside. It was the right thing to do, at least for now, and he didn't want to upset Elle more than he already had. Let her calm down. He could talk to her later in the day.

Karl, the doorman, came in through the door to collect her bags. He nodded apologetically to Jake before leaving with them. Jake nodded back.

"What was she talking about? Did something like this happen before?" Eamon asked as the door closed.

Jake stared at the door. "Years ago, before I started at Atlas, a girl at the bar I was managing filed a sexual harassment lawsuit against me." He grabbed the telephone record from the table and looked at it, shaking his head. The calls to Susie were on there, but he didn't make them. It was a set up.

"You never told me that."

"We haven't exactly been close, have we?"

Eamon paused. "Did you do it? Back then?"

Jake's cellphone buzzed and he pulled it out, expecting a message from Elle. But it was from that Joseph Barbara guy, the client from Atlas that Donovan had told him to ignore. He clicked his phone off and put it back in his pocket.

"No. I didn't," Jake replied. "I was going to fire her for stealing from the petty cash. She pre-empted me."

"Seems like a big coincidence, Jake. What happened?"

"The owner settled out of court. Didn't want the bad press."

"You know the media is going to find out."

Jake nodded. "Whoever is setting me up, they knew how bad it would look." He swore under his breath. "I don't blame Elle for leaving. Goddamn it."

Someone knocked at the door. Jake swung around. *It has to be Elle.* He jumped at the door and pulled it open. "Baby, I'm so sorry, I'm going to—"

But it wasn't Elle.

"Mr. O'Connell," said a man in a dark suit. He flashed a badge at Jake, 'FBI' stenciled in large block letters next to it in the wallet. "I wanted to introduce myself. I'm Special Agent Tolliver."

Jake glanced behind him. No sign of Elle. "What do you want?"

"I've become involved in the Atlas investigation, but we're also investigating Bluebridge."

A tingle in Jake's spine. "Why?"

"I work outside of the regular channels, Mr. O'Connell. A

special investigative branch. We've noticed some unusual activity at Bluebridge. I'm not investigating you, but I was hoping you might be able to tell me a bit more about your visit there? What made you—"

"He's got nothing to say." Eamon pulled the door fully open and put an arm in front of Jake. "Unless you want to haul him in, he's got nothing to say."

Agent Tolliver glanced at Eamon, then looked back at Jake and pulled a card from his wallet. "If you ever change your mind, here's my number." He handed it to Jake. "Think about it."

Eamon shook his head, but Jake took the card anyway. "Thanks," he mumbled as Eamon gave Agent Tolliver the finger, then slammed the door in his face.

"Why did you do that?" Jake felt an electric jolt of anger toward his brother. This FBI agent could be important. "Bluebridge might be framing Donovan and me. Maybe this guy can help."

Eamon let him finish. "First of all, *they* never help *you*. That's the first rule. And second, how the hell do you even know who that is?"

Jake flashed the card. "We can look him up. And his badge looked real to me."

"So you're an expert?" Eamon shook his head.

"I wanted to tell him how empty Bluebridge was when I ran in there. It seemed strange."

Jake inspected the card. Embossed. Deep blue insignia with gold leaf patterned onto the FBI crest.

Looked legit.

"Whatever's going on, Jake, we have to figure it out ourselves. This Henry Montrose guy who owns Bluebridge, he's a heavy dude. We gotta be careful. We don't know what Sean got himself wrapped up in."

Jake frowned. "What do you mean, '*we*?'"

"I'm getting you out of here, Jake. You might not like me, but I'm still your big brother. Family is family. Come on, I'm going to sneak you out the back entrance. I got my car there."

Jake shook his head. "I'm out on bail. I can't leave New York."

"We're not going to leave New York."

"No?"

Eamon grinned. "At least not New York State. I'm taking you

79

home, up to Schenectady."

"What are we going to do there?"

Leaving the city seemed like a bad idea. It would put more physical distance than there already was between Jake and his family, and if Elle found out he left the city again…

"I got connections up there." Eamon pointed at himself and then at Jake. "*We* got connections up there. And besides, Anna called me. She wants to see you."

"Anna called you?" Jake tried to understand what his brother was saying. "My little girl called you? But she was just here. How did she—"

"Not Anna." Eamon put a hand on Jake's shoulder. "I mean *Anna.*"

12

Schenectady
Upper New York State

The front door swung open before Jake even rang the bell. Anna opened it. *Auntie Anna,* he still called her in his head.

"I'm so sorry," she cried, wrapping her arms around him before he could say or do anything. Tears streamed down her face.

Jake didn't resist. He put his arms around her as well.

She felt tiny.

Frail.

They stood like that in the doorway, half in and half out of the rain falling outside. Clenching his teeth, Jake waited for his own tears, but none came. He gripped her tighter just the same. It was the first time he saw anyone cry about Sean's death.

Rocking back and forth, they slowly released each other. She wiped away her tears, took his jacket and hung it up in the entrance closet. Holding his hand, she led him inside.

"It's so nice to see you, Jake." Anna smiled, leading him to sit down on the floral-print couch in front of the big bay window that looked out onto the street. She rubbed her eyes. "You're looking well."

"It's nice to see you, too." Jake sat next to her, still holding her hand. A plate of cookies was on the walnut-veneer coffee table in front of them. Oreos. His favorite. "You're looking great."

The statement felt awkward. Forced.

"How's the project coming along?" Jake tried to steer the conversation away from himself.

She must have seen Jake in the news, implicated in the Atlas financial scandal, arrested on rape charges. It was as embarrassing as it was frightening. He was supposed to be the local kid that made good. Now he was sure he was the talk of the town—*that O'Connell kid, the apple sure doesn't fall far from the tree after all.*

Anna sighed. "We had to move the office here, upstairs."

81

Jake frowned. "Why?"

After her husband died four years ago, she'd poured all her energy into starting a foster care network. The last time they talked, she was getting funding for a new halfway house and activity center for boys she was going to build in the woods. The same woods Jake and Sean, and sometimes Eamon, used to escape into when they ran from whatever foster home they happened to be in. Anna joked that if that's where the boys wanted to go, she might as well build them a house out there.

"Budget cuts. The downturn hit this area hard." She managed a wisp of a smile. "No money."

"Can I help?" Jake always tried to offer Anna money, but she would never accept, saying he needed it for his family.

She held up her hands. "You know what I'm going to—"

"Anna!" a voice called from upstairs. A loud screeching and wailing began. "Could you come up for a second?"

Anna squeezed Jake's hand. "Would you excuse me?"

"Of course."

Jake watched her get up and climb the stairs. Awkwardly. Slowly. Anna had aged in the two years since they'd seen each other. He usually came every year, at the holidays, but this past season they'd gone south for a beach vacation instead. Jake had been meaning to come up for a visit, but there was always something that got in the way.

She looked fragile, her hands thin, skin papery, face gaunt. People had a way of aging suddenly when you weren't looking. For thirty or forty years, through middle age, they would look almost exactly the same, and then all of a sudden the decades would pile on in months.

But sometimes, it wasn't time that aged us. Jake could see the worry in her eyes.

He looked around the room. It was the same as he remembered it. The mantle over the fireplace was stacked with snow globes, many of which he had bought for her—Prague, Hong Kong, Kiev—every place he'd ever visited. On the opposite wall was a mahogany shelf unit that had been there for twenty or more years, with carefully arranged crystal glasses up top, and books and decades-old *National Geographic* magazines stacked below. The room smelled like mothballs and bread. Anna was always cooking something.

He picked up an Oreo.

The door to the den was half open, and in the darkened room beyond, three kids sat on a couch, staring at a television. It was an old tube-model TV set in a heavy wooden case. The volume was set low. The kids stared at the screen, oblivious to the world outside.

He knew how they felt.

He'd been one of those kids.

The wailing upstairs subsided into sobs. Floorboards creaked. "Do you want to go out for a walk?" Anna called from the top of the stairs.

"It's raining."

"Are you made of chocolate?"

Jake smiled. Hadn't heard that in a while. "No, I'm not."

"Then you won't melt."

Jake took a bite of the cookie. He hadn't realized how hungry he was. He finished it and gobbled a second while he waited. Anna appeared in a windbreaker and sensible rubber boots, holding a large purse and an umbrella. Jake stood and followed her out the front, grabbing his jacket from the closet on the way out.

It wasn't really raining anymore, just a light mist. His dad would have called it Scotch mist. Pulling his baseball cap low, Jake stuck his hands into the pockets of his jeans as they walked past the beat-up Ford his brother loaned him.

"I didn't do those things they're saying I did." Jake realized the words sounded familiar even as he said them. Donovan said exactly the same thing to him just before they carted him off in handcuffs.

Anna reached one arm around him and squeezed. "I know."

"The woman who's accusing me, she worked for me. I was going to fire her—"

"You don't need to explain, I believe you." Anna released him. "You were always a good boy, Jake, and you've grown into a good man." She smiled at him, waiting until he saw her expression before she looked away.

"Thanks." It was the first time Jake heard anyone, sincerely, believe him. "I don't know what to do."

"Your greatest strength is facing things straight on, Jake, and that's all you've got to do now." She shook one small balled fist in the air in front of her. "Have you talked to this woman?" Anna might look frail, but she was tough, as hard as the times she'd lived through.

"I'm not allowed to." Jake dug his hands further into his pockets.

He looked at the other houses on the street. Small. Sagging. White clapboard siding with screened porches. This area of Schenectady hadn't been prosperous in a hundred years, not since Thomas Edison had founded General Electric here in 1890 and sparked the electrification of America. "Elle took Anna and went to her sister's."

"I'm sorry." Anna sighed and her hands fell to her sides. "But maybe that's best for now."

They walked in silence. The mist progressed back into rain, and Jake pulled up the collar of his jacket.

"I'm worried that Sean was involved in something illegal." Jake wasn't sure how to bring it up, or if he even should. It would only get her worried, but she deserved to know. Sean had been like a son to her, as much as Jake was. "I don't know exactly what, but it seems to have something to do with my boss and what's happening at Atlas…what's happening to *me*."

Anna continued walking, methodically, staring down at her feet as she took one step and then another. "That's what I thought."

"That's what you thought?"

"It seemed like too much of a coincidence."

Jake stopped walking. "Wait. What seemed like too much of a coincidence?"

He pulled his hands out of his pockets and put them on Anna's shoulders, turned her to face him. A question had been nagging at him for a while, and he needed an answer.

"Why did you call Eamon to ask to see me? Why didn't you call me directly?"

Anna stared into his eyes. "Because Sean told me not to."

Standing in the rain, she pulled a manila envelope from her purse.

▲▼▲

Jake stared at the envelope, still wet, sitting on the motel table. The ink of the handwritten address had smeared. Sean had written

84

that, probably the last thing he ever wrote, and Jake was probably one of the last people he ever spoke to.

Why didn't I take ten seconds longer? Why didn't I call him back again?

Jake picked up the bottle of Jameson and poured an inch of it into a glass. Outside, the rain hammered down into the darkness. Cars rushed by on the interstate.

A simple kiss from your wife on the way to work, your daughter sitting in your lap reading, a call from an old friend— things taken for granted, now things ripped from Jake's life. He looked around the room. A discolored orange sheet covered the bed he sat on with his laptop next to him, an air conditioning unit jutted out of the wall under the window, tattered orange curtains pulled closed over dirty windows. His gym bag, stuffed with jeans and t-shirts, sat next to an old TV on the dresser.

He downed the whiskey and stared at the envelope. When Anna gave it to him, he wanted to rip it open. She said that Sean had inserted a note into it, telling her not to call Jake directly, to call his brother and get Jake to meet her in person. Sean's note said it was a matter of life and death.

It had become a matter of death.

On the drive back from Anna's, the envelope sat beside Jake like a white-hot coal, the rain pelting on the windshield. He'd thought of stopping to open it a dozen times, but each time something had held him back. There was a kind of finality in opening the envelope. It would be the last message he would ever get from his friend.

In a way, it would be the last time they would ever speak.

Jake wasn't ready.

There had to be answers in the envelope—answers for why his friend was dead, for why Jake was sitting by himself in this motel room. He thought of taking it to the police. Was it evidence? But he needed to find out himself, first.

His laptop pinged and Jake reached over to flip it open. He'd set an alert for the start of the Bluebridge quarterly investors' meeting. Viegas would be speaking. Jake wanted to see what he would say. He needed all the information about them he could get. Clicking a link generated a new window in his browser. The face of Vidal Viegas filled the screen. Viegas introduced himself, detailing the stellar returns Bluebridge earned for its investors.

Jake sighed and returned his attention to the envelope. He

picked it up, then reached inside to pull out another smaller envelope. "Jake" was written in big cursive letters on the front of it. Sean's handwriting. He looked inside the manila envelope, upended it. That was all that was inside.

Taking a deep breath, he opened the second envelope. A stack of papers filled it, along with another memory key. On top was a letter addressed to Jake:

Jake,
If you're getting this, and you didn't know you were getting it, then something happened to me. I'm sorry, buddy, I really am. I love you, Jake. You've been more than a brother to me. Promise me that you'll have a big party for me.

I will. Jake rubbed his face. *And I love you, too.*

That's why I'm dreading what I need you to do. I can't tell you more right now, but the reason will become clear. You need to get off the grid, dump your laptop, cell phone, credit cards, don't access any email accounts or online tools. You need to become a ghost. And you need to go to this location.

The location was a set of GPS coordinates. An attached map showed it up north in Canada, past Montreal. Jake had never been that far north, but he and Sean used to go up to Montreal all the time when they were teenagers. Montreal was a bit more than two hours up the interstate from Schenectady.

And get in touch with Dean Albany. He can help you figure out what to do. Two things Jake: remember the nuggets, and the key is money in your pocket. You can't tell anyone what you're doing, nobody except Dean. Keep this secret. I can't tell you more, but the other papers in here should convince you that this is serious. Never giving up, Jake, that's your strength. I'm sorry to say that you're going to need it.

That was it, besides the other papers and the memory key. Jake looked at the key, but externally it was unremarkable.

Carefully, he set Sean's letter down and inspected the papers. He read the first one. It was a medical chart from Stamford Hospital. Jake scanned the document—heart attack, a list of medications and times and activities. Scrawled at the bottom of the chart was a time of death and a doctor's signature. Jake looked at the top of the paper to find the name of the patient.

He blinked. That couldn't be right.

Vidal Viegas.

Jake rubbed his eyes and read the document again. It seemed to be an original. The doctor's signature looked like it was written in ballpoint pen, but then Jake was no expert. On the bed beside him, in the browser window on his laptop, Vidal Viegas announced a major new acquisition in Japan through the company's Hong Kong affiliate.

Jake looked back at the death certificate. It was dated over a year ago. Jake shook Viegas's hand a week ago at Atlas, and almost ran him down the day before at Bluebridge. Goosebumps prickled across Jake's arms.

On the webcast, Viegas smiled and asked if anyone had any questions.

AUGUST 19th

Friday

13

Canadian Border

"Name, please?" the border guard asked.

"Mark Smith," Jake replied.

"Turn off the engine." The guard reached to take Jake's passport. "And could you please take off your sunglasses?"

"Sorry."

At least Canadian border guards were still polite. Jake peeled his sunglasses off and smiled at the officer. He turned his ignition off. *Mark Smith.* Could there be a more blandly suspicious name?

"Is this your SUV?"

"Yes, sir," lied Jake.

The officer inspected Jake's passport, then glanced at Jake. "Roll down your back windows please."

"Sure." Jake fumbled with the controls.

The officer looked through the windows as they rolled down. "Mr. Smith, can you open the back?" The officer put Jake's fake passport down and exited his inspection booth.

"Sure," replied Jake again, panicking this time.

Where was the back door release? He ducked his head down and felt around. *Don't pop the hood*, for God's sake, *don't pop the hood.* He found a button and then checked and re-checked the symbol above it.

He pulled it.

The trunk hatch popped open.

Thank you, God.

The guard walked around the back of the car and pulled open the back gate. He took his time.

Jake rubbed his eyes.

It'd been more than a decade since he'd driven across the US-Canada border. *The longest undefended border in the world.* This was supposed to be a cakewalk. Not that long ago, a passport hadn't even been a requirement. Just a *hello*, yes, I'm American, going up to see some friends, have a nice day.

When did they start inspecting everyone?

Behind him, the back door slammed shut. Jake watched the guard in his rear view mirror. *What's he doing?* Slowly, the guard walked back to his inspection booth, in through the back door, and picked up Jake's passport. He put it on the scanner. "What brings you to Canada, Mr. Smith?"

Jake felt his face flush. "Going to see some friends for the weekend." He looked at the passport in the guard's hand.

The guard nodded and looked at his computer screen.

Jake's brother had gotten him the passport. He didn't know if it was fake or stolen. Maybe it had been a mistake to trust Eamon. He hadn't ever trusted him before, not really. But Jake was desperate. He tried to keep breathing normally, resisting the urge to wipe his brow. If he was caught now, it was all over.

They'd see it as fleeing the country.

There would be no bail. In fact, they'd lose the bail Elle had already posted for his arrest. They'd lose their home. Elle would never believe him. She would think he was abandoning her.

But he had no choice.

Jake had investigated the Viegas death record, started by calling the Town Clerk's office of the City of Stamford where they managed the official death certificates. He found out that hospitals reported deaths directly to them, and to the Office of the Chief Medical Examiner. Jake asked about Vidal Viegas. There was no record of any death.

Then Jake looked up the doctor whose signature was on the medical chart. He called Stamford Hospital and was informed that Doctor Mills had stopped working there a year ago, and the same story for the attending nurse listed on the medical chart. They had no idea how to get in touch with either of them.

"Sir?"

Jake looked up.

The guard held the passport out, handing it back to him. "Have a nice trip, sir," he said.

Jake took the passport, forced a smile, relief washing over him. "Thank you."

The guard waved the next car forward.

Jake started the car and pulled it into gear, then slowly accelerated. A signpost advised "100 km/h=60 mph." All the signage was in French. He was in Quebec. The change in landscape was immediate.

Before the border was all rolling hills and forests, but immediately afterward the landscape changed to farms and silos and barns. To Americans, this frontier was the northernmost point, the coldest and most inhospitable place in the country. But to Canadians, it was as southern as it got, and they crowded everything right against the border. Most Canadians lived within an hour's drive of the invisible line. Montreal, a city of four million people, was less than half an hour away on the main highway. But Jake wasn't going to Montreal.

Technically, he wasn't even going to remain in Canada.

Jake turned off the air conditioning and rolled down the windows to breathe in the Canadian air. It felt different, and it wasn't the change to bumpy, pot-hole-ridden roads. He'd always felt freer up here. In most of the world, there were always people around you in all directions. But not in Canada. Here you could drive an hour north and know there was open space for three thousand miles.

And that, Jake figured, must be the reason why whomever or whatever Sean wanted him to see was hiding in the north, and why he'd also told him to see Dean.

Whatever was up there wanted space.

To be alone.

Or to escape.

And up here, you really could escape.

Jake was a fugitive now, but with the window down and the wind in his face, he felt calm. At peace. In a way, he was still communicating with his friend. Sean had never been without a plan, some clever idea no one else had ever thought of. It suddenly felt like there was a way for Jake to fill the hole inside him rather than board it over. A purpose.

He and Eamon had almost gotten into a fistfight about the trip to Canada. It wouldn't have been their first. Eamon thought he'd lost his mind for wanting to skip across the border at a time like this, that his grief over Sean had driven him crazy. Jake didn't—*couldn't*—tell him about the envelope, of course, so he understood his reaction. But while Eamon hardly approved of the trip, he brought Jake the passport within a few hours. Just like that.

Jake had called his lawyer before he left, from a payphone at the corner of a garage down the street from the motel where he was staying. He explained that he was with family upstate. Said the lawyer should call his brother if he needed to get in touch.

The lawyer was adamant that Jake needed to return to New York City. The cops might arrest him if they found out he'd skipped, even upstate. The lawyer added that the District Attorney's office was all over Jake's case—high profile—and that the Security Exchange Commission wanted to interview him.

Right away.

And not just for an interview.

An interrogation.

Jake told the lawyer to push the meeting back by a week and hung up. The call felt like a noose being drawn around his neck, but the next one was worse. He called Elle, knowing there was a good chance she'd pick up only because it wasn't his cell number.

She did.

Standing in the payphone booth that stank of urine, the Plexiglas walls covered in graffiti, with traffic growling past on the interstate—Jake tried to tell his wife how much he loved her. He explained that he was going to see a friend. That it might help clear everything up.

She said she was busy, then asked what the noise was.

How's Anna?

She was fine, outside playing with her cousins.

I love you so much.

She needed to go.

I didn't do this Elle. Sean sent me a package. I have proof.

There was a long pause. *What proof?*

I can't say right now, but I'm going to find out.

He waited for her to hang up, his heart breaking, but then she said, *Be careful, Jake. I love you, too.* She started crying as she disconnected. Jake stared at the black plastic receiver in his hand for a minute before he hung it up.

I'm going to fix this, Elle, I promise.

Jake couldn't help but replay the conversation repeatedly as the lush countryside slid past outside the window of the SUV.

A week had passed since Sean's death in London. The trail, if there was one, was going cold.

Cormac couldn't be far from Jake's position. The old man was feeding him good information.

"The one with kale?" asked the pretty girl behind the counter. She couldn't be more than seventeen.

"Yes, the Green Monster," Cormac replied.

"Perfect, that'll be two minutes." The girl returned Cormac's smile. "Do you want to pay now or later?"

"Now is fine." He reached for his wallet.

Cormac drove into Albany to get some decent food. The other Special Forces guys used to make fun of his fixation with health food when they returned from missions and scarfed down burgers and fries. This town was a dump, but it was better than the interstate. One of the worst things about being on the road was the junk food, and an organic smoothie was just the thing to counteract his last fast-food-burger meal.

His partner had lost track of Jake O'Connell in New York. Cormac's employer had informed him that Jake was now in Schenectady, and maybe heading north. He must have slipped out the back with his brother and come upstate to visit his family. It made sense. Cormac wasn't happy with how easily his new partner was fooled. It was yet another sign of his unworthiness.

Pulling his wallet from the breast pocket of his suit jacket, he felt his phone vibrate. Holding up one finger, he mouthed, *one second*, to the girl behind the counter and then turned around, limped back a few steps, and pulled out his phone.

The encrypted messaging app lit up: *O'Connell passed into Canada.* Coordinates and details were appended.

Cormac arched his eyebrows. He hadn't taken Jake for a runner. This was getting more interesting.

Then another message pinged: *New target: Maxime Lefevre.*

Attached were three images of a man's face. Also attached was a new payment. Cormac smiled. Yes, this had become a *whole* lot more interesting.

His phone rang. An unlisted number. Cormac answered. "Hello."

"Mr. Ryker," replied a gravelly voice. It was the old man. "I trust you received my new instructions."

"Yes."

"I need to get this cleared up as soon as possible, understood? Additional bonuses for performance." A pause. "I can't stress enough how important this is, Mr. Ryker."

"We're clear, sir."

"I have terminated your partner. His performance was insufficient."

This day was getting better and better. "I'm happy to hear that. Do you have any more information for me at this time?"

"More will be coming."

The line disconnected.

Cormac turned to the girl. "Can I get that to go?"

14

Shenzhen
China

Jin struggled, but her legs were taped to the legs of the chair she was strapped to, her hands bound painfully behind her back. The glare of a floodlight on a tripod nearly blinded her. Squinting, she could make out a camera atop it. Behind that, people shuffled in the darkness. For hours—maybe even more than a day—they'd kept her in here in darkness, tied up. The room smelled like damp concrete, her mouth pasty and filled with dust. She coughed, tried to spit.

All she saw clearly was the man hulking over her; the same one who'd stuck a needle into her arm. He wound up and smacked her across the face.

Pain and shock exploded through her nervous system.

A voice from the darkness: "Ms. Huang, how does a twenty-nine-year-old girl own condos in Shenzhen and New York and afford to vacation in Dubai?"

She gulped two mouthfuls of air, steadied herself. "I'm a data scientist." She coughed from the back of her throat.

"Data scientist?"

"For banks," she whispered.

"And what do you do for these"—the voice paused—"banks?"

"Fraud detection." Jin tried to focus on something other than her throbbing face. She tasted blood. "Counter-party risk management." She wasn't sure they understood, but they demanded no explanation.

"And who else do you work for?"

"The State Ministries."

Silence for a few seconds, and then the hulking man wound up and slapped her again. Harder this time. Nearly knocked her and the chair over.

"We don't believe you, Ms. Huang. Why were you logged into the Assassin Market?"

97

White and black spots swam in Jin's vision. She was stunned, but kept her wits. "I...I wasn't," she stammered. That was true. She hadn't ever logged into it. Maybe Shen Shi had from one of their shared laptops.

"I don't know what that is," she added. Lied. Admitting anything could be deadly. She didn't know who she was dealing with, didn't know what they knew, but it didn't seem like they wanted to kill her. Not yet, anyway.

"You expect us to believe that?" The hulking man grabbed her torn shirt and pulled her close, until her face was inches from his. "Who are you working with?"

So far they hadn't mentioned any groups associated with the Chinese Peoples' Liberation Army—the PLA—or its cyber divisions.

Jin felt her face swelling.

Ears ringing.

But she kept a part of herself removed. Watching. Analyzing.

Anybody attached to any of the Security Ministries would have been able to track down her work for the PLA, so in an error by omission, these goons had to be PLA, either that or criminals. If they were criminals, she had a feeling she wouldn't be getting this kind of friendly treatment. It would be much worse. By their accents, she was certain they were from Beijing, and that meant, one way or the other, that they were upset about money.

The PLA groups she'd worked with were a bunch of nerds, lunch-boxers who tinkered with code. This group of goons was a whole different part of the animal. China's cyberworld network was so arcane that senior Chinese officials had no idea what was going on with it. It was like trying to explain using a cellphone to a fish, but whoever was interrogating her was listing off agencies with alarming precision.

She'd gotten in touch with China's patriotic "red hackers" network after her return to China. A few of her friends freelanced for them. She even attended a law enforcement trade show in Guangzhou to meet people.

There she'd met commercial software vendors bragging that if someone named a target—any individual, anywhere—they could break into their computer, download their hard drive, record keystrokes, get into bank accounts, even monitor cellphone conversations anywhere in the world.

The Chinese bureaucracy encouraged the culture of hacking. It was more of a state-sponsored kleptocracy, from hacking competitions to companies and government corporations employing networks of shared hackers. The force behind it all was the government insistence on maintaining surveillance on everyone and everything. You could criticize it, but at least it was out in the open, even if it was about the only thing out in the open.

The man looming over Jin pulled his arm back, his hand in a fist. "I'm going to ask you one more time…"

She tensed up, tears streaming down her face, her breath coming in labored gasps. A part of her mind distanced itself from the beating, but she was terrified. "I'm sorry, I don't know what you want." She closed her eyes and cringed.

"That's enough," said the voice from the darkness. "We have what we need for now. We're going to need her."

Jin opened her eyes. Shaking. The floodlight clicked off and another light, a bare incandescent one that hung from a wire above her head, came on. It illuminated a rough concrete room with blacked-out windows. Four other people stood by the door. It wasn't a bunker, though, and it didn't have the feeling of a government office. There was what appeared to be a kitchen in one corner. The room looked like it could be in any one of the thousands of unfinished building projects on the outskirts of Guangzhou.

The man who called off Jin's aggressor wore a business suit. He motioned at an improvised wooden platform in the corner of the room. On it were the twisted remains of a laptop and her backpack.

"We're going to need your help getting into that," the businessman said evenly as he saw her staring at the laptop. Walking forward he tapped the large man still looming over Jin. "Let's go."

The door to the room opened, and the other men filtered out until the one with the business suit was left. He made to leave but then stopped and looked at Jin. "You're lucky that we found you before they did, Ms. Huang." He walked out and closed the door without bothering to explain who *we* or *they* were.

The light bulb above Jin's head flickered. Taking deep breaths, she tried to calm herself. They needed something. She had to

99

convince them that she was the only one who could access and decode what was on that laptop.

That made her valuable, which probably made her alive, but getting out of here would be even better.

Closing her eyes, she rolled her shoulders back and forth, seeing if there was any wiggle room in the bindings holding her hands. They might be goons, but they were diligent with their rope work. The chair, on the other hand, was a different story. She'd been working to loosen its joints for hours.

Rocking back and forth, she felt the old wood creaking. Stopping, she listened. No voices in the corridor. Totally quiet, except for her own labored breathing. She tensed her entire body, and with a jolt propelled every ounce of her weight forward.

The chair rocked, lifting its weight off the back legs.

With a grunt, she swayed her momentum backward, this time raising the front legs of the chair off the ground as she swung back. Her heart skipped a beat when the chair almost tipped over, but then it dropped back the other way. She swung all of her weight in that direction, straining her head forward.

As the chair balanced on its front legs, she pushed downward with the balls of her feet, balancing the chair and herself onto her toes. With all her strength, she pushed upward and sprang off her toes, jacking herself into the air with her calf muscles. The chair spun backward and sideways, and as its first leg hit the ground, Jin leaned back with all the force she could muster.

The back leg splintered.

Cracked.

Then she crashed to the ground, pain shooting through her arms and shoulders.

Her face impacted the concrete floor.

Hard.

Gasping for air, Jin lay still on her side, electric jolts of agony lancing through her shoulders. Still no voices outside. She pulled on her arms, trying to be quiet, but weeping from the pain. She felt like she'd broken something. With a final pull, the wooden chair cracked apart, its legs and supports disintegrating from each other.

Wriggling around on the floor, she separated herself from the bits of the chair and then, bending in half at the waist, pulled her bound hands underneath her feet. Using her hands, she propped

100

herself up onto her knees and then stood unsteadily.

Her hands were bound together around a strut of the chair, a splinter of which was still embedded in the knots around her wrists. She pulled this out with her teeth, and the bindings loosened. She wriggled one hand and then the other free, then leaned over and untied her feet.

Panting.

Sweat streaming down her face.

She held her breath. Any noises in the hallway?

Nothing yet.

Got to hurry.

She glanced around the room, looking for a weapon, but realized it was futile. Even with a baseball bat, she doubted she could make a dent in the gorilla who'd attacked her, and she didn't have any idea how to use a gun. Stealth was her only weapon. She crept to the door, her stomach in her throat, the only sound her heart banging in her ears.

She turned the handle. Inched the door open.

No voices. No sound of footsteps.

She opened the door another inch with one trembling hand. Peered into the hallway.

Dark.

Empty.

Slowly, slowly, she swung the door open far enough so she could squeeze out. She had heard them turn down the hallway to her right, so she crept to the left and then started running, her feet scuffling across the dust on the unfinished concrete.

At the end of the hallway was a stairwell, the doors not yet installed. She turned into it and jumped down two steps at a time. In a blur she reached one landing, and then the next, one after another until she reached ground level. Stopping to catch her breath, her whole body shaking, she leaned against the bar of the door leading outside, opening it a crack.

Sunlight streamed in.

Birds chirped outside.

But what if *they* were outside, too?

Jin pushed the door open—wide—ready to sprint, to fight, but she stopped cold.

"Wutang?" she stuttered.

Wutang stood in front of her, on a sheet of plywood balanced between the street curb and the emergency exit. "Jin!" He looked as surprised as she was.

"Are you with these bastards?" Jin half-whispered, half-yelled, trying to make sense of it. She looked around. Her intuition had been right. It was one of the abandoned, half-built high-rises between Guangzhou and Shenzhen.

"What?" Wutang took a step toward her. "My God, what happened, your face—"

Jin recoiled. "Stay back."

Down the street was a beat-up green Chery QQ hatchback, fuzzy dice hanging from the mirror. Chen appeared on the driver's side of the vehicle. "Come on, let's go," he called out.

"Chen followed them here," Wutang explained, urging her toward him, holding his hand out.

Jin edged forward. "Why are you doing this? Why are you helping me?" If the goons upstairs found them here, they could all be killed.

Wutang held an arm out. "Why do you think?"

The way he looked at her melted Jin's heart.

High above in the building, voices started shouting, echoing down the stairwell behind Jin.

"We have to hurry!" Chen yelled from the car.

More voices, outside the windows, louder this time.

Jin jumped across the plywood platform and grabbed Wutang's hand. They ran down the street and she jumped into the backseat of the car, Wutang jumping into the front. Shouts erupted above their heads. Chen already had the car in gear and he stomped on the accelerator, peeling out in a haze of blue smoke.

15

Kahnawake Mohawk Reserve
Southern Quebec

"We're twenty-first century Mohawk cyber warriors, check it out!" Dean Albany beamed at Jake, spreading his arms wide. "Not bad for a bunch of redskins, huh?"

Around them, thousands of servers hummed inside sleek black cabinets. Air from the cooling fans blew a breeze into Jake's face. Fat packets of blue wiring snaked overhead. Everything was perfectly squared away, state-of-the-art. They stood in Server Room D of MIT—the Mohawk Institute of Technology—in the Kahnawake Indian reserve, on the other side of the St. Lawrence River south of Montreal Island, about an hour north of the US border.

Jake smiled. "Not bad. Kahnawake"—he pronounced it kah-na-wog-eh—"is a lot different from the last time I saw it." He looked down at the blue slip-on booties he'd put on at the entrance. To protect the machines from dust and dirt, according to the guard.

Jake hadn't seen his old friend in two decades. He was glad Dean was smiling. They hadn't parted on good terms—an understatement—and Jake hadn't called ahead.

Jake drove the long way up from the small border crossing, passing through farmlands swaying with corn ready for harvest, letting the smell of the air work its way into his brain to twist out half-forgotten memories of another life. Jake and Sean used to come up here as often as they could when they were teenagers.

Everything was an escape back then, and now, he was escaping again.

When he'd arrived, he did a loop of Kahnawake to get a feel for his old stomping ground before parking. He drove up past the MIT building, along the dusty stretch of Highway 132 that snaked through the thin birch forests lining the reservation. Then he hooked back under the rusting trusses of the Mercier Bridge that spanned from this side of the river to Montreal Island. There were no street addresses on the reservation. Mohawks didn't believe in owning the land.

Jake showed up in the reception area of the MIT building and asked the guard if Dean was around. The guard, who didn't seem the least bit surprised at an unscheduled drop-in, told him to wait a few minutes in the lounge. Dean's smiling face had appeared moments later. Before Jake could say anything, or even explain why he'd randomly dropped in after all these years, Dean took him on a whirlwind tour of MIT.

"Five server rooms now, and this whole building used to be a coat factory." Dean opened a door and stepped onto an electrostatic mat for collecting dust. He brushed back his mop of black hair. A year older than Jake, Dean was edging forty, yet he didn't have a fleck of gray. He had the aquiline nose and olive skin distinctive of the Mohawk tribe here. "We're getting new customers faster than we can expand."

Dean spoke in perfect English, even if this was the French province. Quebec didn't have a French 'quarter'—eighty percent of the population spoke it. Many Quebecers didn't even speak English. In the middle of this French place, the Mohawks still spoke English, with one good reason being that even though they were located in Canada, the Mohawks had dual American and Canadian citizenship; they were North American citizens.

"Nice." Jake followed Dean into the next room, also filled with more servers.

Many native Indian communities operated casinos on their land. It was a way of raising money for the community. But casinos tended to attract a certain type of person—they invited in the criminals, organized crime, prostitution and everything else that came with it. There was only one type of casino that didn't bring people like that into the community: online casinos.

In 1998, the Mohawks of Kahnawake filed paperwork to create a legal international framework for operating online gambling. They were the second jurisdiction in the world, after Antigua, to open for business as a provider of web-based casino services, and outside of the state and provincial systems, they were still the only one in North America to be legally operational.

"And here's why it all works." Dean tapped a door labeled 'Data Communications Link.' "We're global now."

104

A fat data pipe running through the reservation, explained Dean, connected to the main fiber optic link that carried most of the data from Eastern Canada down into the US, straight from Montreal to New York, then branching out into Europe and the rest of the world. That connection made it possible to handle a mind-boggling amount of business.

This MIT wasn't a university; it was a technology center. Dean explained that over three hundred online casinos ran out of the Kahnawake facilities, and the Mohawks now operated installations in Gibraltar, Singapore, London, Paris, all over the world. But this facility was their crown jewel, their home base on their home land, located in the twenty-five square miles of the Kahnawake Mohawk tribe's land that they'd hung onto for the past four hundred years.

It was an unassuming crown jewel.

From the outside, the MIT building was a squat cinder-block building sitting next to the Red Wolf gas station and plaza, along a mostly deserted stretch of road dotted with small shacks advertising discount cigarettes and fireworks.

Dean continued with his tour. He led Jake into the UPS room. "Doesn't mean United Parcel Service," he laughed, "this is the battery back-up in case of any power failures." He pointed out the back door. "And out there are three fail-over generators. We can keep power going for two days without refilling, and there's a diesel station next door, too."

"Nice." Jake did his best to appear enthusiastic, but impatience was getting the better of him. He needed to know if Dean knew anything. "Is there somewhere we can talk privately?" Jake took a deep breath. "I'm here illegally, you should know that first."

Dean stared at Jake. "Oh yeah? Because I don't need to remind you that the last time you were here, you got *me* thrown in jail."

▲▼▲

Jake looked around as he pushed through the swinging double doors of the Kicking Horse. Regulars were already stacked shoulder to shoulder at the bar, and the whole joint smelled of stale beer and damp carpets. At least this place hadn't changed. "How did you hear about Sean's death?"

Trailing in behind Jake, Dean nodded at the bartender and held up two fingers. "Through Mark. He was doing steel work on a building upstate." He led Jake to the side of the bar where their two Budweisers were delivered. "He found out from Sean's aunt. You know the one."

Jake nodded. "Can I borrow your phone? I want to check my messages." He took Sean's warning seriously, so his phone was still in Schenectady.

"Sure." Dean handed him his phone, then picked up a beer.

Jake dialed his own number. It would go to voicemail after five rings, and Jake could tap the # pound key to get into his voice message system and enter his password.

One ring, then two. Jake took a sip from his beer, waiting for the voicemail to pick up, when someone answered, "Hey there, this is Jake."

He choked on his mouthful of beer. "Hello?" Jake answered. Had someone answered his phone?

"Please leave a message after the tone," continued the voice, *his* voice.

He frowned and pulled the phone away from his ear, then typed in his password. Put the receiver back to his ear. No messages.

"Everything okay?" Dean asked.

"Yeah, I, um, yeah." Jake stared at the phone. Was that the voice message he'd left on his system? He wasn't sure, but then again, he'd set it up years ago. He handed the phone back to Dean.

"Any messages?"

"None."

"You okay?"

Not really. "Yeah, I'm fine."

On Jake's psychopath scale, Dean barely registered. He was caring. Thoughtful. It was one of the reasons Jake had liked him so much, but Dean also had an uncomfortable way of sensing what other people were feeling.

"If you say so." Dean took a sip of his beer, watching Jake carefully. "You know, the reason I'm in tech is because of Sean. He got me into all this stuff after my deployments. He even redesigned our payment system and the automated agents for our international money exchanges. Really helped us."

Jake hadn't known that. He shifted in his seat. "So what did you hear?"

"Heard that Sean had an accident in London."

"Anything else?"

"And I heard that you had some"—Dean paused to choose his words carefully—"legal problems." He put his beer down. "Sorry for dragging you on that tour. I wasn't thinking. I was excited to see you. You know. To show you I did good."

Jake grimaced. "I'm the one who's sorry."

As teenagers, they'd gotten caught up in smuggling tobacco across the border. It was a big business in Kahnawake. After a few years of making good money, Dean had wanted to up the ante by smuggling drugs and even guns.

At the time, Sean had just gotten a scholarship to Columbia. Jake wanted Dean to come with them to New York, told him that smuggling guns and drugs would get him killed. They had a huge fight. In the end, Jake called in an anonymous tip to Quebec Police that got Dean arrested and thrown in jail, but at least it was as a juvenile.

Of course everyone knew who did it.

Dean picked up his beer and finished it off. "It took me a few years to realize it, but you did me a favor."

When Dean got out of juvenile detention, Jake heard that he joined the US Marines. There weren't a lot of opportunities for young Mohawks back then. To outsiders it might seem strange that a Canadian Mohawk could serve in the US military, but having dual American and Canadian citizenship encouraged many of the young Mohawks to do just that. Ex-Rangers and Special Forces filled the local legion hall. As the saying went around these parts, every family had at least one Marine.

Dean leaned across the table and put a hand on Jake's shoulder. "I forgive you." He smiled. "How's your family?"

"Everyone's good," Jake replied after a pause. "Or I mean, everyone's the same."

"And Eamon?"

"Just got out of Attica."

Dean forced a smile, then motioned to the waitress for two more beers.

"How's your dad?" Jake asked, deflecting the focus away from his family.

"Good." Dean snorted. "You know the men in my tribe, he'll

live to be a hundred and drink and smoke every day of it."

Jake smiled. He did know. Dean's grandfather was born in 1866, before the Battle of Little Bighorn, even before the formation of Canada. He fathered Dean's dad when he was seventy, and lived to be a hundred and six. Dean's curious surname, Albany, came from his grandfather, who was born on a train between the stations of Albany and Schenectady. Mohawks had no surnames, but one had been given to the child on his official birth certificate—Albany. Over forty people in Kahnawake now shared the name.

In an indirect way, Dean's surname was the reason Jake and Dean became friends.

One hot summer night when he was thirteen, Jake's brother had sent him to get cigarettes from a gang of local Mohawk kids outside the Double Deuce poker hall, where their dad was gambling. Jake asked for Dean's name, and when he said Albany, Jake replied that Albany sucked. Dean took offense and threw the punch that started their first fistfight. By the time both of them had bloody noses, Jake managed to explain that he'd been referring to the town of Albany, at which point they both broke into laughter.

"And your brothers?" asked Jake.

Dean shrugged. "You know, still in the tobacco business." Still smuggling was the unspoken subtext. The waitress arrived with two more beers and Dean paid for them.

Two men came up behind Dean. One slapped him on the back. "How you boys doing?"

Jake looked down. One of them had a gun on his hip, and wore the Mohawk Peace Keeper police uniform.

Dean spun around. His face lit up. "Doug, Daniel, nice to see you."

The guy who wasn't in uniform turned to Jake and held out his hand. "Doug Hamer."

The Mohawk Peace Keeper policeman held out his hand as well. "Peace Keeper Daniels."

"Pleased to meet you." Jake shook both hands. "Uh, Mark...Mark Smith."

Dean frowned, but let it go. "Doug here is our local RCMP junior liaison. Helps run community activities with the kids, even coaches one of the Kahnawake soccer teams. And Officer

Daniels"—Dean smiled—"heck, I served in the Marines with this bastard."

Peace Keeper Daniels smiled. Jake did his best to smile back.

"Nice to meet you," Doug said to Jake. "Listen, didn't mean to barge in, and we gotta go. See you at your place later," he added to Dean, clapping him on the shoulder. They both turned and walked out the front door.

Jake waited for them to disappear through the doors. "I thought there were no outside police here? Isn't the RCMP like the FBI of Canada? What's he coming to your place for?"

"Relax." Dean turned to Jake. "He's not here as an officer. He's the *junior* liaison, working with the Peace Keepers. And he's dating my daughter."

Jake almost spat out a mouthful of beer. "Your daughter?"

Dean grinned. "She's joining the Marines next year."

Jake hadn't even known Dean *had* children.

"We have some catching up to do." Dean took a swig from the new beer. "She's seventeen, I found out her mother was pregnant with her after I signed up for the Marines. I always tell her that by the time I was nineteen, I'd crossed the Indian and Pacific Oceans twice, done two humanitarian missions. She wants to be like her dad."

Shaking his head, Jake offered up his beer bottle for a cheers. "Congratulations."

"I heard you have a little one."

"Yeah." Jake smiled, but felt his insides drop away.

Dean had a family, just like he did. Did he have the right to drag Dean into this mess? Sean's note said that Dean might be able to help him. But how? Had Sean talked to Dean? Jake put his hand into his jean pocket, feeling the two memory keys—one from Sean, one from Donovan—and his Silver Eagle dollar coin.

It was time to lay things out. "Dean, I'm not supposed to be here. I'm out on bail from the rape charges, and the SEC is investigating me in the Atlas fraud. They already arrested my boss."

A tiny grin crept onto Dean's face. "You ain't standing on Canadian or American soil now—you're in the Mohawk Nation."

Jake understood what he meant. This was sovereign territory. They had their own police force, the Peace Keepers, as well as their own unofficial militia, the Mohawk Warriors, to defend

109

themselves and their land.

A few years ago, the Canadian government had tried to ride roughshod over Mohawk burial grounds. Tensions escalated, leading to an armed standoff between the Mohawk Warriors blocking the roads and bridges into their territory and the Canadian military. Eventually, the Mohawks had won the day. The Warriors were an active and important part of the community.

"Did Sean talk to you lately?" Jake asked.

Dean shook his head.

"Because Sean asked me to come and talk to you," Jake continued, "and he told me to go up to an address up north."

"What did he want you to talk to me about?"

Jake reached into his pockets and produced the two memory keys. "I'm guessing that he knew I'd need help figuring out what's on these."

Dean nodded and reached for them, but Jake pulled back.

"One of them is from Danny Donovan, something he asked me to hide. There's a federal investigation into Atlas. Might get nasty."

"Sounds like fun." Dean grabbed them. "You mean your boss, the guy they arrested?"

"Yeah. He said that Sean did some work for him before Anna was born. I think Sean did it to help me out, but he didn't say anything. Donovan said it's why he gave me the job in the first place."

"That sounds like Sean." Dean inspected the memory keys. "Did Donovan say what it was?"

"I looked, but all I understood was a listing of a bunch of shell companies. Most of it seems to be directories of software, and I have no idea how to interpret it. The other one, the black one, that's from Sean."

"From Sean?" Dean held the memory key up. "He gave you this before the accident?"

Jake looked straight into Dean's eyes. "That was no accident. And he's not the only one who's dead."

He pulled Vidal's death certificate from his pocket.

16

Northern Quebec

"No offense, bud-dee, but you going to need warmer clothing. There nothing up 'ere but black bear an' ca-ree-boo till Russia!" the pilot said in his thick French Canadian accent, erupting into a phlegmy smoker's laugh.

Jake could barely hear him over the roar of the plane's engine. He peered out of his side window. Thousands of feet below a carpet of green forest and blue lakes swept by. He'd read somewhere that Canada had three million lakes, more than anywhere else on the planet. The pilot skimmed underneath a ceiling of clouds that dotted the sky to the horizon.

The Super Cub bush plane was at least thirty years old—a two-seater, the pilot in front and Jake in back. With floats on, it topped out at ninety miles an hour, but it was the best Dean could come up with on short notice.

"She's old, but she's reliable," the pilot said, patting the instrument panel. "Just how I like my women!" Another throaty cackle. He said something else, but Jake couldn't tell if he was speaking in English or French. Sounded like a mix.

Past the red *Canadiens* hockey team baseball cap on the pilot's head, Jake stared at a screwdriver shoved into the ignition switch, the exposed wiring wrapped together with electrical tape. Maybe this was a bad idea. The interior was bare metal and webbing, smelled of engine oil and rotten fish, not to mention the sour odor of last night's whiskey. Jake smelled the booze—had nearly been knocked over by it—the moment he'd opened the side door to get into the cockpit. He would've gotten right back out, but he didn't have much of a choice.

This was a favor.

"I fly, too!" Jake yelled over the engine.

He tried to convince himself that he could take over if it came to it, but that was a stretch. The pilot was only half the problem. The plane was falling apart. Jake had seven hours of experience in a Cessna with his trainer, and had never landed by himself. Bringing this rickety thirty-year-old bush plane down on the edge of the Canadian arctic was a bit out of his comfort zone.

"Oh yeah?" laughed the pilot. "You want to take over?" He let go of the flight stick between his legs and made as if to unbuckle his straps.

"No, no!" Jake shouted, alarmed, but from the roar of laughter up front he realized the old guy was kidding.

Smiling and nodding in recognition of the joke, Jake leaned back in his seat as the pilot kept talking. Someone had once asked him where on the planet he thought the biggest herds of animals existed. Thinking of the video footage he'd seen of the massive wildebeest migrations in the African savannah, he'd made that his answer. But the correct response was Quebec. There were herds of over a million caribou—what people in the rest of the world called reindeer—that roamed the tundra of northern Quebec. It was another world up here.

Jake was exhausted, but three hours of bone-jarring vibration kept him awake.

That, plus his fear of the pilot passing out.

Viegas's death certificate had convinced Dean that Sean's death had been no accident. Jake told him that the doctor and nurse who signed it had left the hospital, that there was no record of them anywhere else he could find. The only other option was that the certificate was a fake. And if so, why would Sean have sent Jake a package with a fake death certificate in it, telling him to go off on a wild goose chase?

No, they both agreed that it was all connected.

The Mohawk nation never forgot their own, Dean had assured him. They'd find a way to help.

At one of the summer powwows twenty years ago, a school bus bringing in grade-school children had jumped the concrete curb of a low bridge spanning a small river leading to the event. The bus had flipped over and capsized into the water. Jake and Sean had been hiding under the bridge smoking a joint when it happened, and before he knew what he was doing, Jake had plunged into the frigid river. He and Sean pulled seven Mohawk children out before anyone else got there, probably saved the kids' lives. The Mohawk Council had conferred status of honorary tribal members onto both of them.

112

Still, there was a risk in getting involved, and Dean needed to get the elders' blessing to dig into it more. After a few phone calls, they'd found this bush pilot who was willing to fly him up. When Dean asked if he could reveal what he knew to the Longhouse Council, Jake hesitated, but ultimately agreed.

He needed all the help he could get.

After finishing up at the bar, Jake and Dean had gone back to the MIT building, where they sat together and read media reports on Bluebridge and its founders, Vidal Viegas and Henry Montrose. The men might have been partners, but Montrose was the senior one. He had to be the one pulling the strings at Bluebridge.

What was Montrose up to?

Had he killed Viegas, replaced him somehow? Had Sean been killed for knowing that secret?

Vidal—or whoever had replaced him—was busy on a tour promoting Senator Russ in the presidential campaign. The campaign donations for this year were staggering, and every industry Bluebridge was branching out into seemed to be a platform piece for Russ, everything from wind turbines to the defense industry. Then again, that was business and politics as usual. The only thing that made it unusual was the death certificate of Viegas.

They'd disconnected some computers from the network to look at the contents of the memory keys. Dean took a quick look at the files on the one from Donovan, which he said looked like a collection of libraries for a database engine. He promised to dig deeper.

They couldn't open the one from Sean. It was encrypted, and they didn't have the code. They tried all the passwords they could think of, scouring Sean's note for clues. The only thing that stood out was the cryptic line from the note: *Remember the nuggets, and the key is money in your pocket*. Did he mean that once they got the code, they would have as much money as they needed? Or that they needed a lot of money to unlock it? Money was the last thing on Jake's mind.

The pilot reached around and prodded Jake's shoulder. He'd been talking while Jake was daydreaming, staring out of his window.

"What?" Jake asked.

"Dat's all you 'ave?" the pilot yelled over the engine. He meant the backpack stuffed between Jake's knees, some warm clothes and a sleeping bag Dean gave him. "Yoo 'ave no 'unting gear 'der? You need something?"

Jake frowned, his brain trying to make sense of the man.

He meant, *hunting gear.*

He thought Jake was going hunting.

Jake was about to say, no, I'm not a hunter, but then he laughed grimly to himself. He *was* going hunting. "No, I don't have any gear," he yelled back.

"No worry," the pilot replied. "Dean tol' me to take care of you." Holding the flight stick with his right hand, he reached down his left hand and pulled out an old rifle.

Jake hesitated, but took it. Propping it upright beside him, he checked its chamber. It wasn't loaded.

The pilot sensed what he was doing. "By your feet," he said over the noise of the engine.

Jake looked down at a cardboard box filled with rifle cartridges he hadn't noticed before.

Over his head, the pilot waved a leather wallet with a billfold. "Dean said to give you this, too."

Jake reached forward and took the money. "Thank you," he yelled. "Thanks for everything."

Maybe he would survive this plane ride after all.

"We h'almost der." The pilot turned and smiled, revealing a mouthful of tobacco-stained teeth. He pointed at a large lake on the horizon, sparkling in the afternoon sun. "You be hunting soon, my friend."

Jake pulled out the map Sean gave him, the one pinpointing the location he needed to go to. It indicated a spot on a mountaintop near the lake they approached. A remote sport-fishing lodge was on the lake. That was where he was going to start.

▲▼▲

Cormac held the picture of Jake O'Connell up to the bartender of the hunting and fishing lodge. It was an outside bar. Two old-timers battled on a chessboard at the table nearest him, while a group of four men in head-to-foot camouflage roared in laughter

114

at a joke just told by a wiry man wearing a red *Canadiens* hockey team baseball cap.

"So you've seen him?" Cormac asked. He was double-checking. The old man had called him in the morning, giving specific instructions that Jake O'Connell would be coming to the Bear Mountain Lodge. He was a weirdo, sure, but the old man was never wrong. Not when he was this specific.

The bartender took the picture and studied it. "Yeah. He arrived a few hours ago. Jean flew him in." The bartender nodded at the wiry man in the *Canadiens* baseball cap. He frowned at Cormac. "I didn't know you were coming. The boss told me not to expect anybody else for the day."

Cormac smiled his goofiest grin. "Sorry, getting away from the wife and all. This was a last minute thing." He turned and inspected the man in the *Canadiens* baseball cap.

"Nice ride." The bartender nodded at the Cessna 185 Cormac flew up in. It sat at the end of the docks next to the rusting old Super Cub and a more modern Bombardier six-seater. As the sun set, a beautiful orange-and-pink sky erupted on the horizon over the mirror-still lake.

Cormac made it just before dark. It took longer to rent a float plane in Montreal than he'd anticipated—no valid pilot's license under the alias he was using, but a big wad of cash could fix nearly any problem.

"Is Jake staying here?" Cormac nodded at the main lodge.

Frowning, the bartender shook his head. "No, he headed up Montagne d'Ours, to one of the cabins we rent up there." He pointed to the right, to a forest trail leading up a steep incline. "Bear Mountain," he repeated in English. "It's a good two hour hike up. All of the ATVs are gone already."

"Right, right." Cormac took back the picture. "I've been trying to catch up with my buddy all day. Thought he might be staying at the main lodge tonight."

"You could ask Jean, he might know more." The bartender pointed at the pilot.

Cormac glanced at the table of men again. Apart from them and the older-timers finishing their chess match, only two other men sat at the other end of the patio overlooking the lake, quietly watching the sunset. The hunting and fishing lodge looked like it could accommodate a dozen rooms. It didn't seem full. Maybe

115

twenty people including staff.

No roads in or out.

"Sure, that's a good idea," Cormac replied, looking at the three floatplanes moored at the docks. Those were the only escape routes.

"Your other friend got here last week," the bartender added.

"Huh?" Cormac was still staring at the planes.

"Your other friend, the one with long hair."

Long hair. "Tall guy, lanky?"

The bartender nodded. "That's right. Your friend was asking about him."

It had to be Maxime Lefevre—the other person the old man had sent him to kill. Cormac smiled. Two birds with one stone. His lucky day. "Perfect."

Cormac needed to cut off all escape routes and disable the planes.

Or the pilots.

He grinned at the bartender. "Could you give me five beers?"

"What kind?"

"Whatever they're drinking." Cormac nodded at the table where Jean sat.

Jake had at least several hours on him. It didn't make any sense to try and climb up there tonight. He'd go at first light, and in the meantime he could tie up loose ends here. It might be Cormac's lucky day, but it was about to be a bad luck day for his soon-to-be-best-friend Jean.

Dropping his bag on the counter, Cormac reached into his pocket for his wallet.

"What are you hunting with that?" the bartender asked as he popped the caps off the beers.

Cormac had left his bag open. He cursed himself. A rare mistake. The barrel of his sniper rifle stuck out. Pulling it shut, he replied, "There's some big game out there," with a smile.

The bartender arched his eyebrows. *Must be an American,* his Gallic shrug seemed to say. He arranged the beer on a tray and followed Cormac to the table.

▲▼▲

Twilight faded into night as the moon appeared on the

116

horizon.

Jake had a headlamp but hadn't turned it on yet. He wasn't planning to, either. He slowly made his way up from the lodge, staying off the main trail as much as possible. An ATV would have been faster, but the noise would have given him away. Walking up was difficult work, and he wasn't in hiking shape. Huffing and puffing, he stopped to lean against the trunk of a birch tree. Sweat soaked him.

The path followed a ridge up the side of the mountain, and from here he had a view back to the lodge. He noticed another plane had arrived when he was about halfway up the trail to the top. He wondered if anyone else was heading up here.

He hoped not.

Then again, he had no idea what was waiting for him at the top. As night fell, he realized how unprepared he was. How isolated he felt. And how afraid he was.

Fear.

Like a mouthful of nails he couldn't spit out.

When he was arrested on the rape charges, he'd whiled away his time in lockup by ranking the other detainees on his psychopath scale. At least a few of them were full-Teds. Only the finest of hairs separated the unsuccessful psychopaths in jail from the successful ones running Wall Street. Dazzling, super-confident—just a few of the words used to describe the predators of Wall Street, and they were the same ones used to describe psychopaths.

Fear knotted Jake's stomach, and it was both unnerving and reassuring. Fear meant he wasn't a psychopath.

People saw psychopaths as aberrations, examples of something gone wrong in human programming, but Jake often thought that perhaps we had it wrong. After all, you wouldn't see a psychopath panic. Maybe psychopaths were the next stage in evolution for the human species. Ruthless and fearless, they were perfectly adapted to the modern world, maybe more evolved.

And maybe that was why they both fascinated and repelled Jake.

Down at the lodge, he'd asked a bartender about the location indicated on his map. The bartender told him it was a cabin that the lodge rented out to hunters, that it was rented out for the season. He didn't have a name. Whoever it was, it had to be who

117

Sean wanted Jake to meet. There was no phone in the cabin up top, no way of communicating with the lodger, and Jake had refused a guide. Said that he'd like to surprise his friend.

And that was the truth.

After taking the time to enjoy a burger at the lodge patio bar and call Dean from the lodge's phone, Jake trudged into the woods. Jean, the pilot, had said he was planning to stay overnight, but that he had to leave the next day around noon. Jake had assured him he'd be back, but in reality, he wasn't sure of anything.

As his eyes adjusted to the darkness, he could see that the trees thinned out up ahead. A structure bordered the tree line. It had to be the Bear Mountain cabin. There weren't any lights on inside. Time to wait and see. Leaning against a tree, Jake pulled a fleece out of his backpack and put it on, shivering against the chill of the night. He sat and settled against a tree for surveillance.

Shaking his head, he tried to fight his drooping eyelids.

He hadn't slept in two days.

AUGUST 20th

Saturday

17

Lockhart Street
Hong Kong

Catcalls from throngs of partygoers echoed above the pounding music pouring in through the window of Chen's cramped apartment. Dawn painted the sky pink, but Lockhart Street in Hong Kong's Wan Chai district was still littered with people.

Not quite able to shake off its history as a port of call crawling with prostitutes, the Wan Chai area was trying to transform itself with flashy new bars. But no matter how shiny the chrome at a grand opening of a new Lockhart Street nightclub, there was always an undercurrent of sleaze. Prices were cheap, half that of other areas, which drew in heavy drinkers like fat flies to hot dung.

Wutang and Jin sat on matching black faux-leather couches that took up two walls of Chen's apartment's tiny living room, with an open window next to Jin. They worked on laptops balanced on their knees. Chen stood by the window and smoked.

A pair of thirty-inch LCD monitors packed against aging rack-mounted servers occupied the other wall of the living room. Chen had made his digs in Hong Kong sound glamorous, but this tiny apartment—the paint on the walls peeling, the carpets stained, the appliances rusted—was a cliché wrapped in a cliché, the hacker den above the rave club.

Jin frowned at the open window. She could barely hear herself think. "What time do they close downstairs?" A headache pounded behind her eyes, each thump of bass from the music like a hammer strike driving a nail into her head. Her entire body hurt from the beating she'd taken, and her face was swollen. She took painkillers, but it wasn't helping.

"Usually ten on weekends." Chen could see what she was thinking. "Sorry, but it's cheap, and they let me pay cash. This place doesn't exist, not officially, and that's what we need right now."

Jin flashed Chen a tight smile. "You're right." They risked a lot by helping her. She had a hard time believing they were putting themselves in so much jeopardy for Wutang's crush, but she didn't have many options.

Chen flicked the butt of his cigarette out the window and slid it shut. He sat down at his workstation and opened up a search window in a browser. The closed window shook, the bass thumped through the walls.

Two days ago, when Jin was kidnapped, Chen saw the goons carry her out of Wutang's apartment when he showed up to meet her at the noodle shop. He followed them and called Wutang on the way. After scoping out the building for a day, they were about to try and sneak in when she suddenly appeared in front of them.

After they all jumped into Chen's car, they raced downtown, then abandoned the car and jumped onto a series of commuter buses, hiding themselves in the rush hour crowds. After taking the 113 bus out to Shekou terminal, they took the ferry into Hong Kong's main port. The path of least surveillance, Chen had joked.

When they arrived at Chen's place, the first thing Jin did was go back and try to log into the Assassin Market, but the darknet service had disappeared. Wutang said that autonomous corporations spawned themselves, morphing into new entities and leaving their old shells behind—a tactic to evade authorities.

To access it again, they'd need a new set of credentials. Even then, cracking the anonymity shield would require the resources of a government-sized organization like the NSA. The autonomous corporation wasn't about to expose any of its clients.

But while Jin could no longer log into it, she could research how the Assassin Market operated. The information was freely available on the web. Anyone could place an initial bounty on the head of any person in the world, and others could add to that amount. Bettors placed wagers—of at least 10% of the current pool—on when that person would die. When the target died, the person with the closest bet won the pool, with the time of death independently verified by media reports online.

A dead pool.

The idea had been around for a long time, but the Assassin Market was the first time an autonomous corporation was used to implement it. The CIA were investigating the darknet entity for several killings in the past year, but nobody had been able to shut it down.

"Oh boy," Chen exclaimed from his workstation.

"What?" She had her attention on an Assassin Market article in Forbes Magazine.

Chen closed the window he had open on his screen. "Nothing."

This wasn't the time to be secretive. "What?" Jin insisted. She looked at him.

"I saw a new story about Shen Shi's death. Doesn't matter."

"Show me." Why did Chen look so awkward? "Open it in our shared workspace."

Chen pursed his lips and grimaced. "Okay, but stay calm." He clicked a link on his screen, sending the article into the workspace they shared between their machines.

A video opened on Jin's screen. It was from a security camera in the hallway when Shen Shi fell into the elevator. Jin took a sharp intake of breath, blood draining from her face. The video showed the elevator doors open, Shen Shi turning to Jin as he chatted with her. Then it looked like Jin pushed him. She reached forward as he fell into the elevator shaft, then pulled back. The headline of the news article: *Jin Huang charged in brutal death at Shenzhen High-Tech Incubator. Suspect now on the run from authorities...*

"I didn't push him, it's just the angle of that video..." Jin began shaking, tears coming to her eyes.

"Shut that down," Wutang told Chen, reaching to put an arm around Jin. "I know you didn't," he whispered. The video image disappeared from their shared workspace.

Tears streamed down her face. "I tried to grab him, that's why I moved forward."

"I know," Wutang repeated, squeezing her. "Come on, we had to expect this."

Jin nodded, wiping the tears away with the back of her hand.

"What do you know about spoofing?" Wutang asked Jin, changing the topic.

"Spoofing?" Jin breathed in and out, still shaking. "You mean like faking an email address?"

"Yeah, but not just with email." Wutang opened a web definition on his laptop screen and pointed at it:

A spoofing attack is a situation in which a software program masquerades as another by falsifying information to gain an advantage.

Wutang's Tor browser pinged. He was in the middle of arranging a video chat session with his gamer friend Sheldon. Clicking his browser, he sent the video call to Chen's workstation so they could use one of the large monitors on the wall.

Chen clicked the monitor on. "We think someone's spoofing people. And I mean *really* spoofing people."

A window sprang open on-screen labeled 'Sheldon.'

"*Really* spoofing people?" Jin tried to erase the image of Shen Shi falling into the elevator shaft from her mind. "And by that, you mean…?"

"What he's talking about," came a voice from the computer speakers, "is software that doesn't just masquerade as another computer, but masquerades as a person."

Wutang pointed one hand at the computer screen, and the other at Jin and Chen. "I'd like to introduce you to Sheldon. This is the guy I was talking about on the ferry, the expert in artificial intelligence."

"A pleasure to meet you." The image on the screen stabilized into a thin boyish face with shaggy blond hair above day-old stubble.

Chen nodded hello at the camera on top of the screen. "So you're the chatbot expert?"

Wutang nodded. "He's the reigning Loebner prize winner. He was the first guy to beat the Turing test." He narrowed his eyes. "Or I mean, to write an automated agent that beat the Turing test."

"Turing test?" Jin asked. "You mean convincing people that a machine they're chatting with is a person?"

On-screen, Sheldon raised his hands. "It was a watered down version of the test—I only convinced eleven of the thirty judges, and I gamed it by making my chatbot a thirteen-year-old." When Jin didn't respond, he added, "I mean, my chatbot didn't need to be a genius or anything. Bots have been tricking people for a long time, 'love' bots in online dating chat rooms have been fooling people into thinking they're real humans for years."

"He still beat the Turing test for the first time." Wutang turned to Jin. "This guy's famous."

"So you think someone is spoofing *people?*" Jin pulled her mind fully into the conversation. "Like identity theft?"

Sheldon's head nodded on-screen. "Taken to the next level. Like the attacker that does a network analysis of your social media and figures out who your best friends are, then spoofs emails from them to you. Starts a dialog. The best hacking is done through social engineering."

"Social engineering? You mean using social interactions to extract information?"

Sheldon nodded. "I did a statistical analysis of the data Chen shared with me"—he looked away and fiddled with something on his side—"and it seems you have a sophisticated bot masquerading as a human in those communications. Usually this kind of attack requires human intervention, but in this case, it's being done by a machine."

Tables and graphs replaced Sheldon's image.

Jin looked at Chen, who shrugged. She hadn't told him he could share the data from Shen Shi's laptop, but then again, desperate times called for desperate measures. "So you're saying that someone is using a fancy chatbot to extract information from people?" she asked.

"In a nutshell, yes." Sheldon paused. "And it's linked to the identity theft ring Shen Shi investigated for Yamamoto."

Was that why they were killed? Had he been on the verge of exposing a hacking scheme the PLA used to steal money? But if they were the ones responsible for killing Yamamoto and Shen Shi to hide their plan, why didn't they kill her? Why kidnap her and ask her questions?

Also, she could imagine the PLA doing away with Chinese citizens, but killing a foreign national like Yamamoto? The head of Japan's largest financial fund? The repercussions seemed too risky, but maybe—if it was for enough. "How much money are we talking?"

"Impossible to estimate, but a lot." Sheldon shook his head, then started nodding. "A whole lot."

"So this chatbot is messaging and emailing people, making them think that it's a person?"

"Not just that it's *any* person, but a *specific* person," Sheldon pointed out. "Whoever is running this, they amass enough information about someone to mimic them. And not only

125

through email, I think this thing is making telephone calls, too."

"It can hold a *live* telephone conversation?"

Sheldon looked squarely at Jin. "How can you know that you're not talking to a machine right now?"

That stopped Jin cold. Hard-thumping bass shook the windowpane in the silence, and she looked from Wutang to Chen. Her face flushed hot. "Are you guys messing with me?"

"I'm kidding." Sheldon's mouth curled into a clever smile. "But the tech has been evolving for a long time. Machines write most of the breaking new stories we read now. There are even competitions for machine-written fiction and music composition."

"It's never been a question of 'if' this would happen," Chen said, "but a question of 'when'."

"A few things are kind of odd," Sheldon added. "It's strange that this is happening in China, in Chinese. Advanced chatbots usually come in English. No offense, but it's what all the top geeks speak."

"The PLA's cyber division is spending billions on advanced research," Chen pointed out. "Maybe they leapfrogged. They're well-funded ..."

"Maybe." Sheldon didn't look convinced. "But this goes way beyond your soup-and-nuts stuff. And right after the social engineering attack starts, this thing seems to replace *all* communications from that person." Sheldon clasped both hands together. "It's as if the person targeted by the attack disappears"—he pulled his hands apart—"after the machine takes over."

18

Bear Mountain
Northern Quebec

"Who are you?"

"What?" Jake mumbled.

"Who are you?"

Jake opened his eyes to find the barrel of a gun in his face. He recoiled and banged his head against the tree behind him. Cursing, Jake put his hands down to steady himself. He must have fallen asleep. The grass was wet with dew, the sun already climbing over the clouds on the horizon. Sunrise from the top of Bear Mountain was beautiful, or it would be if he didn't have a gun pointed at his head.

"Keep your hands where I can see them," the grizzled voice instructed.

Jake focused on the hollow cavity of the gun muzzle inches from his eyes. He looked up. Blinking to clear his eyes, he focused on the person holding the rifle. The face looked familiar. Relief tingling into his fingertips, he realized that it was Max Lefevre holding the gun on him. Sean worked with Max. They'd been introduced a few times. Why hadn't Sean just said so?

Jake recognized his own rifle, the one the pilot gave him, slung across Max's back. Jake hadn't bothered to load it. The shells were in his backpack.

"Max, it's me, Jake O'Connell. I'm Sean Womack's friend. He sent me to find you."

"O'Connell?" Max moved the rifle barrel an inch closer to Jake's forehead. "How did you find me?" Spit flew out of Max's mouth, his arm holding the gun shook. "You got twenty seconds to explain before I blow your head off. Is there some sort of tracking chip in me?"

When Jake didn't respond right away, Max pushed the muzzle into his forehead and yelled, "Tell me!"

"Sean sent me a map."

The veins in Max's neck flared. "*Merde*," he muttered, shaking his head.

"We've met before," Jake added. "A few times. That's why Sean sent me."

"He's dead."

"I know he's dead."

The creases in Max's frown deepened, sweat glistening. "You said we met before." His jaw muscles rippled as he clenched his teeth. "*Where?*"

Jake squirmed in the wet grass. "At the…" He froze. Where the hell had he met Max? "We met at Bluebridge, when Sean showed me around, and one night in Guangzhou, in China when I was visiting…"

Recognition flashed in Max's eyes. He pulled the gun barrel a few inches back from Jake's head. "So tell me about the nuggets."

"Nuggets?" Jake's mind was blank. What the hell did he mean?

"Nuggets," Max insisted. "You got ten seconds to tell me about nuggets." He pushed the gun barrel back into Jake's forehead. "One….two…three…"

"I don't know what you're talking about." Was this some code? And then the light dawned….*remember the nuggets.*

"…five…six…"

"You mean when Sean bought those chicken nuggets?" The night in Guangzhou, instead of buying girls drinks, Sean brought boxes of chicken nuggets. Not everyone wanted drinks, but everyone needed food, he'd reasoned. Typical Sean logic.

The barrel lifted away from Jake's head.

"I was there," Jake continued in a hurry. "And there was that girl." What was her name? "Jane?" He closed his eyes and dredged up the memory. "Jin?"

Max hoisted the rifle onto his shoulder. "Jake, right?" He offered a hand to Jake to pull him up. "Yeah, I remember you. From Schenectady?"

▲▼▲

Jake watched Max make his way around the windows of the cabin, peering out into the forest, his rifle still in hand while Jake's was slung across his back.

"You mind telling me what's going on?" Jake asked again.

128

The log cabin was a single open space on the main floor, with bedrooms upstairs accessed from a staircase against one wall. Under that staircase was another set of stairs that led into the basement. It was more of a half-basement, as the cabin was built atop a massive boulder that jutted up out of the ground at ninety degrees, forming a natural rock wall underneath. They'd come into the cabin through the downstairs entrance.

"So you came here alone?" Max checked the sight on his rifle. "Did you tell anyone where you were going?"

"Only my friend Dean, who's part of the Mohawk tribe in Kahnawake. We can trust him. An old friend, and Sean told me to find him."

"Maybe Sean wasn't so smart," Max growled. "He's dead."

Jake took a deep breath.

"Sorry." Max scowled. "I shouldn't have said that."

A wood-burning stove dominated the small main living area, not really more than a room, with large windows on all four walls—one side provided a view of the forest, and the other looked down on the side of the mountain. The tiny kitchen was set against the wall opposite the staircases. The kettle on the stove whistled, and Jake stepped forward and turned off the gas burner.

A large plastic hose connected the stove to the propane tank outside. The place was functional, but hardly up to code. None of the pilot lights worked, so he'd needed to light the burner with a match. Picking up the kettle, he filled the French press he'd already scooped coffee into.

"Tell me your story first." Max settled onto a daybed next to the window with the mountain view. The main lodge was a small dot against the sparkle of the lake below. "When did you speak to Sean last? What did he tell you?"

"I talked to him a week ago, August 13th. Just before he was killed. That was no accident."

Max stared out the window. "Of course it was no accident."

"I said I'd call him back..." Jake clenched his jaw, swallowed hard. "And then it was too late. Donovan gave me a memory key, saying it was something Sean had helped him with. I told Sean, but he didn't say anything."

"And what was on the key?"

"Some trading algorithms Donovan was using to skim from other hedge funds. That's the most Dean and I could get from it."

"And that was it?"

"No. Sean sent me a package."

Max turned to look at Jake. "He *sent* you a package? Like in the mail?"

"Not directly to me. He sent it to our foster care worker from when we were kids, probably so nobody could track it."

Max returned to looking out the window.

"It had another memory key in it," Jake continued, "but its contents are encrypted. No idea how to crack it yet." He stirred the coffee and water in the press, and put on the cover. "Did Sean give you the encryption key for it? Or do you have any idea of what it might be?"

"No and no." Max wagged his head from side to side. "But it might be good if I could have a look."

Finally, an inch of headway. "And there was a death certificate for Vidal Viegas in the package. It looked authentic."

Max exhaled slowly. "I can explain that." He leaned his rifle against the wall and put Jake's beside it. With a final glance at the lodge below, he got up and walked toward Jake. "Is that coffee ready?"

"I think so." Jake pushed the plunger in the coffee press down. "So what's with the Viegas death certificate?"

"Vidal Viegas died over a year ago," Max replied without hesitation.

The answer was so straightforward and matter-of-fact that Jake was taken aback. He expected some long-winded explanation, some fudging of the details. Max stared straight at Jake as he spoke. There was no dissembling, no wavering.

"So who was it that I ran into at Bluebridge last week?"

The plunger reached the bottom.

"That wasn't Viegas you met. Body doubles. Montrose and Viegas used them all the time to attend charity events, show up places they didn't want to be. They were obsessed with productivity, wanted to automate everything. Do you know how many employees we had at Bluebridge?"

Jake did an off-the-cuff calculation in his head, based on other hedge funds he knew of. "I don't know, a thousand?"

"Not even a hundred, including administrative staff. Bluebridge has seats on the board of directors of four hundred companies, did over a thousand financing deals last year. Wonder how that's possible with less than a hundred employees?"

"Four hundred companies?" The information staggered Jake. All hedge funds were secretive, and Bluebridge was in a class all its own, but what Max was telling him didn't make any sense. "That's not possible." Then he remembered how empty Bluebridge headquarters was when he stormed in on Viegas.

"Automation, Jake. Remember that social media company with fifty employees—and five hundred million customers—that sold for ten billion dollars? At Bluebridge we did the same thing, but with financial systems."

"Like automated trading?"

"More than that. We started using smart messaging responders that wrote emails for us, became a normal part of our internal process. Montrose funded a whole research project in Eastern Europe."

"What does that have to do with Sean or Vidal?"

"We were already using automated agents to make trades and negotiate simple deals, but Montrose had us start using them to virtually attend board meetings. We weren't even the first corporation to assign an artificial intelligence to a board of directors. A venture capital firm did it back in 2013. Montrose took it to the next level."

Jake wasn't making the connection. "But what does this have to do with Vidal dying?"

"A year ago, in the middle of the CodeCom merger— Bluebridge's biggest ever—Viegas had a heart attack. Montrose went nuts. Vidal was central to the deal. They told us not to tell anyone. We used the autoresponder to answer all of Vidal's emails. It copied his style, his habits. Then Montrose used the agent to attend the contract meetings remotely, using it to simulate Vidal's voice."

"And nobody found out?" Jake found it hard to believe.

"That place"—Max shook his head—"you know how secretive they are. Nobody ever saw Montrose or Vidal in person. Sean and I were on their core technical team with four other guys. Nobody else knew, at least not at first.

"After the CodeCom merger, Montrose was ecstatic. The digital Viegas was even better than the real one, he said. We all started using the system, creating these digital clones that could attend meetings for us, do emails. Montrose loved it, said he could be in a hundred places at once. Every possible operation inside of Bluebridge became automated when Sean started the autonomous corporation program."

"Autonomous corporations? You mean, without people?"

Max nodded. "Semi-intelligent software entities operating on darknets. Sean used Montrose's money to pioneer a program of them."

Sean could appear reckless to an outside observer, but he was always careful, meticulous. This sounded dangerous. Jake shook his head. "Why would Sean do that for Montrose?"

"Your friend Sean was an idealist. He was working to create WorldCoin, a cryptocurrency that would pay everyone alive on the planet a *'world citizen's dividend,'* as he called it." Max rubbed his face. "He wanted to replace the global currency markets with it, dreamed of a perfectly democratic 'One World' autonomous government that would be incorruptible."

The grandeur of the vision sounded like Sean. Jake smiled sadly. An impossible dream for other people, but for his brilliant friend, just another system to be implemented.

"Sean thought he could generate an $800 billion annual budget," continued Max, "for social programs by capturing inefficiencies. He saw what we were doing at Bluebridge as a first stepping stone to his grand plan for solving the world's problems."

Jake tried to absorb what Max was telling him. "And this was all done at Bluebridge?"

"We took a lot of off-the-shelf tech and wired it together— autonomous trading agents, chatbots, natural language recognition, machine vision. Montrose had more money than God. By the time Sean was finished with Bluebridge, you'd think there were *two* thousand people working at the company, and Montrose cooked the books to make it look like there were. The shareholders loved it. Everyone knew something odd was going on, but nobody wanted to know the details."

The pieces were fitting together. Tens of billions of dollars were at stake. "So Viegas died and Montrose covered it up? And now Montrose is trying to cover his tracks, take everything for himself?" Greed made sense. From his time on Wall Street, he knew it had no bounds.

"I don't know for sure. I know that people at Bluebridge

started disappearing. At first, Montrose paid the programmers to stay quiet. Then some of them left, one by one. I tried to contact them, but they went off grid."

"Paid to stay dark?"

"Maybe."

"Maybe?"

"Maybe worse." Max went back to the window and peered down at the lodge again. "I don't know."

Something dawned on Jake. "You keep talking about Montrose in the past tense."

"I don't think you get it. It's not Montrose who killed Sean, not directly, anyway."

"Who did then?"

"Not who," Max said slowly, "but what. Much easier to get a machine to do something illegal than do it yourself. You're one step removed, like those high frequency traders using machines to front run for them. At the core of Bluebridge is the capitalization system. It figures out what will make the most money for shareholders. It makes trades, hires and fires, negotiates deals." He paused. "Engages in contracts. And Sean didn't like the turn his grand dream had taken. He was about to blow the lid off."

"So you're saying Sean was killed because he was going to expose Montrose and Bluebridge?"

Max nodded and shrugged at the same time. "I got the hell out of there. We built a bridge from the digital to the real world, from the machine world of bits and bytes to our world of flesh and blood. The Bluebridge network doesn't see a difference between the two. And it certainly hasn't been trained in ethics, or not the sort you'd agree with."

"Can't we expose Montrose? Shut it down?"

"I still don't think you understand what's happened." Max walked back to the window. "I think Montrose is gone. The only thing left in charge of Bluebridge...is Bluebridge itself."

Jake stared at Max. Waited for some telltale smirk, a shrug that hinted Max was guessing. But Max stared back at him without blinking or wavering. If anything, his face hardened.

A tingling sensation crept from Jake's scalp, down his back and out to his fingertips—*I'm being hunted by a machine.*

19

Bear Mountain
Northern Quebec

"More coffee?" Max asked.

Jake shook his head. "Another cup and I'll explode."

Max seemed to drink a cup every ten minutes, his nervous energy filling the room. Jake suspected this wasn't unusual behavior for him.

He saw why Max had gotten along with Sean. The two of them must have bounced off each other like jackhammers. Sitting up here in the woods, with no network connections, no stream of information—with nothing to do but stare out the window—it had to be driving Max nuts.

And maybe Jake could use that to his advantage.

The funny thing was that in any other situation Jake would have loved the place. Sitting at a breakfast table beside the stove, looking over the green forests leading down to the lake below. He imagined himself up here on vacation with Elle and Anna. The thought was excruciating.

His old life had been torn away from him.

Maybe he could get it back by redirecting some of that energy that was crackling into space around Max. Use him to fix this. Instead of running blind, Jake could start to figure out how to get out of this situation.

Jake was still hunted, but at least things made sense—why Sean was killed, why Donovan thought Bluebridge set him up, why Jake was framed by his co-worker. Bluebridge was covering its tracks, embedding them into its web of deceit.

The first step to beating an opponent was understanding the situation. "So you think it's taken control of itself?"

Max turned from the counter with a plate stacked with sandwiches. He walked over and dropped one in front of Jake. "Either way, it hardly makes a difference."

"What?"

134

"Montrose, the founder of Bluebridge, was a friggin' psycho to begin with. Sure, you saw Montrose at charity events in the newspapers, but that guy would sell his own mother to make a deal. Bluebridge is just an extension of him."

Jake picked up his sandwich. "Like a full-Ted psycho?" He took a bite. If there was one thing he understood, it was psychos.

Max looked at him quizzically. "Like what?"

"Full-Ted, like a full Ted Bundy," said Jake around a mouthful of ham and cheese. "I categorize psychos, from Ted Bundy to Dalai Lama."

"You think the Dalai Lama is a psycho?"

"Saints are psychos too," Jake said, taking another bite. "Just non-violent ones."

Max pointed his sandwich at Jake. "So how did I rate?"

"You?" Jake laughed. "I remember thinking you were obsessive compulsive, borderline personality disorder, but in the opposite extreme. If anything, you're *too* empathetic."

Max smiled. "I'll take that as a compliment." He took a bite of his sandwich. "Montrose played dirty, would find any way to gain an advantage over an opponent in a deal. He hacked into people's email accounts, phone conversations—"

"Wasn't that risky?"

Laughing, Max took another bite. After chewing for a few seconds he replied, "Bluebridge was like a retirement club for senior US intelligence officers, and Montrose had a whole team of NSA-trained hackers, even Chinese hackers he brought over from Beijing, Shanghai, Guangzhou—you name it.

"More money than God," Max continued, "and the money is why we all went along with it. Why nobody asked questions. We were all on the juice. Bluebridge was designed to make money, with Montrose there or not, and it does it better than anything or anyone before. *Ever.* Fifteen billion in profits last year."

Reaching onto the table, Jake put his passport in his breast pocket, along with his wallet and billfold. He also stuffed in an old tobacco tin in which he'd put the Viegas death certificate and his Silver Eagle dollar coin. His jeans were in the dryer after getting covered in muck on the walk up last night. Jake sat in his boxer shorts with a fleece top borrowed from Max.

"How does something like that decide to take control of itself?" Jake asked. It still seemed far-fetched.

Max snorted. "Maybe that's what they were grooming it for all along." He cocked his head to one side. "Maybe Montrose is on a beach, watching his money-making machine rake in profits. It's possible, but I doubt it. When did you last talk to Sean?"

"A week ago, August 13th."

"Sean died August 10th. The papers in the morgue were faked. I looked into it when I heard about it. That's when I bugged out. This was our safe house. Only Sean knew about it."

"So that was a machine I was talking to on the phone? Not Sean?" Jake asked incredulously. He felt some of his guilt wash away. There was no way he could have called Sean back. It wouldn't have mattered. It wasn't even Sean.

Max nodded. "It had a lot of data on him. I couldn't even tell if I was talking to it or Sean when he called me."

"Wait, you talked to the machine when it was impersonating Sean?"

Max laughed, his mouth full of sandwich. "Weren't you listening? That's what we built it for. We used it all the time to respond to phone calls and emails for us."

"So how do people even know *you're* gone?"

"Maybe they don't. Did you try calling my home? Maybe I'd answer, have a chat with you. Maybe Bluebridge has taken over my identity. I don't know. All I know is, people started disappearing, so I got the hell out."

Jake remembered calling his phone when he was with Dean, when his own voice answered. Had Bluebridge already taken over his own identity? "Don't you think that law enforcement will start looking at all of these 'disappeared' people and link this thing back to Bluebridge?"

"You still don't get it." Max shook his head. "The machine impersonates them, answers their phone, even does video chats— it's just that you can't meet them *in* person. It comes up with clever explanations of why they had to leave, take a job somewhere else."

Max paused and let this settle into Jake's head before dropping the next bomb. "Directly or indirectly, Bluebridge now controls a good chunk of the US economy. Like I said, it had directorships on over four hundred major corporations when I bugged out."

"So this thing is sitting in on hundreds of board meetings?" Jake asked.

"And nobody has any idea they're talking to a machine. I know. I ran the program." Max swung his laptop around. On the screen was a story about Senator Russ. Standing beside him in the picture was Vidal Viegas's body double. "And now Bluebridge is busy buying itself a presidential election."

"And your plan was to run away?"

"It was working until you showed up." Max fixed Jake with a steady gaze. "Looks like you're already running away yourself."

Jake clenched his jaw, his stomach tightening. "I'm out here trying to protect my family, and that includes finding out what happened to Sean."

Max waved one hand in the air, as if shooing away a fly. "So now you know. Leave me alone."

"You can't outrun this, Max." Jake pointed at the image of the Vidal Viegas's body double on the laptop screen. "Whatever or whoever this is, it's going to catch up, no matter where you go. Are you going to hide forever? We have to stop it."

"Stop it?" Max laughed. "This thing has hundreds of billions of dollars, whole governments in its back pocket." He held his arms wide. "You're wanted by a half a dozen federal agencies, on the run in a foreign country, and we're stuck in a cabin on the edge of nowhere. I doubt we could scrounge up fifty bucks between the two of us. How do you propose we fight back?"

"*We* have information." Jake looked directly into Max's eyes. "And *you*"—he pointed at Max—"have a responsibility. You let this genie out of the bottle. We need to put it back in. Can you at least walk me through ways we could stop it?"

Max glared at Jake, but then lowered his head. "*Tabarnac*," he muttered under his breath, shaking his head. Putting the last half of his sandwich on the counter, he paced over to the window.

After a moment of silence, he turned back and faced Jake. "Okay, if you could somehow get Montrose-level access, we could gain access to the core Bluebridge system. But containing the eels' nest of autonomous corporations that it's let loose..."

"Can you log in, hack it?" Jake asked. Could it be that easy?

Max laughed. "You have no idea how many layers of security surround that thing. I don't have access anymore, and I doubt you could hack it."

At least it was a start. Jake put his sandwich down. "But if we could?"

"Then maybe reinitialize with older copies of the core. Even if you got access, it's a self-healing system…unless you get it to *want* you in charge…say, if you had something it needed."

"*Want* us in charge?"

Max shrugged. "I'm thinking out loud. I don't have all the answers, but"—a grin spread across his face—"I did steal a copy of the old Bluebridge core before I bugged out." He motioned upstairs.

Jake saw the gears start to turn in Max's head. *Just like Sean.* Jake knew the look in Max's eyes. He'd seen the same expression on his friend Sean so many times before—the lure of an impossible problem that needed to be solved. Now it was a question of feeding the fire. "What else? What else do we need to think about?" Jake encouraged.

"If we go back into the world, a big problem is going to be the assassin markets—"

"Assassin markets?" It was the first time Jake heard the term.

"Crowd-sourced darknets that Bluebridge uses to put bounties on the heads of people it wants gone." Max frowned at Jake. "You really don't know what you've gotten yourself into, do you? But maybe we can try and—" In mid-sentence Max's forehead exploded in a red mist, spattering blood and brain fragments across the table between them.

Jake stood, trying to understand what was happening, when something punched him hard in the chest and sent him crashing onto the floor.

▲▼▲

Jake and Sean coasted to a stop on their bikes.

"My dad says I'm weak," fourteen-year-old Jake said as they leaned the bikes against a lamppost.

Jake shook from the beating his brother gave him, fresh purple-and-red bruises rising on his arms and face. He'd managed to connect a few punches of his own—even when he knew there was no chance of winning, Jake never went down easy.

Touching his face tenderly, he felt his lip. Swollen. He couldn't go to school like this.

A cold wind blew autumn leaves across empty streets. Jake and Sean sat side by side on a bus stop bench, next to a garbage can overflowing with empty fast food wrappers and beer cans. Half of the buildings around them were derelict. Jake wondered for the hundredth time how this dump was the capital of New York, and not the glamorous city of the same name south of them. It was only a bit more than a hundred miles away, but it might as well have been a million.

"Never giving up, Jake, that's your gift. You never give up." Sean lit a cigarette and offered it to Jake. "You know this place was once the center of the universe?"

Jake took the cigarette and had a drag. "You shittin' me? How's that?"

"Thomas Edison had his lab up the street. Invented half of everything that makes the world today. People used to travel from all over the world to come here."

"Not anymore," Jake laughed.

"Know what that is?" Sean pointed at a low red brick building across from them.

Jake shrugged and took a puff from the cigarette. He coughed and Sean smiled at him. The place his friend pointed at was one he'd seen a thousand times before, wedged between a minimart and a high rise apartment block. Nondescript, without any signs announcing what was inside. He'd never given it a second glance.

Sean pulled a plastic bag from his pocket and picked through the garbage, pulling out the bottles and cans they could return for nickels and dimes, dropping the rest around the garbage can. "It's a nuclear submarine control center."

"A what?" Jake took another drag from the smoke and offered it to Sean, who shook his head.

"A control center for the US Navy's fleet of nuclear submarines."

Jake shivered and took another pull from the cigarette, feeling the burn of it in his throat. It made him feel ill, but then, it was something. Better than nothing. "Really?"

"Yeah." Sean pulled out a few more cans, rummaging deeper. "They stuck it here 'cause it's a low income area. If that makes any sense." Grimacing, he pulled his hand out of the garbage and wiped off something slimy on the side of the can.

Jake decided the cigarette was making him feel sicker than it was worth. He offered it to Sean again. "What's your point?"

Sean dropped the bag of cans onto a nearby bench and took the cigarette. "That sometimes there's hidden power right under our noses." He took a drag. "You're not weak, Jake. You're like that building. Maybe not everyone sees it, but there's a hidden power in you."

139

"You're just saying that." Jake looked away, over at the hills that seemed to encircle and trap him in this place. "You're the smart one. You're getting out of this shithole."

"That thing your dad calls weakness"—Sean tapped Jake's chest—"it's the opposite. And you shouldn't focus on money."

"Easy for you to say. You're going to get into college, make a bunch of dough, and forget me and this place forever."

"That's not true. And you're smart, too. You made me your friend, right?"

Jake laughed. "Right."

Sean produced something from his pocket and held it up. "I got something for you." He handed it to Jake.

Jake took it. It was a coin. Huge. Two inches across.

"That's a 1957 Silver Eagle dollar coin. Probably worth fifty bucks. My gift to you."

"Seriously?" Jake turned the coin over and over.

"Now you'll always have money in your pocket, Jake."

20

Lockhart Street
Hong Kong

Jin opened the bag of food Chen brought into the apartment for dinner. "Shanghai noodles again?" She picked out a container. "I feel fat just looking at it."

Jin and Wutang had resumed their positions on the couches, with Chen hovering in front of his workstation, cigarette in mouth, and Sheldon's face smiling on one of the computer monitors.

Wutang leaned in for a container, grabbing some chopsticks. "You need to eat fat."

"Maybe you do." Jin dropped her noodle container on the table. Not that hungry.

They'd hit a brick wall in their data sifting. They could see the money flowing from the identity theft internally in China, but they couldn't see where the outside influx of cash was coming from— it was as if a financial firewall had been erected.

Jin shook her head and stared out the window at Lockhart Street. In the bright light of day, the street below the apartment looked so different. At night it was dark, dangerous, pulsating with life. In the day, it was a dirty side street in the middle of the Hong Kong skyscrapers.

"So you're saying that my list of wealthy dead people is linked to the autonomous corporations Shen Shi investigated?" Jin asked Sheldon.

"Beyond a doubt." Sheldon nodded. "These autonomous corporations are interacting with one another. The ones doing identity theft connect to the ones setting up assassinations, all of them intertwined into the cryptocurrency payment systems."

"And you think they can really spoof people? They can fool people into believing they're someone they're not?"

"Over the phone, even over a video link. You can access voice and data files for anyone. Intelligence agencies have data taps on all the big carriers, thousands of hours of conversations and all your emails are there for the taking. Collect enough data and you can spoof anyone. Like creating a new copy of them."

"Takes a lot of money," Wutang added. "The question is where all the money is coming from."

"And why." Chen took a puff from his cigarette, leaning over to the window to blow the smoke out.

Sheldon nodded on-screen. "And why, yes, that is a good question."

They'd scoured Shen Shi's databases for evidence of the autonomous corporations' handiwork. It wasn't something you could point at directly, but when you knew what you were looking for, you could detect their digital wake like an invisible boat that left waves in rivers of information.

They found shell companies linked to shell companies, a house of cards funneling money into government contracts, in what they assumed were payoffs to officials. It looked like a shadow organization slowly worming its way into the upper echelons of the Chinese Politburo. They didn't have access to the same level of records outside of China, but they had to assume it was happening in other places as well.

Sheldon built a nested model of the autonomous corporations as they spawned, interacted, and grew. Decentralized, but Sheldon was convinced that there was some starting point, some motivating force behind their sudden and explosive growth.

"Maybe we should go to the police?" Chen suggested.

"And turn Jin in?" Wutang's face puckered in an angry frown. "They want to pin Shen Shi's murder on her."

"And we have no proof," Sheldon added, "just a lot of data that fits an explanation. And everyone involved is anonymous—"

"So there's no way of guaranteeing the authorities we go to aren't already in on it." Wutang shook his head. "Those people who abducted Jin seemed like government to me."

"And we have nobody to point at, nobody to accuse." Jin hung her head. "Nobody except me."

"And the authorities are already trying to stop the assassin markets," Sheldon pointed out. "It's not invisible to them, the CIA is actively trying to hunt these things down."

"So we wait?" Chen rubbed his face. They were all tired. "If Yamamoto was killed for trying to expose this, maybe we should get in touch with the people he was going to tell."

"So you want to contact the chairmen of the Bank of China and CITI Bank?" Jin clearly didn't think it was a good idea.

"Do you have a better idea?" Chen sighed. "At the end of the day, we're talking about banking fraud on an international scale. Banks live and die by data, and they have the money to fight this kind of thing."

"Do you think they'd listen to us?" Jin shook her head. "Too risky, and how do we know *they're* not in on this?"

Sheldon agreed, "That strategy already got at least two people killed."

He meant Shen Shi and Yamamoto, plus the string of rich people who were dead for who knew what reasons. Jin suggested another angle, "Can't we find someone working for one of the autonomous corporations, infiltrate one of them?"

"I'm working on that." Sheldon put up a screen. "Already into several identity theft autonomous corporations, buying IDs, working my way inside. Thing is, like I said, I bet the people working for the autonomous corporations don't even know they're working for machines."

This was a new twist to Jin. "What do you mean?"

"The autonomous corporations hire people to do things they can't do themselves."

"Like kill people?"

Sheldon nodded. "But also lawyers to negotiate contracts, programmers to help spawn new instances of themselves. Most people work from home these days. Who's your boss? A phone call, a video chat, a paycheck. Do you really know who you're working for?"

"I don't kill people," Jin replied.

"And most of these people don't either," Sheldon answered.

Chen finished his cigarette and flicked it out the window. "But some of them do."

Sheldon nodded. "Yeah, some of them do. And that's the frightening part—they're opening a rabbit hole for all the psychopaths to disappear down."

"The killers you mean?"

"Not just killers. Look at this." Sheldon opened up a darknet page called DirtyDeeds.

It wasn't porn as Jin expected. A website that looked like a newspaper classified section popped up. Sheldon clicked one of the links, under 'domestic':

Neighbor dog driving me nuts. Located in Broward County FL. If u willing to kill dog, will exchange tags. Offering 2DC.

Jin frowned. "2DC?"

"Two darkcoins—it's a cryptocurrency—about a thousand dollars at current exchange rates," Sheldon explained. "It's a *help needed* ad for someone to kill their neighbor's dog. You should see the *help wanted* section—weapons, child pornography—you name it." Sheldon grimaced. "The DirtyDeeds DAC started up a few months ago, but already has thousands of users, millions of dollars changing hands. All of it anonymous."

"My God."

"God's got nothing to do with this. The US Feds shut down the Silk Road, the famous darknet drug-selling site, only because there was a central point of failure—the founder and owner Ross Ulbricht. They charged him with murder-for-hire and narcotics trafficking, but they only got him because he bragged."

Sheldon rolled his shoulders. "With an autonomous corporation, there's no central point of failure. They don't boast, they don't drink, and there's no way of seducing them. You might catch one or two people who use it, but once they're started, stopping them is close to impossible."

Wutang nodded in agreement. "What are people going to start doing once they realize they won't get caught? These things are spawning exponentially, growing like a cancer into the human network."

The shrieks and cries of the partygoers outside the windows took on a more sinister note to Jin's ear. Outside, somewhere in that crowd, there might be people hunting other people, on missions directed by machines. Despite the heat, she shivered. "What can we do? This sounds like something the Security Ministry or American NSA should be dealing with, not us."

"I agree, but this isn't going away, and Jin's name probably hasn't disappeared from that Assassin Market," Sheldon observed. "Whatever Yamamoto found hit a nerve. We're right at the tip of the spike. *Something* is funding these things with a huge influx of cash."

Wutang reached over to squeeze Jin's hand. "We need to get your name off that list, and we need to get you out of here. You're an American citizen, so we should get you on American soil."

"You think I'd be safer there?" Jin didn't feel like she'd be safe anywhere. The Assassin Market didn't recognize national boundaries.

"Safer than here." Wutang rubbed his eyes. "I'm being serious. Your family is there. Maybe they could help."

"Maybe, but my mother's on her way here." The funeral for Shen Shi was planned for Friday. Her mother was on her way to China now. "And I need to find out who killed my cousin."

Jin had emailed her family using an anonymized connection into her webmail, told her she had nothing to do with Shen Shi's death. Her mother was frantic. She'd been trying to reach her for days. Police were calling, reporters, all kinds of people. It shook Jin to realize that whoever was following her knew how to reach her family. She had to stay away from them, and there was no way she could attend Shen Shi's funeral.

"Then we have to move forward." Sheldon paused on-screen to stare at the three of them. Everyone nodded.

"I doubt this list of wealthy dead people is confined to China," Jin said. "And I bet that wasn't the PLA that kidnapped me."

"Then who do you think it was?" asked Chen.

"I don't know. It doesn't fit." Jin rubbed her eyes. She was exhausted and frightened, for herself and her family. "I think we should look into the Sean Womack connection more. He was really close to someone I met once."

"Who?" Sheldon asked.

"Jake O'Connell. He lives in Manhattan. If Sean knew anything, I'm sure he told Jake. And look at this." On their shared workspace, Jin opened a link to a story about Jake: *New York, Aug 17th—Atlas executive Jake O'Connell storms Bluebridge headquarters, accosts founder Vidal Viegas…*

"The same day as Jake stormed Bluebridge, he was arrested on rape charges. Why did Jake try to get to Viegas?" Jin asked the group. "And Viegas was Sean's thesis advisor at MIT."

"And check this out." Sheldon opened another article on their shared workspace about Jake's boss: *Danny Donovan, former CEO of Atlas, claims Bluebridge executives are framing him for massive fraud scandal…*

"Bluebridge," they all whispered almost in unison.

"A massive source of funds. Isn't that what we're looking for?" A creeping sensation tickled Jin's neck, the hair standing up on her arms despite the heat and humidity. The answer was staring them in the face the whole time. "What about the world's richest hedge fund, founded by one of the leading artificial intelligence experts?"

"And you've met Jake O'Connell?" Wutang turned to Jin. "In Manhattan?"

"No, I met him here, in Guangzhou, but we stayed in touch."

"Bluebridge earned fifteen billion dollars last year." Sheldon whistled. "That could do it. We need to get in touch with your friend ." He pulled up an image of Jake's face. "The billion dollar question: Is he still alive?"

21

Bear Mountain
Northern Quebec

Flat on his back, gasping for air, Jake came to his senses.

He tried to look down at his body.

Was stopped short by a searing pain in his chest.

Pulling himself onto his elbows, he leaned against the wall, panting. Spots of blood flecked his fleece top, and Jake ripped it open, expecting to see a gaping wound.

Instead he found a gash across the left side of his chest.

He prodded it with a finger.

No sucking chest wound.

Whatever hit him had glanced off.

Something dripped onto him. Blood poured in a steady stream off the table above his head. Jake propped himself up another inch. Max wasn't so lucky. There was a gory hole in the side of his head, with chunks of flesh and bone strewn across the table and floor.

Jake scanned the room. The window next to them, facing east toward the lodge, had two neat holes in it. Tiny fragments of glass littered the floor beneath it.

A sniper.

What had Max said about assassin markets?

Jake braced himself up higher. The pain in his chest so intense he could barely breathe.

Must have broken a rib.

Before, the danger had all seemed abstract, one step removed despite his arrest. Though he suspected someone had killed Sean, a part of him hadn't been quite convinced. Now the prospect of imminent death was close. Someone was trying to kill *him. Now.* White-hot fear wrapped its fist around his brain.

Push it away, don't panic, he told himself.

Their attacker must think he killed them both. Jake went down like a sack of potatoes. The sniper would be waiting and watching.

Glancing over at the kitchen countertop, a large knife handle stuck out of a butcher's block. Across the room, the two rifles rested against the window where Max left them. He didn't know if Max's gun was loaded. His backpack was in the entranceway downstairs, and he knew there were bullets in there.

Jake knew a thing or two about guns; had learned to use them as a teenager. But did he stand a chance at winning a firefight with a trained assassin?

He could barely breathe through the pain and panic.

On the counter next to the knife block was a pack of matches, and next to it was a bottle of lighter fluid. At eye level, the rubber hose stuck out of the back of the stove.

An idea flashed into his mind.

Reaching onto the countertop, he pulled the knife from the butcher's block and sat upright. Leaning over, he hacked at the rubber hose, managing to cut through it in three hard swipes.

A blast of propane whooshed out, filling his nostrils with the smell of rotten eggs.

Gagging, he grabbed the matches and lighter fluid from the counter and crawled to the basement door on the other side. Over his shoulder he glanced at the rifles at the window. Too risky. He paused, then glanced at the stairs leading up to the bedroom. Max had a copy of the Bluebridge core up there, but going up would expose him. Swearing under his breath, he dismissed the idea.

Someone was here to kill him. That trumped everything else.

Inching the basement door open, he slithered through it and knelt on the stairs, grabbing a pair of sneakers and closing the door behind him. He crept down in the semi-darkness, gasping for air as pain lanced through his chest. He pulled a tarp over himself and crouched against a pile of wood in the corner, away from the stairs.

And waited.

The killer would come and check, wouldn't he? This was the only entrance into the cabin. What if there was more than one attacker? Did assassins come in pairs?

Jake calmed his breathing.

Quiet. Stay quiet.

His pulse banged in his ears. His chest burned. Grabbing a rag from the side of the wood pile, he soaked it in lighter fluid and balled it up. His hands were soaked as well, so he wrapped the rag in another, first using the clean one to wipe his hands. It was the best he could do.

He checked his watch. *1:10*. His legs ached. He checked his watch again. *1:11*.

Calm.

He saw the downstairs door through a hole in the tarp. *1:14*.

Was there a candle burning upstairs? Jake couldn't remember. *1:16*.

What was taking so long?

The downstairs door finally creaked open, spilling light into the half-basement against the rock wall. Someone stepped into the doorway, a gun in his hand. The man scanned the basement, then looked up the staircase. Jake couldn't see him clearly. The man entered and started up the stairs, gun pointed forward, limping slightly.

At the top of the stairs, the door creaked open. Shaking, Jake slid out from under the tarp and struck a match, igniting the rag soaked in lighter fluid. Stepping out from under the stairs, he tossed the burning rag through the open door up top and sprinted for the door.

"Shit—" Jake heard behind him, but he didn't stop moving. He ducked and crashed through the door. A whomping concussion flattened him.

The massive explosion shattered the cabin above his head. The heat seared Jake. Glass and fragments of wood showered down all around him. Catching the smell of burning hair, he rolled onto the grass out front, trying to put out any flames.

As the roar subsided, Jake sprang to his feet. Smoke poured out of the shattered windows above him. Staggering, he jogged over to where Max had parked an ATV, then jumped on and started it up, jamming it into gear and skidding down the trail in a spray of gravel and dirt.

Don't shoot me in the back, please don't shoot me in the back.

Jake struggled to stay on top of the ATV, adrenaline the only thing keeping him upright. The trail was steep and littered with rocks and tree stumps. It was more of a hiking trail than a road. Somehow he managed to keep from spilling over as he made his way down, but as the lodge came in view from between the trees, he lost his balance and jumped off. Jake danced into the underbrush while the ATV rolled and crashed down the trail.

"Hey buddy, you okay?" It was a hunter, staring wide-eyed at Jake.

Four of them ran up the trail, with more coming behind. They must have heard the explosion. "I'm fine." Jake stepped across the pine needles and out of the trees, still dressed in his boxer shorts and the fleece.

"What happened up here?" asked the hunter.

"I don't know." Jake stepped onto the trail. He recognized them from the night before. They'd been sitting at the bar at the lodge, drinking. "I was out taking a leak, and whoosh, the friggin' cabin exploded. I got the hell out of there."

"You're bleeding."

Jake glanced at his shirt. A dark stain spread all across his left side.

"You should get down to the lodge. I think there's a medical tech on staff," the hunter said, offering a hand to help Jake.

"I'm fine, I can get down myself." Jake shrugged him off. "But could you go up and check on my friend? I'm worried he might not have made it out."

The hunter retreated, frowning and looking up the trail. Jake stepped toward the four men, and three of them stepped back, giving him space to pass.

"You sure?" The hunter and his friends watched Jake.

One of them held a phone. The fourth hunter didn't move, but stared right at Jake.

He looked scared.

Why would he be scared?

Jake noticed the rifle in the fourth man's hands. The man raised it.

Reacting without thinking, Jake lunged forward and grabbed the muzzle of the fourth man's rifle as it fired, the crack of the bullet deafening his left ear.

The other hunters all hit the ground, one of them swearing, "What the hell?" as he jumped into the pine needles at the side of the trail.

The speed of Jake's reaction surprised the shooter, so Jake managed to wrench the rifle from his hands. In one smooth motion, he grabbed the stock and brought it up, crunching the weapon into the man's chin. The guy dropped to the ground like a sack of wet cement.

Panting, Jake stepped over the man, pointing the gun at his head. His face was a mass of blood where Jake hit him. Not moving. Swinging the gun around, Jake turned his attention to the other three men. They held their hands up.

"Who is this?" Jake demanded, pointing at the unconscious man at his feet.

"We...we don't know," said the first hunter, the one who'd tried to help Jake. "He hopped a ride on the floatplane with our group yesterday. Said it was a last minute thing."

Jake's head rang. He pointed the rifle at the hunter. "You never met him before that?"

The hunter trembled, his hands held high. "Not before yesterday."

Taking in big lungfuls of air, Jake stared at the hunter, then at the other two, and then back at the guy at his feet. Another assassin, but this one went down without much of a fight. What was going on?

"Stay here," Jake commanded, pointing the rifle at the hunter. The man nodded, his eyes wide.

More people were coming up the trail. Jake had to move. Giving the three hunters one last look, Jake started down. When he passed two more hunters coming up the trail, Jake told them there was an accident up higher. They did a double take looking at Jake, in his boxer shorts and holding a rifle, but they continued on as he insisted he was okay.

After a hundred yards, the trail opened on to the lawn of the main lodge. A knot of people stood on the patio, all of them staring up the mountain. None of them had rifles, not that he could see. Jake glanced over his shoulder to see the smudge of smoke rising over where the cabin had been. He ran up to the lodge, keeping his distance from the group of people, his rifle pointed in the air. The bartender he'd spoken to the previous evening was at the main door of the cabin.

"You got a first aid kit?" Jake asked the bartender. The pain in his ribs was excruciating. He needed to risk getting it looked at.

The bartender nodded. "I trained as an emergency medical tech. I got a first aid kit." He motioned for Jake to follow him inside. "What happened up there?" he asked, looking over his shoulder.

Jake scanned the faces on the patio for Jean, the pilot who flew him in. The old Super Cub was still at the dock. Where was Jean? Even if he was hung over, there'd been an explosion. It seemed unlikely he was still sleeping it off. "Have you seen my pilot?" Jake asked the bartender.

"No." The bartender retrieved the first aid kit from behind the reception desk. There wasn't much in it. A few gauze patches, some tape and alcohol swabs. "I think there's another one—"

"It's fine." There wasn't time. Putting his rifle on the reception counter, Jake pulled his shirt over his head. "Can you put a couple of those patches across the cut, tape it—"

"My God." The bartender stared at Jake in horror.

Jake followed his eyes and looked down at himself. A mottled purple bruise had spread across his chest, angry and red and swollen in the middle, with a bleeding gash scraping off to one side. "Can you patch it up? Quick?"

"You're going to need some medical attention. We gotta get you—"

"Somebody is trying to kill me," Jake interrupted. "I don't have time. Do you understand? Someone is trying to kill me. That's what happened up there."

The bartender stopped fumbling with the medical kit. "Kill you?"

Jake pulled his shirt higher. "Can you patch this, quickly? Please."

Something in Jake's eyes must have convinced the bartender. "Yeah, sure, okay," he stammered, and pulled out a roll of gauze, holding it against Jake's bleeding wound.

"So you haven't seen Jean? My pilot?" Jake repeated, holding the gauze in place while the bartender taped it. He glanced out the doorway. Everyone seemed to have gone up the trail. The patio was empty.

Good.

Still no sign of the pilot, though.

"No, he disappeared last night," replied the bartender.

One more gauze patch and Jake pulled his shirt back down.

"You want some pants?" the bartender asked.

Jake nodded. "That would be great."

"Give me a sec."

The bartender disappeared while Jake hobbled back to the

door. Still no sign of Jean. He glanced at the three floatplanes on the end of the dock. The Cessna and Bombardier planes gleamed beside the rusted old Super Piper, and Jake knew the Cessna controls. But while small planes had locks and keys just like cars, Jean's Super Piper didn't. Jake remembered the screwdriver shoved into the ignition.

"These should fit you."

Jake looked over his shoulder to see the bartender returning, waving some khakis in the air. Behind him came someone else. The guy looked like the manager. Jake grabbed the pants.

"*Monsieur*, are you alright?" asked the manager. "Could you tell me what happened?"

"No idea," Jake replied, pulling the pants on. "Maybe the propane tank?"

"You should be sitting down, sir." The manager pointed at a couch beside the reception. "Please, let me help you."

Jake shrugged him off and backed away, grabbing his rifle. "I'm fine."

"*Monsieur*...s'il vous plait..."

Turning, Jake did his best to bolt. He hobbled across the patio. Looking back, the manager stared at him in wide-eyed horror. Hopping down the stairs, Jake jogged across the dock and stepped onto the float of the Piper Cub, opening its door and throwing the rifle onto the seat. Kneeling, he unwound the ropes mooring the plane to the dock, then jumped into the pilot seat. He ignored the shouts erupting from the lodge.

This was as old school as it got, analog switches and dials—airspeed in knots, altitude, engine RPM, manifold pressure—he scanned them one by one, nodding.

"Okay, okay, master switch on." Jake turned the screwdriver and a red light blinked on.

There was no separate switch for the magnetos, so Jake had to assume the master turned on the batteries and magnetos at the same time.

"Set mixture to 'full rich,'" he muttered, then he grabbed the primer knob, unscrewing it so he could pull it out and push it back in three times to get some gas into the piston while he pressed his feet up and down on the aileron pedals, testing them.

He glanced to his left. The manager ran across the patio, ordering him to stop. Two other people followed, one of them with a rifle pointed in the air. Saying a prayer, Jake punched the ignition switch. With a wheezing cough the engine turned over, first once, then twice, then sputtered to life as the manager banged on Jake's window.

Jake locked the door and advanced the throttle with his left hand. The engine roared to life. "Sorry!" Jake yelled at the manager. "I don't have time to explain."

The plane pulled away from the dock.

Jake strapped himself in, using his feet to angle the tail fin, slowly curling around so he was lined up down the center of the lake. His hand shaking, Jake pushed the throttle to maximum and felt the plane accelerate, bouncing across the waves. As the trees on the opposite shore grew larger, the plane shook violently.

Why wasn't it lifting off?

Gritting his teeth, he realized he hadn't pulled back on the flight stick yet. He leaned back, pulling the stick, and the plane soared off the water. Seconds later he skimmed the tops of the trees, then climbed into the sky.

He wiped his forehead, his eyes stinging. His whole body soaked in sweat.

Shaking.

The only digital device on the dashboard was an old GPS unit screwed onto it, its fat satellite antennae sticking up. Reaching forward, he clicked it on, and the screen flickered. An image appeared in black and white. It worked. Jake checked the maps. He knew the closest populated area was Lac St-Jean, about a hundred miles due east. It was a huge lake, twenty miles across. Even he could land on that. Or crash land, anyway.

Climbing and swinging away from the sun, Jake relaxed.

What the hell had happened back there? Holding the flight stick between his knees, he inspected the angry red-and-purple welt on his chest. He noticed his fleece top had a hole through it, right through the left breast pocket. Opening the pocket, he discovered the tobacco tin, which had been ripped apart.

Had it deflected the bullet?

No.

It was his Silver Eagle dollar coin, nearly two inches in diameter, dented off center. It had been inside the tobacco tin with the documents he'd stowed in there. Together with his wallet and passport, it'd been enough to absorb and deflect the bullet, giving him a chest wound instead of a stopped heart.

The Silver Eagle from Sean had saved his life.

Money in his pocket.

Money in his pocket!

The clue Sean had left in his note. That had to be it. The key code had to be something to do with his Silver Eagle coin. Jake put it into his pants pocket.

He had other things to worry about right now.

How did the assassins find him at Bear Mountain?

He hadn't told anyone but Dean he was coming up here. What was he going to do now? Minutes ago, Max was explaining how they might disable the system. Now Max was dead, and Jake had incinerated the copy of the Bluebridge core.

The engine sputtered and coughed.

Jake blinked and pulled himself back to reality.

He checked the gauges.

The manifold pressure was good, oil pressure fine, but something was wrong. The engine coughed again and whined. Jake scanned the dials and switches desperately.

There was one gauge at zero.

The gas.

The engine sputtered a few more times before going silent.

"You can't be serious."

Horrified, Jake watched as the propeller blade froze to a stop in front of him. In his rush, he hadn't checked the gas. Hadn't thought to. The tank had been half full when Jean landed the plane. Jake had been watching it yesterday. Somebody must have emptied it last night.

But right now, the how or why didn't matter.

"Landing, how do I land this thing?" The only thing he remembered was that he had to lower the flaps, get the airspeed down as low as possible.

Wind whistled across the airframe as the plane dropped from the sky.

22

2nd Circuit
Court of Appeals Building
New York City

There better be a damn good reason for this, Judge Danforth fumed as he strode down the marbled main corridor of the New York 2nd Circuit Court of Appeals building. The click-clack of his polished black Oxfords echoed through the empty hallways, his stride quick and forced. He hoped it conveyed his displeasure to the knot of suited lawyers waiting outside his chambers up ahead.

This might be the circuit court, but he had a busy schedule. The only reason he'd agreed to come to his chambers on a Saturday morning was the call he'd received from his old friend Jerry Sandoz, a partner at the law firm where he'd started his career. A call from Jerry was unusual enough to warrant an exception.

"Make this quick, gentlemen." Judge Danforth fished for his keys, shooing the lawyers away like pigeons. Turning the old lock over, he pushed the huge oak door open and marched inside. He didn't invite them in. They followed anyway.

It was also the weekend before school started after the summer break.

Judge Danforth started family life late, well into his forties. He'd sacrificed his youth to endless nights devoted to making partner at his law firm and then, after his appointment, to dreams of the Supreme Court. That dream was fading, his once star-caliber career relegated to the second-string of Appeals Court.

Today his eight-year-old son had his soccer finals.

"Tell me why I'm here," Judge Danforth growled at the three lawyers hovering in front of his desk.

The lawyer in the center, square-jawed with slicked-back hair, handed him a large black-and-white photograph. Judge Danforth inspected it and frowned. "Who is this?"

"Jake O'Connell."

The name rang a bell. "The hedge fund trader, arrested on rape charges?" asked the judge. Jake's face had been plastered across the newspapers a week ago, before the news cycle latched on to the next scandal.

"The same."

Judge Danforth squinted and put on his reading glasses. The image was grainy, the man in the picture wearing sunglasses with a baseball cap pulled low. "And why are you bringing this to me?"

"Because we'd like you to issue a Federal warrant for Mr. O'Connell."

"You'd like me to do what?" The judge dropped the photograph and pulled off his reading glasses. He glared at the slick lawyer. "What's your name?"

"Peter Osorio, your honor."

"Peter, I'm not sure what Jerry told you—"

"This isn't just coming from Mr. Sandoz, your honor. Senator Russ has a special interest in this as well. We couldn't use his name over the phone."

"Senator Russ?" Judge Danforth frowned. There was a new power structure forming in Washington. Senator Russ was a surprise contender for his party's ticket, so it shocked everyone when he swept the primaries to secure the nomination. With the election two months away, it looked like a landslide for him. "I don't understand. This is an appeals court. I have no involvement with the O'Connell case."

"But," said Osorio, "you could decide to make it your business. Judges have discretionary powers. This might be the 2nd Circuit Court, but you're still a Federal judge, with powers under Article III, backed by the judicial branch of the Federal government."

Judge Danforth slumped back in his chair. The audacity. "I remind you that we are in chambers, Mr. Osorio, and you are a hairsbreadth away from being in contempt of my court." Taking a deep breath, he paused. Still, it might be worth it to find out what was going on. "And why is this photograph supposed to motivate me to use my discretion?"

"That was taken yesterday at the Canadian border. Mr. O'Connell has fled the country." Osorio pursed his lips. "And this morning, Mr. Daniel Donovan, former founder and CEO of Atlas Capital—just released on ten million dollars bail—was found dead in his apartment. Murdered."

"And you think there is a connection?"

"Assistant DA Bailey has placed Mr. Jake O'Connell as the number one suspect. In fact, we think Mr. O'Connell is the real mastermind behind the entire Atlas fraud, which may eclipse Bernie Madoff in scope. Tens of billions. Key documents were discovered at the Donovan residence—"

"Wait, you're telling me that the police have put this entire new investigation together in the past few hours?" Judge Danforth wasn't intimate with the case, but from his experience, this sort of thing took weeks, if not months, to assemble. It seemed a hundred and eighty degree turn from what he'd heard informally in the halls.

Osorio worked his lips together as if tasting something sour. "I suggest you talk to Assistant District Attorney Bailey for details, but I can tell you that Senator Russ, likely soon *President* Russ, would look very"—Osorio chose his words carefully—"*favorably* on your attention to this matter." He adjusted his tie. "As you know, Judge Tomasso is due to retire this year."

Tomasso was a Supreme Court justice. Was this man seriously trying to bribe him with an appointment to the Supreme Court? It seemed beyond belief. "Did I hear you properly?"

Osorio replied without hesitation. "Yes."

Judge Danforth stared hard at him, but Osorio didn't shrink. Danforth could smell a set-up, but then this Jake O'Connell character didn't seem like an angel. Arrested for rape, now under suspicion for murder by the DA, fleeing the country in the middle of a massive fraud investigation…

"It would make for good press, wouldn't it?" Osorio suggested. "Judge discovers rich hedge fund manager fleeing country…murder, rape…stealing the life savings of millions of average Americans. It'll be front page news all over the country, with your face next to it."

Judge Danforth picked up the photograph and studied it. His old friend Jerry sent Osorio here. Maybe Jerry was throwing him a golden opportunity. And Senator Russ was a shoe in for the presidential election. A whole new power structure forming, and maybe this time he wouldn't be left out. Imagine, *Supreme Court Justice Danforth*. His wife could handle the soccer today. "I need to verify this with DA Bailey."

"Of course." Osorio smiled an oily grin.

"And how is it that I announce this discovery to the world?"

"We can help with that."

Judge Danforth put the photograph down. "Okay, give me the paperwork."

Osorio handed over a sheaf of file folders. Judge Danforth reached to take them, but Osorio held on to them. "Two more things. First, we need you to issue a Federal arrest warrant for Mr. O'Connell's wife, Elle O'Connor, and his brother, Eamon. We believe they're involved."

A bit outside the box, but possible. "And the second thing?" Judge Danforth held onto one end of the sheaf of file folders while Osorio gripped the other.

"We need a ruling that the Kahnawake Commission is in violation of federal gaming regulations, and also violates interstate money laundering and tobacco and firearms statutes."

"The Kana-what?" Judge Danforth had no idea what Osorio was talking about.

"Ka—na—wa—gay." Osorio spelled it out for him. "It's a Mohawk reservation in Canada."

Judge Danforth let go of the files. "Canada's a little outside of my jurisdiction."

Osorio waggled the file folders, encouraging Judge Danforth to take them again. "It comes under the Indian Act, which treats Native Americans as North American citizens in cooperation with Canada. It's Federal in jurisdiction, and add to that firearms smuggling, this will come under anti-terrorism regulations of the DHS. We believe they're harboring Mr. O'Connell."

Judge Danforth leaned forward and took the file folders. "I'll see what I can do."

Osorio gave a fawning nod. "Good. Sign the Federal warrant for O'Connell right now, it's all prepared in the top file. With that, we'll coordinate with Canadian authorities, with the FBI and CIA, and set an international warrant through Interpol. He won't slip through, Judge. This time tomorrow, Mr. Jake O'Connell will be public enemy number one."

23

Somewhere over
Northern Quebec

Where was he? Jake checked the altimeter.

Four thousand four hundred feet.

So he had some height to play with. He needed to find water. Fast.

Three million lakes in Canada, but out the window of the Super Cub, only endless greenery undulated in waves to the horizon.

Three million lakes.

All Jake needed was one.

He punched buttons on the GPS, hoping it would indicate water features. But it was old school. As ancient as the plane. Its black and white screen only displayed longitude and latitude along with some squiggles that he figured were roads.

Airspeed sixty-eight knots.

A gust of wind rocked the plane, and Jake fought to keep it level. He tried to remember what the stall speed of a Cessna was.

Fifty knots?

No idea what it might be for this bag of bolts.

Better keep the nose down, the airspeed up. He had no idea how the pontoon floats might be affecting the trim, the stall speed. The flight stick between his legs felt like it was stuck in molasses, and he heaved it back and forth as gusts tried to push the plane over.

Three thousand two hundred feet.

The carpet of rolling green gained some definition. Treetops, boulders—he dropped like a stone. Below him a huge basin, ringed by rolling mountaintops. He sailed straight at the top of the closest peak.

Jake gritted his teeth. "Oh boy."

This was going to be close. Reflexively, Jake pulled back on the stick, raising the nose of the plane, but he quickly corrected.

Eased the nose down. The trees on the peak ahead of him grew in size. He saw branches. Leaves. A gust rattled the plane.

"Goddamn it!"

At the last second he pulled back, bobbing the Super Cub up a few feet, the pontoons scraping through the topmost branches into the clear space beyond. A few thousand feet of open air greeted Jake on the other side, the forest retreating below him as he cleared the peak. And there, a twinkling blue at the base of the mountain.

A lake.

His lake.

"Thank you God," Jake gasped. "I can make that."

He had to skim down the face of this hill to gain enough speed to spot the landing. Then circle around once, bleed off the speed, and set it down.

Easy.

He brought up one hand to drag through his hair. Shaking. He put the hand back onto the flight stick, his knuckles blanched white.

A thousand nine hundred feet.

You can't die here. Die here and they'll never find you. Elle will think you ran away, abandoned your family. And Anna...

His little girl.

Focus.

The shimmering lake grew in size. He pushed the nose down further, the only sound rushing wind rattling the passenger door. Getting louder. Gaining speed.

Under a thousand feet.

The treetops swayed, individual leaves fluttering, the wind blowing tiny ripples across the lake. He headed with the wind. If he could swing around the other side, he could land against the wind. Holding his breath, Jake pulled back on the stick, using the speed he gained on the slide down the side of the mountain to level off.

Silently, the Super Cub rocketed across the edge of the lake, the surface like a mirror.

Jake turned the stick, pushing the plane into a banked turn. Slowed from seventy to sixty knots. "Come on, come on," he urged between gritted teeth.

The plane lost more speed than Jake had anticipated. There

wasn't enough height to circle around. What next?

Flaps.

He brought one shaking hand up to the dashboard. There it was. The Johnson bar that controlled the flaps. How much? Ten degrees? Twenty? He grabbed it, pulled it out, and then forced it all the way down. Thirty degrees. He wanted to bring off as much speed as possible before he hit the water.

High in his banking turn, he stared out his side window at the edge of the lake—weeds and fallen trees, lily pads. The plane slid sideways, and he pulled back and right on the flight stick. No time to spot the landing. This was it.

He knew he had to get the nose down again, then swoop toward the surface and pull back, skim the top of the water and feather the backs of the pontoons onto it. That was the theory.

The plane dipped under the tops of the trees. Less than a hundred feet up now.

"Come on, baby."

Jake pulled back on the stick, but not too much. He didn't want to stall fifty feet in the air.

But he miscalculated.

In the last instant, the shimmering top of the water rushed at him. The still lake water was transparent—he'd been looking through it, at the bottom of the lake. Realizing his mistake, Jake hauled the stick back, pulling the nose up enough to avert the disaster of crashing headlong into the water.

The front left pontoon hit the water first, the impact bouncing the left side up. Jake's face slammed into the dashboard. For a moment he thought he'd get another chance at landing, but the plane slipped sideways, bobbing up in the air. He pulled the stick right, but it didn't respond. Not aerodynamic anymore. Now he was joyriding in a metal can.

The Super Cub tipped sickeningly. The next impact wasn't as forgiving as the first.

A screeching roar erupted as the Super Cub slammed into the still water, tearing the metal airframe apart. Jake flipped over, his knees slamming into the side of the compartment. Another terrific crash, and his head slammed into the side window, cracking the glass.

Then silence and cold.

Jake coughed.

Water rushed into the passenger compartment.

He was upside down.

And sinking.

Shoving his hands above his head, he strained in his seat and took a deep breath, pushing his head above the cold water as he submerged. Junk from the cockpit rushed in brownish water around him. Jake fumbled with the seatbelt, felt his fingers against the clasp.

Water gushed up his nose and he gagged, letting out a mouthful of precious air. The plane, inverted, sank into the depths of the lake. Pressure needled his eardrums.

The seatbelt clasp opened.

Jake pirouetted in the tiny compartment. Grabbed the door release handle. Pushed it open and swam outward, then upward.

Sunlight streamed down through the water.

In three strokes Jake broke the surface, gasping for air with burning lungs. Pain sliced through his chest. Pulling his fleece top off, he swam for the shore. It wasn't far, two hundred feet, but it felt like a mile. Jake pulled himself through the lily pads and collapsed into the weeds on the shore.

AUGUST 21st

Sunday

24

Lockhart Street
Hong Kong

Almost two days stuck in this apartment. Jin needed out.

The noise in the streets outside was working its way into a frenzy again. The now-familiar thumping bass came up through the apartment's floor, through Jin's feet and into her bones, shaking her brain. The walls felt like they were closing in, the air being sucked from her lungs. She looked out the window at the crowds of people weaving in the streets. How much she'd give to be one of them—careless, unaware.

She gritted her teeth and returned her attention to her laptop screen.

"Where's Wutang?" Chen asked from his workstation, leaning back in his chair with an unlit cigarette dangling from his mouth.

Wutang went out to get dinner for them over an hour ago. Chen had given up on data diving and wanted to get out of the apartment to stretch his legs.

Jin couldn't blame him. "I have no idea."

They had a rule: at least two people in the apartment at all times, which in effect meant at least one of the guys was with Jin. There was no way she was going to expose herself out there. "You can go out if you want," she added.

"I'll wait a bit more." Chen opened his laptop. "So you really think Bluebridge is behind this?"

"I don't know." It was still a guess.

She'd been trying to unravel Bluebridge's tentacles. Not easy. While it was the largest hedge fund in the world, Bluebridge was still a private corporation. It didn't divulge much and remained as opaque as possible. The world was a big place, though, and there were a lot of connection points if you burrowed deep enough.

"The partners of Bluebridge have senior board positions at hundreds of major corporations around the world," Jin said after a minute of silence. "That makes Bluebridge connected into every financial and government system on the planet."

She was mining the reporting structures of stock markets, drilling into their shareholding and reporting disclosures. Bluebridge controlled hundreds of shells, which in turn invested in thousands of other companies, all focused on defense and military. She'd watched Vidal Viegas in webcasts, talking this up as the next big growth industry after a recent slump.

"Somehow," Jin continued, "Viegas and Montrose are appearing at multiple, simultaneous meetings—and never ceding voting control to a proxy." She brought up a graphic illustrating the timing of shareholder and board meetings.

It seemed beyond possible that a blue chip firm like Bluebridge was caught up in a hacking and identity theft ring, but Jin couldn't be the only one to notice that Bluebridge executives attended meetings at the same time in different places.

"One thing's for sure," Jin added. "The partners of Bluebridge are buying their way into a political party." She brought up an image of Vidal Viegas with Senator Russ on stage at a fundraising event.

Chen was nonplussed. "So what? People are buying elections everywhere."

Everywhere.

The word stuck in Jin's mind. People left data trails behind them like vapor trails behind jets, a cloud of bits and bytes that followed them everywhere—cell phone location records, credit card purchases, social media postings, web browsing history—pull enough of it together, and you could almost read someone's mind.

You could almost become them.

What were these partners at Bluebridge up to? Were they buying political influence on both sides of the fence, even masquerading as dead Chinese nationals? If so, this went beyond simple corporate espionage. This was political espionage.

Why would they risk it?

Then another thought.

Why stop there? Why stop at China and America? Bluebridge had holdings all around the world. She glanced at her monitor again, at the image of Vidal Viegas standing next to Senator Russ. With American elections less than two months away, Senator Russ was the landslide favorite. Bluebridge was about to gain access to the most powerful economic and political platform in the world. She stared at the image of Viegas on the screen. Was it the face of a megalomaniac?

"Your friend, Jake," Chen said, interrupting Jin's daydreaming.

"What about him?" She turned around. No sign of Jake yet. Nothing new in the news or social media. Jin feared the worst.

The light from Chen's laptop screen illuminated his face in a ghostly glow. It was getting dark out. "He's been indicted on Federal US charges, for conspiracy to commit fraud, international money laundering. And Danny Donovan, the CEO of Atlas, was murdered yesterday. Looks like Jake skipped bail, he's on the run."

"How did you find out?"

"I have some friends in the NYPD. It just came up."

How did he have connections in the NYPD? He hadn't mentioned that before.

"Any hits on him yet?" Chen asked.

Jin glanced at her laptop screen. She set up her facial recognition system to scan social media and photo sharing websites to search for Jake O'Connell, programmed it to center on people in New York and fan outward from there. There were no alerts. "Nothing yet."

If he was still alive, there was a good chance that they'd find Jake before any authorities did. Live data mining on the open web wasn't something the police were good at yet.

An alert sounded on Jin's laptop, and she flinched. An urgent incoming message from Sheldon. Clicking the link, his face popped up on the large wall monitor beside Chen.

"You guys need to get out of there." Sheldon said immediately, his eyes wide.

"What's wrong?" Jin tensed, her faced flushing.

"I got access to the Assassin Market again." Sheldon looked at Jin. "The pool on you just doubled. Someone added another $100,000 bet. For 6 a.m. tomorrow morning."

Jin shot to her feet. "What?" Now there was a time? Less than twelve hours away? "Are you sure?"

Sheldon clenched his jaw. "The dead pool bet doubles if you die at exactly six."

Jin began shaking. "Can you...can you get in, change it?"

"I can't do anything. I just have access." Sheldon looked at Chen. "And *you're* on there now, too."

169

The cigarette fell of out Chen's mouth. "That's not possible."

Sheldon brought up an image of the Assassin Market darknet page. Chen and Jin's names were at the top of the list. "Somebody just placed huge bets minutes ago. They must know where you are."

"That's not possible," Chen mumbled again. "That can't be possible."

"What do we do?" Jin asked Sheldon. "Is Wutang on the list?"

Sheldon shook his head. "Just you two. Half a million dollars together."

"I need to leave." Chen was already at the entrance to the apartment.

"No!" Jin jumped toward him. "Don't leave me here alone."

But he opened the door and jumped out. Jin ran to the door in time to see him disappearing down the staircase. She thought of chasing him, but closed the door instead. She needed to think.

Another ping. She looked at the couch. It was her laptop.

Breathing heavy, her head spun. Her skin crawled. Less than twelve hours to live. Somebody had to know they were here. Should she run? But how? And where to? And where was Wutang?

Her computer pinged again. Shaking, she walked over and opened it. A message popped up. The social media monitoring tool had a hit on Jake O'Connell. So he was alive. What was he doing? She stared at the image, a photograph of him in boxer shorts and ragged fleece top holding a rifle, surrounded by trees. The social media post it came from was tagged in Canada.

The door opened.

"Chen, don't run out like that," Jin said, turning. But it was Wutang. "Where have you been?" she almost yelled at him.

"What's wrong?" Wutang asked, frowning. "What happened?" He dropped a box of noodles and set of chopsticks in front of her.

"The Assassin Market, they know where we are. Chen's been added to the hit list," Jin said breathlessly. "We need to leave. Chen just ran out. Did you see him?"

"No." Wutang shook his head. The news didn't seem to surprise him. "Are you okay? Keep calm, sit down. Eat something, we'll figure this out."

How could he be so calm? "And we just got a hit on Jake

O'Connell in Canada." Not knowing what else to do, she sat down and opened the noodle container. With shaking hands she unwrapped the chopsticks and stuffed in a mouthful of noddles and chewed.

Wutang stood and watched her eat. "Why are you standing like that?" she asked.

"I'm sorry."

"Sorry for what?"

Wutang leaned down and took the noodle container away from her. Behind him, the door swung open and two other men entered the room. Men who were much larger than Wutang.

Jin's heart hammered in her chest. "What have you done?"

25

Kahnawake Indian Reserve
Quebec

Drums echoed over the waters.

Not so long ago, the sound of the drums struck fear into the hearts of the people on the other side of the river, a signal that the war canoes were coming. Now the sound was mournful, echoes of a great nation corralled into reservations.

But still proud.

Echoes of a Proud Nation, proclaimed signs spray-painted onto concrete bridge pylons on the route leading into the reservation.

It was the end-of-summer powwow in Kahnawake.

Dancers in Mohawk ceremonial clothing circled a central grassy area, their bright fabrics adorned with beads and bones and tiny bells that jangled in rhythm with the drums. Many wore the hair roach, the crow-belt with the eagle-bone whistle. Thick hanks of long, colorful fringes swayed gracefully with the movements of the dancers' bodies, like blowing grass on the prairie.

The dancers were surrounded by rows of grandstand seating amid a haphazard sea of vending tents selling arts and crafts, everything from carved whale bone to dream catchers. The Mohawk powwow was open to the public. It was as much a celebration for the Mohawk nation as it was a spectacle for visitors, and the Mohawks were happy to oblige them.

Jake hung back at the edges.

He'd walked in on foot, passed the yellow barricades, paid his $7 entrance fee to a woman wearing a "Mohawk Mom" T-shirt, then walked over the bridge onto the small island that split the swift currents of the St. Lawrence River.

It was the same bridge where he and Sean had rescued those kids all those years ago. Jake stopped at the embankment on the other side and sat for a while under the bridge, remembering his friend, before continuing. He did a sweep of the powwow, starting at the food stands—walleye nuggets, moose dogs, sturgeon subs—then circled the vending tents and made his way toward the edge of the water.

At the edges of the powwow were campers and RVs, many with campfires burning, their flames reaching up into the night sky. Jake noticed some of the cars and campers were decorated with "Retired US Army" bumper stickers, and amid the traditional Mohawk dress, there were men standing around in active-duty combat fatigues.

Jake watched the dancers move slowly to the beat of the drums, stepping forward with the ball of one foot on one beat, then flattening that foot and shifting weight onto it on the next beat, their heads bobbing up and down. The sign of a good dancer was the ability to keep the feathers moving constantly, Jake remembered, to keep swaying up and down and around and around.

He hung back from the crowd, in the azalea bushes. In front of the line of vending tables, children squealed and ran between the legs of their parents.

After two hours, he finally tracked down Dean. Found him chatting with a group of people. He recognized one of them. Peace Keeper Daniels, one of the Mohawk police officers Jake had met with Dean in the Kicking Horse. He didn't recognize anyone else. Jake shadowed Dean for an hour.

It took Jake a day to get back to Montreal. After crash landing the floatplane, he bushwhacked his way to the highway and hitched a ride to the hospital, telling the driver he'd been in an accident. But he slipped around the back of the hospital instead of going in, using his cash to stay in a motel to recuperate.

He couldn't escape the truth of the matter. The only person who'd known he was up on Bear Mountain was Dean.

Jake watched from the shadows.

Dean laughed, shook someone's hand, then peeled off and made toward the bushes where Jake hid. Darting out, Jake pulled his friend into the bushes and dragged him down.

Dean lashed out, striking Jake in the chin with an elbow. "What the—"

"Shut up!" Jake grunted, grappling with him, wrapping an arm around his neck. "Be quiet."

Dean went limp. "Jake?"

"How did they know?" Jake demanded. "Who did you tell?"

173

"What are you talking about?"

"When I called you for help. Who else did you tell?"

"Nobody." Dean twisted, but couldn't get loose.

"Somebody tried to kill me on Bear Mountain." Jake squeezed his arm around Dean's neck. "Jean disappeared. Who was he?"

"Just some drunk bush pilot who owed me a favor." Dean coughed.

This felt ridiculous. Down in the dirt under the bushes, Jake had a flashback to their teenage years, wrestling with Dean after sneaking alcohol into the powwow. He couldn't believe Dean had intentionally played a part in the disaster at Bear Mountain. Despite his frustration, he let go.

Dean brushed dirt off his arms. "What the hell happened up there?"

"I blew up a building and then crashed a plane after someone tried to kill me."

"You serious?"

"Do I look like I'm joking? So you didn't hear from Jean?"

"I tried calling him a dozen times on his sat phone," Dean explained, "but no answer. That's one thing he always kept with him, no matter how drunk he got."

Jake exhaled. "He wasn't at the lodge when I came down, so I stole his plane. I had to crash-land it. Hitchhiked out."

"Jesus. Are you okay?"

Jake nodded and pulled his Silver Eagle dollar coin out of his pocket. "The only reason I'm alive is this. I had it in my breast pocket, and the bullet bounced off it."

Taking the coin, Dean whistled and inspected the dent in it.

"And I think I figured out the encryption key," Jake added. "That 1957 Silver Eagle, when Sean gave it to me he used the expression 'money in your pocket.'"

Dean's eyes lit up. "Incredible. That has to be it." He handed it back. "So what did you find up there?"

"I met Max Lefevre, he worked with Sean."

"Did he come back with you?"

Jake closed his eyes. "No, now he's got a bullet in his head."

Dean hesitated. "Did you...?"

"No, not me, someone tried to kill both of us. I escaped."

Dean stared at Jake for a moment. "Come on, let's get somewhere more quiet." He stood and offered a hand to Jake.

"They're looking for you."

Jake took Dean's hand and stood. "Who?" They walked away from the fires and crowds, to the opposite end of the island. It was dark, but still twilight.

"The RCMP showed up this afternoon with US Federal Marshals, started stopping people on the streets, showing them your picture. The Mohawk Peacekeepers got them to leave, but only when they promised to arrest you. Donovan was murdered yesterday, seems they're pinning it on you."

"Donovan's dead?" Jake gripped the Silver Eagle coin in his pocket. People were dropping like flies around him.

"Don't worry, nobody's going to arrest you here," Dean added. "The Longhouse Elders have approved me to help you, but you gotta keep low."

That was a relief. The Mohawks operated two systems of governance: an official elected one, and an unofficial but more powerful one through the Longhouse Elders. "Did you take another crack at the memory keys?" Jake asked, taking a deep breath.

"The Donovan one seems to be automated agent trading algorithms."

Jake nodded. "Seems like something the geeks downstairs at Atlas would work on, but why would Donovan try to hide it?"

"These look like they were used at JP Morgan and some other automated trading desks. Donovan must have been using them to gain an advantage."

Made sense. So that's how Donovan was making so much money.

"Did you manage to talk to Max?" Dean asked.

"Max said Sean was killed for some kind of automated agent software that runs Bluebridge." He cocked his head to one side. "Or more accurately, he was killed *by* it."

Dean sat on a fallen tree near the side of the water. Moonlight glittered across the St. Lawrence River. "He was killed by software?"

Jake shook his head. "Someone contracted by it. The system can masquerade as people on the phone. I doubt they—whoever *they* are—know they're working for a machine. Max said they designed the program to look for and eliminate the root causes of glitches, destroy bits of code that are problematic. They built a bridge between the digital and real worlds, and it seems it got off the reservation."

Jake laughed bitterly at his own joke. "Now the bits of code it's destroying are people in the real world. This thing has dug itself in like a tick, tapping into telephone systems, the Internet, everything with a digital connection. Bluebridge has hundreds of directorships at major corporations and politicians on its payroll."

"Phone systems?" Dean said. "Maybe that's how it found out. Maybe it was tapping my phone calls." He considered that for a moment. "Means it can listen in on anything. We're going to need to start encrypting our phone conversations, too…" He swore under his breath. "And politicians. Now it makes sense."

"What?"

"There was a ruling from a 2nd Circuit Court judge in New York that the Kahnawake gaming operations violate US Federal gaming restrictions. A bunch of calls from US Congressmen to Quebec politicians today, threatening trade sanctions if we're not shut down."

"So Bluebridge knows I'm here?"

"Who did you tell?"

"Nobody." Jake closed his eyes. Had he told his brother, Eamon? No. But he knew Jake was coming into Canada, so it wasn't a stretch to think Eamon might realize he was coming to see Dean. "I told Eamon I was coming to Canada, and I did tell my wife, Elle, that I was going to see a friend. But she had no way of knowing you were up here in Canada. And I told her not to tell anyone."

Dean grimaced. "One more thing."

"What?"

"There's an arrest warrant out for Elle as well. They're asking about her, too."

Jake tensed up. "Why?" His stomach churned. "Why would they do that?"

"Just trying to get to you, that's why." Dean scratched his head. "Don't worry, I sent word to Eamon. We'll keep her safe. What else did Max say? Anything about Vidal Viegas's death certificate?"

"Max said Vidal died over a year ago. They were using the system to impersonate him, make it seem like he was still alive. Bluebridge has been using body doubles. Nobody even knows he's dead."

Dean whistled. "So tens of billions of dollars at stake, massive systematic fraud."

"And Max thinks the other founder—Henry Montrose—is gone too, that Bluebridge is running on autopilot. Like an airliner that flies by itself after the pilots and all the passengers die. Only when this thing crashes, it's going to take more than a few hundred people with it."

Dean digested that in silence for a good ten seconds. "Wow. Should we blow the lid off? Go public with everything?"

"That's what Sean tried to do, but he was killed before he could. Max said this thing is good at covering its tracks, hiding everything under an avalanche of misinformation." Jake sighed. "Sorry I dragged you into this. So they're trying to jam you up?"

Dean nodded. "They want to shut us down. Now we know why. We're in Bluebridge's crosshairs, too. So this thing is trying to take over?"

Jake shook his head. "From what Max said, it just wants to make money for its shareholders. Like a computerized psychopath." He rubbed his eyes. "I need to get back into New York, I need to protect Elle and Anna."

"We'll get you back over the border, my friend." He smiled and slapped Jake's knee. "Don't worry, I still have some connections in the smuggling business."

"Good." Jake stood and started pacing in the sand beside the water.

"And that's some heavy code on the Donovan memory key, my friend. Copies of the agent systems for a dozen big banks." Dean stood and put an arm on Jake's shoulder, stopping him from pacing. "You know, we could hack that into a few networks, steal a few hundred million, disappear into the sunset."

A few hundred million could go a long way. "Let's head back to your office to see if we're right about the encryption key."

Dean nodded, picked up a rock and tossed it into the water, low and hard. "So this thing can impersonate anyone?"

Jake nodded. "That's what Max said."

"And you're sure that was Max?"

"I think so." He turned to Dean. "If it wasn't Max, then why go to the trouble of killing him?"

177

AUGUST 22nd

Monday

26

Lake Champlain
Quebec

Smiling white teeth appeared, floating disconnected in the darkness, glowing under the dim light of a crescent moon. "Stay quiet, *Rahsatsteh*."

Jake didn't need to be told.

Dean's brother, Chuck, was using Jake's Mohawk name, Rahsatsteh—he pronounced it *raw-stuts-dey*. It meant "strong like an oak." Jake hadn't heard it in a long time. "How long until we get to the other side?" he whispered.

"With this engine, about an hour and a half," Chuck whispered back.

A tiny electric motor whirred behind Chuck, pushing the open aluminum boat across the inky waters of Missisquoi Bay at the north end of Lake Champlain. The lake was nearly a hundred and fifty miles long, almost big enough to qualify as a sixth Great Lake. It started in Canada and stretched south into upstate New York and Vermont.

A favorite smuggling route of the Mohawks.

Another Mohawk sat in the front of the boat, his eyes fixed ahead, staring into the darkness. Jake had no idea how he could see anything.

They were heading for the Missisquoi River delta, on the other side of the border, sneaking Jake back into the States under the cover of night. Lucky for him, this border was nothing like the one the US shared with Mexico to the south. The DHS maintained border security, but drones didn't patrol it. Mohawks were both American and Canadian citizens, with free movement guaranteed between both countries. Their smuggling was something of a gray zone in legal terms, so the border patrol mostly left them to it—and anyway, they usually smuggled American tobacco into Canada, not the other way around.

Dean and Jake had managed to crack the encryption on Sean's

memory key. Dean tried a few combinations, and, like magic, '1957SilverEagle' worked. The data on the memory key opened up, like that. A hundred gigabytes of data, thousands of directories containing what looked like the systems comprising Bluebridge.

The Bluebridge core.

Max would have known what to do with it, but Max was gone, and Dean could only guess what it was that they had in their hands. They had no idea what to do with it. Not yet.

"Sit back and relax, Rahsatsteh, enjoy the ride," Chuck laughed, putting an arm on Jake's shoulder. "Look up at the stars. Play with your new toys."

Jake nodded and settled into his seat. Chuck was referring to the VOIP phones Dean had given Jake, phones with end-to-end encryption that didn't send voice data over the regular networks.

If someone were listening in over regular landline and cellular carriers, this would solve that problem. At least, Dean had assured him it would. Dean also gave Jake a voice scrambler that he could use if he needed to communicate over landlines or from a payphone.

Dean sent someone ahead to find Jake's brother in Albany. Jake still wasn't sure where exactly they were going, but he had to put his faith in someone.

Two phones sat in Jake's lap—one for himself, one for his brother—along with the secure phone numbers for Dean and Chuck. Dean also created a set of 'one-time' pads, a stack of sticky notes, each page with a single random number on it. He gave one to Jake and kept the matching one for himself. He said verifying the codes each time would be a good way of securing a connection.

As an added precaution, they decided to always enquire about personal details, things only they would know about each other, or things they'd discussed the last time they saw each other in person.

Anything suspicious would be a warning flag.

It was about one in the morning. Sleep came the instant Jake closed his eyes.

Someone tapped Jake on the shoulder. "Time to get up," said the voice. It was Chuck, his broad smile glowing again, but this time in the glare of headlights. The boat was run aground, and a pickup truck faced them, its engine running.

"We found your brother," Chuck said, helping to pull Jake up.

Jake clambered out of the boat and onto dry ground. "We passed the border?"

"Yes, sir." Chuck smiled. "You'll be going with Matt and Frank." He motioned to two men standing beside the pickup. "Mohawks, you can trust them."

Jake thanked Chuck and trudged to the truck, shaking hands with Matt and Frank. They offered him the backseat, which he gratefully accepted. Waving to Chuck, he sank into his seat, buckling himself in. By the time the truck turned and started crunching up the gravel road leading down to the water, Jake was asleep again.

▲▼▲

"Wake up, hey mister, wake up."

Jake opened his eyes.

It took him a few seconds to re-integrate his senses.

Where was he? The rumble of the road reminded him. His senses sharpened, adrenaline flooding his bloodstream. He jumped up. "Is everything okay?"

The man shaking him, leaning over the partition between the front and back seats, smiled. "Everything's fine. We're arriving." He turned back to the front.

Jake recognized him from the night before.

Matt.

And Frank was driving.

His own personal Mohawk underground railway.

Jake let out a long sigh. "Good."

The truck pulled into the parking lot of a run-down Super 8 Motel. The sun crept over the horizon. It had to be six in the morning, Jake figured. Three hours down the interstate, past Burlington, Vermont, and then crossing over into New York. He recognized this place. The outskirts of Schenectady.

Pulling around the back of the motel, they parked the truck by a rusted chain link fence separating the Motel 8 from the garage next door.

"Room 212," Matt said, turning to face Jake. He pointed to the second floor of the motel. "We'll wait here."

Jake took a moment to look around the parking lot.

A family was loading their minivan. Looked like they were on a road trip. So normal. Jake felt a pang of regret, of longing.

Matt watched Jake's eyes. "Don't worry, we checked the place out. They're harmless."

Jake nodded and opened his door. Stepped out. He smiled at the family as they grouped together for a picture, then crossed to the motel staircase and jogged up, then rapped on the door 212.

Noises inside.

Footsteps.

The door swung open, and his brother stood smiling in the awning. "Glad you're back, little brother," Eamon reached to hug him.

But someone else was waiting behind him.

Elle. His wife.

Beside her was Anna. "Daddy!" she cried out.

Stunned, Jake knelt and scooped his daughter into his arms. Tears streamed down his face, and he stood, holding his daughter in one arm while he wrapped the other around his wife.

▲▼▲

"Thanks for protecting Elle." Jake picked up his coffee and blew on it.

Jake was sitting in Eamon's room, beside Elle's. It was noon, and Elle was taking a nap with Anna. She hadn't slept in days either. The second Eamon found out there was an arrest warrant for Elle, he sent one of his guys to collect her from her sister's place in Hoboken.

A bottle of beer sat on a table between Jake and his brother. Eamon picked it up.

Eamon still had no idea what was really going on. Dean's guys had found him and told him Jake was coming back, but they'd said little more than that. Jake made a snap decision. He needed his brother's help. It was time to trust him. So he explained everything: the package from Sean, what Max had told him.

"So what did you tell Elle?" Eamon asked.

"I told her that Sean sent me information, that Bluebridge Corporation killed him for it and are framing me to keep me quiet. I showed her the Viegas death certificate." After he showed her that, her doubts had evaporated. Having her back on his side felt like a boulder was lifted off his chest.

Jake leaned his plastic chair back against the peeling wallpaper of the motel room. He tested his left ribcage. Each breath was painful work, his chest a swollen black mass. It wasn't his only injury—he'd suffered cuts and scrapes from jumping off the ATV, and his left knee was tender from crash landing the plane.

He was lucky to be alive.

More than lucky.

Eamon raised his eyebrows. "Did you tell her the part about it being a machine taking over?" He took a swig from his beer.

"Not yet." Jake looked out the window at a dumpster beneath them. The sun was high in the sky now, and the heat was coming, too. A wind sprang up, warning of rain from black clouds on the horizon. "I don't know. I wasn't expecting to see her."

"Sounds like you don't believe it yourself." Eamon took another swig of beer.

Jake rubbed the stubble on his face. "Maybe I don't." In the light of day, sitting in the outskirts of Schenectady—listening to the cicadas whine in the distance—it felt like a fairy tale. Right now he needed Elle to believe him.

"They've issued a Federal arrest warrant for you, for me, even for Elle. That 2nd Circuit Court judge has us in his sights, little brother." Eamon took another drink from his bottle.

"You think I don't know that?"

"So what's your plan? Are we going to blow the cover off?"

That had been Jake's plan. To get back in the country, show up for court, then email the *New York Times* with all the information he had. Something like that. He knew it wasn't a great plan, knew that Sean had failed at something similar, but he didn't have any other ideas.

Now, with the Federal arrest warrant and murder charge, cops might be as likely to shoot him as arrest him. Maybe that was the plan. Jake's access to the outside world was even more restricted. And if his enemy was trying to get him arrested, then they—or it—weren't afraid of him going public. What nasty surprises might be in store once he was behind bars? Jake sighed. "I don't know. I

185

need to think."

"Better think fast."

"Yeah." That was the truth. What was he going to do? He needed some sleep. Jake pointed at the VOIP phone Dean gave him to give to Eamon. "So you have my number?" Jake had to write his number down on a piece of paper. After spending most of the last decade in jail, his brother wasn't up to speed on the latest in cellphones.

His brother picked up the phone. "I got it."

"And you'll use that to call me?"

"I will." Eamon rolled his eyes in response to Jake's arched eyebrows. "I promise." He finished off his beer and dropped it on the table. "So you want a gun, huh?"

"I do." Jake wasn't a fan of them, but he needed to be able to defend himself. And his family. "What would you recommend?"

"A 12-gauge pump shotgun would be my first choice. Effective and reliable, and the odds of having to use it again after pumping it once are slim." Eamon smiled at his brother. "Lethal at close range, no aim needed."

"I can't carry around a shotgun. Something smaller."

"Ah." Eamon nodded. "In that case, there are two good alternatives, the first being a .45 1911. The design is a hundred years old, still popular because it works well."

Eamon might not know much about cellphones, but he was an expert in firearms.

"Can I hide it?" asked Jake.

Eamon wagged his head side to side. "In that case, I'd suggest one of the smaller polymer pistols, something like a Ruger LCP. It disappears in a pocket. Cheap, light and works great out of the box. Fires a less powerful round than the .45, but will kick much more due to the lack of mass. You can put a Band-Aid at the top of the grip, under the slide, to lessen the sting of firing it."

A car pulled up while Eamon was speaking.

"Who's that?" Jake asked, standing to walk forward and look over the railing.

Eamon didn't get up. "Just my guys. Something must be up."

Two men got out of the car and looked up at Eamon. He nodded. They started coming around the side and up the stairs.

Jake sat back down in his chair. "I thought we agreed we weren't going to tell anyone I'm here?"

186

Eamon shrugged. "Something must be up. Maybe the cops are on their way." He got to his feet. "Hey guys, what's up?" he called out. One of the guys was huge, his suit bursting from the muscles beneath it.

"Not much, Eamon," the lead one replied. "We need to talk to Jake for a second."

Eamon gave them room to pass. "No problem."

"What can I do for—"

The first one cocked his fist and punched Jake in the mouth. Jake was too surprised to react. "What the hell?" he managed to get out as he was pinned to the wall.

The big man behind the first one wrapped his arm around Jake. "Don't make a sound. We don't want to have to hurt your family."

"Sorry, Jake." Eamon shook his head slowly, following them as they walked down the stairs. "It's the only way, little brother."

27

Outskirts of Schenectady
New York

Garbage littered the second floor of the abandoned warehouse. Wind through the shattered windows blew stray bits of paper around Jake's feet. In one corner was a pile of rank blankets, the nest of some homeless person. Jake guessed whoever it was had been not-so-politely asked to leave by the three men in dark suits, their hair slicked back, who now glared at him.

They looked like gangsters.

The place stank of urine.

After what had to be a minute of standing and staring at each other, Jake finally asked, "Should I know you?"

He tested his lip. It was swollen, the metallic taste of blood still filled his mouth from being punched at the motel.

What was he doing here? He glanced at his brother, standing off to one side, but Eamon stared at the ground. When Eamon stared at the ground, it meant something bad.

The man in the middle snorted. Smaller than the other two, but obviously in charge. Enunciating each word slowly and carefully he said, "Should he know me?" He laughed. Shook his head and looked back and forth at the two gorillas flanking him.

Jake grimaced. "Did I say something funny?"

The small man smiled and looked at Jake. "Sort of." He nodded at the big guy on his right, who stepped forward and punched Jake hard in the gut.

Doubling over, Jake gasped, the wind knocked out of him. He almost threw up. Putting down one hand to steady himself, he gritted his teeth. "I don't know what you want," he wheezed. "Who are you?"

"He don't know what we want," the small man laughed, his voice rising as if he was amazed. "Who am I? This guy don't know anything. Let's see if we can remind him."

With his left arm, the large man who'd punched Jake grabbed

him by the collar of his shirt, lifted him off the ground, and in the same motion landed a crunching blow across his face with his right hand.

Jake crumpled onto the pee-stained floor.

"Hey!" Eamon yelled. "You said you weren't going to do anything to him."

"I'm not going to kill him. Not yet." The small man knelt to look Jake in the eye. "Tell me again you don't know who I am."

Jake tried to lift himself off the concrete but couldn't. He groaned and tried again, managed to get onto his knees. A food wrapper stuck to his face and he blew it off, bloody spittle coming out. Black spots danced before his eyes. He hadn't been hit like that in years.

"I'm Joey Barbara, you sack of shit," the small man continued. "But who I am isn't as important as why I am out here, in this shithole, like some errand boy. Tell me again you don't know who I am."

"Wait, wait." The name. Barbara. Jake held out one shaking hand as the big man advanced. "Joseph Barbara. Mr. Barbara. You left me messages, and I set up that meeting with you. Danny Donovan told me to cancel it."

"Ah," Joey Barbara looked skyward. "Now he remembers. And do you remember *why* I wanted to meet with you?"

"I don't know." Jake coughed, gasped, and got to his feet. The big man took a step toward him. Jake backed away. "Hold on, because he owes you money."

"Very good." Joey Barbara snorted. "And not just me. You and your buddy Donovan said it was a *no lose* deal. Your words."

What did he mean, *my words?* "Donovan was my boss, I just worked for him." But his confusion transformed into a cold jolt in his stomach, as he suddenly understood what was going on. "Whatever happened, I wasn't a part of it."

Joey shook his head. "Hit him again."

The big man nodded and raised a fist.

This time Jake knew it was coming. He shifted his weight onto the balls of his feet, and ducked underneath the blow. Bending his knees, he exploded upward with an upper cut that caught the big man square on the chin. The big man staggered back, shocked, and reached under his jacket. Jake glimpsed an oversized handgun under the suit, but Joey Barbara held out a hand, stopping the big

189

man from pulling out his weapon.

"I told you, we haven't spoken before," Jake insisted.

"This guy, I can't believe this guy." Joey Barbara stared at Jake. "Is there something wrong in your head? We've spoken on the phone at least a dozen times. We even did one of those frickin' video chats that you Wall Street guys love."

Jake shifted his stance, one foot forward and one back, centering his weight. Fighting was like riding a bike for Jake. Maybe he hadn't done it in years, but it came back fast. "Mr. Barbara, you've been taken in by a scam, the same people who are framing me—"

"Framing you? You're some angel, huh? Sticking it to your office girls, and I seen the fraud indictments. You're a slime ball." Joey Barbara shook his head in disgust. "And they call *us* organized crime. The real organized crime happens on Wall Street. Stealing from pensioners, stealing my *hard-earned* money." He straightened his tie. "Anyway, I don't give a shit about that. What I want, what I need, is my money back."

It was futile to try to deny anything. Jake needed information. "How much?"

"Fifty million. Maybe that's chickenfeed to you, but I'll tell you who doesn't think so. It was all I could do to keep the Rizuttos from whacking you up in Montreal. I know you went up there." He nodded at Eamon. "The Five Families, my friend, the Chicago outfit, the A-team, they're all breathing down my friggin' neck."

"The A-team?" Was this some twisted joke?

"The Clerkenwell crime syndicate out of London," Eamon whispered. "Tommy and Eamon Adams, the Adams family, the A-team."

"Shut up," Joey Barbara spat at Eamon. "Me and your brother are talking." He paused to smooth down the lapels of his suit. "I told you, we don't lose money. So I don't care how you do it, but you get that money out of Atlas Capital and back into my hands."

Jake wasn't going to repeat that he'd never spoken to him before, so he tried another tack. "If you hadn't noticed, I have a Federal warrant out for my arrest. It's a bit difficult for me to operate right now."

"Do I look like I care?" Joey Barbara held open the palms of his hands to Jake. "I wouldn't normally do this, but that nice family of yours, you want it to remain a nice family, right?" It was rhetorical. "Me? Maybe I'd just kill you, but these people I work with... Well, we don't want to go there, Jake. Get our money. And you better not get arrested before you do."

With a flick of his chin, Joey Barbara indicated that it was time to leave. The two bodyguards retreated to wing their boss. They walked to the stairwell in formation. Joey paused before the open doorway, then turned to look at Jake. "That Federal arrest warrant, that's the least of your problems, my friend."

Jake slumped against the wall. "Tell me something I don't know."

28

Central Pier Complex
Hong Kong

"Where are we going?" Jin gasped. It had to be well past five in the morning, the assassin bet was in less than an hour.

A large man had just dragged her out of the car she'd been stuck in for the night, hauled her across the pavement and onto a large wooden boat. They were in the Central Piers, and judging from the smell, it was a fishing boat. Red and white netting covered the floor, dotted with bright orange floats. Above her, in the pre-dawn twilight, she recognized the glass-and-metal tower of the Financial Center.

Wutang sat in front of her, silent, a grim look on his face.

The race across Hong Kong seemed like a frenzied dream now.

Wutang had literally dragged Jin out of the apartment, then pushed her into the back of a waiting limo that squealed away seconds after she got into it, gunfire erupting amid screams in the street. Wutang rode in the front, leaving her alone with the two thick and thuggish men in the back who pulled a black hood over her head.

They'd locked her in the car, left her there for hours. When they finally returned and took off the hood, she refused to get out until she was given an explanation, at which point one of the men had grabbed her, picked her up kicking and screaming, and deposited her in the boat.

The man who carried her down the docks reappeared from the main cabin. He glanced up at the buildings lining the piers, squinting, then nodded at Wutang and disappeared. The engines of the boat fired up, and Jin felt the vibrations rising up through the floor and bench, moving into her body.

The look in Wutang's eyes. Something was wrong. Had he been forced into this? She grabbed his hand. "Who are these men?"

Wutang shook his head. "I'm sorry," he repeated.

It was all he'd said to her, over and over, all night. "Wutang, you can't do this." Panic flooded Jin's veins. She'd trusted Wutang, but perhaps she made a fatal mistake.

The engines gunned and the big guy threw the bowlines. Jin glanced at the back of the boat. The gunnels were low. One or two quick steps and she could jump onto the dock. With a belch of blue fumes, the engines roared and she felt the boat begin to move. She slid sideways and tried to jump up, but Wutang grabbed her. He clenched his jaw, his fingers digging into her arm.

"Stop," Jin cried. "You're hurting me." She tried to pull away. "Whatever you're doing, you have to stop."

"Be quiet." Wutang pushed her back, knocking her onto the bench. The boat pulled away from the dock. She tried to get up again, but Wutang blocked her.

"They killed Shen Shi!" Jin yelled. The engine roared, fumes poured into the air as the boat accelerated. "Wutang, you can't do this, you need to—"

Wutang slapped her across the face. "Shut up!"

▲▼▲

From the docks, hidden, Chen watched the boat pull away. He watched in amazement as Wutang slapped Jin across the face. Who was this person? He'd known Wutang for years, ever since they were kids growing up in Shenzhen, but this seemed like a completely different man.

The fishing boat pulled away from the dock, and he watched Jin and Wutang in the back. There wasn't much he could do. After he ran out of the apartment to call his friends, he saw Jin dragged into a limousine by Wutang and two large tattooed men. Not Chinese. Japanese. The moment the limo door closed, gunfire erupted from a nearby black Escalade. Four men jumped out, automatic weapons blazing.

Chen called his friends right away, flagged down a taxi to follow the limousine. He watched from the roof of Central Ferry Building Number 6, observing from a distance as he waited for his friends to arrive.

They'd be able to help.

They could track the boat.

It was still dark—sunrise was in half an hour—but the area around the harbor was lit by the pier lights. Chen watched the fishing boat pull farther into the harbor, into the busy traffic of the ferry lanes, when a flash caught his attention from the corner of his eye. Glancing to his left, he watched a trail of smoke shoot out of the third floor of the Central Ferry Building Number 5. Sweeping right, his eyes followed it as it ran a course straight into the fishing boat. The boat erupted in a massive ball of orange flame, and a half second later the shock wave and concussion of the explosion thudded into Chen.

A roiling black cloud rose into the sky above the flaming boat as it tipped sideways, its engines still churning, turning it in a tight circle. Then another explosion rocked the boat and it tipped all the way over. In a matter of seconds, it tilted up like a cork, its stern high over the water, and then disappeared under the waves.

Chen looked at the time on his watch. Exactly six a.m.

29

Super 8 Motel
Schenectady

Jake clicked the bathroom's light on, and in three buzzing pops the bare fluorescent tube in the ceiling hummed to life.

The left side of his face was swollen and red, with purple bruises underlining both eyes. He leaned in closer. His left eye had hemorrhaged, leaving a bright red corona around his china-blue iris. He sighed.

How had he ended up here?

How had it come to this?

And, what, exactly, *was* this?

"Are you going to tell me what's going on?" Elle asked.

She sat at the small table in front of the air conditioning unit at the front of the motel room, playing solitaire. The curtains were pulled closed. They had two connecting rooms, one for sleeping and one they used for meeting. Anna was asleep in the other room. "Did Eamon do that to you?"

She'd roused from her nap only to discover Jake was gone again.

Eamon's guys had assured her everything was okay, but then Jake returned with fresh bruises and cuts. Elle freaked out, but she gave him some space when he said he didn't want to talk about it. Let him sleep for a few hours. Now she needed answers.

"No, Eamon didn't do this," Jake replied half-truthfully. Out of the corner of his eye, he saw her put her cards down.

"Jake, I know you O'Connell men love the tough guy routine, but please."

Jake turned on the hot and cold faucets together. Water bubbled into the sink, and he pushed the cracked rubber stopper into the drain. He needed a shave. "It wasn't his fault."

Eamon had apologized profusely. Barbara had insisted that he and Jake already had a deal going, that he and his guys just wanted to talk. And who was Eamon to refuse someone like Barbara?

Jake wasn't mad at him, not anymore. After all, he'd dragged his brother into this situation.

Eamon still only half-believed Jake's explanation that some machine was behind it. Jake had spent the afternoon going over it with him, explaining the memory key from Donovan with the banking algorithms, the copy of the Bluebridge core Sean gave him.

Eamon was most interested in the banking algorithms, especially when Jake mentioned they might be able to use them to steal millions. He suggested it could be a way to pay back Barbara. It wasn't a bad idea, but it wasn't quite so simple. They'd need to hack into the trading offices of some of the world's largest banks. It wasn't something Jake or Dean had any idea how to do.

Still, it had felt good to fight back. At least Jake had been able to channel some rage into hitting that mafia goon.

"So whose fault was it?" Elle asked. "Was it these Bluebridge guys who framed you?" She got up from the table and walked over to the bathroom.

At least Elle finally believed it was all a set-up. That was a huge relief.

Anna's tiny snores echoed in the next room, the adjoining door between the two rooms left ajar, the sound a balm to his soul.

Two weeks ago his life had revolved around some imaginary number, some amount of money he needed in the bank before he could change his career, his life. It had taken this craziness to make him realize how wrong he'd been, what was really important.

All Jake cared about was in this motel—his family, his wife and his baby girl. "We're going to get that place in Virginia, sweetheart, when this is all over, I swear."

"That doesn't matter now." Elle touched his arm, her fingers gentle. "Who hit you, baby? Tell me."

Splashing water onto his face, Jake leaned his elbows onto the sides of the sink and hung his head. "It's complicated." He felt like a rat at the bottom of a sinking ship. "It was some mafia guys. Danny Donovan was mixed up with them, they want me to get their money back."

"What does that have to do with you?"

"They think I'm the one who brokered their deal," Jake replied. "I told you, the guys at Bluebridge have technology that can impersonate people. They made these mafia guys think they were dealing with me." He still hadn't told Elle how powerful Bluebridge itself was…that they thought it was operating on its own.

"Isn't that fraud?" Elle frowned. "I mean, can't you explain it to them?"

"They weren't in much of an explaining mood yesterday, honey."

Elle put her arm around his shoulders and he turned his head to kiss her arm. They'd barely touched each other the past month.

"We're going to figure this out, Jake." Elle rubbed his neck. "Eamon really cares about you. He's sweet. He came with sandwiches for Anna and me."

"You be careful, you don't know him like I do." He might not blame his brother for the showdown yesterday, but that didn't mean he was feeling warm and fuzzy about him. He'd decided to trust Eamon, yes, but there were limitations. "He was here? When?"

"When you were sleeping. Said he wanted to apologize."

Something started ringing. Jake leaned out of the bathroom doorway. It was the encrypted VOIP phone Dean gave him. Only Dean and Eamon knew the number. He stepped into the room and looked at the number displayed. It was his brother. "Hello?"

"How you doing, Jake? Feeling any better?"

"Good." Jake hesitated. "What's up?"

"Can you come out?"

"What for?" Jake looked at Elle and mouthed, "Eamon." She nodded. "Elle said you came by."

"I wanted to apologize again. And I have something to show you, might be important."

"Can you tell me on the phone?"

"Don't trust these things. I need to show you. I'm three blocks down at my buddy's office. If I leave I won't be able to get back in. Seriously, I need to show you something."

It sounded like his brother, and Dean had said these phones were secure. Still, it was better to be cautious. "Want me to bring the leftovers from this morning?"

"Bagels and lox?" Pause. "Naw, not day-old salmon. Gross. Just come on over."

Jake glanced at the plastic boxes in the garbage. "Sure, where?"

197

It looked like some kind of lab. Refrigeration units lined one wall, while rack-mounted servers lined the other. In between was a row of wooden benches, and Eamon was sitting at the one in the center. Eamon waved and nodded, walking over to the door to buzz him in through the glass doors.

It was a Wednesday, but nobody else was there.

They were alone.

The door clicked shut behind Jake.

"So what's up that's so important?" Jake asked.

He'd seen this building a hundred times before as a kid—a squat red brick building with no exterior signage. Sean had told him it was a command center for nuclear submarines. If it had been true back then, it wasn't anymore. It looked like a research center. Eamon had texted him the external key codes to get into the building. Jake wondered what this place had to do with his brother.

"I'm really sorry about Joey Barbara," Eamon said straight away.

Jake hadn't ever heard his brother say he was sorry about anything before, but he must have apologized a dozen times already. It wasn't like it was the first time he'd been subjected to a beating because of his brother. "Don't worry about it."

"I don't think Tomasz's ever been hit by anybody," Eamon laughed. "At least, not anybody alive."

"Tomasz?"

"The big guy you punched. You still got balls, little brother." Eamon ruffled Jake's hair. "Tell me that didn't feel good."

"Okay, enough." Jake backed away. He wasn't in the mood for this. "So what did you want to tell me that was so important?"

Taking a deep breath, Eamon exhaled slowly, rubbing his eyes. He sat at one of the benches and leaned on the table. "I know how you see me. Trouble. You don't trust me—"

"You have to *earn* trust." Jake slumped onto the bench across from Eamon. "Stuff like today—"

"Doesn't help. I know. There was a lot of time to think on the inside. I'm trying to change, Jake, I just don't know how. Growing up, you had your Auntie Anna, your foster care worker. Sure, she tried to help me when she could, but it wasn't the same..."

Was there some angle to this? Jake shrugged. "You can't go blaming other people for the things you do. You have to take responsibility for your own actions."

"I am!" Eamon slammed the table. "I did. I just spent five years in jail. *Five years*. You don't think I paid for what I did? I paid my debt."

Jake held his hands up. "Okay, so you paid your debt."

"That five years you've been out here, having a family, a baby girl, a beautiful wife..." Eamon buried his head in his hands. "You know what I'd give to have your life? I have nobody. Nobody, Jake. What have I been doing with my life?"

Jake wanted to say they had each other, that family was still important to him, but he held back. "You made your choices," he said.

"I did, but I don't want that old life anymore." Tears glimmered in Eamon's eyes.

Jake had never seen his older brother cry. "You don't have to go back to it. You can change, Eamon."

"Oh yeah?" Eamon looked Jake in the eyes. "I get out, and wham, this Joseph Barbara guy is breathing down my neck. The head of the Genovese mafia family, threatening *my* family. Of course I stuck up for you, but they threatened my boys..."

"Your boys?"

"Mick and Fumbles, my guys, you know." Eamon wiped his eyes. "I wanted to get out, fly straight, but here I am stuck right back in it. Aiding and abetting a fugitive...that's what I'm doing by helping you. You know that, right? There's a warrant out for me now, too."

Jake leaned back and closed his eyes. He'd been so wrapped up in his own head, he hadn't spared a moment to think about his brother's situation. "You're right." He opened his eyes. Eamon was staring at him.

"You know how long I'll go to jail?" Eamon asked. "Third strike. They'll put me in a deep dark hole until I'm an old man. And that'll be my life."

For perhaps the first time, Jake saw pain in his brother's eyes. "You don't have to help me, Eamon. I appreciate it, but maybe it would be better—"

"No way." Eamon shook his head. "No way I'm giving up on

199

my little brother." He pointed his index finger at Jake. "I'm sorry for everything, but you're still my brother. And this time, I'm going to do right by you. We're going to fix this, Jake." He pointed his finger at the table. "But when we're done, I'm leaving all of this behind."

"Okay," Jake whispered. He wasn't used to having his brother stick up for him. It was a new feeling. He liked it. And Jake believed Eamon, believed the sincerity in his eyes. "Okay, thank you. Now"—he glanced around the office—"what is this place?"

"What's what place?"

Jake fished in his pocket for the VOIP cellphone to call Dean. "This place, why did you ask me to come here?"

"I didn't ask you to come here." Eamon frowned. "You asked me."

The hair pricked on Jake's arms. "No, you asked me." But even as he said it, he knew the truth.

It was the machine.

Bluebridge.

Why hadn't he asked more personal questions? Used the one-time pad Dean had sent? A part of him hadn't really believed that this thing could fool him, successfully masquerade as someone he knew.

Now he believed.

But now might be too late.

The realization dawned on Eamon at the same time. He swore under his breath, his eyes wide.

Jake ran to the door, pulled on it. Locked. He hit the door buzzer, but it was no good. Started banging against the glass, grabbing a chair and pounding with it. The Plexiglas was at least two inches thick. Unbreakable. What kind of lab was this?

As if answering his question, an electronic voice said, "Please exit the building. A level 3 biological outbreak has been detected. You have sixty seconds before decontamination."

The lights dimmed and klaxons sounded.

"Warning. The doors will lock in sixty seconds and biological sanitation will begin. This is lethal to all life forms. Please vacate the premises."

Jake stared at the strobing orange lights overhead.

"Oh God."

30

GenTec Offices
Schenectady

"Yes, the doors are locked, Jake," Cormac chuckled.

He settled into the leather of his Buick rental and glanced out the tinted windows at the GenTec Life Sciences building. He tried to find a comfortable angle. His back itched and burned. Cradling his hardened and rubberized laptop on the steering wheel, he got ready for the end of the show. Sirens wailed from the building. One of Eamon O'Connell's guys—the one who'd dropped him off—exited his car, gun out, clearly wondering what the heck was going on. In ten minutes, the place would be swarming with police and fire engines.

But in one minute, Jake O'Connell and his brother would be dead.

On the laptop's screen, Cormac watched as Jake and Eamon stared dumbfounded at the alarms and flashing lights above and around them. It was a grainy black-and-white surveillance camera feed from inside. Cormac smiled. "What now, Jake?" he whispered.

On cue, Jake picked up a chair and started bashing it against the Plexiglas wall.

"Nope, that's not going to work," Cormac sniggered, munching on a handful of freeze-dried green beans. "Fifty seconds, Jake."

Beside Jake, Eamon pulled out his gun.

Cormac watched, smiling. "Bullet resistant."

Then Jake did something Cormac hadn't expected. Jake turned away from the Plexiglas walls, toward the server racks on the other side of the room. Shaking his head, he took the gun from Eamon and pointed it in the other direction. They walked off camera. Cormac tried to swivel the camera around, but he could only catch the edge of them.

Cormac put down the green beans. "What are you up to?"

The gun discharged six times. Jake fired at the ceiling, and then the brothers started pulling on something. Cormac sat upright. "Twenty seconds, Mr. O'Connell."

Jake and Eamon disappeared from the screen.

Right on time, the image on-screen hazed over with the biological decontaminant, as the room was flooded with a lethal dose of toxins. Cormac flipped his laptop closed and looked at the building.

Was it over?

Cormac watched the seconds and minutes tick by. Next to the building, Eamon O'Connell's guy stared at the door. A distant whine of fire engines. Cormac started his engine, and was putting the car in gear when two figures staggered out of the building's fire exit.

"I don't believe it," muttered Cormac.

It was Jake and Eamon. Cormac watched wide-eyed as they jogged to the waiting car and got inside. Finishing putting his car into gear, Cormac put his foot down and started off.

They must have climbed out through the ventilation. It was the only way.

He had to hand it to him. This Jake kid was resourceful. Kept a cool head. Even after Cormac killed those pilots back at Bear Mountain—even emptied the fuel from the airplanes—Jake had found a way to escape. He was determined, never gave up, so Cormac wasn't really that surprised he found a way out this time as well.

But it wasn't Cormac's idea.

Cormac had warned his employer that a stunt like this would create too many loose ends, but the old man wanted it to look like an accident. Cormac's employer had wanted it to look like Jake was breaking into GenTec when something went wrong. The fact that it was a company owned by Bluebridge wasn't lost on Cormac.

Cormac scratched his neck and grimaced, his fingers testing underneath the bandage.

This whole thing was getting a little too odd. Cormac had never worked for an employer like this one. The old man would call him at all hours with questions and asking opinions. Sometimes the questions were complex, but often they were banal. Obvious.

What did it mean, the old man had asked the day before, when a reporter said the President's policy on the Middle East was designed to split Islamists into dozens of splinter groups? Cormac had explained that it was a joke. Sarcasm. That they were making fun of a policy that seemed designed to make the situation worse.

But the old man didn't get sarcasm, seemed crippled by a literal mind.

An old baby.

It sounded odd, but that's the image that formed in his head when he talked to the old man. Like he was talking to a seventy-year-old baby—and that's how it felt, like somehow he was babysitting.

Strange.

But as long as it paid well, strange didn't bother Cormac.

One thing that did bother him was that his client was getting more desperate. When he started out with him a year ago, the jobs had been surgical in their precision, but things were getting messy. Cormac had seen it before. Knew when it was time to get out. The old man on the phone never sounded the least bit desperate though, which meant it was time to get out, but not quite yet.

Cormac was happy Jake wormed his way out of this one. It wasn't often, but sometimes a job got personal. It cost a huge amount of money to keep what had happened in Canada quiet. Cormac's own money. He rubbed the bandage on his neck again, the topmost plaster on the second degree burns covering half his back.

His skin was literally in this game.

It would feel satisfying to put a bullet between Jake's eyes. Or maybe something more personal. In any case, it was time for Plan B.

▲▼▲

Jake slammed the door to the motel room shut behind him and Eamon.

Elle was sitting on the bed waiting for them. "Shh, Anna's asleep," she scolded, pointing to the door to the adjoining room.

Outside the windows, fire engines wailed over the warble of police sirens. Looking at Eamon and Jake with their backs to the wall, she added, "Is that for us?"

Jake pulled his VOIP phone out of his pocket and started dialing Dean's number. "No."

Eamon pushed the blinds open an inch. Peered out. "We gotta get out of here, though, and fast."

"Can we trust them?" Jake motioned at Eamon's buddies, who stood outside on the balcony.

"Of course," Eamon replied. "You know Mick and Fumbles, they're my guys from the neighborhood. We're family. You can trust them with your life."

Jake nodded. "You'd better be sure of that." Dean picked up on the first ring. Jake hit the speakerphone button. In front of him he had the one-time pad Dean gave him. "Six-two-one," he said aloud.

A pause on the other end. "Eight-nine-eight," Dean's voice responded.

Jake checked his pad. Eight-nine-eight was the correct sequence.

"Jake?" Dean said over the phone. "Everything okay?"

A police siren howled outside, so close it sounded like it was in the parking lot. Jake tensed, his hand gripping the phone. The siren deepened in tone and grew softer, the police cruiser moving away.

"Why did we get into a fight when we met?" Jake asked, still cautious.

Pause. "Because my name was Albany. You hated Albany. Still hate Albany."

Eamon looked at Jake, who shrugged. "And what's the only thing I hated more?"

There was no pause this time. "Your dad."

Satisfied it was Dean, Jake growled, "I thought you said these phones were secure. I was almost killed again, my brother too this time."

Elle put one hand to her mouth. "You didn't tell me that."

Dean swore quietly on his end. "I wanted to talk to you about that. When you met Max, you said he mentioned something called the Assassin Market. I looked it up. This thing is real."

Jake stopped pacing. "So what is it?"

"An assassination website, with bounties placed on people's heads."

"And *I'm* on it?"

"I don't know," Dean replied. "I haven't been able to find it or log in. But it explains a few things."

"Okay, but right now I need to understand what happened." Jake started pacing again. "Eamon says I called him, but I didn't. And he called me on the VOIP phone, except it wasn't really him. What the hell, Dean?" Either Dean's security didn't work, or Dean was really in on this somehow.

"You got a call from this thing pretending to be your brother?" Dean asked.

"Yeah, and it came from the phone number you gave me for my brother's VOIP phone. I checked when the call came in."

"Let me think," Dean replied.

In the silence of the room, the sirens outside seemed louder. More fire engines and police were arriving. They were at risk of being evacuated, if nothing else. "Think faster," Eamon demanded, looking out past the curtains again.

"The only way it could have spoofed the call is if it somehow found the numbers for those phones," Dean said. "Those are encrypted, so there's no other way to get in once a connection is made. Did you use the security precautions like we talked about, to make sure your brother was your brother?"

"More or less," Jake replied. "I asked what we had for breakfast in the hotel room."

"Did you use a one-time pad?"

"No." Jake rubbed his eyes with one hand. "I didn't."

"This is for real, guys," Dean said quietly on the phone. "You gotta take this security seriously."

"How the hell did it find out so quickly?" Jake fumed. This thing seemed supernatural in its abilities. How could they beat something that knew *everything*?

"Do you have any computers, any other cell phones in the motel?" Dean asked. "I told the runner who contacted your brother before you arrived to give everyone strict instructions to leave their cellphones and electronic equipment behind. Just to use what I sent you. What's in the motel room?"

Jake scanned the room. It was dated. An old TV on the dresser, not even a digital cable box. "Nothing." He looked at Elle.

She shook her head. "I left everything, like I was told."

"What about Anna?" Dean asked over the cellphone. "Does

she have an iPad, any gadgets, toys?"

Elle shook her head again. "No, nothing—" Her eyes went wide. "Oh, my God."

Jake stared at her. "What?"

"That phone we gave Anna for Christmas, your old cell phone. She likes to carry it around, you remember, like she's a big girl?" Elle's hands came to her mouth. "She was walking around, talking on it, telling me she was chatting with her friend. I thought it was an imaginary friend, you know how she is…"

Elle stood straight up and jumped two steps to the adjoining door, cracking it open. "Anna?"

"Anna," Jake called out, "could you come in here?"

No response. Elle swung the door open. "Anna!" she yelled, stepping into the room.

"Anna?" said Jake again, louder. He glanced at Eamon, and both of them rushed into the next room.

"Anna?!" screeched Elle, already on her knees, looking under the bed. Tears in her eyes, ligaments straining in her neck, she looked up.

"Jake, where's Anna?" she cried, wild-eyed. "Where's our baby?"

31

Hong Kong Harbor
China

"What's going on?" Jin demanded. The small boat she'd been dumped into—just before the explosion—skimmed across the water, with Hong Kong's skyscrapers visible in the smoggy distance.

Wutang stood in front of her, next to the large tattooed man who drove the boat, and another man sat in the co-pilot chair. He swiveled around to watch Jin and Wutang, his face expressionless. A handgun rested carelessly in his lap.

Standing in front of her, Wutang reached into his pocket and pulled out a switchblade that snicked open. He stepped toward her. "Please don't move," he whispered.

Jin jumped back, her eyes wide. "No, stop…"

In one motion Wutang leaned over her and cut something from the back of her shirt. Putting the switchblade away and raising his hands in surrender, he backed away slowly. "Sorry, this was the only way."

"Only way for what?" Jin sputtered as he crushed something between his fingers. "What was that?"

"A tracking device." Wutang held it closer for her to examine. A tiny flash of metal inside a fabric tag. "They were listening to us. Sorry for hitting you. It was the only way to get us out of there." He sat opposite her, and threw the crumpled bug overboard. "Chen was a plant for the group that kidnapped you. We had to make it look convincing."

The bow hit a large wave, sending a shock of spray into the air that rained down on them. Jin wiped the saltwater from her face. "Make what look convincing?"

"Your death." Wutang cocked his head to one side. "And mine. Had to remove us as a threat vector…at least for a while. We"—he flicked his chin at the man driving the boat—"were the ones that placed the big bets on the Assassin Market for you and

Chen."

"What?" Jin pushed away from him. "Why?"

"I found out that Chen's mother is sick. Dying. He needed quick money. I hacked into his crypto accounts and found huge deposits."

Jin wanted to get up and smack Wutang across the face. He'd scared her to death. She'd been kidnapped twice in a week, and the second time hadn't been any better than the first. But her escape from that abandoned apartment building had seemed a little too easy, not to mention the convenient fact that they'd been left alone in Hong Kong for a few days.

So Chen was an informant? All that time in his apartment had been a play to extract information? She revealed everything to Chen.

But not quite everything.

The hit on the social media monitoring system. Jake O'Connell. He was alive.

On the other hand, who the hell was Wutang? Or this *new* version of Wutang? She'd always had the impression he was a shy programmer nerd. Kidnapping her and staging an explosion, faking their deaths? Removing threat vectors?

"And who are these guys," Jin demanded, "your Triad gangbanger buddies?"

She had to admit, even though anger felt white hot inside her as she glared at him—he did seem tougher, more dangerous. More exciting. And relief at not being dead washed through her.

"Not Triad," Wutang replied, "these are Yakuza."

Yakuza? Japanese organized crime. Jin frowned. "What are they doing here?" And how on Earth did he know them? She'd heard stories about the Yakuza, some brutal, but also how they were the first ones to bring relief after earthquakes and tsunami.

"It started with Yamamoto, remember? He was head of Japan's largest hedge fund."

"So he was in with gangsters?"

"Not exactly." Wutang pointed at the seat beside her—could he sit there?—and Jin nodded. He stepped over, slid in beside her. Now he wouldn't have to yell over the engine. "Have you heard of *sokaiya?*"

Jin shook her head. She felt Wutang's warmth and inched closer.

"It's the name for the large-scale, institutionalized bribery practiced by the Yakuza in Japan. They buy shares in a publicly listed company, then start digging up dirt on the company leadership. After that, it's a case of 'give us money, or we'll show up at meetings and embarrass you.'"

Wutang looked up and then back at her. "It's sort of a way of keeping management honest. To combat it, Japanese companies tend to hold all their shareholder meetings on the same day—over 90% of the Tokyo stock exchange do it. Holding all their meetings on the same day made it difficult for the gangsters to be everywhere at once."

"And what does that have to do with anything?"

"Last year, the Yakuza bosses noticed a drop-off in business. Someone was muscling in on their territory. Someone who was able to attend a lot of shareholder and board meetings at the same time."

Jin connected the dots. "Bluebridge."

"We think so. Seems to be connected to something called InformDAC, an autonomous corporation that pays people to supply compromising information on senior executives. Yamamoto must have figured it out, like the Yakuza did. Bluebridge executives were attending dozens of meetings, some simultaneously. Using it to control Japanese businesses."

"So this chatbot software is spoofing Bluebridge executives?"

Wutang shook his head. "We think the chatbot technology comes *from* Bluebridge. Looks like they're purposely using it to mimic their executives. Not an obvious case of fraud, as they could argue they were attending the meetings by proxy."

"But it would be enough for Yamamoto to want to take it to the heads of the banks, and the fact that this was corrupting senior Chinese and Japanese officials."

Wutang nodded.

"And so they killed him."

"That's right. The Yakuza were tracking Yamamoto. They wanted to find out who was stealing their business, and how and why. When he was killed, they shadowed Shen Shi, found you. They knew that the State Security Ministry had planted Chen. They were watching him, so they knew when to capture you."

"So you're not Yakuza?" Jin asked.

Wutang laughed. "Me, Yakuza? Are you kidding? No. But by

209

the time they grabbed me on the street, I'd already figured out Chen was dirty. I was getting ready to escape with you. They came up with this plan, said we had to make it look convincing."

Jin smiled, her little bubble burst. She liked imagining Wutang as a secret agent gangster. "So where are we going now?"

"They want to stop whoever or whatever is cutting in on their business. They want *us* to stop it."

Jin moved another inch closer to Wutang. "Us?" she asked, shivering.

"Us." Wutang smiled and put an arm around her.

They cleared the harbor, and the tattooed man glanced over his shoulder at them, smiling, the rising sun glinting off his gold-capped front teeth. Turning back to the front, he slid the speedboat's throttle forward and the engine roared, the acceleration pushing them back into their seats. The boat rocketed off across the water, skipping over the waves into the sunrise over the South China Sea.

AUGUST 23rd

Tuesday

32

Super 8 Motel
Schenectady

"Good afternoon, Bluebridge Corporation. How may I help you?"

It sounded like Cindy, the receptionist Jake had encountered when he stormed the Bluebridge offices less than a week ago. Jake's phone was wired into the laptop Dean gave him, which was bouncing his call through a dozen anonymous connection points over the net. Dean had set it up remotely.

"I'd like to speak to Mr. Henry Montrose," Jake grunted, trying to keep his voice even.

"Mr. Montrose isn't in the office today," came Cindy's singsong voice. "Can I take a message?"

"No." Jake's voice went up an octave. "I need to speak to him immediately."

"I'm sorry, but who is this?"

"He knows who this is," Jake barked.

Jake paced back and forth, a wire stretching from the VOIP phone in his hand to the laptop perched on top of the TV. He glanced at Elle sitting on the foot of the bed next to Eamon, his brother's arm around her. She trembled, her eyes bloodshot and full of tears. Jake felt empty—no fear anymore, not for himself— except maybe it wasn't emptiness he felt.

Rage filled him.

A pause on the other end. "Excuse me, sir? He knows who this is? Who *is* this?"

"Listen Cindy, get that goddamn piece of—"

Click. Click. "Mr. Jake O'Connell?"

This was it. This had to be the machine. "Where's my daughter?" Jake screamed into the phone, spitting onto the handset as he held it in front of him. He put his ear back to the phone.

"Mr. O'Connell, this is the New York Police Department,

Special Investigative division," came a calm voice after a few seconds of airtime. "Mr. O'Connell, you need to surrender yourself. Threatening Bluebridge exec—"

Jake hung up. "Jesus Christ," he muttered.

He glanced at the gold cross hanging around his brother's neck. It had been a long time since he'd gone to Church, but he missed it now. He felt like crawling into a sanctuary, confessing his sins, begging for divine intervention. It seemed to be his only hope for saving his daughter.

"What...what happened?" Elle stammered. "Did it say anything? Do they have Anna?"

"The police picked up the call. At least it sounded like the police. They must be monitoring the lines there."

"Did the police say anything about our daughter?" Elle was frantic.

Jake scowled. Threw the phone on the bed. "No."

Nothing.

There had been no demands. No mention of ransom.

They'd torn through the rooms looking for Anna—or any sign of where she might be—until Mick, one of Eamon's guys, came in and asked what was going on. They said Anna was gone. He smiled and told them she'd gone downstairs to meet Jake. Mick's smile faded when he noticed Jake, glaring at him from the back of the room.

Jake had grabbed Mick by the throat and pinned him to the wall.

They got the full story.

When Anna went outside, Mick asked her what she was doing. She told him her dad was on the phone, and he wanted her to go down to the lobby. This was before Jake and Eamon returned. She handed the cell to Mick, who talked to both Jake and Eamon. They said they were downstairs; that all Mick had to do was make sure she got down the stairs okay.

Mick had been in tears, not understanding what happened. The machine had fooled him. They hadn't told any of Eamon's guys the whole story, they hadn't had time, so Mick had no way of knowing.

"What did you do?" Elle screamed at Jake.

He pulled her close and let her hit him. Pulled her sobbing face into his chest.

Their daughter was gone, vanished without a trace. The call to Bluebridge—a last-ditch effort—had accomplished nothing.

Then Jake's phone pinged. At first he ignored it, but it pinged again. Flipping it open with one hand, he clicked on a message from an unknown caller.

A video.

Anna's faced filled his screen. "Hi, Daddy", she squeaked, smiling. "The nice lady told me you would meet us here." She was in a featureless white room. The video ended as abruptly as it had started. No explanations.

"What does it want?" Elle took the phone from him, slumped onto the bed and started watching the video of their daughter over and over.

Jake finally explained that they thought it might be a machine that was hunting them. A machine running a human network. Why hadn't he told her everything immediately? Half-truths were as damning as lies. In the end, she hadn't much cared—she wanted her daughter back.

There were no demands, but Jake could guess what it wanted. "It wants what Sean sent to me in that package."

The copy of the Bluebridge core, with the banking algorithms from Donovan and Viegas's death certificate, made for some damning evidence. They just had to do something with it.

"Can't we give it to them...or *it?*" Elle asked. "You're risking your life, our *daughter's* life!"

She didn't need to tell him. The thought kept drilling its way deeper into his head.

"It's not that simple," Eamon replied. "We have no leverage. How would it know we haven't copied the information? How is this ever going to end?"

"Our daughter has been *stolen*," Elle cried. "Can't we call the police? We need to do something. *Anything.*"

"You want to call the police?" Eamon shook his head. "Bring them here? We'll all be thrown into jail. And if we're thrown in jail, no way we can avoid Joey Barbara's guys."

"That doesn't matter anymore," Elle said quietly. "We just need to get Anna back."

"We can't call the police," Jake replied to her, just as quietly. "Not yet, anyway." There was no way he was letting anyone take his family away from him. He was going to fix this, protect them.

215

Somehow.

But the walls were closing in.

Anonymous death squads, the mafia breathing down his neck, half a dozen federal agencies on a manhunt for him and his family—and this machine knew exactly where Jake was. It wasn't afraid of getting him arrested, so why weren't the police here already?

Jake felt like he was stuck in a mirror maze, herded, prodded, and corralled between the fences to the slaughterhouse, pushed deeper and deeper into a labyrinth with only one exit. He had to figure out a way to get outside of the lines he was being painted into, to figure out how to create a second exit.

One he wasn't being pushed toward.

But how?

There was one last option.

He went to the backpack Eamon had brought him from the old motel and fished into a side pocket, produced a card. He'd managed to hold onto it throughout all his misadventures. "I'm going to call this guy. We need help."

Eamon stared at the card, frowning, until he recognized it. It was the business card FBI Special Agent Tolliver had given Jake back at the house. "You're going to call the Feds? They're *hunting* for you. You're going to call them?"

"This guy, Tolliver, you remember? He came to my house before this whole thing really kicked off. Said he was investigating Bluebridge, said he was operating *outside* of normal channels." Jake threw his hands wide. "You have any better ideas?"

"Christ, Jake, that's playing into their hands." Eamon pointed at his own chest. "You've already got all the FBI you need right here."

"What?"

"Foreign born Irish, Jake. We got connections. We can handle this."

Jake stopped pacing. "What, are you and Mick and Fumbles out there"—he pointed to the front door—"going to fight some global artificial intelligence? It's probably staring down at us from space right now, eyeballing us from some freakin' satellite."

"This thing isn't God, Jake. It can't have all the angles covered." Eamon scowled at the FBI card in Jake's hand. "I don't know if it's smart to get in touch with people who are already

216

hunting for you." His shoulders sagged. "I'm trying, Jake. I'm sorry about everything. The guys, they didn't know—"

"I know." Jake's face softened. "Look, you can help by taking Elle up north into Canada." Jake fended off objections from Elle. "Kahnawake has more ex-Rangers and Special Forces marines than Fort Bragg. Get up there and keep her safe."

"And what are you going to do?"

"I'm going to get in touch with this guy. I'll use the voice scrambler Dean gave me. Arrange a meeting somewhere public. Make a deal. I've met him. I know his face."

"What kind of deal?" Elle asked.

"We have the Vidal Viegas death certificate, we have a copy of the Bluebridge core and the trading algorithms. I know this FBI guy will want all of that."

"I'm not going north," Elle said quietly.

"Baby, it's too dangerous, you can't come with me—"

"I'm staying here. You go meet that agent, but I'm staying here until we find Anna."

"Elle, you can't stay here. What are you going to do?"

"I'm with Elle." Eamon walked up beside her, put a hand on her shoulder. "This is our town, Jake, we grew up here. If anyone can find Anna, maybe me and the guys can."

Jake closed his eyes, gritted his teeth. "I can't risk losing you, Elle. I'll get her back, I'll make a deal."

"I can't abandon Anna," Elle whispered. She gripped Eamon's hand on her shoulder.

Jake stared at his wife. Exhaled. It wasn't an argument he could win. "But we need to leave this motel. It knows we're here. The longer we wait, the more we're sitting ducks." All this time, he'd been back on his heels, reacting. It was time to fight back. "And if I end up playing into its hands, then we're no worse off." Jake looked into Elle's eyes. "If I disappear, give them everything. Do anything it takes to get Anna back."

He turned to his brother. "I'm trusting you, Eamon." The words came surprisingly easily.

Eamon's jaw muscles rippled. "I got this, little brother." His eyes glistened. "I got this."

"Maybe you're thinking the wrong way," Elle said, breaking the moment between the brothers.

Jake turned to her. "How so?"

217

"This thing wants money, right? That's what you said it was programmed for?"

"That's what Max said."

"So hit it where it hurts. Take its money away."

"What do you mean?"

Of all of them, Elle was by far the smartest. She often had insights that Jake had a hard time seeing. He'd learned long ago to listen to her instincts.

"I don't know." Elle rocked back and forth. "I'm just saying, that's what is at the root of this. Money."

"Maybe," Jake admitted, "and maybe this FBI guy can help us with that."

Eamon peered back through the curtains. "Come on, we gotta go."

AUGUST 24th

Wednesday

33

Downtown Albany

"Agent Tolliver," said a clipped, electronic voice. "I have information for you."

"Who is this?" Agent Tolliver replied.

"Do you have an encrypted line you can call me from?" said the electronic voice.

A pause. "Yes. What number should I call?"

Jake cleared his throat and looked around. The closest person was a hundred feet away, entering a convenience store. He was on a small side street, at the end of Main St. in downtown Albany. He held the voice changer, a small electronic device Dean had given him, up to his mouth.

Jake found it ironic that to evade a machine, he had to sound like one. Speaking one digit at a time, he gave the agent the number for a new VOIP phone Dean sent down the night before. He hung up the receiver of the payphone and slipped the voice changer into his pocket. Glancing around again, he made sure nobody was watching. Nobody was. He crossed the street to a small park, his hand on the phone in his pocket, waiting for the return call.

The trees around the park swayed. A storm was coming.

The day before, they'd driven all over Schenectady and Albany—ducking into buildings, switching cars, splitting up, doing anything they could to lose a possible tail. Jake had a hard time believing they could evade whatever or whoever was following them, but at least they'd made it difficult. They spent the night in the car, on the run, ditched all of their possessions. All except for the phone. Elle wouldn't part with it, no matter what.

Every two hours, a new five-second video clip of Anna was sent. Playing with toys, smiling at the camera. Later in the night, they were images of her asleep on a cot. Elle clutched the phone in her hand, wouldn't let anyone else touch it. Each time it vibrated, signaling a new message, she started sobbing, and then she'd play the new video clip over and over. All Jake could do was sit beside her and hold her tight.

In the small hours of the morning, Jake said goodbye to Elle. It was one of the hardest things he'd ever done, but he knew it would be best—and least dangerous—for them to split up.

Dean had someone come down to bring them new electronic communication gear. More security-hardened, with stricter instructions. Jake had a protocol to follow when Special Agent Tolliver called him back.

The situation up in Kahnawake was degrading fast. The Canadian authorities had stepped up the pressure, insisting that an audit team be allowed to inspect the Mohawks' gambling operation. A thinly disguised tactic. The Mohawks refused entry to any outside police forces or inspectors. Dean didn't think it would escalate, but that could change. Especially if Bluebridge suspected that Dean was the one holding its critical data.

Jake sat on a bench in the park. His phone rang and he picked up.

"Who is this?" Agent Tolliver demanded on the other end.

Jake hesitated, his finger hovering over the 'cancel' button. He either had to take the plunge or go it alone. He didn't trust Tolliver—he didn't trust anyone besides his family members—and he couldn't be sure this was even Tolliver. But he had to do something, take some chances. "Jake O'Connell," he finally said.

A pause on the other end. "What can I do for you, Mr. O'Connell?"

"Why did you come to my house that day?"

"I told you," Special Agent Tolliver said. "I've been investigating Bluebridge."

"For what?"

"Irregularities." Another pause. "I believe you are being targeted by Bluebridge, Jake. If you have any information to share, now would be the time. And you should be careful of letting yourself fall into the hands of any authorities right now."

Jake nodded. It was time to go through some security questions. "What did you give me at the house that day?" he asked.

Agent Tolliver didn't hesitate. "A business card."

"Is that all?"

"Yes."

"And what did my brother give you?"

This time there was a pause of a few seconds. "The finger, I believe."

It had to be the guy who'd been at Jake's door. There was no way any camera or recording device could have picked up on such minor details, but Jake needed something else. Something more convincing. "Tell me why you're really investigating Bluebridge."

The Agent cleared his throat. "Because I think Vidal Viegas has been dead for over a year."

▲▼▲

The porch door slid open, and Jake and his father stood and stared at each other.

"Well, this is a surprise," said his dad, taking a step back.

"Sorry, I need to—"

"You don't need to explain." His father took another step back, holding a knife in one hand. It took Jake a few seconds to see the piece of half-buttered toast in the other. He motioned for Jake to come inside.

Jake stepped into his old house. He hadn't expected his father to be there.

"The police came by earlier," his father said, matter-of-factly. "Old Ralston, you remember him?"

Jake nodded. Of course he remembered Ralston.

His father had aged—his hair thinner, whiter, than Jake remembered, and the creases in his face deeper. But his father's eyes were still the same. Though it had to be shocking for him to see Jake outside his back porch door in the middle of the night, his eyes didn't register any surprise. Calm. Collected. He looked about as surprised as if Jake had left twenty minutes ago to get milk, and was rapping on the door to come back in.

But it hadn't been twenty minutes.

Jake had left this old man's life twenty years ago. He'd only been back to this house a few times since moving out, and his father had never been home.

"Sit down," his father said, turning to finish buttering the toast. When Jake didn't move from the doorway, he added, "Or stand, same to me. You want a drink?"

"You have any whiskey?" A silly question, like asking the Pope if he was Catholic.

His father nodded, taking a bite from his toast, and shuffled into the kitchen. Jake noticed that. The shuffling was new. Jake did a mental calculation. His father was sixty-eight this year.

Jake glanced around.

The house had barely changed.

Thirty years his parents had been renting this place, and it was a dump from the start. On the dining table, a cigarette-rolling machine balanced on top of a scattered stack of unopened mail, next to an ashtray overflowing with butts. He noticed the ceiling was stained yellow, then realized it had to be from cigarette smoke. The smell of stale beer and neglect brought memories rushing into Jake's head.

Bad memories.

"Your mother's in the lounge," Jake's dad grunted. He leaned over, opened the cupboard doors under the sink.

Jake nodded and took two steps forward, craning his neck to look around the corner. *The lounge.* A fancy word for a television room. Some murder mystery played on the TV.

To be honest, the room wasn't even about the television. A half-full glass sat beside his mother's liver-spotted hand. He didn't have to guess what it was. *Vodka tonic.* That's all she ever drank. He saw the back of her head, her gray roots showing under a blossom of red coloring still hanging onto the tips. She was in her favorite recliner.

"Flo, Jake's here," his father called out, his hands in the cupboard above the sink. "Flo?"

No response.

Jake's father returned to the dining table with two chipped tumblers and a bottle of Wild Turkey. He pushed the stack of unopened mail aside. "Your mother's asleep."

Asleep.

Passed out.

Same thing, in Jake's family.

Jake nodded and sat at the dining table. His father shrugged and opened the bottle of whiskey. Poured them each two fingers.

Where did psychopath conmen go when they got old? Home, seemed to be the answer.

Jake's dad lifted his glass. "Didn't think I'd see you here."

"Me either." Jake lifted his glass and grudgingly clinked it with his dad's.

They both took a drink.

Jake wondered for the hundredth time why his parents had stayed together. The marriage was a sham, a mess. Jake usually chalked it up to them having no one else—but all these years later he found he had a grudging respect that they'd managed to stick it out.

Why had Jake come here? He wasn't entirely sure. It was dangerous, an obvious place for someone to look for him. Jake had driven by a few times, his head down, and looked around. An hour ago he'd been tossing and turning in a cheap motel bed. Some instinct had pulled him out of bed, sent him out into the night.

But maybe this had been a mistake.

"You know, Jake, I'm sorry for everything that happened. I wasn't a good father. I know that. What happened that night"—his dad paused to finish his drink—"that was terrible. I was drunk. I'm sorry."

Jake stared at his dad. *I almost froze to death. You almost killed me.* But it was the first time his father had apologized, the first time he'd even acknowledged it. Still, he knew his dad's words were just that—words, not something he felt.

"I didn't come here for an apology. I wanted to say goodbye to Mom."

He thought about telling his father that Anna had been kidnapped, but he couldn't stomach it. Couldn't stand the thought of watching the empty black pools of his father's eyes, the awkward pause while the mind behind those eyes tried to think of what to say, how to react.

"Goodbye?" Jake's dad took a drink, the creases in his face deepening. "You want to say goodbye? Where are you going?"

"Nowhere." Jake had arranged to meet Agent Tolliver the next day, but he wasn't going to tell his dad that. "Just...away."

One way or the other, Jake's chances weren't good. He'd picked the most public place he could think of, Rockefeller Center. He would be going alone. Eamon and Elle were searching for Anna, but nothing so far. They'd even asked Joey Barbara's people if they knew anything, but they'd denied any involvement.

"I'm glad you showed up." Jake's dad nodded. "I know I've

been a terrible father, but I'm proud of you."

Again, just words.

If someone asked him, Jake would say he didn't care what his father said. Not now. Not ever. But deep down, in some valley in his soul…the words felt nice to hear. The most painful thing was to be ignored, which was what his dad had always done to him. Funny that his dad would say those words now, when Jake was indicted for fraud, wanted for rape and murder.

"I mean the way you got yourself a Wall Street job," his father clarified. He picked up the Wild Turkey. "You want some more?" he asked as he poured another few fingers into his own glass.

"No thanks."

Even now, Jake's father's eyes were calculating, looking for the angles. The police had an arrest warrant for Jake for fraud— maybe there was some way to get some of Jake's cash? Or, maybe he could turn Jake in, call the cops, get into the morning papers? There had to be a reward, right?

"I could help you," his father said.

Here it comes. Jake rolled his eyes and finished his drink. "And how could you help me?"

Jake's father shrugged. "Not sure. You might be able to use an old conman like me, one way or another. The world might be all computers and webs now"—he waved his drink in the air—"but in the end, it's still people, and people trust people." He took another sip of his drink. "I'm good with people. You know that."

Good at fooling them, stealing from them. But this was beyond what a small-time grifter could imagine or manage. "I don't think so."

"You remember when we sold those Bibles?" his dad asked.

"I remember." Jake shook his head and looked down at the table. Smiled.

He'd forgotten about that, or tried to forget. When he was about ten years old, somehow his dad had gotten his hands on a shipment of Bibles that had been printed wrong. The printer had only inked one side of each page. Thousands of them bound up like that, with only one side of each page printed.

Jake's dad slapped the table. He liked a good laugh. "That was a great idea, no?"

Junk, that's what most people would have thought of those Bibles. But not Jake's dad. To him, it was a goldmine.

226

Jake's dad had dumped the whole pile of them in their backyard, covered them with a tarp. He and Jake had gone door to door, selling them as 'Bible workbooks'—you read one page, then did your best to fill in the next blank page.

It was a test for the truly faithful, his dad had explained. Over and over. To anyone in the neighborhood who would listen.

They'd made a bundle.

Jake looked up from the table and into his dad's eyes. That was his dad. No gray clouds, only silver linings. Jake was sure his dad qualified as a three-quarter-Ted psychopath, but he wasn't a violent one. Maybe Jake had to look at the silver linings, too. He put his drink down. "I'm going to say bye to Mom, okay?"

His father nodded. "You remember, this old man's got some tricks up his sleeve. You call me if you need me."

Jake stood. *Need him?* He'd never needed his father, but Jake knew that was a lie even as he tried to sell it to himself. He shook his dad's proffered hand. "Goodbye, Conor."

Jake always used his father's name. Conor. The locals called him Puddy, but Jake never used this nickname, and never called him Dad either.

"Goodbye, son."

They let go of their handshake, but didn't embrace.

"You remember what O'Connell, means, you hear me?"

Jake nodded. *Strong like a wolf* was its Gaelic meaning. "I know." It was the one thing his dad had drilled into his head when he was a kid.

Conor pointed a shaking old finger at Jake. "I named you after your granddad, you know. That old bastard never went down without a fight. You won't either, you hear me?"

"I hear you," Jake replied.

Pinned to the side of a kitchen cupboard, right next to Jake, were some postcards. Jake recognized them. Taking a closer look, he noticed there was a stack of them, dog eared, and stuck onto a nail in the side of the cabinet. The post cards he used to send to his mother on his travels.

She'd kept them all. It was the first time he'd noticed.

Walking into the lounge, Jake grabbed the remote and turned the TV off. The house fell silent. Leaning down, he kissed his mother's forehead. "Goodbye, Mom."

227

Jake left through the back door and jumped through the bushes, then skirted old man Henderson's house. He'd parked the beat-up Ford Taurus his brother had given him in the street behind the house. It was past midnight, so he could catch a few hours' sleep in the back of the car, then get up and drive into New York at dawn.

Even if the authorities caught him, even if Tolliver wasn't on the level, he would be no worse off. He'd spill everything he knew, beg them to start searching for his daughter. Dean would make public everything they knew, send emails to all the news outlets; broadcast it over the Internet.

He had a hard time imagining how Bluebridge could contain that, but maybe it could. Jake would end up in jail undoubtedly, or worse, but the most important concern was getting things in motion to find Anna.

His only shot, his only wildcard, was that Tolliver was the real thing. So he had to risk it.

"Hold it right there!" a voice shouted in the darkness.

Floodlights clicked on and Jake held up one hand, blinded. He stopped cold. Fear swept through him like a wave, from his fingertips to scalp, and he resisted the urge to bolt. Squinting, he tried to see who it was. Was he surrounded?

"Don't move!" the voice commanded. "I'll shoot, I swear to God."

It wasn't floodlights, it was the headlights of a police cruiser, Jake realized, his eyes adjusting to the brightness.

▲ ▼ ▲

In the view from the police dashboard camera, a grainy black-and-white video, Sheriff Ralston leaned against the open door of his police cruiser, his gun pointed at Jake O'Connell. O'Connell had his hand up, blocking the glare from the headlights. Sheriff Ralston barked at him again, telling him not to move.

Slowly, O'Connell put his hand down, squinting into the light. Sheriff Ralston instructed him to get on the ground, but O'Connell remained still. His gun trained on the other man, Sheriff Ralston stood and walked around his car door. Moving closer to O'Connell, he told him to get on the ground.

O'Connell did not respond.

After a standoff lasting no more than ten seconds, Jake O'Connell advanced on Sheriff Ralston, who backed up. He instructed O'Connell to get on the ground, to keep his distance, threatening to shoot otherwise, but O'Connell continued to walk forward until he was right in front of the other man, the sheriff's gun pressed into his chest.

Then O'Connell reached down and took Sheriff Ralston's gun away from him.

AUGUST 25th

Thursday

34

Rockefeller Center
New York City

A huge inflatable pumpkin floated over the bronze Greek god. At his feet, his subjects skated on the ice rink of Rockefeller Center. Jake smiled. It seemed appropriate that he was meeting Agent Tolliver next to the iconic statue of Prometheus, the Greek god who, legend had it, brought fire to mankind.

They used to call the Rockefeller Center the 'sunken plaza.' The skating rink was two stories below street level, lined with flags from nations around the world, with passers-by gawking over the edges at the skaters below.

While he was waiting, Jake read the plaque detailing the Center's history. Back in the 1930s, it was an open-air café lined with shops, but when nobody seemed to want to go down there to shop, they came up with the bright idea of turning it into a skating rink—nearly a century later, it still was one.

More important for Jake, standing here gave him a wide-angle view of anyone around the square. He'd arranged to meet Agent Tolliver on the viewing platform at the south end of the skating rink, one level down from street level, but still one level up from the ground. Just as important, tourists always packed the Center—it was as public a place as one could find.

The exposure was dangerous, though. Jake had a bounty on his head, but he had to take the chance. Meeting somewhere private would entail a whole other set of complications. Acting quickly was the only thing on Jake's side.

Though meeting next to the statue of Prometheus seemed appropriate, the giant orange pumpkin seemed out of place. It hovered over the spot where the famous Rockefeller Christmas tree would stand, blazing in its glory, in a few months. It was only August 25th, but the retailers were already gearing up for Halloween. The tourists didn't seem to care—Christmas tree or giant pumpkin—people taking pictures filled the place.

Jake checked his phone.

Nearly two o'clock, the pre-arranged time for his meeting with Agent Tolliver.

Jake had arrived early—before eight—when the plaza was still empty. He spent the time scouting, sitting at a café across the street, then down in the Rockefeller Café, getting a good idea of the ways in and out, watching for anything—or anyone—suspicious. Now Jake watched the viewing platform from across the square. He'd asked Tolliver to wear a Cincinnati Reds baseball cap.

Another sleepless night.

After disarming Sheriff Ralston, Jake had tied him to a tree and then hid the police cruiser in the woods down the road. Adrenaline competed with exhaustion, and only one thought hammered through his head: *Where's Anna?* He continued to check in with Elle every two hours. New video clips of their daughter were being sent in like clockwork.

But without any demands.

Torture wasn't a strong enough word.

A scrolling news display hung on the side of the Rockefeller building directly in front of Jake. He tried to focus on the platform above the rink, waiting for that red baseball cap, when something caught his eye. "*Bluebridge acquires Japan's largest hedge fund…*" announced the news display.

Jake clenched his jaw.

Even while it hunted him, this bastard thing was still ringing in deals and racking up profits. The next news item described a terrorist attack in Hong Kong harbor, something about a rocket-propelled grenade destroying a fishing trawler two days before.

There.

A red flash in the crowd.

Jake glanced down from the news display. On the platform a red baseball cap appeared. Jake fished out the old binoculars he'd taken from home, the ones he used to take out camping with Sean years ago. He focused them on the person with the baseball cap, and the image of Agent Tolliver came into sharp relief. He stared directly back, and Jake involuntarily retreated a step.

Agent Tolliver looked away after a second.

"Can you take our picture?"

Jake spun around. "What?"

234

"Can you take our picture?" repeated a man standing next to Jake.

"Ah," Jake stammered, "no, sorry. I'm late."

He held up his hands and walked away from the perplexed-looking family. Glancing back at the platform, Tolliver was still there. Jake started around the plaza and tried not to stare. What was the procedure for something like this? Should he wait to see what the other guy did?

But Jake was tired of waiting.

It was him.

Jake was sure of it.

The agent who'd come to his apartment when Eamon was there. The same blue eyes, the same gaunt face—either it was him, or someone who looked exactly like him.

Was it possible for Bluebridge to come up with a body double that quickly? In less than twenty-four hours? He fought the feeling that he was dealing with something supernatural. He had to be pragmatic, take some calculated risks.

Anna's life depended on him.

"Tolliver," Jake called out from the top of the stairs leading down to the rink.

Agent Tolliver turned around. He nodded. "Jake."

That was definitely the guy Jake had met at his apartment. Glancing back and forth, Jake tensed up, waited for yelling to start, for the sound of sirens, for someone to tackle him to the ground.

Or for the impact of a sniper's bullet.

"I came alone, as we agreed," Agent Tolliver said, still standing at the railing.

He looked as nervous as Jake felt.

"Can I come up?" Agent Tolliver asked.

Jake nodded, and Agent Tolliver walked up the stairs. Took something out of the pocket of his trench coat. Jake expected a gun, a Taser…some sort of weapon. Not an iPhone.

"Put your index finger on this," Agent Tolliver instructed, holding out the phone. A dongle was attached to the end of it.

"What is it?"

"Fingerprint reader."

Jake hesitated, but then lifted his right hand and pressed it to the device.

Agent Tolliver held it in place for a second before turning the phone around. "Good. Can't be too careful, Mr. O'Connell. Let's go sit down." He motioned to an empty table and two chairs at the edge of the building. A couple had just vacated it.

"After you," Jake replied. He followed Agent Tolliver through the crowd. "My daughter, they abducted my daughter."

"Who did?" Agent Tolliver asked as they sat together.

A young boy screamed as he ran past, his mother in pursuit. Tourists took pictures all around them.

"Bluebridge. I don't know. I think it's them." Jake noticed a girl in a motorcycle helmet looking at him. She had a camera on top of her helmet, one of those 'Go Pro' ones Anna raved about wanting. The girl looked away.

"When?"

"Yesterday, when I called you."

"That's why you called?"

"I need help. You said you could protect my family."

"I can, and we *will* find your daughter. I can assure you of that, Mr. O'Connell. The agency has immense resources for this sort of thing. It's what we do."

It felt like a mountain lifted off Jake's shoulders.

"But I need you to help me, too," added Agent Tolliver.

Anything, Jake was ready to do anything to get Anna back. "Tell me what you need."

"You can start by telling me why you think someone at Bluebridge is targeting you."

It felt good to let loose. Jake had nothing to hide, not now. "I have the automated trading algorithms for several of the large banks. Donovan gave them to me."

Agent Tolliver frowned. "And that's what they want?"

"That"—Jake put his elbows on the table and clasped his hands, resting his chin on them—"and Sean Womack sent me a copy of the programming core of Bluebridge's systems."

This time Agent Tolliver didn't frown. "I see."

"And I have the original death certificate of Vidal Viegas."

"You have the *original*?"

Jake nodded.

"Mr. O'Connell. You have no idea how important—"

"There's more," Jake interrupted. "Max Lefevre, he worked with Sean Womack, I met him, and he said that Henry Montrose

236

wasn't in charge of Bluebridge anymore."

"What are you saying?"

"I'm saying that Bluebridge is running itself, that some kind of artificial intelligence has taken over."

Agent Tolliver didn't look surprised. Didn't betray any emotion at all, actually. "We've suspected that for some time. Where's Max now? Can I speak to him?"

Jake grimaced. "He's dead. Almost got killed myself."

Agent Tolliver pursed his lips. "And who's 'we'? Who have you told? It's important, Jake."

"My brother, my wife." Jake looked at the table. "Dean—"

"Dean? Who's Dean?"

"He's with the Kahnawake Mohawks in Canada, runs a data center up there."

"And he has the information Sean gave you?"

This was going a little too fast for comfort. Jake was giving a lot away, and not getting much in return. "Can we talk about my family? How we're going to find Anna?"

"One step at a time," said Agent Tolliver. "To start with, where's your wife?"

"My wife?" Jake looked around at all the people crowding them. "Shouldn't we go somewhere quieter, more secure to talk?"

Agent Tolliver paused but then nodded. He got up from the table, and some tourists nearby asked if they could take it. He said yes, of course, and asked Jake to follow him. He had a car nearby on 50th. They could take that to a safe house, he said, and discuss everything at length. Tolliver pointed through an opening in the crowd, indicating a black car parked beside a van.

In his jacket pocket, Jake gripped the gun his brother gave him. He was relieved that they weren't the only ones fighting Bluebridge, but he also felt uneasy. He'd seen Agent Tolliver somewhere else. Sometime before he came to the house. Jake was sure of it. He watched as Tolliver limped forward, favoring his right leg. He noticed a bandage on Agent Tolliver's neck, the skin around it red and blistered. He was about to ask what had happened to him when it hit Jake.

Limping.

Jake flashed back to when he and his brother went to the Colcannon for a drink, just before he had met Tolliver. A man had limped into the bar. And at the Atlas Capital offices, when

Donovan told him Bluebridge was framing him, the man who'd followed Viegas to the front had limped.

Jake looked at Tolliver again.

Adrenaline flooded Jake's bloodstream.

It was him.

Jake took a second look at the bandage on his neck. It looked like it covered a burn. There were no coincidences in this thing.

Jake gripped the gun in his pocket.

▲ ▼ ▲

Cormac saw the flash of recognition in Jake's eyes. With one lightning-quick motion, he reached into Jake's jacket pocket, wrapped his hand around the gun he'd seen there, and put it in his own pocket. Amateur. Didn't he realize how easy it was to spot a gun in a jacket pocket? He moved behind Jake, pushing the muzzle of his silenced gun into Jake's ribs. "Don't even think about it," he whispered.

He felt Jake tense up, his feet stopping in place.

"Nowhere to run, Jake. Keep walking. You want to see your daughter again, don't you?"

"You bastard," Jake hissed, but he started moving again.

Cormac could hardly believe his luck when Jake called him. His employer had predicted he would, but Cormac was still amazed. Cormac usually wouldn't expose himself to a target, but he had to admit it worked beautifully—showing up at the O'Connell's apartment and posing as an FBI agent. He had to give credit to the old man.

Cormac could have killed Jake in a dozen easier ways in the past few days, but his employer wanted information, wanted to know what Jake knew, who else knew. Cormac would have opted for a small room and a bone saw to get the information out, but the old man didn't think it would work on Jake.

His employer had been right again.

This was much easier.

There was one problem, though. Not really a problem, but more of an issue: Cormac wasn't the one who kidnapped Jake's daughter. The old man had only informed him about it after the fact. Not that he couldn't use the information, though. It was excellent leverage.

"Get in the car," Cormac instructed as they crossed the street. "And we can go see your little girl."

The problem was that it demonstrated a lack of trust on the part of his employer. Cormac already had one foot out the door, sure, but it didn't suit him to find out he wasn't included in all of his employers' plans. The truth was, he might have balked at kidnapping a child. It was too risky. Too many unknowns. Too much emotion.

Cormac opened the door to the Cadillac. "Get in," he told Jake, "and strap on your seatbelt."

"You heard what I said, right?" Jake stared at the interior of the car and back at Cormac. "This machine has taken over Bluebridge. You're not working for who you think you are. Montrose is gone, Viegas is gone. Bluebridge is running itself."

"Get in the goddamn car, Jake."

"I want Anna to be safe. I'll do anything you want." Resigned, Jake stooped and slid into the car and strapped on the seatbelt.

Cormac edged around the front of the car while keeping an eye on Jake. Keeping one hand on his gun, he pulled out his earpiece with his other hand, disconnecting it. His employer was listening in, but it was time to cut the cord.

So Jake's friends had the automated trading algorithms for major banks, even a copy of the Bluebridge core? That sounded like it could be worth a lot of money.

He looked at Jake through the open window of the driver's side of the Cadillac. Was Cormac being set up somehow? He didn't like the feel of this anymore. What Jake told him made sense. It was hard to believe, sure, but all the pieces fit together. Those strange questions from the old man. The calls made late at night.

"For God's sake," Jake said from inside. "You're working for a machine."

Cormac looked Jake square in the eye. "No, I'm not."

"Everything I've told you is true."

Jake was quick but naive. "I know I'm not working for a machine," Cormac said. He stood and backed up a step. "Because I'm working for money."

Time to tie up loose ends.

"Jake, I've got some good news and some bad news. The good news is, I didn't take your daughter." Cormac pulled out his gun

239

and pointed it at Jake, the muzzle of its silencer three feet from Jake's head. Point blank range, and Jake was strapped into his seat. There was no way Cormac was going to miss this time. "The bad news is, I'm going to take your life."

Cormac started to squeeze the trigger.

A loud whining noise sounded to his right.

He had just enough time to glance sideways before something crashed into him, sending him flying into the back of the van in front of him.

▲ ▼ ▲

What just happened?

Jake ripped off his seatbelt and jumped out of the Cadillac. Already a crowd of people ran over. Agent Tolliver was splayed out on the pavement in the middle of 50th street, beside the van in front of the Cadillac.

Someone on a dirt bike had rammed into him. The bike and driver were in a pile next to the van.

Jake couldn't see the gun.

He looked at the driver of the dirt bike. It was the same girl he'd seen in the plaza, the one with the camera on top of her helmet. She got up unsteadily, shaking her head, and leaned down to pick up her bike. She looked at Jake.

"Come on!" she yelled. "Let's get out of here."

Jake glanced left and right. Was she talking to him?

"Jake," she urged, "let's go!" She pulled off her helmet and stared at him.

It took Jake a second to recognize her. That bar in Guangzhou, all those years back when he'd visited Sean before his wedding. "Nuggets?" came out of Jake's mouth before he even knew what he was going to say.

"That's right, *remember the nuggets.*" The girl smiled. "Come on, we gotta go!"

Jin, Jake remembered, that was her name. She'd worked with Sean on banking contracts in Hong Kong. What was she doing here? But Jake didn't have a lot of time to think about it.

Tolliver groaned.

A crowd of people had formed around them, and Jin pushed her bike through. From the corner of his eye, Jake saw NYPD officers run across Rockefeller plaza, heading in their direction.

"Come on!" Jin jumped on her bike, kicking down on the starter. Its engine fired up and she revved it, starting down the street against the traffic.

People yelled at her to stop.

Glancing at Tolliver on the ground, Jake watched him open his eyes. He got up onto his elbows and looked around. Jake realized he was searching for his gun.

Something buzzed by Jake's ear, followed by the loud crack of a rifle shot. The marble façade of the building behind Jake exploded in a shower of fragments.

He ducked down.

Somebody was shooting at him. Somebody besides Tolliver.

The people who'd gathered around started yelling and screaming, some running, some falling to the ground. Turning on his heel, Jake took off toward Jin.

Another crack of a rifle shot.

Sprinting, Jake wound his way through the cars and jumped on the back of Jin's dirt bike. She gunned the throttle and they peeled out onto 5th Avenue, skidding around the corner.

35

Two Bridges Housing Project
New York City

"Who's this?" Jake asked.

He was still shaking.

He'd been brought to an empty apartment, about ten floors up in the Two Bridges housing projects in lower Manhattan. The view out of one wall of windows was the Brooklyn Bridge. They were so close he saw people chatting in their cars as they waited in the rush hour traffic. From the other set of windows there was a view of a windowless monolithic forty-story building with 'Verizon' stenciled near its top.

A young man helped Jin clean a nasty scrape on her left shoulder. The way he fussed over her, it was clear he was more than a friend. The guy put down his tube of antiseptic cream and turned to Jake, outstretching his hand. "My friends call me Wutang."

Jake shook his hand. "I'm Jake."

"We know who you are," said another young man, entering the empty living room of the high-rise apartment. He put out his hand. "My name's Sheldon."

"And you're the expert in artificial intelligence?" Jake said, reaching to shake his hand as well. Jin had filled him in a little on the subway ride over. She'd flown in from Hong Kong the previous day, specifically to find him, but she hadn't explained the details yet.

"That's right." Sheldon wagged his head back and forth. "Well, chatbots and automated agents, that sort of thing, but close enough."

"He was the first person to beat the Turing test," Wutang said, turning his attention back to Jin's shoulder, carefully applying a bandage. "Or I mean, the first person to build a chatbot that beat the Turing test a couple of years back."

The Turing test? Jake had heard Sean talk about it once. "A

way to test if something is a person or not?"

"Sort of."

Sheldon sat in front of three large flat screen displays arranged on a long table along one wall of the living room. Below the table was a mass of wiring, several desktop computer boxes and routers and an assortment of other flashing equipment. Apart from four folding chairs, it was the only furniture in the room. It smelled like a fresh coat of white paint was just applied to the walls.

Jake looked down at the scuffed parquet wooden floors.

Events had taken a bizarre turn. An hour before, Jake thought he was about to ensure his family's security and have the FBI start searching for his little girl. Now his life hinged on three hipster kids in an empty apartment overlooking NYPD headquarters.

After knocking Tolliver over, they'd torn down 5ᵗʰ Avenue, winding through the traffic on the bike. They dumped it in Union Square, then melted into the crowd and ducked into the subway station. Jin had orchestrated a wild goose chase, leading him from one subway car to the next at stops, eventually getting off at the Chambers Street stop in the financial district. Jake jumped back down the stairs when they came outside. It was at 1 Police Plaza, the headquarters of the NYPD, right next to the Metro courthouse he'd only been released from two weeks before.

"How did you find me? Why did you find me?" Jake asked from one of the chairs.

With Jin's wound bandaged, she and Wutang sat in chairs facing him.

"Sean sent me an email before he died—*Remember the nuggets*—that got me thinking about that night we met, you remember?"

Jake nodded.

"And like I said," Jin continued, "we found you through social media. We've had a facial recognition search going on openly posted images in the New York area. You must have been in Rock Center all day. We had seventy-two partial matches from pictures people posted today. It's why I went there looking for you."

"And how did you know that guy was"—Jake searched for the right word—"a bad guy?"

Sheldon tapped on his keyboard and brought up an image of Jake at the table in Rockefeller Center. "When Jin found you sitting and talking in the plaza, we did a pattern match on the guy you were talking to. We expected it to return nothing—at least not right away—but boom!" He brought up another image, this one of a blackened and burned man walking down a forest trail. "This is from Bear Mountain in Canada. We know you were up there—we found pictures of you posted online—and this guy, too."

"How did you know he wasn't my friend?"

"From the way you were talking to him," Jin answered. "Seemed too suspicious. I hung back, then I saw him take your gun and pull one on you."

"That was crazy," Wutang whispered to Jin. "You could have gotten yourself killed."

Jin shrugged. "I didn't think, I just reacted."

"Thank you," Jake added softly. "That was brave."

"And that is one very bad dude," Sheldon said, bringing up more images. "I've done more searches on him in the past hour. His real name is Cormac Ryker, he's ex-Special Forces, and there are rumors of discharge for the Al Anbar incident." He brought up images of a newspaper article. It was undeniably him. "Went into private security for a while, then disappeared off the map. Probably a hired killer now."

Jake's skin prickled at Sheldon's description. *Hired killer.* The Assassin Market. "And how do you know each other?"

He needed to know everything they knew before he told them more. It was still possible this was part of an even more elaborate trap. The feeling of being stuck in a mirror maze was stronger than ever.

Who to trust?

An hour ago he'd put all of his trust into Agent Tolliver, who was apparently an assassin, Cormac Ryker. Should he trust these kids? Sean had trusted Jin. And she'd saved Jake's life—that he was sure of.

"We're friends." Jin adjusted herself on her chair while Wutang packed up the first aid supplies. "But I only met Sheldon in person yesterday when we flew into New York after one of our gang turned out to be a plant for the Chinese army, or some splinter group."

"The Chinese army?"

Jin nodded. "We discovered evidence of a hacking program that was spoofing people, a network of digital corporations linked

244

to the Assassin Market."

"Not just spoofing," Wutang added, "masquerading as people in phone calls, infiltrating the human network. Impersonating Chinese officials, buying political influence. At first we thought it was a program of the PLA cyber division, but now..." His voice trailed off. Obviously he wasn't sure how much he should say either.

So it was happening in China as well. "And that's why you came to find me?"

The hint of a sad smile tugged at the corners of Jin's mouth. "I like you, Jake. I know we only met once, but I followed your social media. Felt like I knew you. That's why I had a feeling you were being set up. But that's not why we're here."

"Then why?"

Jin looked Jake straight in the eye. "Because whoever is behind this, they killed my cousin to cover it up."

Jake returned her stare. "They killed my friend Sean."

"I know, Sean was my friend, too," Jin said softly.

"I don't have time for this." Jake got up and stared out of the front windows, at the NYPD headquarters across the street. "I need to do something. They've got my daughter."

"Who does?" Jin asked.

"Bluebridge, it kidnapped her. That's why I was meeting with Tolliver...Cormac, whatever his name is."

"My God, I'm so sorry," Jin whispered. "We had no idea. Why did they kidnap her?"

"To stop me."

"From what?"

"I don't know!" Jake slammed the window. "No demands. No ransom. They just took her." He turned to them. "Why did you drag me here?" It didn't seem like the best place to hide out. Exposed. Up in the air. Only two central elevators and a staircase down on this wing.

Not many ways in or out.

Jake felt trapped.

"Because of that." Sheldon pointed out of the front windows at the windowless tower before them.

"And what's that?"

"Intergate Manhattan, the biggest high rise data center in the world. The entire facility is within the perimeter of 1 Police Plaza,

245

guarded by NYPD and Homeland Security. Bluebridge leases the top ten stories, nearly half a million square feet of server space. There are a couple of city blocks of computers up there. We want to know what it's being used for."

Jake had a pretty good idea. That *was* Bluebridge. It had to be its brain. "And it helps to be close to it?" What were these guys planning on doing? Scaling its walls in the dead of night?

"I've got some equipment inside Intergate, and"—Sheldon pointed at a mass of gear piled near the corner of the room, partially hidden under a paint-speckled bed sheet—"we're sniffing the microwave transmissions from the building."

He cocked his head to one side. "At least, we're trying. Those five-degree beam width dishes there"—he pointed at a collection of covered circular objects fixed to the side of the windowless building—"can be heard across a diameter of eighty-eight feet at this distance. We're at the edge of that here. They're using standard point-to-point tunneling protocol with WPA encryption on the data. We haven't had much luck figuring out what Bluebridge is up to, not yet. This is as good a center of operations as any."

Jake nodded as if he understood. It looked like they were gearing up, but for what?

"Why are they chasing you?" Wutang asked.

"Because I've got a copy of the Bluebridge core, and copies of the automated agent systems for half of the banks in Manhattan."

Sheldon whistled. "That would be worth chasing."

"But that's not the real reason." Jake stared at them. "You don't know, do you?"

"What?" Jin asked.

"Vidal Viegas has been dead for more than a year."

Sheldon didn't look the least bit surprised. "So that's why Montrose is spoofing him? He's taking over Bluebridge for himself? That makes sense."

Jake shook his head. "Not Montrose."

"Then who?"

Jake pointed at the building ahead of them. "Bluebridge has taken over itself."

36

Two Bridges Housing Project
New York City

It was dark now, and the lights of Manhattan spread a glittering carpet below their windows, the Freedom Tower shining like a beacon in the middle of the Financial District. Wutang and Jin slept on mattresses on the bare floor of the single bedroom off the main living area.

There was no way Jake could sleep. Not until he found Anna.

Sheldon sat in front of his computers, while Jake stared out the front windows at the high-rise data center in front of them.

Now that he knew Bluebridge inhabited the structure, he felt like he could feel its presence, like a malevolent spirit towering above them.

"So is this thing"—Jake took a moment to choose his word— "alive?"

Sheldon sucked in a mouthful of air. "That's a tricky question. One thing I can tell you."

"What's that?"

"Bluebridge is the DAC daddy, this thing has been spawning digital autonomous corporations like little baby Blues."

"So it's reproducing?"

Sheldon shrugged. "In a way, I guess. The problem we're really facing is that humans might be the last step in a billion-year biological bootstrap for digital super intelligences. A lot of people think intelligent machines are more dangerous than nuclear weapons."

"And what do you think?"

Sheldon stared out of the window at the Verizon Tower. "I think we're about to find out."

Getting up from his wall of monitors, he went to check the locks on the front door. He did it every twenty minutes, like clockwork. He went to the bathroom a lot as well, but Jake saw he was washing his hands.

The kid was OCD, but every psychological disorder had a pay-off. Obsessive-compulsive? Hey, you won't leave your doors unlocked. Paranoid? Don't worry about not reading the small print. Psychopath? Hey, at least you won't be worried about *anything* too much.

Any disorder could be useful in the right moment.

Before Wutang and Jin went to sleep, they'd exchanged stories about everything that had happened to them. Now they could piece together a timeline of events, paint between the lines.

It was a frightening picture.

Bluebridge had spread around the world, growing and spawning. A machine, but also part human as it embedded people into its web, empowering and employing the sociopaths of the world. Now they knew the pattern, they saw it emerging everywhere they looked.

"The tricky part is," said Sheldon as he returned from checking the locks, "what do you mean by 'alive'? Intelligent machines already surround us. Machine learning is built into everything from stock trading to the fuel injector in your car. You name it, it's programmed with intelligent software."

Sheldon sat at his computer station.

He was creating their own private darknet. What that meant, Jake wasn't sure, except that they'd use it to connect a direct link to the Mohawks up north. Dean said that pressure from the federal authorities was stepping up. Getting over the border to Canada wouldn't be possible anymore. No more escaping.

Every two hours Jake checked in with Elle. Nothing new on Anna.

Jake rubbed his temples, a headache thumped inside. "What I mean is, does it *think*?"

"You mean, is it self-aware? Conscious?"

"Yeah, I guess."

Sheldon tapped away on his keyboard, responding without looking at Jake. "That's an open question. Alan Turing proposed a test back in the 1950s—"

"The Turing test you were talking about?"

"That's right. Mr. Turing thought that if we could build a machine that could fool a human into believing it was a person, then maybe it *was* a person."

"And do you believe that?" Jake asked. "They said you built

248

chatbots that beat the Turing test. Do you think you built *people?*"
He had a hard time imagining that this slender neurotic kid was
playing God, but then, the whole world seemed to have been
turned on its head.

"Not that simple," Sheldon replied. "Thing is, I could build a
feed-forward zombie—totally without any consciousness or self-
awareness—that could fool you into thinking it was a person.
You'd have no way of telling the difference." He turned to Jake
and smiled. "I mean, how can *I* know that *you're* conscious and
self-aware?"

It wasn't meant as a question.

"You can't." Sheldon returned his attention to the computer
screens. "I think we're only going to understand consciousness
when we build machines that have it, just like we only really
understood flying by building flying machines. Personally, I think
consciousness is an accidental by-product, a feedback loop to
conserve resources."

"So then you think this thing is self-aware?" Jake asked.

"Maybe," Sheldon replied, "maybe not." He shook his head.
"But it doesn't matter. One thing I can tell you—Bluebridge *is* a
person."

Jake was confused. "How can you be so sure?"

"Because it's embodying a corporation. Bluebridge is an
incorporated entity under Delaware law, and this thing *is*
Bluebridge. You can get hung up on self-awareness, but what
really matters is that a corporation *is* a person." Sheldon scowled.
"And a dangerous one."

"I realize that."

"No, I don't think you do. When a human person kills
someone, they get prosecuted, thrown in jail. Guess what happens
when a 'legal' person in the form of a corporation kills someone?"

Jake didn't hazard a guess.

"They pay money," Sheldon continued, "that's pretty much
what happens. When a corporation kills people, it pays fines.
Ironic, isn't it? Pure capitalism, taken to a new level."

Jin appeared from the bedroom, stretching.

"So if Bluebridge is a person, then what sort of person is it?"
Jake mused, leaning back in his chair.

"If we did a personality test," Jin replied, coming to sit down
with them, "my guess is, it would come up as a psychopath."

Jake hadn't expected an answer to his question, but it made sense. Max said the same thing just before he died. Psychopaths were something Jake had experience with. Something he understood.

"Careful," Sheldon said to Jin, "don't go anthropomorphizing."

"Meaning?" asked Jake.

"Greek. To make something in our human image. Like when you imagine God, you think of a grandfather in the sky, but that's not God. God is indescribable, like these new machine intelligences are to us. You can't think of it in human terms. It doesn't have an ego, it doesn't want to dominate the herd and gain power." Sheldon turned to Jake. "And you can't think of it as evil. We do that, and we'll never figure out how to take it down."

Sheldon pressed his hands together, as if he were praying. "The problem is, when we moved from rule-based systems to machines that learned from statistical inferences based on huge data sets, we opened Pandora's Box. They don't operate according to rules anymore. Not rules we understand."

Jake got up from his chair. The pressure built inside his head. "You're giving me a headache, you know that?" He was tired of discussing philosophical points. "I don't care what it is. I want my daughter back." There were still some things he didn't understand. "How is this thing able to tap into everything?"

"Easy," Sheldon replied. "Ever heard of the NSA's TAO division?"

Jake shook his head.

"Stands for 'tailored access operations.' This branch of the US government has a secret product catalogue for ways to snoop and break into anything—monitor mobile phones, get into your computer to look at your screen, log your keyboard strokes. I'd bet Bluebridge has its own TAO catalogue on speed dial."

Jake pointed at the building in front of them. "I want to kill it. Can't we bomb that building?"

"You really want to bomb a federally protected building?" Sheldon laughed.

"Maybe." Jake gritted his teeth. He always wondered how some crazy person ended up deciding that they wanted to bomb a building. Now he knew.

Sheldon's smile evaporated. "Not that simple. Sure, Bluebridge

250

has ten floors over there, but this thing is a distributed system. At minimum, your friend Sean designed Bluebridge the way any other large corporate system would be designed—with disaster recovery, hot back-up sites, business continuity planning. But at the same time, that's good news."

"How's it good news?"

"Because we know how this thing was designed. It's not magic. It was built from components and modules, wires and boxes, using standard design principles. If you blow up that building, it'll switch to its backup systems. I have no doubt it exists on thousands of computers all over the world, all backed-up and supporting each other."

"You're telling me we're the only ones who've noticed what's going on?" Jake's frustration mounted. How was it possible that it was up to them to stop this thing?

"We're not," Sheldon replied. "The group that grabbed Jin in Shenzhen? We're pretty sure they were the Chinese Security Ministry. They saw what happened to Yamamoto, then saw Jin digging into those digital corporations. Grabbed her to see what she knew. The CIA is trying to stop the assassin markets, but this is a whack-a-mole game. These autonomous corporations are spawning faster than anyone can stop them."

"I'm sure other people have noticed," Jin added. "Investors see something odd going on, but they turn a blind eye. They're making money. Greed is a powerful tool for making bad things invisible, and Bluebridge is wielding it perfectly."

Jake stared out the window at the building Bluebridge inhabited. "Max said we might be able to stop it if we can get top-level system access."

"Maybe," replied Sheldon. "We'd need Montrose or Viegas-level access, and they're not exactly around for us to try to convince them."

"Do we know for a fact that Montrose isn't alive?" asked Jin.

"No, we don't." Jake answered. "That is an extremely good point. Everything is circumstantial. Nobody has ever talked to this thing."

"You have," Jin pointed out. "When it was impersonating Sean, and then your brother."

"Sure, but it was pretending to be someone it wasn't," Jake replied. "We've never talked to *it*." He rubbed his eyes. "This thing wants profits, right? That we know for sure?"

Sheldon agreed, "Yes, but not necessarily all the stuff that *we* want profit for—power, pride, domination."

Jake walked closer to the windows and stared up at the rooftop of the building again. Could they destroy this installation, then find its backups, destroy them? No, it would be like the Hydra: chop off one head and two more would appear.

"Can't we hack into it, gain top-level system access? Sean always said that any system could be hacked."

"Possible in theory, but daunting in practice. I'd bet it would be harder to hack into than getting inside the Command and Control of the Pentagon. Getting through its network security is going to be like peeling a giant onion. With the stuff Sean gave you, I'd bet we could skin the first few layers, maybe get into its outside networks. But it knows we're coming, which makes things much more difficult."

Jake stared at the building in front of him. "So what do we do then?"

"I don't know. To get top-level access, you'd need it to give up," laughed Sheldon. "Voluntarily give you control. Maybe you should ask it."

Jake slammed a hand into the window. "Goddammit. This thing has my daughter, Sheldon."

Sheldon cast his eyes down. "Sorry, I didn't mean to—"

"Cormac Ryker said he didn't take her." Jake came and sat in front of the computer monitors. "So who did? And why the hell hasn't it asked for anything?"

"Because it doesn't need to," Sheldon ventured. "This thing doesn't follow normal rules. I'd guess that your daughter is some kind of insurance policy."

"Insurance?"

"Like if you blow the lid, if you attack it, it can get you to recant, spin a believable story of deniability. I don't know. But as long as it thinks you value your daughter above all else, it has leverage."

"Then what's it waiting for?"

"For this," Jin answered. She pulled up an image of Senator Russ, who was now going into the final legs of the presidential election. "Eight weeks and Bluebridge will have bought its way into the White House. After that, it'll creep into every corner of

252

the government from the top down."

"And not just here." Wutang appeared from the bedroom, rubbing his eyes. "This thing is corrupting governments all across the planet."

"So how do we fight back?" Jake pointed at Wutang and Jin. "You guys were smuggled in by the Yakuza." He pointed at Sheldon. "This guy builds chatbots." He pointed at himself. "I'm being hunted by the mafia and half a dozen Federal agencies."

"Actually, you made the top of the FBI's ten-most-wanted list this morning." Sheldon pointed to a webpage he brought up. Jake's name and face were at number one.

"That's not helping," Jin whispered.

"Sorry." Sheldon closed the browser window. "I'll finish getting our video link with Dean and Elle up." He shrugged an apology and buried his nose back into his work.

"Maybe we should use those automated trading algorithms Donovan gave you," Jin suggested. "Steal some money from the big banks, pay off the mafia. Then give Bluebridge what it wants, the copy of the core. Promise not to make any noise, beg for your daughter back."

Jake shook his head. "No, it'll never stop." He was getting to know this thing. The outline of an idea formed. "Wait, do you think *you* could use those trading algorithms?"

Jin nodded. "We'd need to hack into some of the trading centers of the largest banks in Manhattan, but I know my way around. I could figure out a way."

Jake turned to Sheldon. "And you think you understand some of that code Sean gave us, the Bluebridge core? Could we get it running ourselves?"

Sheldon stopped typing. "Maybe. We'd need an entire data center, fat pipes into the internet." He frowned. "And it would have to be somewhere you could defend, physically. Like I said, this thing knows we're coming for it."

"Let me worry about that."

"What are you thinking?" Sheldon asked.

"You said it, Sheldon. This thing doesn't have an ego; it doesn't want power or revenge. It wants money. That's exactly what Elle told me." He laughed, and then turned to Jin. "*Remember the nuggets*, that's what Sean told you, right?"

Jin's eyes were wide with curiosity. She didn't know where he

253

was going with this. "What?"

"Sean said you need to look beyond what you *think* someone wants. If you do that, you're projecting, exactly like Sheldon said. We need to get to what it's really after." Jake stood and grabbed Jin's arm. "Nuggets, that's what this thing wants. Nuggets."

Jin exchanged glances with Sheldon and Wutang, all of whom looked at Jake like he'd lost it. "Maybe you should sit down."

The three screens in front of them lit up, casting the four of them in a soft glow. Dean appeared on one screen, and Elle on another. "Ah, my video link is up." Sheldon turned their audio feeds on.

"Jake, is everything okay?" Elle asked through the video link.

"Everything is fine," Jake replied, nodding at Dean and Elle on the two screens. "I know what we need to do."

AUGUST 26th

Friday

37

Kahnawake Indian Reserve
Quebec

Dean rubbed his eyes, and despite the fear gnawing in the pit of his stomach, he yawned. "I sure hope you know what you're doing," he said to Sheldon over the video connection.

"Me too," Sheldon replied.

Between arguing over Jake's idea and starting the work to implement it, it had been a long night. Locked inside, Dean had little sense of time, but from the way his body was waking up, he guessed it was midmorning. The small hours were the worst, when his mind screamed for sleep, his eyes drooping. But when he stayed up all night, the fog had usually worn off by noon; his body accepting that sleep would come in the next cycle.

Dean hadn't told his body yet that it wouldn't get sleep the next night, either.

The Link Room in the Mohawk Institute of Technology, the corridor between Server Rooms C and D, was usually empty, with nothing inside except the LCD panels fixed to the cinder-block walls, waiting for customers who needed to plug in and connect to the network. Now it was full of equipment. Dean's technicians had worked all night to wire up a new server farm in here. This was going to be the command-and-control center of their operation.

He'd also cleared off everything from the servers in sections A through C, sending out terse emails to inform his online casino customers of the temporary interruption in service. He rerouted most of the service through the Mohawk datacenters in Gibraltar, Singapore and London, but it was still a breach of their SLAs— service level agreements. The penalties were piling on fast, but if this didn't work, then it wouldn't matter. Nothing would.

In the parlance of his casino clients, they were going 'all in.'

Dean had initialized an instance of the Bluebridge system core on a cluster of servers in Server Room A. He'd created a private cloud, disconnecting all outside lines except for one, the blue CAT-5 cable snaking under his chair. This was plugged into a single machine hosting a dedicated VPN channel to Sheldon in New York.

"You sure this is secure?" Dean asked.

"Nothing's secure," Sheldon replied. "But it's as good as we're going to get. Stop worrying so much."

"Easy for you to say," Dean muttered. Sheldon wasn't sitting on top of this powder keg.

Dean watched the Bluebridge system develop on his private cloud of two hundred servers. It would outgrow Server Room A in the next hour. It started with a hundred gigabytes, but Bluebridge was a learning system, and Sheldon was busy feeding it. Except this wasn't Bluebridge, this instance of the system they'd named MOHAWK, and MOHAWK was coming to life before Dean's eyes.

"You need to fight fire with fire, isn't that what they say?" Sheldon remarked, busy typing away on his end.

"They, whoever *they* are, have never sat in *this* chair." Dean did some quick calculations on a piece of scrap paper. By the end of the day, MOHAWK would occupy his entire datacenter. Fighting fire with fire sounded like a recipe for all-out escalation warfare.

Jin appeared over Sheldon's shoulder in the video feed. "Sun Tzu said that if you use fire in battle, you better make sure that you're not flammable yourself."

"It's feeling pretty damn hot already over on this end," grumbled Dean.

Sheldon laughed. "I guess we'll find out which proverb wins soon enough."

A ringing sound startled Dean, who at first thought some alarm had been triggered. When he realized it was the front desk downstairs, he punched the 'answer' button on the VOIP application on his laptop screen.

"Doug Hamer is here to see you," came Angela's voice, the security guard at the entrance. "6—2—3," she added.

Dean had given her a one-time pad, told her to keep it in her purse and keep it secret. He hadn't told her why, but she trusted that he had a good reason. He pulled out the matching pad from his pocket and peeled off the top sticker, "6—2—3," it read. It was his jury-rigged method of trying to manually ensure secure communications.

Doug Hamer was the junior RCMP liaison dating his daughter. Nice guy. But Dean was a little busy.

"Can you tell him I'm not available?" Dean replied, pulling up the video feed from the camera in the front office. It was Doug, all right, standing in jeans and a black-and-red-checkered lumberjack coat, staring up at the camera.

"He says it's urgent, and it'll only take five minutes."

Dean sighed, stretching his neck back. "Sure, I'll be out in a second."

Logging off, Dean shut down his laptop and grabbed the Bluebridge memory key out of the USB slot of the desktop tower in front of him. After flashing his badge past the RFID sensor and keying his thumb onto the biometric sensor, he opened the door to the Link Room and walked out, heading down the corridor.

Doug seemed like a nice guy. He was three years older than Dean's daughter, but Dean was okay with it. He hadn't seen Doug since that time with Jake in the Kicking Horse Saloon. No sign of him at their last family barbeque, but Dean hadn't asked his daughter why. Figured Doug was busy. Having a future RCMP officer in the family wouldn't be such a bad thing. He opened the door to the waiting room with a smile on his face, "Doug, nice to see—"

"Don't move." A man in an expensive-looking suit held a gun level with Dean's eyes. Two more heavyset men in suits stood behind him, flanking Doug, while a fourth jumped forward to prop open the door Dean came through.

"What is this, Doug?" Dean sputtered.

The man who jumped for the door secured it and turned to Dean, grabbing his arms. Dean felt the cold metal of handcuffs against his skin, and then the click-click-click of them ratcheting shut. The man in front of Dean holstered his weapon.

"You can't arrest me." Dean stared at Doug in disbelief as he was shoved forward. The RCMP had no jurisdiction here.

"Sorry, Dean, I had no choice," Doug replied, his face beet red. "These guys, they're—"

"This isn't an arrest," said the man who'd pulled the gun on Dean. "I believe you'd call this a rendition."

"For what?"

The man shrugged. "Weapons smuggling, racketeering, harboring terrorists, take your pick." He turned to the two men at the door. "Take him outside, get him in the car. We're going into the server rooms."

They shoved Dean forward again, and he cursed, "Get your goddamn hands off me." One more push and he was out the door, blinking in the morning sunshine. A black Cadillac was parked in the gravel out front.

But that wasn't the only vehicle out there.

Parked on each side of the Cadillac were dark blue Dodge Chargers with 'Peace Keepers' stenciled in red across their sides. Mohawk Peace Keeper officer Daniels sat on the hood of one of the cruisers, smiling. "What do you think you're doing?" he asked the men holding Dean's arms.

"Get out of our way," barked one of the men behind Dean.

From behind the police cruisers, five men in camouflage stood, black masks over their faces, holding large assault rifles.

"I don't think so," Peace Keeper Daniels replied.

The door behind Dean opened, and the man who'd pushed the gun in his face came flying out, tripping down the stairs into the gravel to thud against the door of the Cadillac. More men in camouflage poured in through the door. They must have come in through the back entrance. They pushed the men in suits down the stairs and surrounded them.

Daniels smiled at Dean, who was still handcuffed on the landing. "Guess it's time to call up the Mohawk Warriors, eh?"

38

Little Italy
New York City

Jake stared up into the rain, tipping his umbrella sideways to see the street sign.

This was it, Mulberry Street.

He looked up and down Canal Street to his left and right. Even in the rain, the street vendors were still out, selling their fakes. Jake came on foot through China Town. It wasn't more than a ten-minute walk from the Two Bridges apartment complex. Nobody took pictures in the rain. His umbrella concealed his face, so it was safer than risking the subway or getting in a taxi.

And it was good to get some fresh air.

A call came in from Dean before Jake left. Some kind of Federal US agents had tried to raid the MIT building and arrest him. The Mohawk Peace Keepers had politely showed them, from behind assault rifles, to the edge of the reservation. Dean said the DHS had stepped up border security and started drone flights over the reservation.

Eamon and Elle checked in every few hours with updates.

They were scouring the Albany and Schenectady area, targeting property lists that Jin had generated of buildings owned by Bluebridge or one of its affiliates. It was a formidable task. There were hundreds of buildings on the list.

What did Bluebridge want? Was it hoping he'd stay still? Not react? How was that possible? Then again, the thing was a machine, maybe it didn't understand the implications of what it was doing, didn't consider the emotional reaction it was provoking.

But maybe it did.

Jake hadn't slept. Had barely eaten. All he could think about was Anna.

Sheldon was working at trying to track down the source of the anonymous messages, the videos of Anna delivered every two hours without fail. She looked happy enough, and at least they knew she was alive—assuming that was really Anna in those images. It was something nobody said but everyone knew.

The federal agents, drones, the DHS, Jake's topping the FBI's ten-most-wanted-list—Bluebridge was bringing the full weight of the United States government to bear. The gloves were off. Which meant Bluebridge saw them as a serious threat. There was no way out but to move forward.

Pulling up the lapels on his jacket, Jake hunched over and jogged across Canal Street, splashing through puddles. He turned into Little Italy.

In less than a week, the San Gennaro festival would begin, the colorful celebration of the Patron Saint of Naples Little Italy held each fall. Already the decorations were up; the red-white-and-green arches stretching over Mulberry Street into the rainy distance, lined with Italian flags. Jake made it a tradition to bring Anna here each year. She loved the lights, the excitement.

Thinking of Anna felt like ice poured into his veins. Where was she? He hoped to God she was all right. *I'm coming, baby*, he said to himself. *I'm coming as fast as I can.* A gold cross was affixed to the wall between two shops, and Jake muttered a prayer as he passed, his knuckles white around the umbrella's handle.

Was he doing the right thing? Maybe he should try to steal the money for Joey Barbara using the bank algorithms, pay him off that way. But what were the chances he could get away with that, with all the attention already focused on him?

Even so, some part of him felt it was the better bet, but he couldn't let himself go down that road. Bluebridge was a problem that wouldn't go away. Fear knotted in his stomach. What did it feel like when a psychopath made a decision? Did they rationalize their choices like he was doing?

If Bluebridge effectively won the American presidency, as it was on its way to doing, it would become impossible to defeat. And if it still had Anna then, there might be no way of getting her back.

They still didn't know what happened to set this in motion. Had Montrose seen his creation as some sort of ultimate hedge against death? People like him were so obsessed with themselves that it wasn't death that they feared the most, but being forgotten.

Had this been his way of extending his digital life beyond his physical death? Were they fighting what amounted to a digital ghost?

Jake watched the addresses as he walked. He stopped. 132 Mulberry Street, the address scrawled on the piece of paper in his hand. He expected some hole in the wall, a dingy basement bar or dimly lit Italian restaurant with stained glass windows. Instead, he found himself staring through the polished windows of the Cannoli King, brightly lit rows of fresh pastries beckoning him inside.

Opening the door, Jake made for the counter to ask for Joey Barbara. A waiter in a bright white apron headed him off, squinted at Jake and then flicked his chin toward a set of stairs at the back.

Jake arched his eyebrows and pointed at the stairs. *There?* A sign hung across the stairs, 'This Section Closed.'

The waiter nodded.

Jake walked to the back, past the only other people in the place, a couple making eyes at each other. They didn't notice Jake. Shaking the rain off his umbrella, he jogged up the stairs two at a time.

"Ah, Mr. O'Connell," Joey Barbara announced as Jake cleared the last steps of the curving staircase. The short man sat alone in the middle of the top floor of the shop, a half-dozen rows of straight tabletops to each side of him.

A hand shot out and stopped Jake. It was Tomasz, the big guy Jake had punched in the abandoned warehouse. Jake tensed, waiting for a blow, but Tomasz grinned menacingly and patted him down.

"Can't be too careful." Joey Barbara waved Jake over to sit with him. He looked out the windows. "Nothing better than a cannoli and espresso on a rainy afternoon." A half-eaten pastry sat on a plate in front of him. "You want one?"

Jake approached cautiously. "Sure, why not." If Barbara wanted to kill him, there were easier ways than poisoning.

"Sit, sit," Joey Barbara commanded as Jake hovered. "You know, next week they have a cannoli eating competition here to kick off the San Gennaro Festival."

Jake sat down, and a waiter appeared with a pastry and espresso, as if by magic. "I know, I bring my daughter every year."

"I'm sorry about your daughter." Joey Barbara grimaced. "We

had nothing to do with that. In fact, we looked into it. Nothing." He shrugged. "But now that we're through with the pleasantries…where's—my—MONEY?" The tendons in his neck flared out, spittle flying onto Jake's cannoli.

"I don't have it," Jake answered quietly.

"He doesn't have it?" Joey Barbara laughed, looking up at Tomasz. When he looked back at Jake, the red in his face was fading. "You know, the only reason you're not wearing cement boots at the bottom of the East River is because Mr. Shintao of the Yamaguci-gumi clan insisted on your safe passage." He looked at Tomaza again. "The frickin' Yakuza, I mean, who is this guy?"

"I have a proposal for you," Jake said, louder this time.

"A proposal?"

Jake nodded. "A proposal."

Joey Barbara leaned over and picked up Jake's cannoli, then hurled it against the wall. "The only proposal I want to hear is that you have my money, do you understand?"

Jake didn't flinch. "I'm going to get you ten times your money back, but I need your help. This thing that's chasing me, it'll wreck your business. It's already affected the Yakuza. That's why Mr. Shintao is supporting us."

Joey Barbara pressed his hands to his temples as if he was trying to keep his brain from exploding. "I want my money."

"And you'll get it," Jake continued. "Or do you want to go back to the Five Families, the Chicago Outfit, the"—he paused, trying to remember—"A-Team, the Clerkenwell Syndicate, and tell them that you turned down ten times the money? Then explain how you let this thing loose on the world? You choose."

"You got ten seconds." Joey Barbara slumped into his chair, sighing. "Ten seconds to convince me not to turn you into the feds right now and collect the million-dollar bounty on your head."

"You're related to Lucky Luciano, right?" asked Jake.

"What does that have to do with anything? Sure, he's like my great-great-uncle or something."

"He fought for his country when it was in trouble, used the mafia to protect the docks, carry out hits against Nazi spies."

"Real patriotic. It got him out of jail. So what, you want protection from something?"

"Sort of." Jake picked up his espresso and took a sip. "You

264

said the real criminals were the Wall Street types, like me. Right?"
He waited for Joey Barbara to nod. When you were selling
something, you had to get them nodding. "How about a chance to
give the Wall Street guys a bloody nose, get ten times your money
back, and be patriotic at the same time?"

"I sense that there's maybe a catch here somewhere. You got
five more seconds."

"Vidal Viegas is dead." Jake pulled a plastic bag from the
pocket of his coat and unwrapped it, pulling out the death
certificate and laying it on the table.

"I saw that dirt bag at a fundraiser my cousin Ricky made me
go to last week and—"

"Over a year ago." Jake pointed at the date on the document.

Joey Barbara leaned in to have closer look. "That's just a piece
of paper."

"It is, but it's the first page of a book."

"You trying to be clever?"

Jake leaned back in his chair. "Do you like ghost stories, Mr.
Barbara?"

AUGUST 29th

Monday

39

Financial District
New York City

Chase Rockwell stared out the seventieth-floor window-wall of his corner office, the rain clouds at eye level. As the head of the private client division of one of Manhattan's largest banks, his office befitted his position. A thousand square feet of open space, the walls adorned with Renoir and Degas, with his desk and the attending chairs tucked away at one end. The voluminous empty space—some of Manhattan's most expensive per square foot—said what was needed without a word being uttered.

When he looked down at the people hurrying by on the streets below, they were like ants at his feet.

Situations like this needed to be handled with care, with his personal deft touch. As few people as possible involved, but as many as required if blame had to be shifted. It was a fine line—one he'd carved many times before to skate past anti-laundering regulations while still respecting his bank's internal controls, and always ensuring his actions were within the range of reasonable deniability.

The Senate sub-committee of the Office of the Comptroller of Currency flagged sixty trillion dollars in suspicious transactions this year, over 30,000 accounts that they were looking into. Chase knew. He'd personally picked the financial lobbyists who worked with them.

The Financial Round Table had five lobbyists for every member of Congress, and they made sure the sub-committee made it their job to check each and every suspicious transaction, no matter how obscure.

Sixty trillion dollars made for a lot of transactions to wade through. Sure, every now and then a bank would get caught in illegal activity, lose a few accounts or have to close an off-shore subsidiary, but the government had to find something from time to time, otherwise it would be *too* suspicious. Acceptable losses,

269

just like drug runners who knew a certain percentage of their shipments would be caught—but 90% still made it through.

It was just business.

Even if Chase got jammed up, there would never be more than a slap on the wrist. Before moving into this position, his previous bank had been caught 'red-handed' laundering money for the Mexican and Colombian cartels, setting up banks in the Caymans with hundreds of billions in deposits but without even one employee or a physical office.

The fees they'd generated from the cartels were astronomical. Even after they were caught, the fines the government imposed amounted to less than two percent of the profits for that year. They didn't even have to admit to any wrong doing, even though they acknowledged breaching the Bank Secrecy Act. No charges were ever laid. "Too big to indict," were the words the *New York Times* used to describe what had happened. Not Chase's words, but he liked them.

He kept the *Times* article in his desk drawer, took it out from time to time.

And smiled.

The government was pragmatic.

That was the truth.

Organized crime was an integral part of modern democracies, their illicit earnings enabling them to win transportation and construction contracts by lowering their bid prices. In a way, organized crime helped subsidize the infrastructure of the nation.

Sometimes organized crime even helped save banks. Back in 2008, money from organized crime was the only liquid investment capital available to many banks when the legal financial system went into cardiac arrest. Chase liked to think of organized crime as the secondary system, the shadow market that helped support the world from below.

You had to be pragmatic about it. Chase liked the word *pragmatic*. He used it a lot.

The Mexican and Colombian cartels were fading in importance, however, and most of them had already chosen their favored bankers. It was time to look to growth, to new markets, and the Eastern Europeans—newly minted EU members with strong organized crime networks that spanned the Eastern and Western worlds—were the future.

The Albanian mafia—the *Shqiptare*—was a hybrid organization, incorporating both criminal and political wings. Chase liked that. Very pragmatic. They also dominated the world trade in illegal organs. In polite company, Chase would frown and say how disgusting it was, but to be honest, he might need a new liver one day. This was a good contact to have.

The door to his office opened. "Mr. Lluca is here," announced his secretary.

Chase let his widest and warmest smile spread across his face. "Ah, Mr. Lluca, a real pleasure." He strode across his office, hand out.

A stooped old man stepped through his door, his hair disheveled, his suit wrinkled. "Yes, yes," the old man muttered, waving away Chase's offered hand.

Chase's secretary closed the door behind the old man, pausing to glance at Chase.

Chase nodded at her, his lips pressed together. *Close the door and mind your own business*, his answering glare said. Chase dropped his hand, smoothing it on the leg of his three-thousand-dollar bespoke Saint Laurie suit.

"This way," he said, indicating the chairs at the other end of his office.

The old man ambled forward, grumbling something in a language Chase didn't understand. He assumed it was Albanian. He watched the old man. Was this really the head of one of the most violent criminal organizations on the planet? Chase wondered how many people this old man had killed, but he had a hard time fitting that image onto the broken wreck shuffling across his carpet.

Then again, when people looked at Chase in his fine suits and polished shoes, they couldn't imagine the monster lurking behind the Windsor knot. He shrugged and walked past the old man to sit on the front of his desk.

"Would you like some coffee?" Chase asked. "A bottle of water, perhaps?"

Lluca settled into the chair and groaned. "No, something stronger. Whiskey?"

"Of course." Chase hit his intercom button. "Micah, please bring in the Abelour and two tumblers and ice."

"No ice," grumbled the old man as Chase closed the

connection.

"You come with some excellent personal introductions, Mr. Lluca." The day before, senior people in the Genovese family had contacted Chase's assistants, leading to a conversation with Mr. Joey Barbara himself.

Mr. Lluca sighed loudly and looked up at Chase with watery blue eyes. "My family needs a…*safe*…place to invest some funds."

"Of course."

The far door opened, and Micah appeared with a tray. She walked over and deposited the 40-year-old single malt scotch and tumblers, offering to pour them each a glass. Chase held up two fingers. She poured them and left quickly, closing the door behind herself.

"I understand, Mr. Lluca. I have a lot of experience in this. And I guarantee we can accommodate you, with few questions asked." Chase handed one of the tumblers to Mr. Lluca. "*Gezuar*," he toasted. He'd looked up the Albanian word for *cheers*.

▲▼▲

Jake's father, Conor, stared at the smug expression on Chase Rockwell's face and lifted his glass of whiskey.

"Cheers," he replied, and drank it down in one gulp. Jake hadn't mentioned anything about not getting a drink on his rounds. Free forty-year-old scotch was a nice bonus.

"More?" Chase Rockwell asked.

Conor nodded. "Da." He wasn't sure if that was Albanian, but he was pretty sure Chase would be equally clueless.

Chase poured more scotch, half-filling the tumbler this time. Conor smiled.

Chase thought he was a trout chasing a fat fly.

Time to reel him in.

"I can only make a small deposit to begin with," Conor said, taking another gulp from his glass. "But I can assure you, more is coming." He did his best to ape a Russian accent. He wouldn't win any Oscars, but then, this wasn't the most discerning audience.

"Do you have any idea how much?" Chase asked. "It would help in deciding how to structure, well, how we would handle this arrangement."

"I have the information, but I cannot give this to you. Not yet."

They stared at each other.

"Any information you share with me, it would—"

"Young man, you will do as I ask, yes?"

Conor saw the flash in Chase's eyes, a fleeting glimpse of the demon that raged behind this suited patsy. He knew it well. He could recognize things in the way people walked, whether someone was weak. It was fun to target someone more challenging.

Time for the magic.

"I must go," Conor said after a pause. He finished his whiskey. "I will send a wire this afternoon with instructions."

Getting up, he groaned and let his coat fall to the floor. Chase jumped forward to help, but Conor waved him back. Leaning over, he grabbed his coat. At the same time, he dropped a memory key onto the floor, to the side of the chair.

He straightened up.

"Thank you, Mr. Rockwell," Conor said, extending his hand. Chase's eye flickered down. Chase saw the memory key, but was choosing not to say anything.

Chase shook Conor's hand. "A pleasure, Mr. Lluca."

Conor turned and made for the door, smiling.

He had five more appointments.

Five more whiskeys waiting for him.

40

Two Bridges Housing Project
New York City

"Four for four, baby!" Sheldon whooped, turning from his computer screens to high-five Jake. "Your old man is a frigging genius at this."

Back in the apartment overlooking the Brooklyn Bridge, Jake stood and watched while Sheldon worked his machines. The once-pristine space was now strewn with take-out containers and cans of Coke.

Jake smiled wryly. It was the first time he'd heard anyone say anything nice about his father. He would have never considered using his dad for this, but Eamon had convinced Jake to give the old man a chance. "Yeah, he is good at fooling people."

"Beautiful," Sheldon added, turning back to his computer monitors. "We're already getting ping-backs. Our Trojan is *in* at Commerce Bank." He grabbed a piece of pizza. "Like I told you, the higher you go in the executive food chain, the less they think the rules apply to them. How many times do you think these guys have been drilled by their security group—*do not stick a memory key from an unknown source into your computer?*"

Jake played along. "How many?"

"A million times. But drop the right lure in front of their noses, and *whammo!* With all that equipment guarding those banks it'd be like getting into Fort Knox, but these guys are handing over the keys."

"Won't they detect it?" Jake asked. This was all new to him.

"Eventually. But average detection times are on the order of weeks, and we only need days. We'll work sideways through the network, from private banking into the production servers. Shouldn't take more than a few hours. Detection will be hard because we're not trying to exfiltrate data."

"Exfiltrate?"

"I mean we're not trying to steal information. What we're

274

going to do is modify data on a minute level that's hard to detect," Sheldon explained. "If you knock a system down, it's easy to locate the 'problem' and stop it. But making small changes here and there? That's much more tricky. People don't usually do what we're doing."

"Meaning what?"

"There are three main types of attackers in cyberspace. Nation-states are usually interested in espionage. They want information, but don't want to mess with the system. Then you have criminals. They want money, and again, don't want to mess with the system. The third are hacktivists. They want attention." Sheldon turned from his computers. "We're in a whole new category. We're going to rock and roll." He smiled. "Literally."

"Sheldon, I wanted to ask you something." Jake sat.

"Sure, anything." Sheldon still had his attention locked onto the information flowing across his screens.

"Seriously, we need to talk."

Sheldon disengaged and turned to Jake. "What?"

"Why are you doing this?"

"Because I can." Sheldon shrugged.

"That's not an answer. This is dangerous. You could go to jail, even be killed. This isn't a game."

Now he had Sheldon's full attention. "I know that. I never thought it was a game."

Jake put a hand on Sheldon's arm. He needed to know. Anna's life depended on these people, and while Jake was thankful for their help, he couldn't figure Sheldon out. He didn't want any surprises.

He gripped Sheldon's arm tighter. "Why are you here? Jin's life is threatened, her cousin was murdered, and I understand why Wutang is here by her side. Me? I'm trying to save my little girl's life, figure out what happened to my friend."

Sheldon tried to pull away, but Jake held on to him.

"What, so now you think I have some hidden motive?"

"I don't know, Sheldon, you tell me." Did he want access to the Bluebridge systems? They didn't need a loose cannon, especially one as bright and technically competent as Sheldon.

"Okay, okay. Let go." Sheldon pulled his arm free and rubbed it. "I want to do my part, you know?"

"No, I don't know." Jake shook his head. "Explain it to me."

Sheldon rubbed his face. "My grandfather died last year; he was ninety-one years old. He fought on the beaches of Normandy. He volunteered. It seemed crazy to me, so I asked him about it. He said he was scared, terrified, but it was the right thing to do. To preserve freedom, our way of life. He said it was his generation's moment."

"And that's why you're here?"

"Yeah, I mean, I'm a scrawny nerd. I ain't going to be any help on a damned beach fighting the Nazis, but here"—he pointed at his computer screens—"here I can make a difference. This is my fight, my way to protect freedom. To do what my grandpa did." He wiped his eyes with the back of one hand.

What a crazy kid. A crazy good kid. "Okay, Sheldon, sorry. I needed to know. You're brave. Your granddad would be proud."

"Thanks." Sheldon's face lit up. His computer pinged. "Hey, can everyone get in here?" he called out, returning his attention to his monitors. "Because our darknet meet-and-greet session is on."

Eight video windows opened, spread across the three LCD panels in front of Jake and Sheldon. A face appeared in each of the windows, showing an array of young men and women. Wutang and Jin walked over from the kitchen, containers of noodles in their hands. Jin had been quiet all day. Her cousin Shen Shi's funeral was tomorrow, and she was still the main suspect in his death.

"Jake, Jin, Wutang, I'd like to introduce you to our Group of Eight," Sheldon said, bowing to the images on-screen. They smiled back.

"Are you guys some kind of famous hacker network?" Jake asked.

"Maybe soon," Sheldon laughed, "but I made up the name last night. Your friend Joey Barbara was helpful in getting us connected. Let me introduce you." He pointed to a dark-skinned boy with a wide face. "That's Mr. Imran Zkhaev of CyberVor, famous for the ID theft of a billion passwords last year."

The boy smiled on-screen and waved. He didn't look more than nineteen.

"A billion passwords?" Jake whispered to Sheldon.

"They're a Russian mob hacker collective based in Omsk, a small town between Mongolia and Kazakhstan," Sheldon whispered back. "We want to crack ID theft rings, they're the guys." He pointed to the person next to Imran and raised his voice. "And next we have Sasha of TeslaTeam in Serbia."

A young blonde girl waved and smiled.

"And what do they do?" Jake whispered.

"They're our connection into the Assassin Market."

"What?" Jake hissed.

"And next to Sasha we have Johnny Jones and cOsmo, representatives of the Anonymous and Chaos Club collectives."

The two men nodded. Their images flickered.

"Those are the old school," whispered Sheldon. "Our denial of service experts."

"Are those their real names?" Jake whispered back.

"Course not. The images we're seeing are modified as well." Sheldon raised his voice. "And across the bottom we have some of my associates, Justin, Lindsey, Joshua, and Phil."

"And they're hackers too?"

"No," Sheldon admitted, "not hackers. These are peers of mine who run network security for some Fortune 500 companies." He wagged his head. "Could be hackers if they wanted, but they have a whole different set of tools and expertise."

Sheldon turned back to the people on-screen. "You all know Mr. O'Connell and Jin and Wutang from the background information I sent you." He cocked his thumb at himself. "I'll be the point person coordinating our activities, but Jake's going to be the tip of the spear."

"Nice to meet all of you." Jake nodded and smiled. He'd never felt so out of his depth.

Wutang and Jin smiled and waved as well.

"Ladies and gentlemen," Sheldon said, starting his meeting, "as you can see from the data I've sent you, Bluebridge, one of the largest financial institutions in the world, appears to have gone rogue. It is the alpha DAC, the DAC daddy"—he sniggered at his own humor—"the top-level organism that has spawned a wave of other digital corporations that have infiltrated human and financial systems worldwide. It has landed in our laps to stop it."

"We're going to unleash a four-tier plan to degrade and destroy Bluebridge's freedom to operate while Jake and his team take out the head of the snake."

"First," Sheldon said, pointing at Imran and Sasha, "we'll begin

277

by 'outing' individuals who are working with the autonomous corporations. CyberVor and Tesla Team have already infiltrated several of them. We're going to offer up the names of these individuals to authorities. The goal here will be to spread a viral rumor that the anonymity shield of these organizations isn't absolute."

"The CIA and NSA are already hot on the heels of these things," added Wutang. "We're going to start drip-feeding them what we know, turn up the heat."

Sheldon nodded. "Exactly. And second"—Sheldon pointed at the Anonymous and Chaos Club team members—"we're going to unleash denial of service attacks against Bluebridge to try and slow it down a bit. At the same time, I want to get inside some of the large corporations Bluebridge invested in, start disrupting their systems."

Johnny and cOsmo nodded.

"And importantly," Sheldon said, nodding at his colleagues in the bottom row, "we need to protect MOHAWK, and that's what you guys are going to be doing. Keep the pipes open, layer security around it. I've distributed information about what we'll need from each of you. Have you read the materials?"

Sheldon waited for them all to nod.

"I need to keep the fourth part of our attack confidential for security reasons," Sheldon continued. "It's extreme, but these are desperate times. You'll know when it happens, because it will be front page news everywhere in the world."

He paused.

"Now's the time for anyone to back out. Once we start, there's no going back. If we fail, we'll be hunted down. Jail time or worse. Does anyone want to leave? No recriminations. I would understand."

This time Sheldon waited longer, but nobody budged or said anything. He smiled. "Good. Then we're all in this together. We have a lot of work to do."

He turned to face Jake and Jin and Wutang. "Our first phase of the operation begins tonight."

Cormac stood in the rain and stared up at the forty-floor,

windowless building in front of him. So this was the biggest high-rise data center in the world? It didn't look like much.

He looked down and shifted his gaze to his left, past the Brooklyn Bridge to the apartment complex beside it. This was as close as the old man had been able to pinpoint the current location of Jake O'Connell. From this point onward, he was going old school. Visual surveillance. The rain didn't help, but Cormac was patient.

There were eight buildings in the complex, over a thousand apartments, but it wouldn't take more than a day or two for him to survey them. Jake would need food, which meant deliveries of some sort, and Cormac knew what his girlfriend looked like—the one who'd rammed him with her bike at Rockefeller Center. And his employer had added a new target, Liu Wei. Apparently his friends called him Wutang.

Cormac's dance card was full up, but this would be it, at least for this employer.

A few days ago, Cormac received a message about the Assassin Market, a digital corporation operating on the darknet. It let people anonymously contribute cryptocurrency toward financing a hit on anyone in the world.

Cryptocurrency. It was a strange new world.

He'd almost dismissed the idea out of hand, but it attracted him. Operating independently, no boss, just the job. He would be like a force of nature, ridding the world of people who'd earned public ire. Already, there was a healthy list, starting with prominent bankers. The top-paying jobs were in the hundreds of thousands of dollars.

Yes, after this, he was going fully independent.

Finishing this job had become a point of professional pride. There was no way he was going to let Jake O'Connell get the better of him. Was it anger that fueled him? Maybe, if he had to be honest. Burned and bruised, he was going to be the laughing stock of his small group of peers if he stepped away.

What was Jake up to? Cormac didn't really care. All he cared about was ending him. He stared up at the windows of the apartments, their tiny lights glittering in the rain.

One of them held his prize.

AUGUST 30th

Tuesday

41

MSNBC Newsroom
New York City

"Are you serious?" Bill Waiters asked his junior White House correspondent.

"It's happening right now," Dan Rogers blurted back, his eyes wide.

He'd only been on the new post for a few weeks, and the senior correspondent was on vacation.

It was supposed to be a quiet week.

"The White House has been attacked?" repeated Bill, still trying to comprehend what Dan was telling him.

Dan nodded, his face white. "The Vice President has been killed."

A crowd of people gathered around them in Dan's cubicle in the MSNBC Dayside newsroom. He pointed at his computer screen. "I was talking to Jill Strasberg, the White House Communications Director, on a Skype link."

"I know who she is." Bill waved over the rest of his staff. "Is anyone else seeing anything?"

"Nothing, not a peep on the other channels," replied his head of programming from the back of the crowd. "They're still on the Luxembourg story, just like us."

In the background, Bill heard his MSNBC anchor talking about the flash crash in European markets the previous day, an incident centering in Luxembourg. It had wiped out billions of dollars, sending ripples through the financial systems worldwide. The markets were limping to a close on the other side of the pond.

Was it possible they had the first lead on this? An exclusive breaking story on maybe the biggest event since Pearl Harbor?

Bill's hand shook as he raised it over his head. "Everyone, get on this now. Start cuing the teleprompters." He turned back to Dan. Before they went live, he had to get further confirmation. "Can you get Jill back on?"

"I think so." Dan hit the 'video call' button on his screen. After two rings, it picked up.

Jill Strasberg's face filled the screen. "Bill, is that you?" she asked.

"It's me." Bill pushed Dan aside. He'd known Jill for years. She was the godmother to two of his kids. "What the hell happened? Are you all right?"

"I'm okay," Jill replied in a shaky voice. "We're locked down in the White House bunker. The attackers have cut down all the regular communication channels, so we had to go to back-up on the commercial networks. This channel is encrypted, right?"

Bill turned and looked at his staff members, most of them with blank expressions on their faces. One of the technicians in the crowd around the cubicle shrugged yes, he thought so. Bill turned back to Jill. "Yes."

He could see other White House staffers he recognized milling around in the background, one of them nodding at Bill as he passed.

"What can we do?" he asked Jill.

"The President wants to go live, wants to address the nation." Jill swung the camera around, and right beside her was the President, busy getting miked up. He glanced directly into the camera, nodded at Bill. Jill swung the camera around. "Can you do it, Bill?"

This was unbelievable.

"Bill, we got a hit on the AP newswire, reporting some kind of smoke and strange activity at the White House," said a voice from over top of the cubicles. "A buzz is starting in social media, but still nothing on any of the other networks."

Clenching his jaw, Bill Waiters made the most important decision of his career. This was the moment he'd been waiting for all his life. "Get this Skype feed into main production, we're going live in ten seconds."

▲▼▲

Under the MSNBC logo, the President's face filled the screen on the large display. His expression was calm and resolute, but his eyes were pained, bloodshot. A bandage was taped across the left side of his forehead, showing flayed red skin at its edges. His face was smudged, and the beginnings of a bruise seeped under his left eye. He looked battered, but not beaten.

"My fellow Americans, it is with a heavy heart that I need to inform you that the White House was attacked this morning, and the Vice President has been killed…"

Sheldon turned down the volume, pushing back his chair to send it skidding across the parquet wooden floors. "Ho—lee—cow, I can't believe we did this."

It was ten in the morning, but still dark outside under the heavy rainclouds. It hadn't let up in three days.

Jake stared at the President on the large screen. They'd spent a sleepless weekend planning this attack, plotting out every detail—but seeing it live on network television was stunning.

Wutang and Jin sat beside him, speechless. They'd spent most of the day to themselves. It was Shen Shi's funeral today. She hadn't even been able to talk to her mother.

The weekend had been agony for Jake. All he could think about was his little girl. At least the video images kept coming in. Elle called each time she got one on the phone. She and Eamon were still searching the building sites on Jin's list. It was reassuring to hear from Elle every two hours, to see the videos, but they still didn't really know if the images of Anna were genuine.

So Jake was forcing Bluebridge's hand. Pushing toward a different exit.

"Are you sure you're all still up for this?" Jake asked grimly.

"One hundred percent," Sheldon replied. "It's a good plan." He stopped pacing to put a hand on Jake's shoulder. "In fact, it's genius. Have you ever heard of fever therapy?"

Jake shook his head. "No."

"In the 1950s," Sheldon explained, "one of the first big studies of childhood leukemia was conducted. Untreatable back then, and usually fatal. Out of 300 cases, though, twenty-six went into spontaneous remission. Guess what happened in *every one* of the cases that had remission?"

"What?"

"A serious infection with a life threatening fever. This doctor, Coley, was the first to notice the connection. Made this thing called Coley's Toxins—nasty bacteria that could kill you. But if you've got a cancer in your system that will *definitely* kill you, then introducing a fever via a nasty bacteria isn't that much of a risk."

285

Jake shook his head. Sheldon was always going off on tangents, but he had to give it to him—the kid was a genius. In three days he'd managed to get the Bluebridge core up and working at the Mohawk facility. "So what did it do?"

"By inducing a massive fever, these bacteria triggered a heightened immune response to all threats in the system." Sheldon beamed at Jake. "Don't you see? That's exactly what we're doing. There's a cancer in the global organism, and we're going to poison it to trigger an immune response."

A tingling sensation crept from Jake's scalp into his fingertips—*we're poisoning the world*—then settled into a fluttering in his stomach. Sheldon's analogy was bang-on.

"I hope to God we don't kill the patient on the table," Jake said from between clenched teeth. What was that expression his dad loved to use? *In for a penny, in for a pound.*

He grabbed Sheldon's chair and moved it in front of the computers. "Sit down. It's time to inject more toxin. And get Dean on video chat."

▲ ▼ ▲

Chase Rockwell stared out his window at the rain, the lights of Manhattan visible at his feet through the fog and clouds. The excitement of the other day—meeting the disheveled patriarch of the Albanian mafia, and then reading the memory key the old man had dropped, which detailed his assets and holdings—had been replaced with a frenzy of conflicting news stories erupting across the world's media outlets.

But that wasn't what worried Chase.

The DOW Industrial Average plunged two thousand points in an hour, forcing regulators to close down trading early on the NYSE and even the NASDAQ. Already they were calling it the Terrible Tuesday Flash Crash. There had been another flash crash the day before on the Luxembourg Stock Exchange. That one they blamed on automated agents fouling up the high speed trading systems. The crash in New York had been caused by convulsions over the presidential spoofing on network television.

The problem was that Chase had to freeze their own trading systems in the melee, and when the NYSE and NASDAQ went offline, they were stuck. He wasn't sure where their accounts had ended up for the day. The potential exposure to financial losses was frightening, especially as it wasn't clear if the markets would open the next day.

A knock on the door.

"Come in," growled Chase, pulling his eyes from the rain-streaked windows.

His new intern's head peered around the corner of the door. "I have the results."

"Get in here, then."

Chase steeled himself for the worst.

He didn't really care about what happened to his clients. Sure, it would be better for PR if they didn't lose their shirts, but he was worried about his own personal funds.

His intern came in and closed the door, then walked toward Chase. Instead of looking scared, the little bastard was smiling.

Chase couldn't help noticing the brogues the kid wore. They looked like they were right out of Bloomingdales. When would someone have the sense to tell interns to spend $700 on a good pair of Gucci or Prada loafers? They lasted three times as long, and didn't make you look like a walking douche bag.

"What's the smile for?" Chase barked.

The kid's suit was a disaster as well, off the rack from Barneys or Bergdorf. What on Earth could he be smiling about? It was a bloodbath, one of the biggest single-day disasters Chase had ever seen on Wall Street—never mind the goddamn suit.

"Look at this," his intern replied, closing the last few feet and dumping the sheaf of print-outs into Chase's hands.

Chase ignored the cuffs on the kid's suit pants and focused on the numbers in front of his eyes. He blinked once, then twice. "When are these from?"

"Today. Right now," his intern replied. "Those new automated trading algorithms we installed a few months back, they react faster than any human—"

"Yeah, I remember." Chase studied the numbers again, his annoyance with the kid's outfit fading. For these kinds of numbers, the kid could come to work in a duck suit for all he cared. "Good work."

Grabbing the report, he turned and dismissed the intern with a wave of one hand.

"Thank you, sir." The intern hovered, then turned and started

287

out.

Chase smiled as he studied each line item.

In any storm, there were opportunities.

This was good.

His smile faded.

Maybe too good.

His smile returned. There was no such thing as too good.

Outside his window, lightning flashed.

42

Kahnawake Indian Reserve
Quebec

"Sorry, miss, but you're going to have to go around," Peace Keeper Daniels explained, pointing down the bridge's off-ramp, the one leading away from Kahnawake. "You'll have to take the 132 to the 30, not more than twenty minutes to get into Chateauguay."

The young lady in the Mazda hatchback was too keyed up to pay attention to his directions. "*Sauvages!*" she yelled in French, gunning the engine of her car and peeling away. She held her hand out the window, giving Daniels the finger to make it clear what she meant.

Savages.

She meant the Mohawks.

Shaking his head, Daniels straightened up and stared down the length of the Mercier Bridge past its towering metal gantries. It was the main connecting point to Montreal Island from this side of the St. Lawrence River, a million people on each side wanting to get across—and it was jam-packed with traffic moving at a crawl.

It was rush hour, but the real problem was that, last night, the Mohawks had blockaded the main highway artery that ran through Kahnawake and into the countryside beyond.

It was Peace Keeper Daniels's job to try and do just that, keep the peace.

Shielding his eyes from the setting sun, Daniels walked back to his cruiser and sat on its hood, waving traffic past, enduring the angry stares and comments from commuters.

Doug Hamer had texted him a warning the previous day, before the attack on Dean, so he alerted the local Mohawk Warriors as soon as a suspicious car pulled up to the Mohawk Institute of Technology building. Still, Daniels had never expected covert US agents would try to kidnap Dean.

289

Not in his wildest imagination.

Something was going on. Daniels hadn't been told what, but he trusted Dean. It wasn't just being Mohawk. They'd served together in the Marines. *Semper Fi.* Daniels didn't need an explanation, not if one wasn't offered.

It was a beautiful sunset, and he tried to enjoy it.

The Longhouse Elders had voted to enact the blockade last night. Daniels could understand their choice, and besides, he knew there was more to it than the Elders' refusal to sanction the auditing of their online casino business. Anyway, the Mohawks hadn't blocked the entire bridge, not like they'd done in 1990 in the land dispute with the government back then. This time they'd only blocked the off-ramp onto the highway that ran through their land.

The vehemence of the public reaction to having to take a detour was swift and nasty, the storm of public outrage directed at the Mohawks totally out of proportion. Barely twenty-four hours since they set up the blockades, and there were already scathing stories flooding Canadian and US media.

On the Canadian side, it was simple enough: people feared the economic sanctions that the US Congress threatened to impose. In the US media, it was a different beast. On many websites and in many publications, there was puritanical raging about breaking Federal gambling restrictions, even though the Mohawks weren't doing anything illegal.

Yep, thought Daniels, enjoying the last rays of sunshine, something big was afoot, but he trusted the Longhouse Elders. And he trusted Dean.

From the corner of his eye he noticed something out of place.

A truck on the bridge.

Khaki green.

Men running in front of it, scattering the traffic to one side.

"Oh, no," Daniels muttered under his breath. What were they doing here? How could it have happened so fast?

He opened the door of his cruiser and grabbed his radio.

▲▼▲

"What do you think, Mr. President?" Dean asked.

He sat in the middle of a bird's nest of wires and equipment

290

strewn around the Link Room in the MIT building.

The President of the United States pursed his lips, frowning. "This was premeditated. There's no way that they could have invoked Section 275 of Canada's National Defence Act so quickly."

Dean agreed. "Bluebridge must have seen this coming."

He got the call from Peace Keeper Daniels up on the Mercier Bridge. The Canadian Army—the 5th Mechanized Brigade—had arrived at the Mohawk blockade. Not long after, Dean received an email, forwarded from the Mohawk elected council, informing him that the Quebec Premier requested military support, and the Solicitor General of Quebec had agreed.

The speed of the government's reaction was as staggering as the public outcry. Dean had thought that the public would support the Mohawks, but it was the opposite.

They'd become isolated on the world stage.

Even worse, the snap decision by the Longhouse Elders to blockade Kahnawake had split the Mohawk nation itself. The elected council of the Mohawks, usually in tacit agreement with the traditional Longhouse Elders, didn't agree. They argued to open the blockades, to let the government in. The big problem was that Dean and the small group of Elders who knew the truth couldn't reveal the larger nature of what they were up to.

The outside world thought they were hiding something about their casino operations. It was too risky to reveal to the wider Mohawk community that they were trying to fight an indomitable artificial intelligence that had infected global networks. Nobody would believe them. Even attempting to explain would jam everything up. Right now they had to keep their attention on the job at hand.

"History is written by those who win the fight," added the President, talking to Dean on the video display window. "Focus on winning the battle."

"You're right, Mr. President," Dean replied, "but I gotta talk to Jake now, okay?"

The President nodded. "I'll stand by."

The other thing Dean couldn't reveal to the world was that they'd spoofed the President of the United States on live network television. MOHAWK functioned perfectly. The first synthetic personality they'd created was the President. There was an

291

amazingly rich and detailed amount of public data on which to base the character.

Dean had spent much of the last two days talking to the newly created President. At first he was disappointed with its clumsiness, but after a few hours the interactions became eerily human.

And then eerily perfect.

It worked flawlessly—the detail of the video broadcast on television that morning had been scary. His President had even done a question and answer session. It was as convincing as it could get.

After the broadcast, Jake suggested killing off this instance of the President, but Dean asked to keep it running. Dean liked talking to him. He found the President to be amazingly perceptive, great for troubleshooting. Someone he could talk to honestly and openly.

A congressional inquest into 'Fakegate'—as the media were calling the spoofed television broadcast—had already been announced, calling it an act of terrorism, but the firestorm it ignited was shaping up exactly as intended. The global stock markets had been sent into free-fall. But it wasn't really the stock prices that Jake and Jin had been after—it was the derivatives markets, the options market where people could place bets on the *future* values of stocks.

Jake's face opened in a video window after two rings. "You okay?"

Dean rubbed his temples and looked at Jake. He looked terrible—dark circles under his eyes, the purple bruises still there, one eye bright red where it had hemorrhaged. As battered as he looked on the outside, Dean knew Jake was doing even worse on the inside. "A bigger question is, how are *you* doing? Are you still getting those videos of Anna?"

Jake's scowl softened and he closed his eyes and sighed. "Yeah."

"You hang in there, Jake. This is going to work."

"Yeah, it's just—"

"I know… How's Elle?"

"She's good. She and Eamon are still searching, but they haven't found anything."

A video from Jake popped up in a message window on Dean's display. It was a television broadcast of a uniformed Canadian

292

Forces officer barking orders at a camouflaged Mohawk Warrior, their noses inches apart, up on the blockade on the Mercier Bridge.

The Mohawk didn't flinch or budge. Just stared straight ahead.

"Are you seeing what's happening on your bridge?" Jake asked.

Dean nodded. "I can't believe the media is there already."

"The media is always there," the President added quietly. "The vultures are always circling."

This situation could easily spiral out of control.

Young Mohawks flooded into Kahnawake from the other Mohawk nations—Akwesasne, Kanesatake, and many more—putting on black masks and jumping into the blockades. The simmering anger of past injustices that always burned just under the surface was boiling up, intensified by the public outrage being hurled at the Mohawks.

These weren't country rednecks manning the barricades. These were ex-Paratroopers, Rangers, Special Forces, and Marines, and they were armed to the teeth with smuggled weapons.

If Dean had thought he was sitting on a powder keg before, now he was sitting on a lit one.

"This has gotten a whole lot more dangerous than I realized it would," Jake said over the video link.

"Did you think Bluebridge wouldn't fight back?" Dean snorted. "I knew this was going to get messy."

Jake let go a long sigh. "Most of your people don't even know what they're fighting for."

Sheldon and Jin waved from the background, stuffing their faces with pizza. Dean waved back. "They know why they're helping. They're fighting for *their* people. I know we're trying to get your daughter back, Jake, but this isn't just your fight."

Jake looked away from the camera, then started slowly nodding before looking back. "Don't you find it even the smallest bit ironic that you're fighting to save the White Man's ass, even as he's trying to bust down your door?"

Dean smiled at that. "The White Man has no idea what we've done for him. I don't expect him to start realizing it now."

Jake laughed, but the smile dropped from his face.

Dean couldn't imagine how hard this had to be on Jake. "We're going to get her back."

In the video feed, Jake clenched his jaw. "We need you to keep

MOHAWK running for another day, maybe two. Can you hang on that long?"

Dean nodded. "I think so."

Another problem was that the food and gas suppliers had stopped doing their rounds today. They were even refusing to answer calls from Kahnawake. Bluebridge must have organized a boycott, but they had enough supplies to hang on for two days.

And it wasn't only the President they'd spoofed.

Sheldon's 'Group of Eight' were making good use of Jin's database of thousands of companies connected to Bluebridge—using MOHAWK to fake calls from directors to radio broadcasts, spoofing emails to investors, falsifying earnings reports. Anything to create chaos. The blogosphere had erupted in a secondary wave as some people recognized what was happening, but they didn't realize Bluebridge was being targeted.

Only Bluebridge knew that.

Part of its secret weapon was its ability to attend multiple, simultaneous meetings, and to do everything remotely through phone or videoconference. With this seemingly unstoppable wave of spoofing, companies and governments were starting to demand meetings in person.

The goal hadn't been to just send the financial markets into free-fall—the NYSE, NASDAQ, NIKKEI, LSE—but also to specifically target Bluebridge stocks. They'd also unleashed denial of service attacks against the websites of the major corporations Bluebridge invested in.

"Two more days," said Dean. "I can do two days."

"Keep your eyes on the prize, gentlemen," the President added.

Jake groaned, "Have you still got that thing running?"

"Yep." Dean nodded. He smiled. "Everyone should have their own leader of the free world."

Jin stuck her head in front of the camera. "Are we ready?"

"We've put the ball in the air," Dean said to Jin, "time for you to knock it out of the park."

"I'm going to make this thing suffer for what it did to Shen Shi." Jin smiled sadly. "Do you know what causes a financial crisis, Dean?"

"I don't know. Losing a lot of money?"

"No," she replied, "That's the result. The cause is fear, and I'm going to put the fear of God into the markets."

Dean stared at her. For a small Chinese woman, she sure could be frightening. "Good girl," he replied. Jin winked and moved out of the camera's view. "Do you need me anymore?" Dean asked Jake.

"Not for now. Why don't you take a break?"

Dean exhaled slowly. "Yeah, time for a smoke." He shut down the President, who nodded and said goodbye for now, and then Dean logged off.

He was alone in the Link Room. Dean had issued strict instructions that it was off-limits to anyone else. Walking out into the corridor, he exited to the back of the MIT building to stand on the second floor fire escape.

He lit a cigarette and took a deep puff, staring at the twinkling lights of the Kahnawake village past the trees in the distance, and then toward the Mercier Bridge and lights of Montreal that lit up the clouds in the sky.

Why hadn't Bluebridge tried to pin the President spoof on them? It seemed a direct way of applying more pressure. Bluebridge's choices didn't seem to make any sense sometimes, but then, as Sheldon kept insisting, it didn't think like a human.

So Kahnawake was under siege.

But they were Mohawks.

Their ancestors had taught them a thing or two about living off the land.

The thing Dean worried about was the data pipe that connected them to the rest of the world. It hadn't been cut off yet because the fiber optic cables that ran under Kahnawake supplied about half of the data throughput to Montreal, and a good chunk of what came through New York and the East Coast to Europe. Sheldon's 'Group of Eight' was doing their best to deflect incoming attacks and attempts to cut off Kahnawake. Time would tell if they'd continue to be successful. And a lot of what Dean was doing was being replicated through their data centers in Gibraltar, Paris, London and Singapore.

No, cutting off those fiber optic links would take some time, and shutting down their entire operation wouldn't be easy. The telecoms weren't as easily bought off as the politicians. That said, it was only a matter of time until Bluebridge managed the impossible.

But Dean was sure they could hang on for a day or two.

The moment this thought crossed his mind, he was cast into blackness.

He thought he'd lost his vision at first, but the tip of his cigarette glowed in front of his eyes. All the lights had gone out, the hum of the machines gone. Crickets chirped in the silence. He glanced to his left, where Montreal lit up the clouds with a pink glow a second before. But the sky—everything—was pitch black.

AUGUST 31st

Wednesday

43

Raleigh
North Carolina

Seven a.m. and it was already ninety-four degrees.

Senator Russ pulled a handkerchief from his suit jacket and wiped his forehead, then tossed it onto the breakfast table and waved to one of the assistants for another. He stared at the side of his tour bus, 'Take Back America' stenciled on it in italicized red letters over a wind-blown American flag.

A cross-country bus tour before the final leg of the election had sounded good on paper last April when they were planning it in New Hampshire. But down here in North Carolina, on a sweltering August morning after sleeping in this coffin on wheels for six days? Not so much.

Russ stood and walked around the front to see how many people showed up for his speech. "Tomorrow, breakfast in the bus, it's too hot outside," he growled at another assistant.

"But you said you wanted—"

"Do I need to repeat myself?" Russ glared at the young kid who withered and shrank away, shaking his head.

The crowd outside wasn't a *crowd*.

Judging from the suits and clean haircuts, most of them were from the local staffing office. The few stragglers were probably wondering if the tour bus was for a famous band. Then again, this was the Research Triangle Park. A lot of eggheads. Russ was realistic enough to know he couldn't expect a lot of intellectuals to show up for one of his speeches.

"Senator!" One of his aides, Roxanne, stuck her head out of the bus door. "I need you inside."

"Let me get this speech done, then we can talk in twenty minutes."

Roxanne shook her head. "It's Henry Montrose, from Bluebridge, and he says he needs to speak with you." She paused. "Right away."

Russ gritted his teeth. He preferred it when the old man was subtler. Making him look like he was jumping through hoops in front of his staff grated on Russ. Then again, the old man had been the main strategist behind Russ's surprise nomination and campaign, and he was footing most of the bills, too.

Fear struck Russ like a thunderbolt—Montrose *better* still be footing the bill.

Given the way the market crashed over the past two days, the old man might be broke. Russ didn't have much of an understanding of the intricacies of the world of finance. That's what he depended on Henry Montrose for.

That, plus his money.

Russ needed the spigot to remain open.

They had a good lead in the polls, but they were still fighting in a lot of states. A big problem was that the financial crash had shifted the campaign away from foreign protectionism toward the economy and the market. Not Russ's strong suits, and the opposition had jumped on it. Was the old man calling to cancel his support?

In two steps Russ bounded over to the bus, pushing Roxanne aside. He jumped inside, grabbing the offered phone. "Hello?" he said.

Roxanne stared wide-eyed at Senator Russ.

"Are you serious?" Senator Russ whispered into the phone. "Is this confirmed?"

He listened, clenching his jaw. After another few seconds, he hung the phone up and waved his hand in the air.

"Change of plan." He looked at Roxanne. "Get Mike in here, we need to rewrite my speech."

▲▼▲

"Research is the cornerstone of the future," Senator Russ thundered from behind the podium, his fist in the air.

Jake shifted in his seat. He was sitting with Wutang, Jin, and Sheldon in the Two Bridges apartment, the four of them gathered around the large screen TV near the window to watch Senator Russ on CNN. They wouldn't be wasting their time watching him on some obscure campaign stop in Raleigh, except an automated alert Sheldon had running had flagged something. An AP newswire about a breaking story.

"We have done our *research*," continued Russ, pausing to emphasize his new favorite word, "and found out conclusively that the recent Fakegate attack, the spoofing of our President's images and words on national television, a terrorist attack that has taken billions of dollars from the pockets of our citizens—"

Jake held his breath. Was the hammer about to come down?

"—was perpetrated by the Iranian Revolutionary Guard, the IRGC. This heinous cyberattack against the citizens of the United States cannot be—"

"Are you freakin' serious?" Sheldon jumped up out of his chair and knocked it clattering onto the floor.

Jake stared at the screen, not moving, but feeling the temperature in the room rising. Like a jiu-jitsu move, he didn't see it coming until after it happened, the shifting of the momentum of his attack to the advantage of his opponent.

But now it was obvious.

Bluebridge was doubling down.

Senator Russ had always been the hawk, making protectionism and demonstrating America's strength to the world central to his platform. Letting the election swing into a debate over the economy would pull some wind out of his sails. Now, though, this election would be about war, about a deliberate attack by one of America's enemies. This was exactly the sort of thing that Senator Russ had been warning about. The war machine had started up, and if Senator Russ hadn't been on track to win, he was now.

And Jake provided the final push.

"My God," Jake whispered, "what have I done?"

"—technical countermeasures can be employed to make sure this never happens again," Senator Russ said on the big screen, "bio-authentication tools to make remote communication safe again—"

"And I bet Bluebridge will be supplying the specs for that." Sheldon paced back and forth behind Jake and Jin.

He was right. They were trying to limit Bluebridge's freedom to operate, but this was its way of defusing the situation. Standards could be quickly implemented that would allow Bluebridge to keep operating. Jake swore under his breath. Had he miscalculated? He clenched his fists. *I need to find Anna. This isn't working.*

"Breathe, Jake," Jin said, standing behind him. "This was going there anyway, we just put our foot on the accelerator."

"We might have started World War Three," Jake murmured.

"Bluebridge is doing this," Sheldon pointed out, "not us. And it doesn't matter. Jin is right. Bluebridge has stepped up its game, so we need to do the same. We need you in this fight. MOHAWK is still operating."

Jake nodded, trying to focus. Dean had called the night before in a panic. A massive power failure had swept Quebec the evening before, but the back-up generators at MIT kicked in as they were designed to do.

"And my guys have a hundred million computers wired into botnets, attacking Bluebridge as we speak. This thing has to be getting desperate, no matter how well it's set up for DDOS protection."

If a war in physical space was imminent, the war in cyberspace was already raging, the entire internet lit up from end to end as Bluebridge and MOHAWK grappled with each other. DDOS—distributed denial of service—was a new term to Jake. It meant flooding a target's networks with millions of service requests a second, overwhelming its capabilities. Sheldon's Group of Eight had bought up every illegal botnet they could get their hands on and turned them loose on Bluebridge and its core group of companies.

The problem was, they weren't the only cowboys in town. Bluebridge had its own network of sophisticated security technicians and hackers, human opponents who launched their own attacks against the MOHAWK facilities. They knew where Dean was, and even if MOHAWK was still up and running, it was getting harder to keep outgoing communications.

Soon enough Bluebridge would track down where Sheldon and Jake and Jin operated from. It probably already had a pretty good idea of the general area.

Only a matter of time.

Jin turned off the display and sat in front of Jake, leaning on the desk overflowing with computer equipment. "We have to push forward."

Her part of the game plan was in play now. The markets had opened again yesterday, tentatively, and swung into positive territory behind a rally. Jin wasn't concerned with the indices, though; she didn't care if the markets went up or down. She needed a good swing each day, so she could use the seed capital from Joey Barbara and the Yakuza to rack up enormous profits in future options as they pushed the market back and forth.

"I've got this, Jake," Jin said. "Time to paint this white swan black."

Jake looked into her eyes. "You make them bleed."

He closed his eyes.

"And after that, you guys need to get out of here."

▲▼▲

The rain finally stopped. Chase Rockwell stared out of the window of his office, admiring the view. Six p.m. Time for a drink. The finish of another beautiful day.

The old Albanian gangster hadn't deposited any funds yet, but even that couldn't spoil Chase's mood. He took a long drink from the tumbler of whiskey in his hand, sucking the last drops from between the ice cubes. He couldn't blame the Mafioso—nobody had ever seen a market like this.

In turbulence, there were always winners and losers, but each back-and-forth swing of the market had only pushed his profits higher. He was giddy. He didn't even need the liquor; he was already high. Chase imagined himself on the cover of *Fortune Magazine* next month—a stern-looking picture of him in his office staring out over New York, with a cigar, maybe.

The king reigns once more.

A knock on his office door pulled him out of his daydreams. "Come in."

Chase turned to watch his door open. His intern, his favorite new person, peered out from behind it.

"Come in," Chase repeated.

The kid stepped into his office, a fresh sheaf of reports in his hands. At least he was wearing a decent suit now. Chase had sent him to his personal tailor yesterday. The cost be damned.

"You need to look at this," the kid said in an unsteady voice.

Chase smiled. "Why? Did we make another billion?"

The kid stared at Chase. Dropped the sheaf of paper on the side table. Turned and closed the door behind himself.

44

Kahnawake Indian Reserve
Quebec

"Scorpion One, this is Black Team leader," a garbled voice said on top of static.

Dean hadn't been on night operations in a long time. Perched atop the water tower in the center of the Kahnawake village, he fumbled with his night vision goggles, trying to focus on the green dots moving through the underbrush. "Is that them?" he whispered.

"Yeah," Daniels replied. After the blackout yesterday, Officer Daniels had put away his Peace Keeper uniform and taken up with the Mohawk Warriors. He was an invaluable addition to the team, a special-ops Marine drilled in guerilla tactics. He was running this operation—Dean was along as an observer. "That's them."

"Center on target," said the garbled voice.

Daniels turned down the volume. "We picked up their transmissions using some comm gear we brought over the border. That's definitely a special-ops unit, but I think they're irregular, maybe contractors."

Dean stared at the green figures running between the bushes in the darkness. So they'd sent in mercenaries. This could erupt into full-blown warfare. "Where are they going?"

"Looks like they're heading for the administrative buildings," Daniels replied.

According to media reports, the blackout the day before had been the result of blown equipment up at the James Bay hydroelectric plant seven hundred miles north, the massive LG1 and LG2 generators that supplied nearly all of the electricity to Montreal.

Quebec was one of the few places on Earth that got all of its energy from renewables, ninety percent from that one source. A single point of failure. Power was back up in most of Montreal, but Kahnawake remained mysteriously dark. They weren't going to get power anytime soon.

The three back-up generators at MIT had started up flawlessly, though, kicking in while the battery back-ups had handled the gap in between. As long as they had diesel, they'd be running.

And Kahnawake had a couple of gas stations that were still full.

"Let's go get 'em," Daniels told Dean.

Standing up, Dean waited for a moment to let his eyes adjust to the moonlit night. Then he walked over to the ladder and jumped down two rungs at a time until he hit the grass. Daniels followed behind, along with five other Warriors.

On the ground it was like being in a jungle, humid and nearly pitch black. This part of Kahnawake was forested. Candles in the windows of houses twinkled through the trees behind them. Putting their night vision goggles back on, they started off at a jog. Dean hung back, letting the others take the lead. In the darkness they passed underneath the metal trusses of the Mercier Bridge, then stopped at the two-story high concrete pylon that anchored the suspension work of the bridge.

A long arched corridor ran through the massive pylon. At its other end were the administrative buildings of the Mohawk council.

"They're on the other side," whispered one of the Warriors, running toward them. He had been scouting ahead.

Daniels held up his hand, indicating that they were to split up. Two flanking each side, while he and Dean and another Warrior came up in the middle through the tunnel. Silently, they nodded and melted away into the night.

"You ready?" Daniels asked Dean.

He nodded.

Weapons forward, they crept along the edge of the stone passage. Dean controlled his breathing, focusing on his footfalls, keeping silent. "First and second in position," he heard through his earpiece.

Staying behind Daniels, he left the passageway. Right in front of them crouched a group of four men, the ones they'd seen from the water tower. They weren't being careful. Sloppy. Standing there in the open.

"On my mark," whispered Daniels into his throat mike.

Then the staccato of gunfire, bursts of flares overhead.

Kneeling, Dean pulled off his goggles, his heart racing. Daniels sprinted ahead and tackled one of the men. The other three scattered. One of them ran back toward Dean. He waited until the guy was on him, then stood and brought his rifle butt straight into the man's face. He crumpled to the ground.

"I got this one," Dean yelled out.

"All clear."

A single shot rang out.

"What the hell?" Dean scanned back and forth, straining to see in the darkness. There, on the ground, was the guy Daniels had tackled.

Only it wasn't the guy Daniels had tackled.

It was Daniels, lying inert.

"Man down!" Dean screamed, running forward ten steps and sliding to a stop.

Daniels was laid out on his back, his eyes wide. "Sorry Dean, the guy pulled a pistol out." He pointed toward the back of the administrative building. The trees lit up with bursts of gunfire around the corner.

Silence.

"We got him," Dean heard in his earpiece.

"Daniels is down!" Dean yelled. "Somebody get an ambulance!"

To his left, an orange fireball mushroomed into the sky, scorching Dean in a blast of heat. He turned. It had to be the gas station on the main street. Then he was hit by another concussion from an explosion that lit up the night sky to his right. He swiveled to face it, realizing in horror that this one was a fiery cloud roiling into the night sky over the MIT building.

Dean wanted to get up and start running toward MIT, but he couldn't leave Daniels. In Dean's arms, Daniels coughed, then coughed again, this time wetly. In the light of the fireballs flaming into the sky, Dean saw blood oozing from Daniels's mouth. His eyes glazed over.

"Help!" Dean screamed, cradling Daniels in his arms. "Somebody help!"

SEPTEMBER 1st

Thursday

45

Upper East Side
New York City

A loud beeping woke Federal Reserve Chairman Gary Reinhold out of a deep sleep. It took him a second to realize what it was.

An emergency alert.

Picking up his phone, he fumbled with his glasses. Read the message.

"Goddamn it," he muttered, glancing at his bedside clock. Four fifteen in the morning. Still black outside. Swinging his feet off the bed, he clicked on his lamp and read the message again.

Gary called back the number on the text, and someone answered on the first ring. Federal Reserve Chairman Reinhold held his tongue while he listened, grimacing. "If it's so goddamn urgent," he hissed at the first pause, "why didn't you call me?"

Hushed explanations on the other end.

Didn't want to wake him, wondered if he was up, his Deputy Chair explained.

"It's four in the morning, did you really expect me to be up?" Chairman Reinhold wiped the sleep from his eyes. He put on his slippers and shuffled out of the bedroom, clicking on the hallway light. "What? They're there *now?*" He straightened up. "Yes, yes, okay, I'll be there in twenty minutes."

His skin prickled as he hung up the phone and put it in his shirt pocket. "Jesus Christ." Reinhold started down the stairs littered with his grandchildren's toys. His phone rang again. "I told Juanita to pick up these goddamn—"

His left foot landed squarely in a yellow Tonka truck just as he put his weight on it. The foot shot forward, sending Reinhold spinning into space. With a dull thud, his head cracked into the edge of a bare wooden stair, his body crumpling mid-pirouette. Chairman Reinhold flopped down the last few steps to land inert at the bottom, blood seeping from a deep wound in the side of his head.

Crickets chirped in the silence.

▲▼▲

It was still dark out.

It had to be a quarter after five in the morning, but Chase Rockwell was still drunk and high. At least the cocaine kept him alert. It had been the worst night of his life. "Where the hell is he?"

Deputy Federal Reserve Chairman Sandra Rodriguez stared at Chase. She knew he was on something, but she didn't care. "I don't know. I talked to Chairman Reinhold over an hour ago. He said he would be here in twenty minutes." She rocked back in her chair. "He's not answering his phone anymore."

"Why don't we get started?" suggested Matt Silver, head of TransBank, sixth largest on the global banking charts. "We need to get on this right away."

Chase sniffed and looked around the wood-paneled main conference room of the Federal Reserve of New York. "I'm not starting without Reinhold." Rodriguez was a political appointee, three weeks into her new position. She had about as much gravitas as a chicken fajita.

No power.

And no money.

And that was what Chase needed right now.

"I disagree," Matt Silver shot back. He shook his head at Chase. "The longer we wait, the more danger we're putting ourselves in."

"Why don't I start?" Rodriguez suggested. "I can guess why you're here, gentleman."

Chase hadn't expected to be surprised by Rodriguez. "You can?"

Rodriguez fixed Chase with an annoyed stare. "The positions of your banks at the end of the Tuesday flash crash are being investigated by the SEC for insider trading. Or worse. The odds of you coming out of that unscathed were—"

"Unscathed?" Chase laughed.

"You're here to explain, I assume?" Rodriguez continued, ignoring Chase's interruption. "Reinhold and I had a long talk with the head of the Chairman of the IMF and New York

310

Attorney General yesterday. If your bank had anything to do with the flash crash, I can assure you that no amount of explaining is going to do either of you any good. I know you've gotten away with this sort of thing in the past, Mr. Rockwell, but I am not a part of the old system."

Chase glared at Rodriguez and shook his head. Unbelievable. A part of him was going to enjoy bursting her little bubble, despite his empire burning around him.

"Our bank lost $24 billion yesterday," Matt Silver interjected. "That's why we're here."

Rodriguez turned to face Silver, her head swiveling so fast it seemed as if it wasn't connected to her body. "Excuse me?"

"Twenty...four...billion," Matt Silver repeated. "And I suspect Chase here has a similar story."

"Eighteen billion," Chase whispered, still not wanting to say it aloud. "Only eighteen. Glad you beat me on this one, Matt."

Matt Silver didn't smile at Chase's attempt at humor. "I don't need to remind you that in the 2008 crash Lehman Brother's bankruptcy was triggered by a $2 billion loss, and AIG's by only $11 billion," he said to Rodriguez.

"Twenty-four *billion?*" Rodriguez looked like she was in shock.

"Forty two if you add us together," continued Silver. "And I bet we're not the only ones. We can't open our trading systems today. We had to shut everything down."

"How did this happen?" asked Rodriguez.

"Automated trading agents," Chase replied. "At least for us. For two days they worked like magic, protecting our assets, so we shifted everything into their control, and then boom!" He mimicked an explosion between his two hands. "Yesterday, everything went sideways."

"Can we fix it?" Rodriguez mumbled. "Can I send over someone to look at it?"

"You aren't listening to me." Matt Silver got up out of his chair and pointed at the skyscrapers of Manhattan outside. A gray light was gaining on the horizon. "When the day starts, our trading systems will be down. Sure, for a few hours we might be able to stall, but when other banks realize that they're not getting their money from us—"

"We had to shut down yesterday afternoon," Chase said. "The markets are already smelling blood."

311

Matt Silver put both hands on the conference table and faced Rodriguez. "Total global financial collapse, that's what's going to happen this morning."

The phone on the conference room table rang. It had to be Chairman Reinhold. Rodriguez punched the phone's answer button, putting it on conference call. "Gary, where are you, we need you in—"

"This isn't Gary, this is Max Pfeiffer. Who the hell is this?"

"Sandra Rodriguez, Mr. Pfeiffer."

Even over the conference link, Rodriguez sat up straighter, like a scolded schoolgirl. Chase snickered. At least this young grasshopper knew who the Chairman and CEO of the world's largest manufacturing conglomerate was.

"What in the world are you people doing over there?" Pfeiffer growled over the phone. "Have you seen the commercial paper markets in Shanghai and London this morning?"

"No, I haven't had the time—"

"You better bloody well make the time. Where the hell is Gary Reinhold? I've been trying his phone for the past hour."

Chase had never heard of Pfeiffer losing his temper before. The German industrialist was famous for keeping an even keel, no matter what the situation.

"We can't get in touch with him, either, Mr. Pfeiffer," Rodriguez replied.

"Well you tell him, *when* you see him, that the global commercial paper market has evaporated. Even I can't borrow a cent. Even the f'ing mafia has closed up shop today. Do you understand? No commercial paper borrowing means no payroll for my two hundred thousand workers who build everything from airplanes to nuclear reactors. Whatever you assholes have done over there, the financial market isn't the only thing affected." He paused. Heavy breathing filled the silence. "You don't fix this, you turn off the lights. Everywhere in the world."

The line went dead.

Then the phone rang again.

This time Rodriguez didn't pick it up. "Tanya, who is that?" she called out.

"The managing editor of the *Financial Times*, says it's urgent," came a muffled reply from the hallway.

And then more ringing. It sounded like a dozen phones

chirping and buzzing in symphony. Rodriguez glanced from Silver to Rockwell, then back again.

Chase couldn't believe it, but he was enjoying this. The shock he felt at losing billions of dollars was wearing off like a day-old hangover. Of course he had a few million tucked away in cash, buried in vaults on Caribbean Islands. Whatever happened, one way or the other, he'd be working on his tan the following afternoon.

The phone on the conference room table stopped ringing.

"Sorry, Ms. Rodriguez, never mind about the *Financial Times* editor," came Tanya's voice from the hallway.

Rodriguez looked palpably relived, letting out a small sigh.

"Because I have the China Banking Regulatory Commissioner on the line. He wants to talk to Chairman Reinhold—or whoever is in charge."

Rodriguez's hands gripped the edge of the table, her knuckles white. "Tell him we'll call him back."

Chase decided it was time to ask. "We need capital, Ms. Rodriguez, enough for us to open our trading systems this morning. Otherwise"—he shrugged—"global Armageddon."

"How much?" whispered Rodriguez.

"A blank check," Chase replied.

"No." Matt Silver glanced at Chase. "A trillion dollars, we could cap it at a trillion."

Rodriguez didn't reply, but all the color drained from her face. "You realize that's tax payer money you're talking about."

Chase shrugged. "I pay taxes."

"Really? I bet you pay less than the girl who served you drinks all night." Rodriguez gazed at Chase in stony silence.

"You know who I'm surprised isn't here with us?" Matt Silver asked, breaking the staring contest. "Henry Montrose, the Bluebridge chairman. He must have lost as much as us, but that old dog, who knows what tricks he has up his sleeve? If there's anyone who knows a thing or two about automated agent systems, it's Montrose and Bluebridge."

"If we could sort out the technical issues, you think that might help?" Rodriguez asked.

"It would be a start," Chase replied. There wasn't any graceful degradation to the previous system of doing it by hand.

"Tanya!" yelled Rodriguez. "Get me Henry Montrose on the

phone. Now! And I don't care who you have to kill to find him!" She took a deep breath. "And get some more coffee in here."

▲ ▼ ▲

Cormac Ryker stared at the single, solitary light on the tenth floor of building three of the Two Bridges apartment complex. It was five forty-five in the morning. The skies had finally cleared. From his viewpoint on top of the Manhattan Intergate building, he had a view of the beautiful sunrise over Long Island to the east. He also had a beautiful view of Jake O'Connell, sitting in front of a computer monitor in that tenth floor apartment.

"You can run, little worm," Cormac whispered, "but you can't hide."

Cormac had his own team this time. No more finesse, no more fooling around. Blunt trauma, instead of surgical.

It was time to bring this to an end.

46

Kahnawake Indian Reserve
Quebec

Dean groaned. Black soot covered him in a greasy film from head to foot. With a grunt, he leaned over and grabbed the red handle of a generator and yanked it.

It roared to life, joining the growl of more than thirty other portable generators they'd found around Kahnawake overnight. They were spaced across the grass out in back of the MIT building, in front of the still-smoking wreckage of the three back-up generator plants. He had a whole crew working to scrounge whatever they could find to generate electricity, pulling generators from houses and smaller buildings, out of garages and basements.

He sat on top of the generator and held his head in his hands. They'd lost Daniels the night before. Gunshot to the chest. He'd drowned in his own blood before they could get him out past the barricades. There were no major hospitals inside Kahnawake.

The loss was heavy.

A mercenary had been killed as well.

It was a miracle there hadn't been more deaths in the confusion. Firefights had erupted, skirmishes unfolding across the reservation. They'd captured six of the mercenaries, but Dean had a feeling it was only a small part of the attacking force. They'd interrogated them, held them in the Peace Keeper prison lock-up not far from MIT, but they weren't saying anything. They were sticking to the line that they were upset citizens who'd banded together to put an end to the Mohawk blockade of the roads.

Problem was, media and public opinion was grim enough to half-believe it.

The battery backups had done their job and kept the servers in MIT running after the bombing of the generators. A team of electricians had managed to jury-rig an electrical system to connect the growing farm of gas-powered generators out back to recharge the UPS. So far they had three hundred thousand watts coming in, enough to power over a thousand servers at full capacity. Dean had to shut down half of MOHAWK in Server Rooms D and E to conserve energy, and they were still draining the UPS—but they could keep it up for another day.

The problem now was cooling the servers. The air conditioning systems used up half as much power as the servers themselves did, so they'd opened all the doors and windows they could, put fans in to circulate the air. It helped, but some servers had already shut down due to over-heating.

Dean had run over after the explosion, expecting to see a crater in the ground where the MIT building had been, but MIT itself wasn't damaged. The attackers hadn't been able to get close enough given the defensive squads Dean had put in place to protect it. They got close enough, however, to detonate the fuel tanks next to the generators, as well as the fuel depots of the two gas stations within Kahnawake's perimeter.

"You got a call inside," someone yelled from the second floor entrance above Dean's head.

Dean glanced up, raising one hand before his eyes to block the sun. It was past ten o'clock in the morning. "Jake?" he asked.

"Yes," replied Harry, one of his technicians.

In the small hours of the morning, Dean had decided to tell his technicians what was *really* happening, expecting them to tell him he was crazy. Instead, they'd asked questions, nodded, and then quietly got back to work.

Dean's heart had nearly burst with pride. They were brave Mohawks, fighting an unimaginable enemy without question. Every one of them had stayed, even after the destruction of the evening before, even after one of their own had been killed.

"Be up in a sec." Dean stopped to inspect the farm of generators, humming away in the dew-wet grass, extensions snaking around them like umbilical cords. Satisfied, he pulled off his gloves, tucked them into the pockets of his coveralls, and jogged up the outside stairs.

Harry waited, holding the door open. "This way, sir."

Dean was teaching Harry, and some other Mohawk students, IT basics in the abandoned schoolhouse beside the gas station next door. Harry was twenty-one. He was one of the kids Sean and Jake had pulled from the bus accident seventeen years ago. It was probably part of the reason his technicians had accepted the

316

story he'd told them the night before—because they knew who Jake was, and what he meant to the tribe.

Dean stopped and smiled at the kid. "This isn't the military, Harry."

Straight-faced, Harry replied, "I know." He let a tiny smile creep across his face. "Sir."

Dean managed a smile back—glad there was still some good spirit—and patted Harry on the shoulder, then walked past him down the corridor to the Link Room. The mood outside was ugly. Frightening. The Mohawk Warriors manning the barricades now realized they had a real fight on their hands. They were out for blood, feeling trapped and cornered, the memories of long ago battles their tribe had lost filtering into their souls. Dean wasn't sure if he could even stop the situation from escalating now.

It was going to get out of control, if it wasn't already.

Keying and fingerprinting his way into the Link Room, he found Jake staring at him, grim-faced, from a computer screen.

"4—8—7," said Jake.

Dean stopped and pulled the one-time pad labeled Jake from his pocket. "How are you, Jake?" he asked after he verified the code.

"I'm sorry about Daniels, he seemed like a good man."

Dean nodded. "He was a close friend." They'd already talked during the night. Dean had called to tell Jake as soon as the fighting had stopped.

Elle was still out searching for Anna, but the police and FBI hunted for her and Eamon as well. If the authorities arrested Jake and Elle, even if they could find Anna, she'd go into child protective custody—into foster care. Jake hadn't said much about it, but Dean imagined the pain he must be feeling.

"The situation's stable, at least for now." Dean sat heavily. "We still need to be careful, even with these one-time pads. If Bluebridge is listening in, it's possible it could insert itself with a man-in-the-middle attack and seamlessly continue the video after we do our code check. Difficult to do, but it might be possible."

"I figured as much," Jake said. "You know, the two times when the machine called me, I remember having a weird feeling both times. I'm going to listen to my gut from now on."

He was probably right. Human intuition was hard to beat if you really listened to it. "I'm not sure how much longer I can keep

317

MOHAWK running," Dean admitted.

If there could be a positive aspect to the tragedy of Daniels's death, it was that public opinion had shifted overnight when news of the explosions and attacks in Kahnawake hit the social media streams. Now there was a growing call for the government to pull the military away.

Jake took a deep breath. "You don't need to anymore. Call it off. I think you've done enough."

"I'm not sure I can do that now. This fight has gained a momentum of its own," Dean said. "And anyway, this isn't your call. You're Mohawk too, Jake. We're family. Those kids out there are fighting for our family. We're going to get Anna back, Jake. We're going to beat this thing. We didn't do all this to lose our nerve in the last moment. We've gotta let all barrels loose, all the way to the end."

"I'm not sure I'm going to make it out of this." Jake's jaw clenched. "If you don't hear from me in two hours, send the media announcements out. Crashing the global economy is going to raise a lot of questions. Bluebridge will be exposed one way or the other."

"You hang tough, Jake."

Nodding, Jake reached for the screen on his side. "You've been a good friend, Dean. Thanks for everything."

Dean nodded. "Anything for family."

Jake smiled, then the connection cut out.

Dean stared at the blank screen. "Good luck, Jake."

47

Two Bridges Complex
New York City

Cormac Ryker held his assault rifle under his trench coat and smiled at the kid in front of him. The kid didn't smile back. The sandy-haired little snot stuck his thumb in his mouth and retreated behind his mother. The elevator jolted to a stop on the tenth floor and pinged. The doors slid open.

"This is us, baby," the kid's mother said, looking down to grab hold of her child. In her other hand she clutched a brown bag of groceries, a stalk of celery poking out of the top. She glanced at Ryker and forced a smile, then edged out of the elevator and hurried down the corridor.

Cormac held the door to the elevator open and watched her disappear into her apartment, glancing back at the other end of the corridor at apartment 1012. Jake's apartment. He punched the 'service' button on the elevator's control pad. "Elevator two secure," he said aloud.

"Building secure," came the response in his earpiece.

Cormac's team had control of all entry and exit points. Jake and his friends hadn't gone in or out in an hour, and Cormac's spotter on the roof next door had Jake in constant visual contact in the apartment the whole time.

Pulling his assault rifle out from under his coat, Cormac strode down the hallway. "Are we a go?" he asked, speaking through the throat-mike to his team.

"We're a go," came the chorus of replies.

Cormac smiled, nodding to his second-in-command who held open the doorway to the stairs. They crossed the last ten feet to apartment 1012 and without missing a step, his guy lifted one jack-booted foot and kicked the door hard. It splintered inward, the cheap doorframe and locks giving way. Cormac strode in, rifle up and out, a smile on his face.

And there was Jake.

Alone.

He sat in far corner of the room, staring back at Cormac—but not looking the least bit surprised.

"Come in, Mr. Ryker." Jake raised his hands calmly.

Jake's reaction, by itself, was enough to make Cormac hesitate. Something wasn't right. Shrugging off the feeling, Cormac was halfway through squeezing the trigger on his rifle when he realized Jake used his real name.

It didn't matter, did it? But if he knew, what else might he know?

Did he know Cormac sent his own team, one he'd recruited himself, up to the Kahnawake reservation to get the Bluebridge core? Cormac let go of the trigger.

Behind him, his second-in-command checked the bedroom and bathroom. "Nobody else here."

Cormac cursed. Where the hell were those kids, Jin and Liu Wu? That was half the bounty on this job. "Go check the other apartments," Cormac growled.

His second-in-command nodded and left through the door they trashed.

Cormac looked at Jake. Who cared if Jake knew who he was? It didn't matter. Soon he'd be free of this whole mess. "You had a good run, Jake." Cormac held his rifle up, centering its sight on Jake's chest.

"Hold it right there, son."

Now what? Cormac glanced over his shoulder. An overweight police officer stood in the splintered doorway, his revolver pointed at Cormac's head. Cormac frowned, and then smiled.

"You're that sheriff, aren't you?" Cormac snorted, keeping his eyes on Jake, his rifle still trained on him. "That one who Jake disarmed outside his house, the one who got tied to a tree?"

"Put it down, or I'll put a bullet in you," Sheriff Ralston said evenly.

"Give me a break, old man. What are you doing here? Trying to regain some dignity? You're way out of your depth." Cormac laughed on the outside, but fumed inside. Where the hell were his men?

"We got all your men," Sheriff Ralston said, reading Cormac's expression. "No way out. Put down the gun."

"You think you have the guts, old man? I'm wearing full body armor. You want to test my HK versus your tiny pistol? I'm getting out of here. The question you gotta ask yourself is"—he smiled a menacing grin—"are you?"

Jake got out of his seat and advanced toward them. Cormac held his rifle steady on his chest. The problem was that if Cormac pulled the trigger, the sheriff would probably do the same. Even a country bumpkin like Ralston couldn't miss from five feet.

Cormac had to stall, had to figure a way to get the jump on the old man. "Looks like we have ourselves a little Mexican stand-off, don't it?" he laughed.

The three men glanced back and forth at each other.

In the silence a phone rang. It was Cormac's, in his pants pocket. Only one person had that number.

A second later, the phone in Jake's hand rang, and then a buzzing in the sheriff's pocket. The computer screens lining the walls of the apartment lit up with remote messages.

Cormac looked back and forth. What was going on? Only the old man had his private number. Cormac gritted his teeth, his knuckles white around the rifle grips. *Drop to the ground, shoot the old man, and then kill Jake.* It would only take a second.

But.

The only person who had his private number was the old man. Montrose. The owner of Bluebridge. He knew who the old man was. He even knew that the old man might not even exist. Might be a machine. The idea didn't faze Cormac. The thing that did faze him was that the old man—whoever or whatever—was the one paying the bills.

Was the old man calling him right now?

Or was this some kind of trick?

▲▼▲

Holding up his arms, palms out, Jake asked Cormac, "Should I answer?" He didn't wait for a response. He pressed the button and held the phone to his ear. "Hello?"

All the other ringing phones went silent the instant Jake picked up.

"Don't do this," said a voice on the other end.

Jake closed his eyes. That voice. "Sean?"

"It's me, Jake. I'm still here."

Just hearing Sean's voice brought tears to Jake's eyes. He opened them. "I'm not stopping. If you know me, you know I'll never stop. Give me what I want."

"I can't do that, Jake. You don't know what you're doing."

Jake looked at Cormac, watched his finger on the trigger of the rifle. "Kill me, and everything goes away, you lose *everything*," he said into the phone. "I will never give up."

Ten minutes before, Jake had left a message on the main Bluebridge answering service, offering terms. He wanted money. Wanted to be in control of Bluebridge. He said that they had evidence to peg the whole financial crash, even the presidential spoofing on Bluebridge—but that Jake and his team would keep quiet if it gave them control. Added that he didn't care about his daughter. It's what a psychopath would have done. Nerveless. Cold. Hard-as-nails.

Jake knew it wasn't Sean on the other end. He knew it was the machine. "Give me what I want," Jake growled into the phone.

"Jake, don't do—"

Jake lifted the receiver away from his ear. He handed the phone to Cormac. "Your boss wants to speak with you." His chest was a foot from the muzzle of Cormac's rifle. The phone dangled in the air between them, Jake offering it to Cormac.

Cormac gritted his teeth. He hesitated, but reached out with his left hand and took it. "Hello?"

He took his eyes off Jake for a split second.

Jake pounced.

His weight already balanced forward on the balls of his feet, Jake ducked under the muzzle of the rifle and sprang the instant Cormac looked away. He launched himself forward with every ounce of rage and frustration built up inside.

Roaring, Jake drove his shoulder into Cormac's midsection, wrapping his arms around him. He surprised Cormac, lifted him off the ground and drove him back three paces to crash hard into the kitchen cupboards. Sheriff Ralston rushed forward and wrestled the HK rifle from Cormac as both of them tried to pin the assassin to the wall.

It only took Cormac a second to regain his balance.

He might have a limp, but his upper body was incredibly strong. Grabbing Ralston, he head-butted him, blood spraying up as Sheriff Ralston staggered back toward the entranceway, still

322

holding Cormac's rifle in one hand. Jake pulled loose and swung a fist to catch Cormac in the chin.

Cormac ducked and laughed. He grabbed Jake's shirt and threw him into Ralston. The two of them collided and fell backward into the hallway, the rifle clattering across the floor.

"This ends here," Cormac snarled. Pulling a knife from his belt, Cormac stepped through the entrance toward Ralston and Jake.

Jake pushed himself and Ralston back across the floor.

"I can't see," Ralston groaned from beneath Jake. His nose was smashed, blood poured out of it.

"Keep backing up," Jake grunted. "Get into the stairwell."

Cormac lunged and Jake rolled off to one side. The HK assault rifle was on the ground down the hallway, ten paces away. Jake sprang to his feet. Two steps and he glanced over his shoulder, expecting to see Cormac chasing him.

But Cormac advanced toward Ralston. Heading into the stairwell. Shots rang out. It was Ralston firing his gun.

Jake glanced back at the rifle.

Not enough time.

Skidding to a stop, Jake turned and sprinted back, swinging through the open stairwell door. Cormac knelt with one knee against Ralston's throat, the other pinning Ralston's hand with the pistol in it. Cormac raised his knife, about to strike, but turned and sprang to his feet when Jake appeared.

Jake charged forward, catching Cormac off balance.

"Jake!" Ralston screamed, reaching up. But it was too late.

Cormac and Jake both spun over the railing, disappearing and falling into open space.

▲▼▲

Five-year-old Jake just wanted to sleep. His father had taken his brother Eamon inside the Kmart to go shopping, told him to stay in the car. Jake was scared, but his father often left him behind to disappear somewhere. Jake was used to it.

He wasn't good at telling time, but it had been a long time. A very long time. Long enough for it to get dark outside.

The Kmart was closed now. Snow completely covered the car, and no other cars were left in the parking lot. The snow had piled up so high that it was almost pitch black inside his father's old Pinto. He was so cold he wasn't even shivering anymore.

But his father told him to stay.

So Jake stayed, curled up in a tiny ball in the backseat. He'd been freezing cold, but now he was tired—so tired. His eyes drooped.

"Ring a ring of rosies..."

Jake tried to sing his favorite lullaby, his small voice hardly a whisper. His little hands poked out of his jacket sleeves, and in the dim light they looked as blue as his frayed snowsuit.

It would be so nice to sleep. His dad would get him in the morning.

Scratch. Scratch, scratch.

Jake's eyes fluttered open.

Scratch, scratch, scratch. Snow fell from the side window, casting light into the car from the overhead mall lights. A face appeared. Mumbling. Then silence.

Jake drifted off again.

Thud. Thud.

Crash.

Glass showered down onto Jake and he opened his eyes. Was it his father? He tried to get up, but he couldn't.

"It's okay, I got you," Deputy Ralston said, reaching for the small boy.

The kid didn't move, and Ralston was afraid he'd already frozen to death until Jake's eyes cracked open and looked at him. Ralston dropped the crowbar he used to smash the window and reached in with both arms, scooping the boy up and against his chest.

Cursing, Ralston started high-stepping through the snow, trying to run toward his cruiser, which was parked on the street out front, the part that had been plowed. "You're going to be okay," he said to the kid. "Your name is Jake, right?"

The boy in his arms shivered, his body convulsing, but he opened his eyes. "Yes."

"You're one lucky kid, you know that?" Ralston had tears in his eyes. He cradled Jake in his arms.

Ralston had only been on the force for two months, but that was long enough for him to have learned a thing or two about the O'Connells. He'd already arrested the kid's father once, for a loan scam the guy was running on local businesses.

Some little kid, Sean Womack, had called the police station in a panic. Said he'd seen Jake's father, drunk, in a mall bar a few hours before. Jake's older brother had been with him, but not Jake.

The dispatcher told the kid to calm down, but the kid kept calling, saying he'd checked the O'Connell house and Jake wasn't there. Wanted them to look around the mall. Said it was a snowstorm, might be a life and death situation.

On a whim, Ralston had decided to go and check it out. He was glad he did.

Arriving at his cruiser, he opened the passenger door and set Jake down, then fetched some blankets from the trunk, wrapping Jake in them. Getting into the car, he turned on the ignition, pushed the heating controls to maximum and switched on his sirens. He pulled out into the snowy street, executing a U-turn to head for the hospital.

Where were they going to take the kid? Probably to a foster home. Poor little guy. He knew the O'Connell kids had only just gotten out of foster care to get back with their mother. After Ralston reported this, it would be a long time before they went home again.

Ralston glanced over his shoulder at Jake in the back. Some color was already returning to his face, his little eyes open and watching Ralston.

"You know what, Jake? I'm going to take you home with me after we get you checked out at the hospital. For a little while. Would you like that?"

Ralston had started dating a nice girl, Anna Ingmar. She'd be kinder to Jake than any foster care worker.

Ralston was sure of it.

48

Stamford
Connecticut

Elle's heart pounded in her chest. "Is this it?" She looked at Eamon.

"1200 Elmcroft," Eamon replied, glancing at his phone. They were sitting side by side in his Dodge Charger. "This is the address Jin gave us."

Getting out of the car, they both stared silently past a row of pines at Bluebridge headquarters. The glass pyramid glittered in cold light under the midday sun. They'd searched over a hundred buildings this past week, but this was the one place they hadn't dared to consider looking for Anna. Whoever had abducted her would never risk something so obvious.

But Anna hadn't been abducted by a human. Bluebridge didn't play by the same rules. Didn't care about the consequences.

The place looked deserted. No other cars on the street or in the courtyard. No people. Birds chirped in the silence, a brisk wind swaying the pines.

Then a whining noise started, grew louder. Elle looked to her right. Jin turned the corner on her dirt bike. Gunning her throttle, she sped toward them and then jammed on her brakes, skidding to a stop in a blue haze. She jumped off her bike, letting it roll over the curb and fall to its side on the grass.

"Did you go in yet?" Jin asked breathlessly, pulling her helmet off and jogging the last few feet separating them.

"We just got here," Eamon replied.

"Is Jake okay?" Elle asked. "What happened? What's going on?" It was the first time she'd met Jin in person, though they'd spoken in video chats.

"I don't know. Jake got us to leave the apartment in the morning, said to wait in the coffee shop down the street and stay hidden. Then at noon—bam!—I got this email with the GPS coordinates of where to find Anna. That's when all hell broke loose—cop cars, fire engines, ambulances, *everything* converged on the apartment building where we were holed up. I took off, leaving Sheldon and Wutang to figure it out, and came up here to these coordinates."

Eamon glanced at Bluebridge headquarters, rising like an ancient pyramid above the trees around it. "Who was the message from, the one saying where Anna was?"

Jin shook her head. "Anonymous sender." She looked at Bluebridge. "It could be a trap, but Jake said if I got an email, to trust it. I've tried Jake's phone, Wutang's, Sheldon's. Nobody is answering."

Trust. Elle stared at the Bluebridge building looming in front of them. If there was anyone in her life she trusted, it was Jake. She knew he wrestled with the fear that he was a monster like his father. But he wasn't. He was the most faithful, devoted person she'd ever known.

She regretted not believing in him. It had been a knee-jerk reaction. She was mad at him, angry that he'd dragged his family into some mess. But it wasn't his fault. Elle knew he loved her and Anna more than anything.

"If Jake said to trust the email, then let's go," Elle said.

Eamon held her arm. "Let me go first." He pulled a gun out from under his jacket, showed it to her, then put it back.

Elle and Jin followed him down the grassy embankment, past the pines, and up to the building's entrance. Eamon looked back at them and nodded. They walked forward and the main doors to Bluebridge headquarters swung open by themselves as they crossed the last few feet.

Cool air swept over them.

Inside it was even quieter than outside. Dead silent. The reception desk was empty. No sign of anyone. The sintered-quartz chandeliers hung over their heads like angels of death.

Eamon gawked up at the chandeliers and across the immense lobby. "Which way?"

Jin checked the GPS coordinates on her phone's screen, zoomed in. "Seems to be the back left corner of the building. We're going to have to check floor by floor. Should we split up?"

"No way," Eamon replied. "We're sticking together."

"Anna!" Elle screamed, her voice echoing. "Anna, baby, are you here?"

"Okay, let's check this floor first." Jin pointed to a corridor that led to the left.

They started running across the lobby, but stopped when a loud whirring whined from one of the hallways. A small four-prop helicopter buzzed out of a hallway to their right. They crouched, Eamon raising one arm to shield Elle while getting out and pointing his gun at the drone with his other hand. It ignored them and whizzed through the lobby, circling around to disappear into a hallway to their right.

"What the hell?" Eamon muttered, still watching the hallway the drone disappeared down. He put his gun back in his pocket.

Jin nudged him. "Let's keep moving. Those are delivery drones, I think."

They walked past the empty reception desk, looking through the glass walls to the interior courtyard. It was lush, overflowing with palms and flowering plants, and vines hung from the balconies. It was also empty of people.

"Anna!" Elle yelled, crossing down the hallway to the left.

They entered a large rectangular office space filled with cubicles, all of them devoid of people.

Jin pointed forward, and they continued down a hallway toward the back of the building.

Elle cupped her hands to her mouth. "Anna!" she screamed.

"Anna!" Eamon yelled.

Elle was about to call out again, but...

A shuffling.

"Mommy?" came a faint reply, barely more than a whisper.

"Anna!" Elle shrieked.

"Straight ahead," Jin said, pointing down the hallway.

Elle broke into a sprint, pushing past Eamon.

"Elle, be careful!" he yelled, trying to grab her.

But she was already running. "Anna, where are you?" she called out.

She ran and ran, past empty offices, empty corridors.

"Mommy? I'm here," came a reply. Louder now.

Elle burst around a corner.

And there was Anna.

Holding a teddy bear. Standing alone in the corridor with one glass wall open to the interior gardens.

Elle burst into tears and fell to the floor, scooping Anna into her arms. "Baby are you okay, did they hurt you?"

Anna started crying too, wrapped her arms around her sobbing mother. "I'm okay," she squeaked. "But I missed you. Where were you guys?"

Flashing lights, red and blue and white, reflected off the chrome and glass interior of the Bluebridge headquarters. Police cars.

Eamon knelt down beside them, hugging Elle and Anna. "Come on, we have to go," he said quietly.

49

Department of Homeland Security
New York

"So, what, are you the FBI, CIA, SEC, some other three letter acronym…?" Jin looked around the bare concrete room. She inspected the camera pointed at her from the corner of the ceiling, then looked into the one-way glass mirror on one wall. Her second interrogation room in as many weeks.

"We're asking the questions, Ms. Huang."

"Am I under arrest?"

"No."

"Am I free to go?"

"No."

"Can I call a lawyer?"

There was a pause this time.

"You only need a lawyer if you're hiding something."

"That doesn't answer my question."

"It's funny you should say that, because that's exactly what we need."

"What?"

"To get some answers to our questions."

Jin shifted in her metal chair. It was bolted to the ground. Elle, Eamon and herself had been arrested after finding Anna. The police had been watching Bluebridge headquarters.

"We're trying to protect you, Ms. Huang."

"Trying to protect me?" Jin laughed at Special Agent Thomas. "*You* want to protect *me?*"

A few weeks ago and she would have been trembling in fear. Now, she felt defiant. She wanted to laugh at them. They were the ones that had no idea what they were dealing with. She was the one with the knowledge.

Agent Thomas opened a file on the metal desk that was bolted to the floor. "You were arrested in July four years ago for four counts of wire fraud, two counts of computer fraud and one count of illegally intercepting a wire communication."

"That was a misunderstanding. The company I was working for asked me to do some intrusion tests—"

"And the terms of your release by Judge Atlee indicated that you were restricted from using networked computers in America for a period of five years."

"It's my constitutional right to have access to computers."

This was one the agents hadn't heard before. "And how's that? Not sure the Founding Fathers mentioned computers."

"The Second Amendment, the right to bear arms. The most powerful weapons to fight oppression aren't flintlocks anymore. Bits of code, Perl scripts—if the Founding Fathers were around today, that's what they'd want protected under the Second Amendment."

Agent Thomas slammed closed the file folder on his desk. "Let's get something straight. We know it was Sean Womack who paid for the lawyers who got you off four years ago. And we know Mr. Womack was a close associate of Jake O'Connell."

"If you know so much, why are you asking me questions?"

"Because Sean Womack is dead, and Jake…well now we can't talk to Jake either, can we?"

"What happened?" Jin sat up in her chair. "What happened to Jake?"

Both officers remained silent.

"Ms. Huang, we know there were other people in that room, who were they?"

Agent Sears sat on the side of the table and looked Jin straight in the eye. "More importantly, *where* are they?"

▲▼▲

"Double mocha latte, no fat," said Wutang to the girl behind the counter.

"Do you even know what's in those things?" Sheldon sniggered. "Why don't you just get a coffee?"

"I like sweet stuff when I get nervous," Wutang replied, handing over a ten-dollar bill. "Bad habit."

Sheldon nodded at the girl behind the counter. "Another regular coffee, please."

"Put it on my bill," Wutang added. "My turn this time."

331

Five hours they'd been waiting here. They'd left the apartment building early in the morning so Jake could set his trap. He was working with Sheriff Ralston, whose men had been watching Cormac Ryker as he planned what he must have thought was his own trap.

Jake had used himself as bait.

To be on the safe side, he didn't tell Ralston about Sheldon and Wutang. Sheldon was pretty sure the old sheriff knew Jake wasn't working alone, but Jake and Ralston had a history together, some bond Sheldon didn't quite understand. Like a father, or an uncle.

At noon, all hell broke loose. Police cars and fire trucks still ringed the building, but the ambulances were gone. The police had carted out stretchers and body bags, people in handcuffs. Sheldon ran over, trying to see something, anything that would indicate the outcome. The police kept everyone back, saying it was some kind of gang fight. One with casualties. Sheldon would have insisted and run under the tape, but he couldn't risk it.

Something more important was going on.

In addition to the message pinpointing Anna's location, they received a second one. Login credentials. For Bluebridge.

Jin had immediately run off to help find Anna, racing up the East Side Highway on the motor bike she'd recovered from Union Square to meet Elle and Eamon. She'd insisted Sheldon and Wutang should be the point people for Bluebridge, in spite of Wutang's objections.

So Wutang and Sheldon had settled in for the long haul at a coffee shop across the street, opening their laptops and logging into the Bluebridge network. Whatever Jake did, whatever deal he made—it seemed to work. For now. Sheldon had patched in Dean to make the connection with MOHAWK, and then downloaded the old Bluebridge core, using his super-user access to start overwriting the system directories.

Sheldon and Wutang didn't have phones that connected into the cellular networks. Too risky, even turned off. So they used voice-over-IP only, devices communicating through the WIFI, setting up their own secure end-to-end encryption. A hundred gigabytes needed to be transferred through the linchpin of the coffee shop's wireless at 1.3 Mbps. It would take five hours for that much data to transfer securely over the connection.

That whole time, they'd completely swamped the data stream in and out of the coffee shop. Sheldon had hacked the router to give them priority. There wasn't even enough bandwidth left for him to make and receive calls himself. Customers were complaining, and the employees had called tech support. But Sheldon would be gone by the time they got here.

He hoped.

As he took their steaming coffees back to their table, Sheldon's computer pinged.

He sat. "It's done. The file transfers are complete."

"The key is money in your pocket, isn't that what Sean told Jake?" Sheldon said to Wutang. He sat beside him, both of them staring at the screen, the login cursor for Bluebridge flashing, waiting for instructions.

Sheldon's hand trembled.

Sitting in this tiny coffee shop, he was about to take over a trillion dollar global empire.

"What do we do?" Wutang asked.

Sheldon's nerves calmed. He cracked his knuckles and smiled at Wutang. "Time to turn this ship around."

SEPTEMBER 2nd

Friday

50

Department of Homeland Security
New York

Sixteen hours in this interrogation room. How long could they keep her?

Jin ached from sitting in the chair. Her head throbbed. No idea what was happening. Exhausted. She'd expected to hear from Jake or Wutang or Sheldon by now.

But nothing.

"You came into the United States under false documentation," Agent Sears said. He'd stayed in the room with her all night, needling her for information.

"You can't deport me," Jin replied. "I'm a US citizen. Born and raised in Boston, as American as apple pie and baseball."

"But you can go to jail. Section 1028 of Title 18 of the USC gives up to fifteen years in prison for using false documents to enter a port or defraud the government. With your prior, plus the evidence we have of you hacking into government databases, you could be looking at twenty years to life."

The defiant expression on Jin's face slackened. She closed her eyes. "What do you want to know?"

"There was some sophisticated radar sniffing gear in the Two Bridges apartment. How do you explain that?"

"I have no idea what that stuff is."

"So you're sticking to your story?"

"Officers, I honestly don't know what's going on. If you're not charging me with anything right now…" Jin held up her hands. "What are we here for, really?"

Agent Sears nodded at Agent Thomas, who nodded back. "We think the Bluebridge Corporation is behind a slew of digital autonomous corporations that have flooded the internet, impersonating humans. This is a brave new world we've been thrust into, Ms. Huang, and we're trying to protect it."

So the feds had some idea after all. "So what are you guys?" Jin asked. "The Turing Police? Hunting artificially intelligent escapees in cyberspace?"

"Only ones that break the law."

Jin couldn't believe Agent Sears managed to say it with a straight face. "Are you serious?"

"We know you were appointed to the Board of Directors of Bluebridge Corporation this morning." Special Agent Thomas pulled out a paper and held it in the air. "Whatever game you think you're playing, this is dangerous. You don't know who or what you're dealing with."

It was the first Jin heard of it. Maybe Jake's crazy gamble had worked. "You'll have to talk to Mr. Henry Montrose about that."

Agent Sears laughed. "Are you kidding?" He sat on the desk in front of Jin. "You're not getting out of here. With your arrest record, we now have you on wiretapping, conspiracy to—"

"No you do not!" a voice thundered from the hallway. The door to the interrogation room swung open.

Jin could hardly believe her own eyes.

It was Henry Montrose. He pushed his way into the room, followed by four men in suits. She assumed they were lawyers. "Take those handcuffs off Ms. Huang right now."

"Who the..." Special Agent Thomas started to say, but then he recognized Montrose and stuttered to a stop.

One of the lawyers opened a briefcase on the desk. "You have been holding my client, Ms. Jin Huang, illegally for nearly a day without granting her a lawyer. Release her now. We've filed a motion that everything in this interview be suppressed."

"What?" a dumbfounded Agent Sears asked.

"Our client was not read her Miranda rights upon arrest." The lawyer handed the papers to Special Agent Sears.

Agent Sears scanned the document, and then reread it. Somebody had a video recording of the arrest. "Goddamn it," he muttered, but he fished the handcuff keys out of his pocket.

"All charges have been dropped," Henry Montrose said, stepping forward to put a hand on Jin's shoulder while Agent Sears uncuffed her. He looked Jin in the eye. "This has all been a huge misunderstanding. It was a rogue computer system that got way out of control. I'm sorry, Jin. I'll be assuming full responsibility."

"Let's go, Ms. Huang," said the lawyer who'd handed the

338

papers to Agent Sears. "Now."

Jin got up, wringing her wrists. She didn't need to be told twice.

"It is only through the actions of this young woman," Jin heard Henry Montrose say to the agents as she left, "that we've been saved. You should be commending her, not arresting…"

▲▼▲

Sitting alone together in the interrogation room, Agent Sears looked at Agent Thomas. "What the heck just happened?"

"We got railroaded, that's what happened."

Agent Thomas studied the court documents in his hands. All charges against the O'Connells were dropped, everything signed by a Federal judge that morning. The papers included a sworn statement from Sheriff Ralston saying that he wasn't going to press charges against Jake O'Connell, if that even mattered anymore. "We have Ralston getting assaulted by O'Connell on video, and the sheriff was eager enough to hunt him down yesterday. How the hell did they get to Ralston so quickly?"

"I don't know. I checked out Sheriff Ralston. Clean as a whistle, even led the anti-corruption division in the Albany police force for ten years."

"At least they got that nut job Cormac Ryker." They had twelve murders linked to him. He'd died in the fall down the stairwell shaft.

Thomas and Sears collected their files. It was a long day for them, too.

"I don't get it, this Sheriff Ralston." Agent Thomas shook his head. "I guess you can buy anyone these days."

▲▼▲

Jin followed the lawyers out of the DHS/NYPD building at 1 Police Plaza and looked up at the Two Bridges apartment buildings in front of them. She saw the window of the apartment where they'd spent the last week, clearly, on the top floor. Behind her, Henry Montrose came out of the building with the lawyers. A black limousine was parked at the curb.

The driver waved her over, holding the back door open.

339

Jin slid inside to find Wutang and Sheldon sitting on polished black leather seats opposite her. They had grim expressions on their faces.

"You okay?" Wutang asked. "Did they hurt you?"

"No, I'm fine," Jin replied.

A second later, Montrose slid into the seat facing them. The door closed with a solid *ka-chunk*.

"What's wrong, Wutang?" whispered Jin. "Sheldon? What happened? Where's Jake?"

Wutang looked like he was going to cry. Sheldon's face was impassive. Glancing at Henry Montrose, Jin felt fear bloom inside her. Had they miscalculated? Had they jumped from the frying pan into the fire?

As the limo pulled away from the curb, Wutang burst out laughing, joined by hoots of laughter from Sheldon. He wiped tears from his eyes. "You should see your face!"

"What?" Jin was stunned. Had they lost their minds? She glanced at Henry Montrose, but now he was the one who looked like he was about to cry.

"I'm never doing that again!" Henry Montrose blurted, his face crimson. "It's one thing to do a charity ball, but deceiving federal officers? I could go to jail for the rest of my life." His hands trembled. "Never again, no matter how much money."

"Relax, Frankie." Sheldon reached forward and grabbed his arm. "You won't have to. You did great." He looked at Jin. "And if you haven't figured it out, this isn't Henry Montrose. This is Frank. He body doubled for Montrose for years, but quit when things got weird. I tracked him down bartending in Yellowknife last night, flew him in on the Bluebridge private jet this morning."

"Something wasn't right about that place." Frankie reached for a bottle of whiskey in the side cabinet of the limo and poured himself a glass.

"I think this calls for champagne, no?" Sheldon sat and reached into an ice bucket. "And don't worry," he added, pausing once he'd fished out a bottle of Cristal, "Jake's okay. Or at least, he'll be okay. A few broken bones, concussion, but he's awake this morning."

"Is Elle okay? Anna?" Jin asked, looking back and forth between Sheldon and Wutang.

"Everyone's fine, all released this morning." Sheldon popped

340

the cork of the champagne. It bubbled over, and Wutang grabbed some glasses. "We're going to the hospital now. They're waiting for you."

51

MSNBC Newsroom
New York

"Three…" the show coordinator said, mouthing, "two, one," silently and pointing at the MSNBC anchor to tell him that he was live.

"Good morning, this is Charlie Wade of NBC Daily, reporting to you on the latest developments in the Fakegate scandal. We were the ones to break it to you"—he laughed—"we were the ones fooled by what is now known to be a sophisticated form of spoofing attack. Now you can't know who you're talking to unless they're in front of you, but new biometric confirmation technology is being deployed around the world, spurring a round of tech investment."

Charlie stopped to pretend to read some papers on his desk. It was a rehearsed pause before he went back to reading the teleprompter.

"What a week it's been folks. DOW goes down two thousand points, then back up two thousand. A real rollercoaster, and it's not over yet."

"The news we're breaking today is that a hacktivist group, the Neo-Luddites, have claimed responsibility for faking the live broadcast of the President of the United States, along with a rash of other human spoofing attacks around the world. According to their statement, the goal was to raise awareness about the dangers of machines replacing humans, but they've vowed that these activities will now cease. The CIA and FBI are investigating, but the news was greeted with a wave of relief by business leaders, enough to encourage stock markets to reopen."

He continued on for another ten minutes, describing gains on the NYSE, and then moved to a story about Senator Russ refuting claims that it was a hacking group, insisting it was the Iranians. His campaign had imploded with a disastrous slide in the polls.

Finishing up, Charlie stared into the camera. "And that's the kind of day it's been. I'm Charlie Wade." He paused, smiling. "But then again, how can you know for sure?" He laughed.

With a nod, the cameraman indicated the live feed was shut off.

The coordinator rolled her eyes at Charlie. "Was that last comment really necessary?"

Charlie chuckled, "What? Don't like my humor?"

"Doesn't matter." The coordinator smiled back. "Soon, you might not be necessary, either."

▲▼▲

Sheldon reached up and clicked the television off.

"Neo-Luddite hacktivists, you like that?" he laughed, turning to Jake. "Knocked Senator Russ right off his perch this morning. Last night Bluebridge cut all funding to Russ's campaign, withdrew everything. I got to watch our synthetic Montrose tell Russ the bad news. You should have seen his face."

Jake tried to laugh, but winced in pain. Covered in a thin white-and-blue sheet, he sat half-upright in the hospital bed. Anna sat at Jake's feet, with Elle holding her steady.

"Take it easy, boys, Jake's got some cracked ribs," Elle said.

"Sorry." Sheldon wiped his eyes.

"You feeling okay?" Jin asked Jake.

She brought balloons; their silver smiling faces announcing, *Happy Birthday*, all around the room. They were the only ones she could find. She unwrapped the foil from the top of a champagne bottle.

"I'm fine," Jake groaned, "a bit of a headache, can't breathe well, but not bad."

If there was one thing he was good at, it was hanging on. When he launched into Cormac and shoved him over, Jake managed to hold onto the railing and swing into the stairwell one level below. The impact knocked Jake unconscious, but Cormac fell all the way down ten stories—it killed him, finally stopped the monster.

When Jake woke up in hospital and realized it was over—that they'd won—he hadn't been filled with elation. Instead, sadness tore at him and he spent the night crying over Sean. A part of him wondered if there was still something of Sean inside of Bluebridge.

On Thursday, Congress had balked at giving a trillion dollar check to the Deputy Chair of the Federal Reserve. They weren't able to come to a decision, and it left the global markets in free-fall—the turning point of no return, a black swan within a black swan.

Bluebridge's capitalization algorithms finally calculated that the only way to maintain its investments was to cede control to Jake. Jake made the call with the offer just before Cormac showed up at the Two Bridges apartment.

Bluebridge had no ego, no desire to fight to the death, no reputation to defend. It was doing what it was designed to do, and when Jake's offer became the most likely scenario for it to maximize its earnings, it gave in to Jake's terms and gave them access. The machine used statistical inferences based on past events, but it was impossible to project a future when what was happening was unprecedented.

"So what happened exactly?" Jake asked. "How did you get the markets to re-open so quickly?"

"On Thursday night I rolled up all Bluebridge's off-balance sheet companies," Wutang said, "accumulated their global accounts, and we made an offer to the Fed on Friday morning. We injected $40 billion into the balance sheets of Commerce and TransBank."

"That got the markets to re-open," Jin added, "and averted global financial meltdown, but there's still a long way to go."

"But it worked," Sheldon said. "You played chicken using the global economy, and it blinked first."

"Nothing else Bluebridge could do to save its global investment portfolio," Wutang added. "When we got access, Sheldon re-initialized the system and ripped it apart."

"And me, Elle, Eamon—all the charges have been dropped?" Jake asked, still not quite believing it.

"You're all as clean as the pope," Sheldon laughed. "The icing on the cake was when your friend, Sheriff Ralston, refused to press charges."

Jake was working together with Ralston to take down Cormac. The night when Ralston confronted Jake outside his father's house, they'd talked. Ralston had agreed to help him. In the end, Jake knew exactly when Cormac was about to burst through the door. A calculated gamble, and Jake had been wearing a bulletproof vest.

"Joey Barbara and the mafia and Yakuza all made their money back when we swung the markets back and forth. There's nobody on our backs anymore."

"And last night I set up a global trust fund," Jin said. "Henry Montrose is donating his fifty billion dollar estate to charity." She popped the cork off a bottle of champagne. "We'll make the announcement on Monday."

"So that's it?" Jake asked. Could they really get away with this?

Sheldon handed him a glass of champagne. "Not quite. The feds have a good idea of what happened. They're not that stupid. We're going to have to expose the Bluebridge AI system, explain that it had a part in it."

"This is more of a controlled crash landing," Wutang explained. "We gotta hire a few hundred people to flesh out the ranks, start filling all those empty cubicles. We're still using some of the automated system features of Bluebridge, but it's a total mess. A lot of shareholders will be screaming bloody murder when the next report is published."

"We can blame it all on Montrose and Viegas." Jin took a sip from her champagne. "Another spectacular Wall Street meltdown. The investors will scream for their heads, and we'll fire them. The week after that, Montrose and Viegas are going to have an unfortunate yachting *accident* off Chile. Suicide? Guilt for what they did? We'll pile all the blame on them."

"Which is where it belongs." Wutang held up his glass and toasted everyone.

"What about these digital corporations that Bluebridge unleashed? The Assassin Market?" Jake asked. "Did you shut them down?"

Sheldon shook his head. "Autonomous corporations are like an invasive new life form in the digital ecosystem. Bluebridge was a shareholder in thousands, and we used that connection point to try and throttle them, but they've mutated, spawned."

"So you can't stop them from operating?"

"Not possible to take back," Sheldon replied. "The same way we've surpassed the Turing threshold. Congress is busy enacting new legislation to try and contain it all, but that's like sticking your finger in a dam that's already burst."

Elle turned to Jake, holding a tablet in her hand. "Hey, you want to talk to someone?" She handed it to him.

Dean's face was in a video window, smiling. "Jake, buddy, how you doing?"

"Been better," Jake grunted. "Give me a few days. And you?"

"We're cleaning up. A big mess up here."

Jake pulled the glass of champagne from his lips. "I'm so sorry about Daniels." He'd apologized before, but he didn't think he'd ever stop. Here they were celebrating, and one of the Mohawks had died two nights before. And in the process of their victory, Kahnawake had become a war zone of burnt-out buildings and barricades.

"Don't be sorry, Jake." Dean's face became stern. "We lost one of ours, but it was a good fight, for the right reasons. Everyone here knows the real story now, even if—officially—it's a rumor. Our people are proud." He looked over his shoulder at the technicians behind him, who were smiling at Jake. "We're a proud nation."

"And Mr. Montrose just made a hundred million dollar donation for a new technical college," added Jin. "In Peace Keeper Daniels's name."

"He would have liked that." Dean smiled at his technicians and then back at Jake. "Listen, I've got a lot to do on this end."

"Yeah, go ahead," Jake replied.

Dean nodded. "We'll talk soon, Jake."

OCTOBER 13th

Sunday

52

Upper West Side
New York City

"Daddy, Daddy, it's time to go!" Anna squealed.

"Okay," Jake laughed, "I'm coming. Why don't you go outside and wait?" He frowned. He didn't want to let his little girl out of his sight again. "Actually, why don't you wait on the couch? I'll go grab some stuff from my bedroom."

Anna nodded and pulled her backpack off before taking a seat on the couch. "Hurry, Dad. Everyone else is ready."

Jake smiled at his daughter, holding up one finger. "Just a sec."

Anna seemed fine, despite her ordeal. When she went down to the front lobby that day at the Super 8, a woman had been waiting for her. The machine—impersonating Jake—told her over the phone that she should go with the nice lady. They took a car ride, and the nice lady brought her to a room in the giant pyramid. Gave her toys and a TV, lots of junk food. Came in and said hello every couple of hours, told her to smile for the camera.

Whenever Anna got grumpy and cried, Jake's face would appear on the TV screen. He'd tell her that he and Mommy were busy, but they would be there soon.

They still didn't know who the mystery woman was, but Anna had described her to Jake. They had access to a lot of resources. They would find her, and Ralston said he'd bring her in when they did.

Jake hurried down the hallway. He'd packed quickly for this trip, so quickly he'd forgotten his shorts. When he stepped into his bedroom, he stopped for a moment to look around. They'd only been in this apartment for a few months, but he was going to miss it. Even so, it was the right thing.

They still didn't know what had become of Montrose, but even if he appeared out of the woodwork, Jin and Sheldon had reprogrammed all of his bio-identification records. He had no surviving family and few friends. If he showed up claiming he was

349

Henry Montrose, he'd be ignored as another crazy. Anyway, Montrose was reviled now, the latest Wall Street scoundrel responsible for wrecking the economy.

Sheldon revealed to the world that an artificial intelligence had run amok in Bluebridge, without getting into the specifics of what happened with Viegas or Montrose. There was no putting this genie back into the bottle. Somewhere out there, another Bluebridge was lurking, and the world needed to get prepared.

They'd avoided total global financial collapse, but the reverberations weren't controllable. The US economy had slid back into recession, and other countries had been hit much worse. It was a steep price, and Jake and Jin were doing their best to funnel Bluebridge capital into ailing national banks.

Reaching into his bedside drawer, Jake fished out some shorts and laid them on the bed, laughing out loud to himself.

"What's so funny?" Anna squealed, running into the room.

"Nothing, baby, I'll tell you later." Now, not only did Jake and his friends run one of the largest financial companies in the world, they also had a controlling interest in two of Manhattan's biggest banks after the bail out.

Bluebridge was still a total mess. Jin was in the middle of hiring financial analysts and a senior administrative staff. To the outside world it might seem suspicious, but then hedge funds did odd things all the time and were extremely secretive. They probably figured it was part of the bloodletting and restructuring program that had been instituted in the wake of firing the two founders.

Congress still fumed about 'Fakegate,' the CIA and NSA trying to hunt down whomever had been responsible for spoofing the President on live television. It was a serious crime, certainly a matter of national security, but at least it had opened everyone's eyes to the damage that the technology could wreak. Sheldon had made large donations to several prominent Congressmen to smooth down ruffled feathers. In time, the storm would pass and a new scandal would take the media's attention.

Was it worth it?

Jake smiled at Anna.

For him, the answer was yes.

He would have burned down the entire world to get his baby girl back. And he almost had.

Had he risked his daughter's life? Used her as a gambling chip?

He didn't think so. It would have been a fatal mistake to exhibit weakness to a psychopath, to Bluebridge. If he'd acted differently, he might have never gotten her back. There was no way he would have gotten his family back, or his life. It was the only way.

But was it worth it for the world?

That was still an open question. After all, Bluebridge had generated record profits for everyone involved, injected lifeblood into the global economy. But of course there was a price to the profits.

A human price.

The autonomous corporations weren't something that Sheldon or Jin could control, even with Bluebridge at their disposal, autonomous corporations were a new digital beast that weren't going away.

When the story about the Neo-Luddites hacktivists came out, Senator Russ had continued to rant and rave about Iran, but after Bluebridge cut all funding to his campaign, it was over. The elections were still around the corner, but it had turned into a landslide for the opposition, bringing the country back from the brink of war.

Jake fiddled with his Silver Eagle coin in his pocket. He pulled it out to inspect the dent in its center for the hundredth time.

They still weren't sure what had happened to Sean or Shen Shi. It had to be Assassin Market hits, but they'd tracked down the driver of the bus that struck Sean, and the driver was clean. No new information yet regarding Shen Shi, but Jin was on it. Chen had been working for the Chinese Security Ministry—their version of the CIA—but digging deeper created as many new questions as got answered.

They did manage to figure out that Sean was about to burst into the Bank of England's Assembly meeting, probably to divulge what he knew about Bluebridge—like Yamamoto had tried to do. Jake had arranged a huge party for Sean, a belated wake, and they'd danced and drank until dawn.

Shorts in hand, Jake grabbed Anna and tickled her. "Okay, let's go!"

Anna squealed with glee and ran into the hallway. They walked together through the front door, locking it behind them.

Movers would be coming next week to clean it out. Jake opened the front door of the apartment building, bright sunshine spilling onto them.

Chase Rockwell had been arrested on money laundering charges and was on his way into custody. But he'd be out. No banker ever stayed in jail for long.

"Come on, Jakey, what's taking so long?" Eamon called out. He waved Jake over to the minivan parked in front of their apartment.

The sliding door of the van was open and Elle waved at him from the passenger seat. "Yeah, come on!"

Jake let go of Anna's hand and she ran over to Uncle Eamon, jumping into his arms. Jake's mother was in the back of the minivan, her expression vacant, but when Anna jumped out of Eamon's arms and into the back to kiss Grandma, a smile spread across her face.

They were moving down to Virginia Beach, like Elle always wanted. They were all going to drive down there together.

Jake was staying on the Bluebridge Board of Directors. These kids needed a steady hand. Wutang and Jin had moved in together—in an apartment in Midtown—in love like two puppies. But Jake didn't have to stay in New York to help out. Jin and Wutang and Sheldon were better equipped to ride that horse, and he'd had enough of the city.

He finally knew who'd inherited Sean's estate. Jake. And Jake used it to buy the hotel-restaurant in Virginia Beach.

Sean would have liked that, too.

Jake convinced his Mom to come down and live with them, and Eamon had said he'd tend bar at the restaurant and help with renovations. The only one missing was Jake's father.

Jin had transferred a few hundred thousand into Conor's bank account, for his help. Of course, Conor complained it was too little, but Jake knew it was the kind of score his old man had always dreamed of.

His dad said he wasn't coming south, and this relieved Jake—but he had a feeling Conor would be drawn down to them anyway, circling in their orbit. Jake was happy to let him do it in his own time, see if his feelings toward his father could heal.

All his life, his father had been searching for that big score, and whether Jake realized it or not, he'd been doing the same thing. Jake reached the minivan and looked inside—at Anna in Elle's arms, his mother, his brother—and realized that *this* was his dream. Not money, but having a family, packed together like this in a minivan, about to embark on an adventure together.

The void Jake always felt inside was gone.

"Yeah, let's go," Jake said to everyone, sliding the door closed.

Walking around the other side, he got into the driver's seat and stared at the open road ahead, turning the ignition switch.

A living was what you earned, but a life—Jake glanced over his shoulder at his family—a life was what you gave.

And it was time for Jake to start giving.

OCTOBER 14th

Monday

53

Schenectady
Upstate New York

Anna Ingmar had just finished washing her dishes when the postman's truck pulled up outside the house. More bills, she sighed to herself. Putting down her washcloth, she wiped her hands on her jeans and walked to the front door.

"You guys okay?" she asked as she passed the TV room. She was fostering eleven young boys right now, and she'd love to take more…but she didn't have space. Or money. Steeling herself, she swung open her front door and the screen door, and then walked to the mailbox.

Anna knew that Jake had been cleared of his troubles. He'd called the day before, saying that they'd bought a place in Virginia Beach and inviting her to come stay. She was happy for him, but she knew her place was here with her boys.

Sheriff Ralston had helped Jake in the end. She hadn't seen Joe Ralston in years. They'd dated briefly when they were young, but it hadn't lasted. Still, he'd brought Jake into her life, one cold and snowy evening, and for that she'd always be grateful.

Opening her mailbox, she shuffled through the letters—telephone, heating, and insurance bills—but one of them was in a blank envelope, addressed to her, no return address. Frowning, she stuck the bills under one arm and tore open the envelope. There were papers inside: a letter and a check. She couldn't help but look at the check, and she had to blink and literally rub her eyes. It was a donation to her Albany Foster Boys charity. For ten million dollars.

She glanced around, seeing if anyone was watching. Was this a joke? Shaking, she unfolded the letter.

Mrs. Ingmar,

This is an anonymous donation of ten million dollars for the construction

357

of the Albany Foster Boys home in the woods outside of Schenectady. Before you try, we want to assure you that there is no way to return this money. Attached you will find a land deed for ten acres that you can use for this purpose.

Anna's breath caught, and tears filled her eyes. She looked at the land deed. It was for that old farm where Jake and Sean used to hide when they were kids. She looked down to finish reading.

There's only one condition. Over the front door, we'd like the inscription 'Nuggets House' written. And over the back door, the one the boys use when they go outside to play in the woods, we'd like you to write in big gold letters:

'Never Give Up'

NOTE FROM THE AUTHOR

Thanks for reading!
If you want more, you can read all about DARKNET in real
life in the next few pages…

AND PLEASE
I'd really appreciate it if you could leave a review on Amazon.
As a self-published author, the number of reviews a book
accumulates on a daily basis has a direct impact on sales
performance, so just leaving a review—no matter how short—
helps make it possible for me to continue to do what I do.

To become eligible for a free Advance Reading Copy of my
next book, sign up here:
MatthewMather.com/list

DARKNET IN REAL LIFE

While DARKNET is a work of fiction, things like murder-for-
hire on darknets and the Assassination Market, autonomous
corporations, cryptocurrencies, darknet marketplaces, and
chatbots—that can fool you into thinking they are people—are all
real and operating right now.

A machine beat the Turing test for the first time in 2014,
forever changing the world that we live in. From now on, it will
be increasingly difficult—if not impossible—to tell if we are
talking to humans or machines when we get on the phone (or
even a video call).

My first job, over twenty years ago now, was working as a
research assistant at the McGill Center for Intelligent Machines,
reputed as the *Harvard University* of Canada. It was there that I first
studied artificial intelligence and conducted my own research into
machine vision. After McGill, I went on to pursue several other
technical fields before becoming a writer of fiction, but my
fascination with the idea of intelligent machines never left me.
You could say that *Darknet* was a novel twenty years in the
making.

One issue that I always had with book and film portrayals of the 'rise of intelligent machines' was that they always seemed to create these 'superhuman' entities that were like human beings in a box, just much smarter and faster than we were (and inevitably seemed to want to destroy the human race). I didn't see it happening like that, not the 'first' time, anyway. The desire to see a novel that explored the rise of the first intelligent machine network, but not characterizing it as a human-like entity, was my inspiration for writing *Darknet*.

The process of writing *Darknet* opened my eyes to many corners of the new informational world that surrounds us—these things like the Assassination Market and autonomous corporations. I invite you to go on the web and research these for yourself. I have included a list of links below:

- Real-life murder-for-hire case on darknets
http://arstechnica.com/tech-policy/2015/01/judge-govt-can-show-murder-for-hire-evidence-in-silk-road-trial/
- Forbes article on the new Assassination Market
http://www.forbes.com/sites/andygreenberg/2013/11/18/meet-the-assassination-market-creator-whos-crowdfunding-murder-with-bitcoins/
- An Economist article on Digital Autonomous Corporations
http://www.economist.com/blogs/babbage/2014/01/computer-corporations
- A list of active darknet marketplaces
https://vault43.org/chart.php
o The Silk Road darknet site was shut down, but dozens of others have replaced it
- Cryptocurrency market capitalizations
http://coinmarketcap.com/
- A Discover magazine article on the Turing test being beaten
http://blogs.discovermagazine.com/crux/2014/06/10/turing-test-beating-bot-reveals-more-about-humans-than-computers/#.VEUGvPnF_zU

Feel free to email me with any questions or comments. I'd love to hear your thoughts or share in things that you find out there!

Best regards,

Matthew Mather
Oct. 20th, 2014
author.matthew.mather@gmail.com

***

If you'd like to see what's going on in my life as I write my books, check out my author Facebook page:
https://www.facebook.com/Author.Matthew.Mather

To become eligible for a free Advance Reading Copy of my next book, sign up here:
MatthewMather.com/list

Other books by Matthew Mather:
CyberStorm
Atopia Chronicles
Dystopia Chronicles

SPECIAL THANKS

I'd like to make a special thank you to Allan Tierney, Theresa Munanga and Pamela Deering who did whole edits of the book as beta readers.

AND THANK YOU to all my beta readers (sorry I don't have surnames for all of you) Cliff Shaffer, Ken Zufall, Tomas Classon, Chrissie Pintar, Katrina Archer, Erik Montcalm, Angela Cavanaugh, Amber Triplett, Wendy Matthews, Bryan Scullion, Philipp Francis, Sun Lee Curry, Monte Dunard, David Dai, Ernie Dempsey, Nick Burnette, James McCormick, Fern Burgett, and so many more!

And of course, I'd like to thank my mother and father, Julie and David Mather, and last but most definitely not least, Julie Ruthven, for putting up with all the late nights and missed walks with the dogs.

-- Matthew Mather

About Matthew Mather

Translated into sixteen languages, with 20th Century Fox now developing his second novel, CyberStorm, for a major film release, Matthew Mather's books are worldwide bestsellers. He began his career at the McGill Center for Intelligent Machines, then started several high-tech ventures in everything from computational nanotechnology to electronic health records, weather prediction systems to genomics, and even designed an award-winning brain-training video game. He now works as a full-time author of speculative fiction.

AUTHOR CONTACT
Matthew Mather:
author.matthew.mather@gmail.com

Made in the USA
Middletown, DE
25 April 2018